THE GREAT WIZ AND THE RUCKUS™

THE
GREAT
AND THE R

Cover by
Joey McCormick
With Colors by Whitney Cogar

Designer Chelsea Roberts
Editors Whitney Leopard & Chris Rosa

THE GREAT WIZ AND THE RUCKUS, February 2019
Published by KaBOOM!, a division of Boom Entertainment,
Inc. The Great Wiz and the Ruckus is ™ & © 2019 Joey
McCormick. All rights reserved. KaBOOM!™ and the
KaBOOM! logo are trademarks of Boom Entertainment,
Inc., registered in various countries and categories. All characters, events, and institutions depicted herein are fictional. Any
similarity between any of the names, characters, persons, events, and/or institutions in this publication to actual names,
characters, and persons, whether living or dead, events, and/or institutions is unintended and purely coincidental. KaBOOM!
does not read or accept unsolicited submissions of ideas, stories, or artwork.

For information regarding the CPSIA on this printed material, call: (203) 595-3636 and provide reference #RICH - 825778.

BOOM! Studios, 5670 Wilshire Boulevard, Suite 400, Los Angeles, CA 90036-5679. Printed in USA. First Printing.

ISBN: 978-1-68415-315-2, eISBN: 978-1-64144-168-1

LIZ RUCKUS

— WRITTEN & ILLUSTRATED BY **JOEY McCORMICK** —

COLORS BY **WHITNEY COGAR** • LETTERS BY **WARREN MONTGOMERY**

SPECIAL THANKS TO **LIZ McCORMICK**

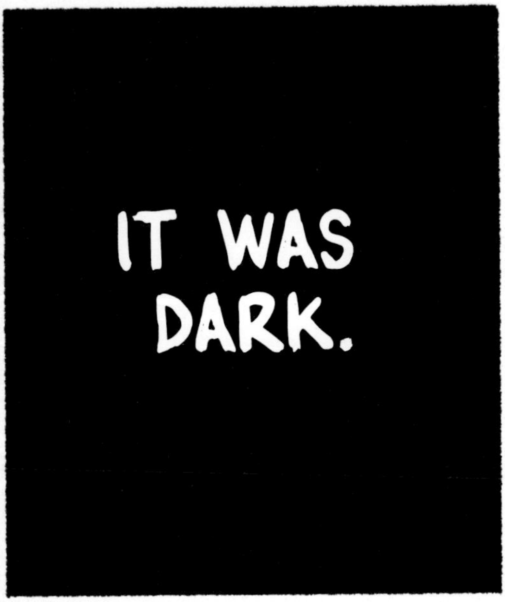
IT WAS DARK.
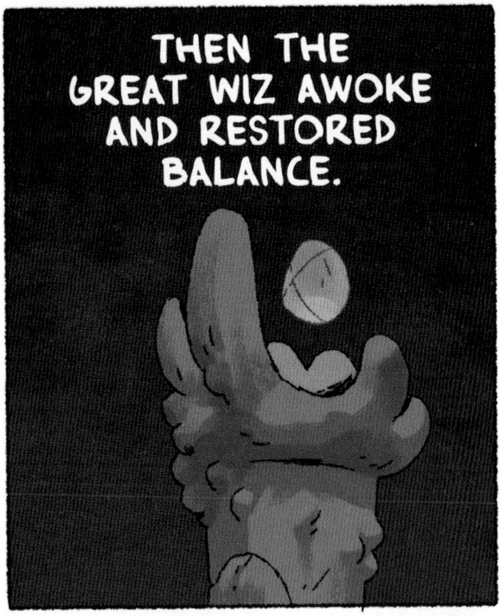
THEN THE GREAT WIZ AWOKE AND RESTORED BALANCE.
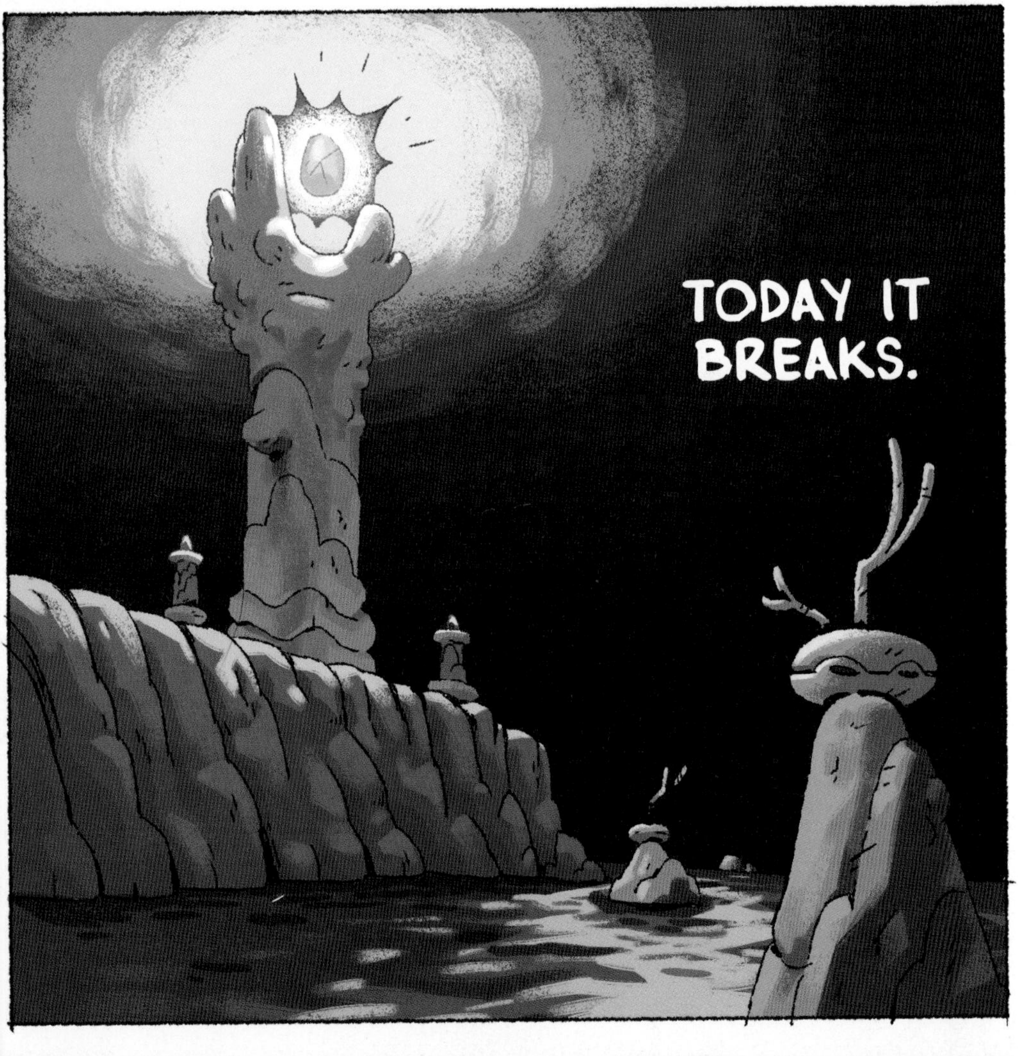
TODAY IT BREAKS.

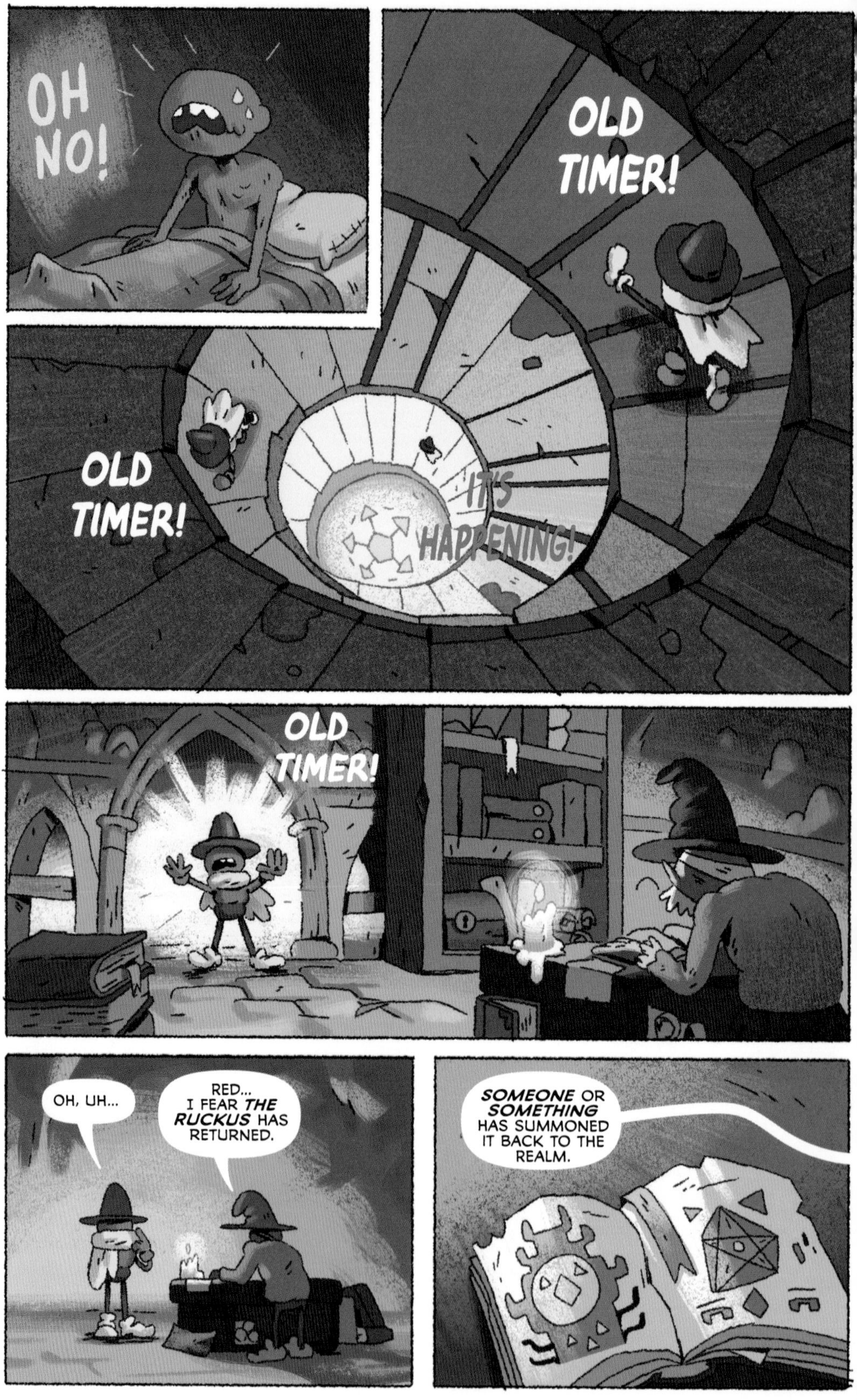

OH NO!
OLD TIMER!
OLD TIMER!
IT'S HAPPENING!
OLD TIMER!
OH, UH...
RED... I FEAR THE RUCKUS HAS RETURNED.
SOMEONE OR SOMETHING HAS SUMMONED IT BACK TO THE REALM.

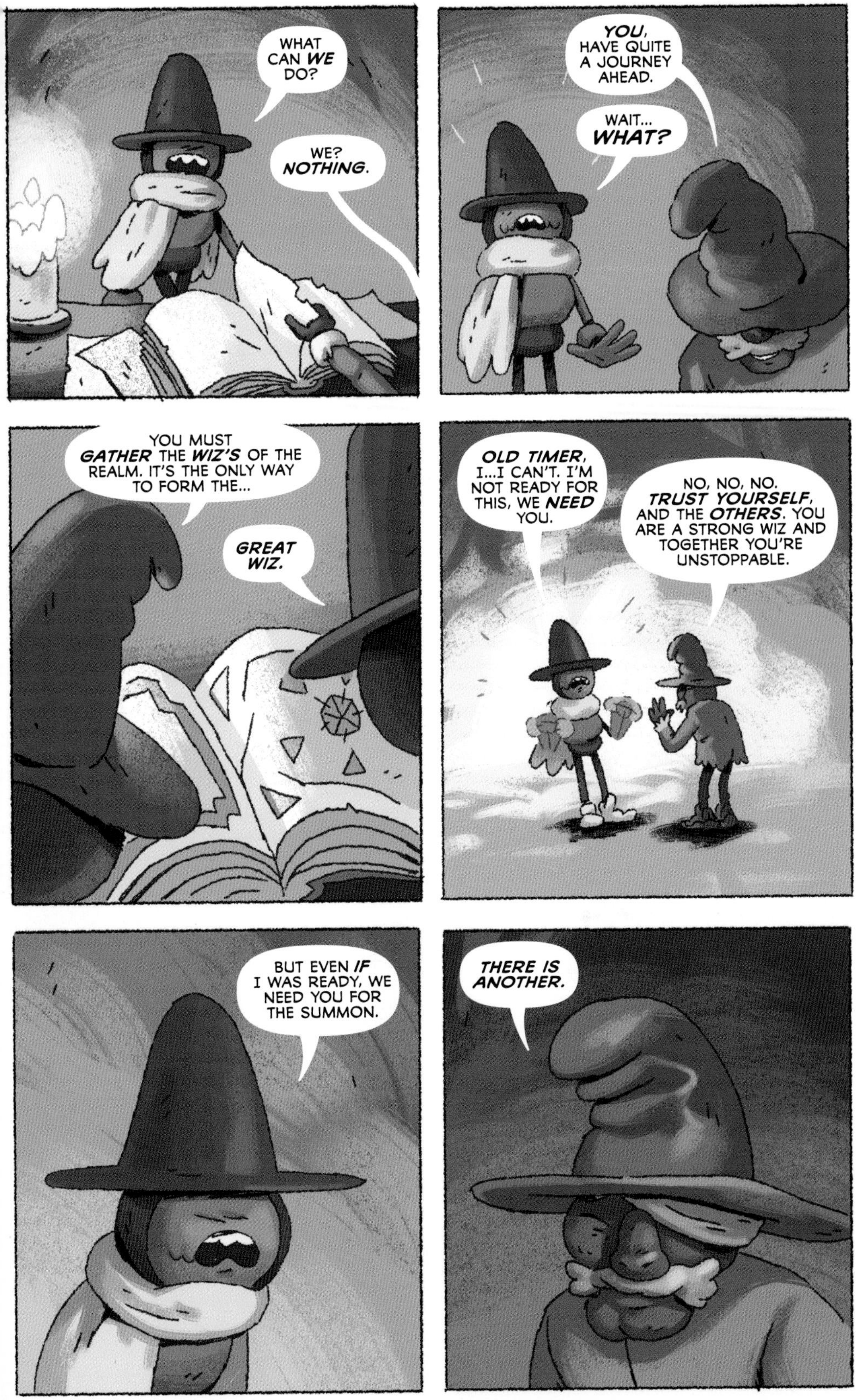

WHAT CAN WE DO?
WE? NOTHING.
YOU, HAVE QUITE A JOURNEY AHEAD.
WAIT... WHAT?
YOU MUST GATHER THE WIZ'S OF THE REALM. IT'S THE ONLY WAY TO FORM THE...
GREAT WIZ.
OLD TIMER, I...I CAN'T. I'M NOT READY FOR THIS, WE NEED YOU.
NO, NO, NO. TRUST YOURSELF, AND THE OTHERS. YOU ARE A STRONG WIZ AND TOGETHER YOU'RE UNSTOPPABLE.
BUT EVEN IF I WAS READY, WE NEED YOU FOR THE SUMMON.
THERE IS ANOTHER.

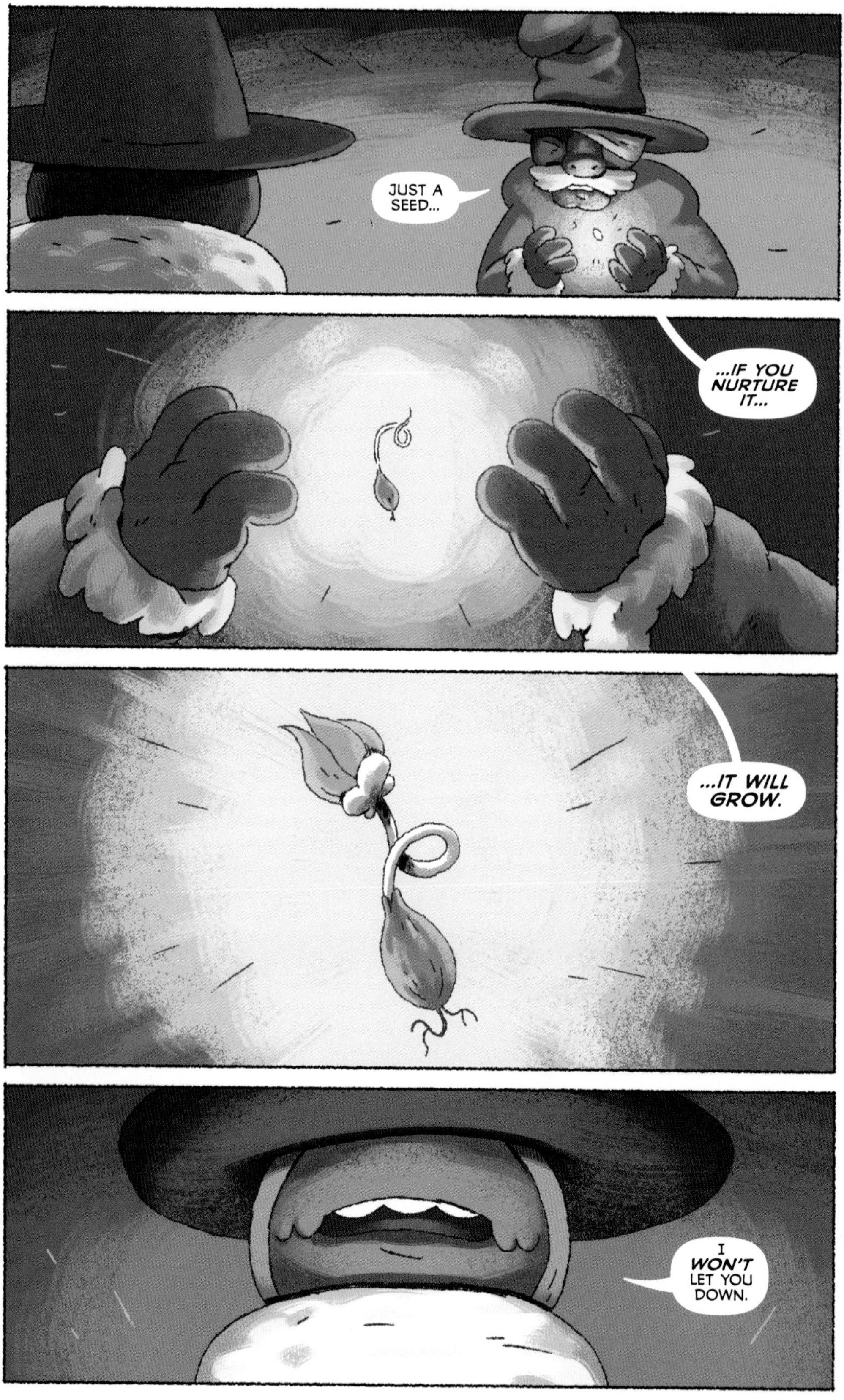
JUST A SEED...
...IF YOU NURTURE IT...
...IT WILL GROW.
I WON'T LET YOU DOWN.

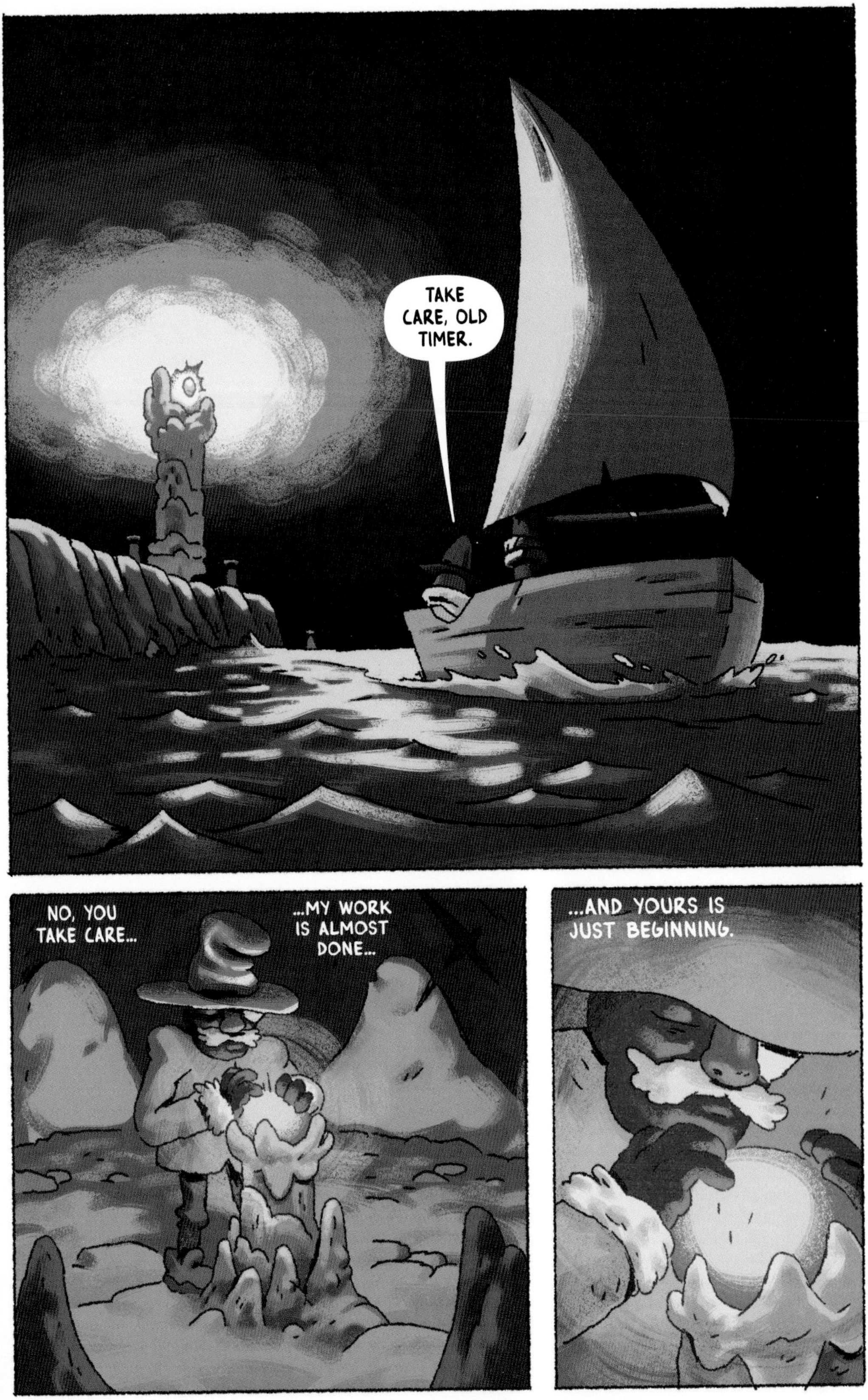
TAKE CARE, OLD TIMER.
NO, YOU TAKE CARE...
...MY WORK IS ALMOST DONE...
...AND YOURS IS JUST BEGINNING.

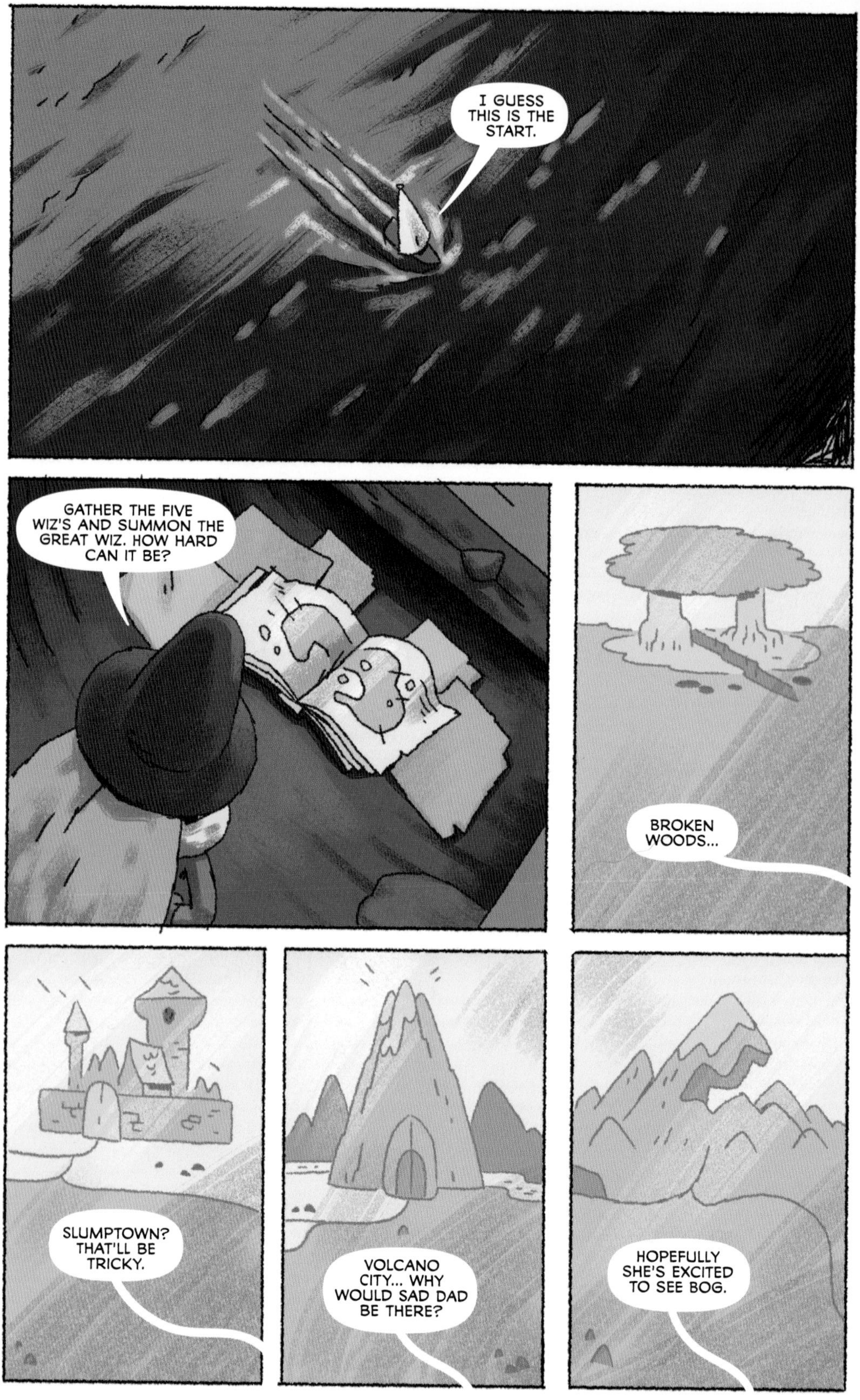
I GUESS THIS IS THE START.
GATHER THE FIVE WIZ'S AND SUMMON THE GREAT WIZ. HOW HARD CAN IT BE?
BROKEN WOODS...
SLUMPTOWN? THAT'LL BE TRICKY.
VOLCANO CITY... WHY WOULD SAD DAD BE THERE?
HOPEFULLY SHE'S EXCITED TO SEE BOG.

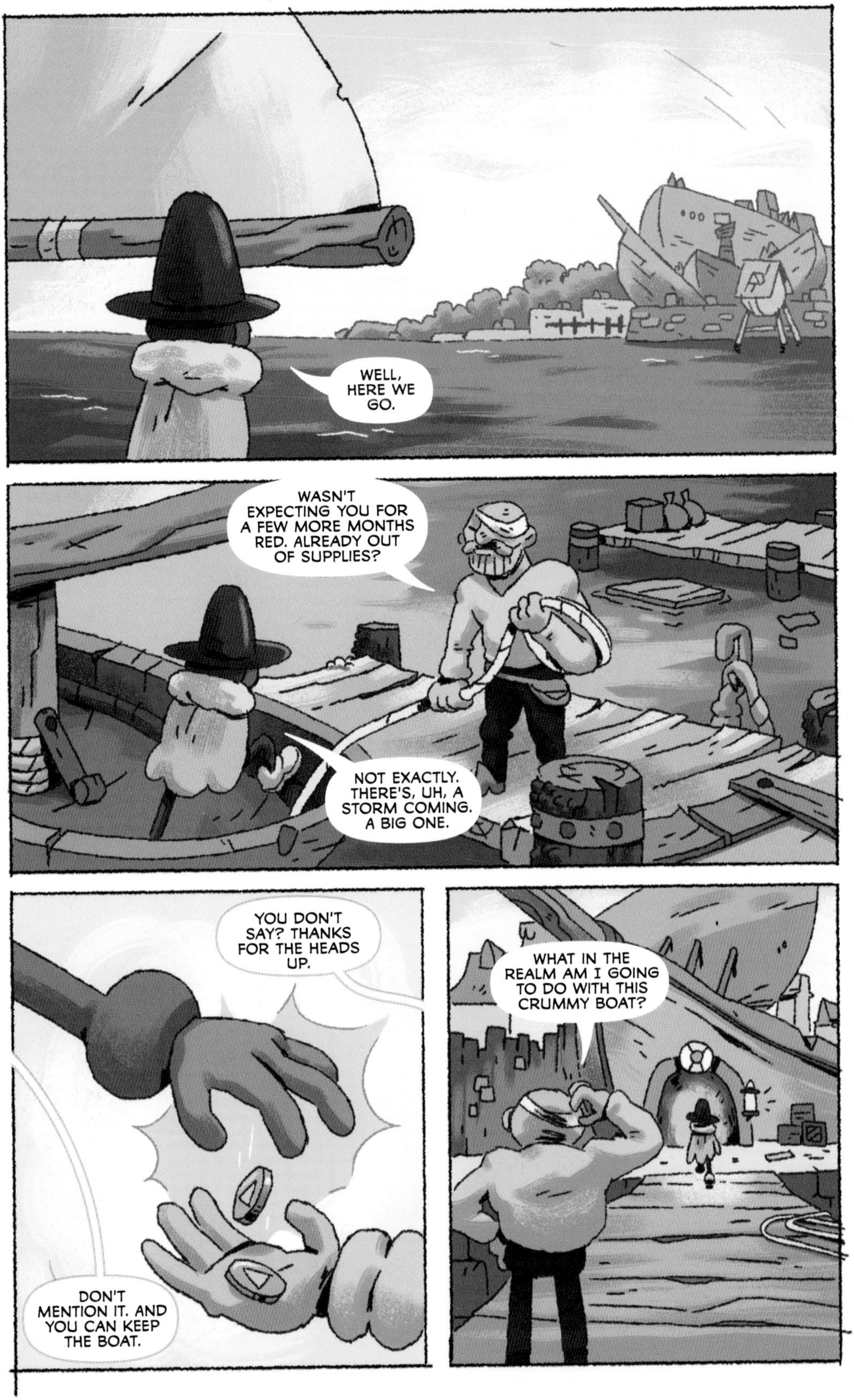
WELL, HERE WE GO.
WASN'T EXPECTING YOU FOR A FEW MORE MONTHS RED. ALREADY OUT OF SUPPLIES?
NOT EXACTLY. THERE'S, UH, A STORM COMING. A BIG ONE.
YOU DON'T SAY? THANKS FOR THE HEADS UP.
DON'T MENTION IT. AND YOU CAN KEEP THE BOAT.
WHAT IN THE REALM AM I GOING TO DO WITH THIS CRUMMY BOAT?

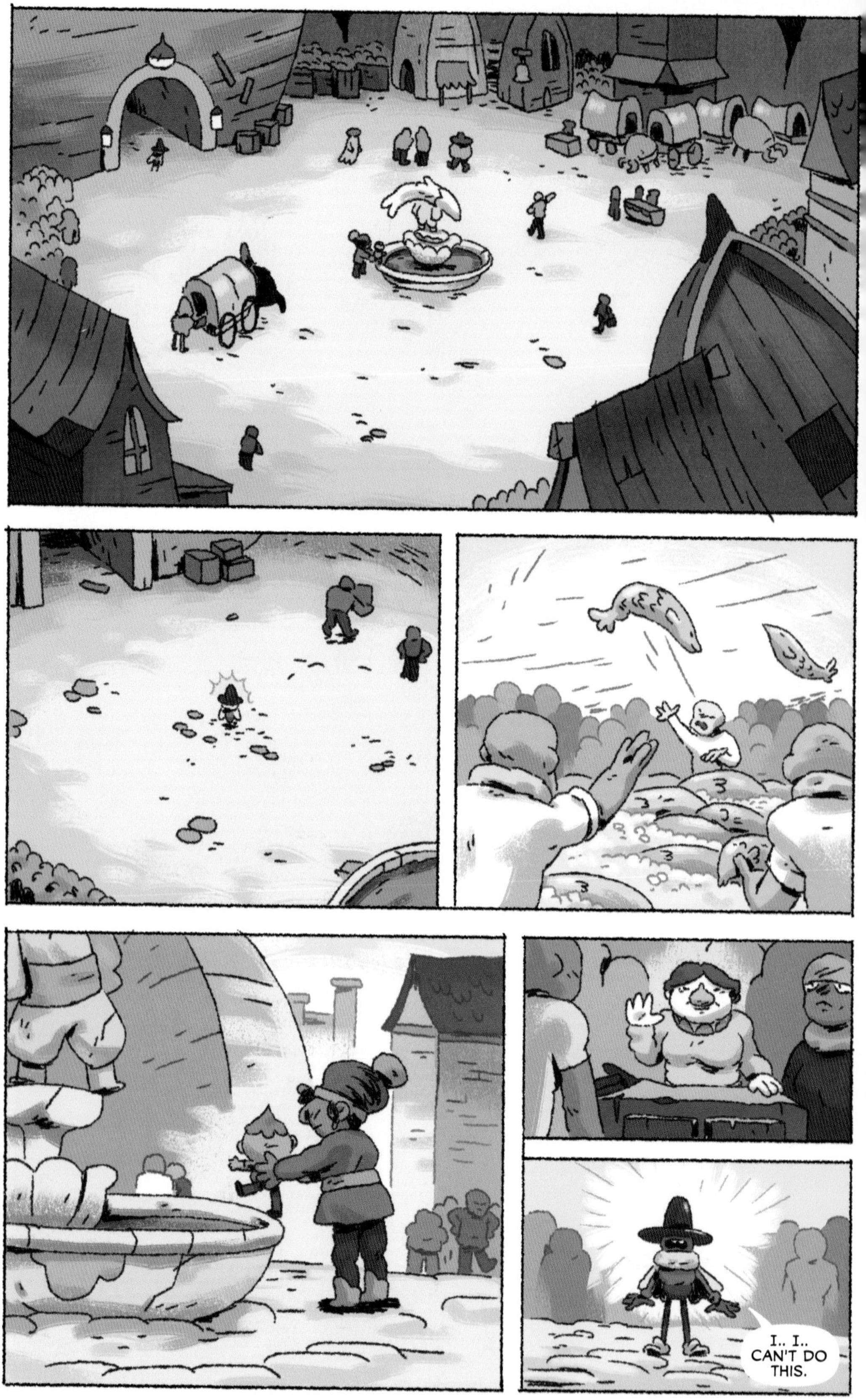
I.. I.. CAN'T DO THIS.

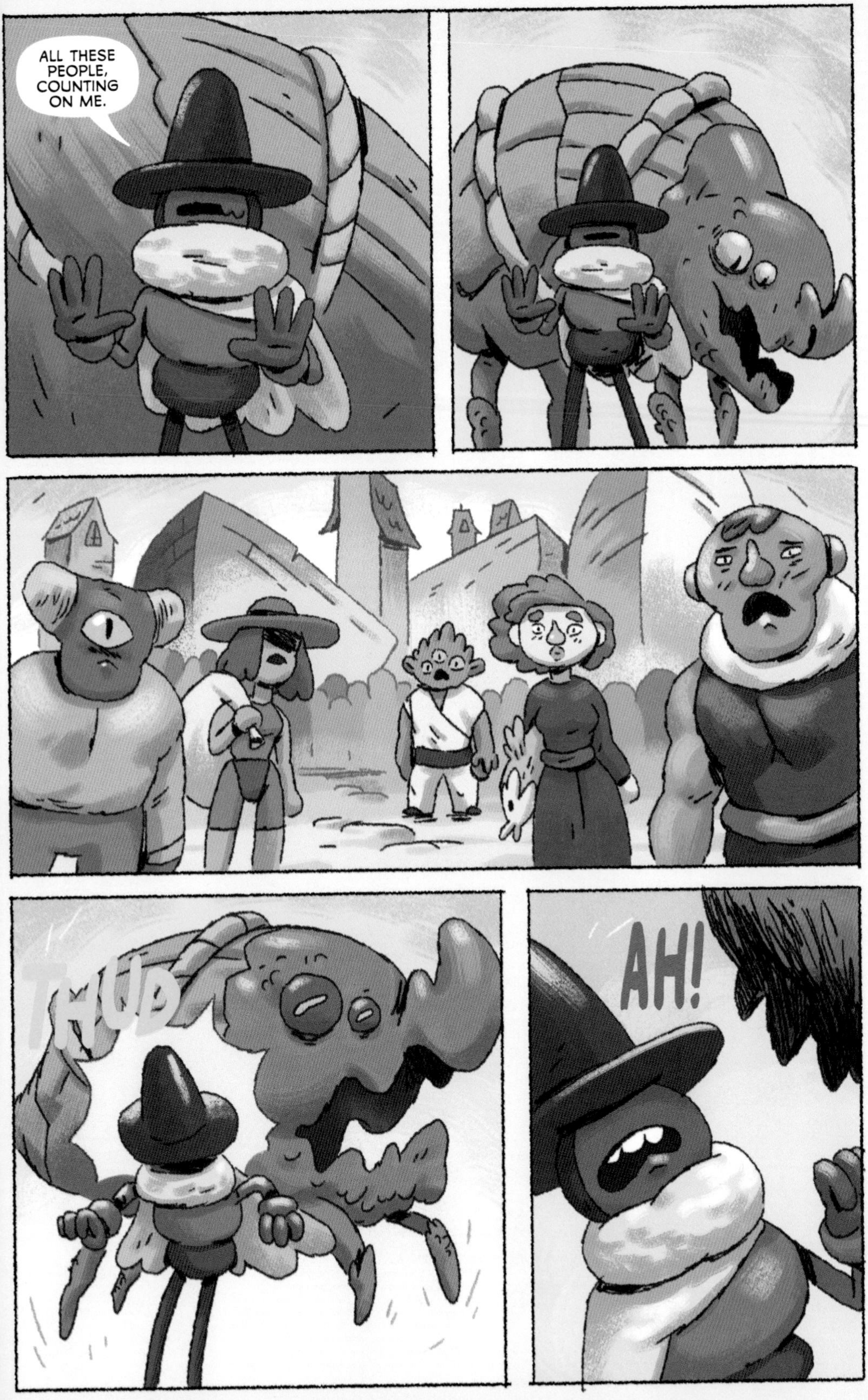
ALL THESE PEOPLE, COUNTING ON ME.
THUD
AH!

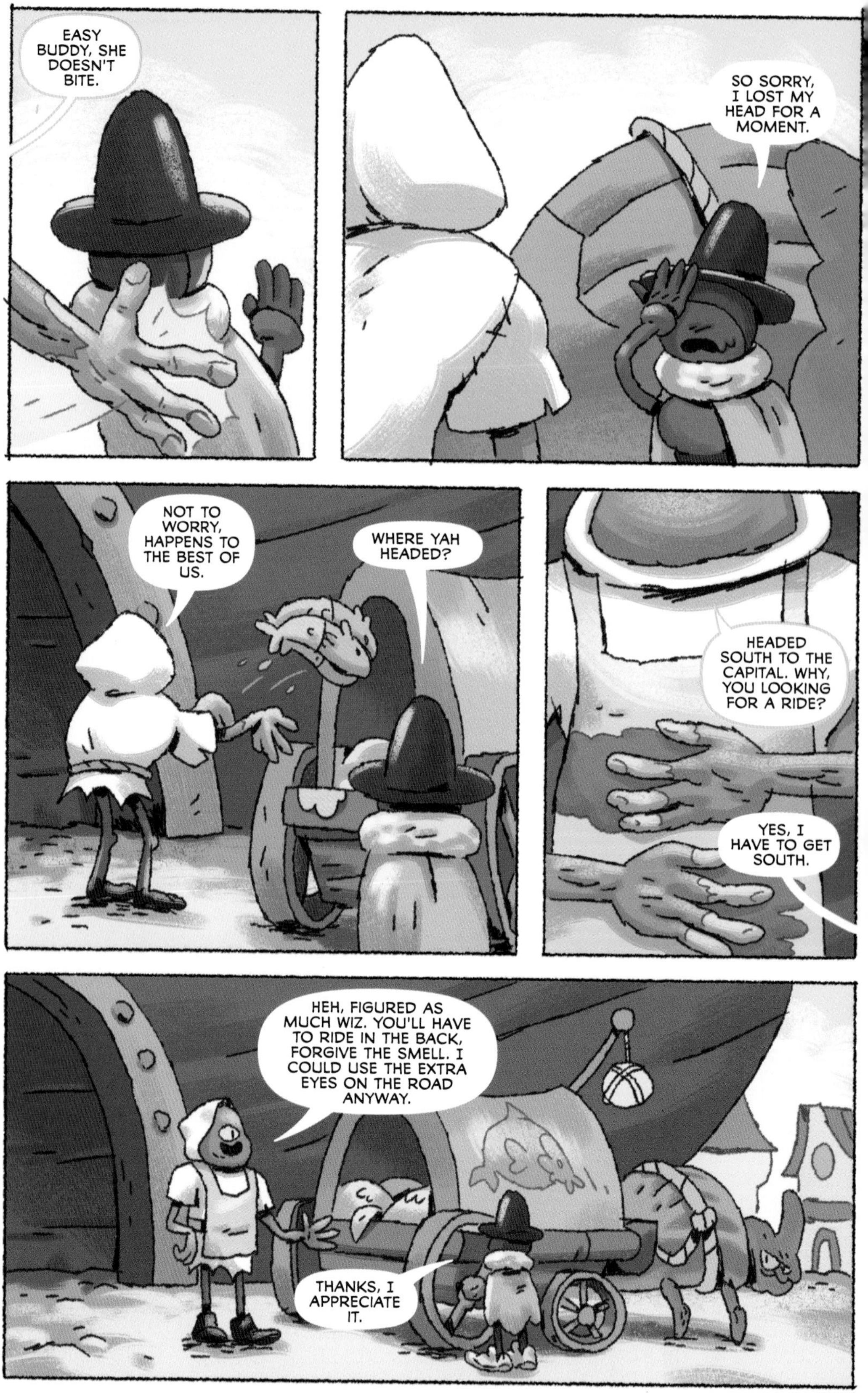
EASY BUDDY, SHE DOESN'T BITE.
SO SORRY, I LOST MY HEAD FOR A MOMENT.
NOT TO WORRY, HAPPENS TO THE BEST OF US.
WHERE YAH HEADED?
HEADED SOUTH TO THE CAPITAL. WHY, YOU LOOKING FOR A RIDE?
YES, I HAVE TO GET SOUTH.
HEH, FIGURED AS MUCH WIZ. YOU'LL HAVE TO RIDE IN THE BACK, FORGIVE THE SMELL. I COULD USE THE EXTRA EYES ON THE ROAD ANYWAY.
THANKS, I APPRECIATE IT.

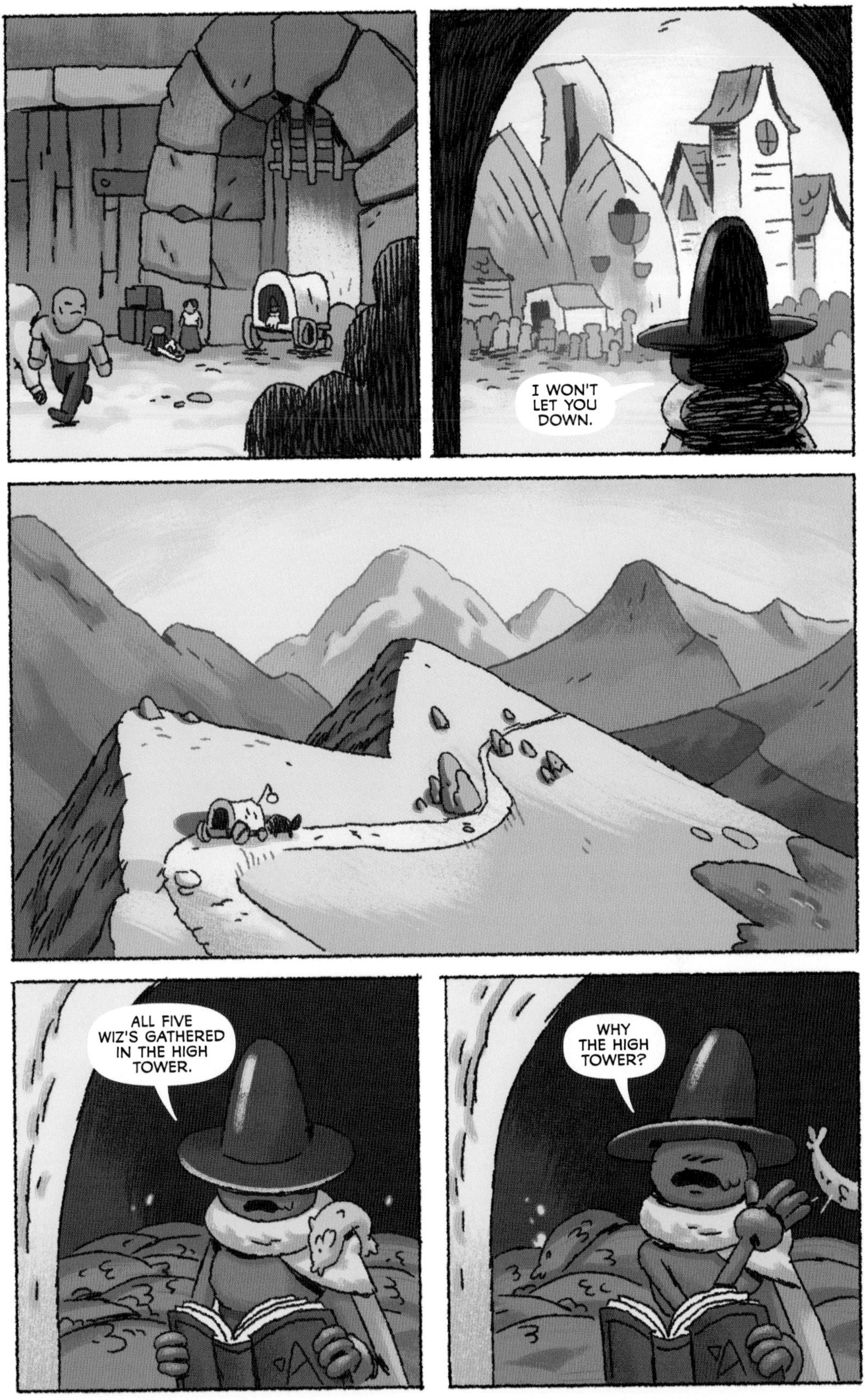
I WON'T LET YOU DOWN.
ALL FIVE WIZ'S GATHERED IN THE HIGH TOWER.
WHY THE HIGH TOWER?

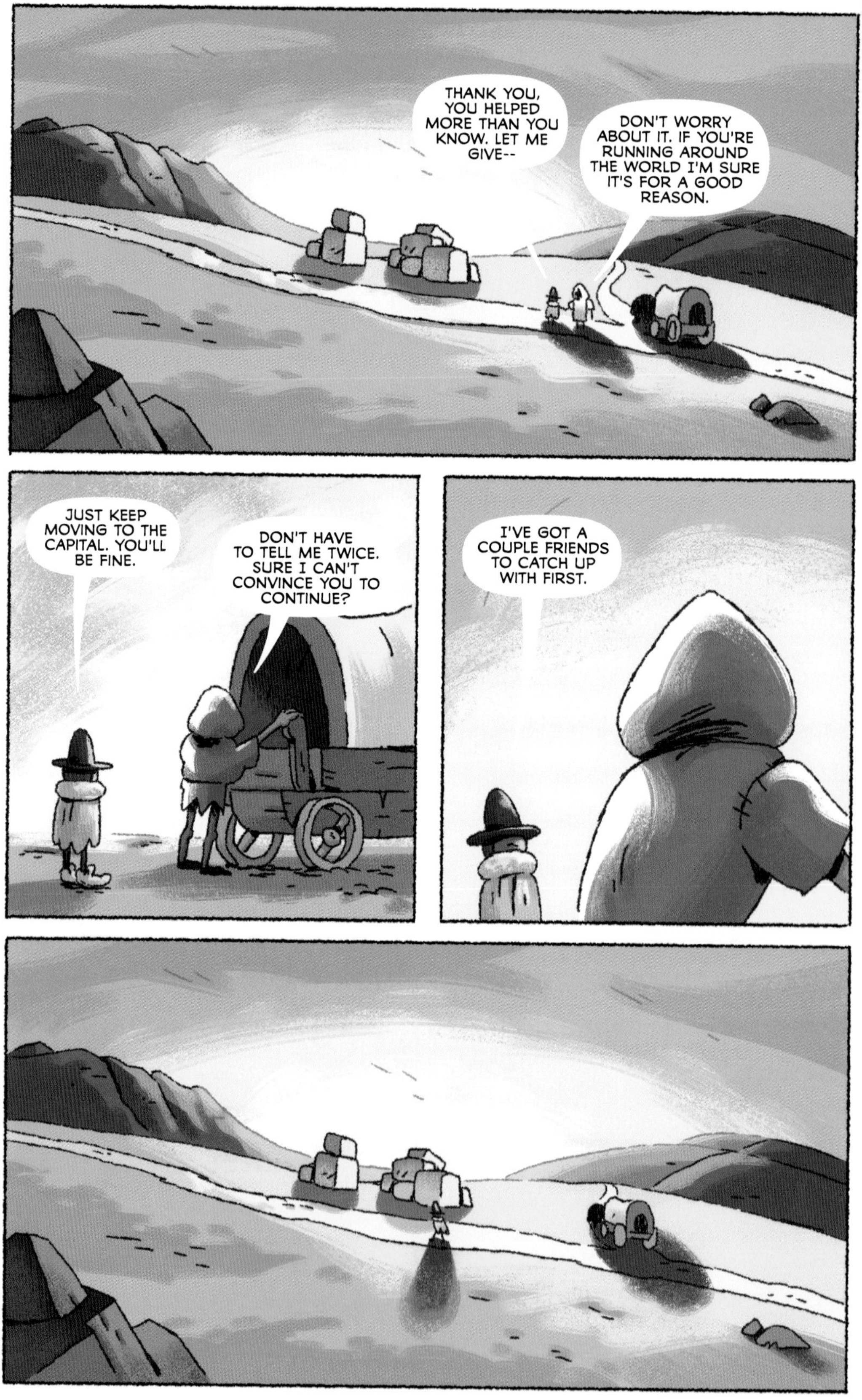
THANK YOU, YOU HELPED MORE THAN YOU KNOW. LET ME GIVE--
DON'T WORRY ABOUT IT. IF YOU'RE RUNNING AROUND THE WORLD I'M SURE IT'S FOR A GOOD REASON.
JUST KEEP MOVING TO THE CAPITAL. YOU'LL BE FINE.
DON'T HAVE TO TELL ME TWICE. SURE I CAN'T CONVINCE YOU TO CONTINUE?
I'VE GOT A COUPLE FRIENDS TO CATCH UP WITH FIRST.

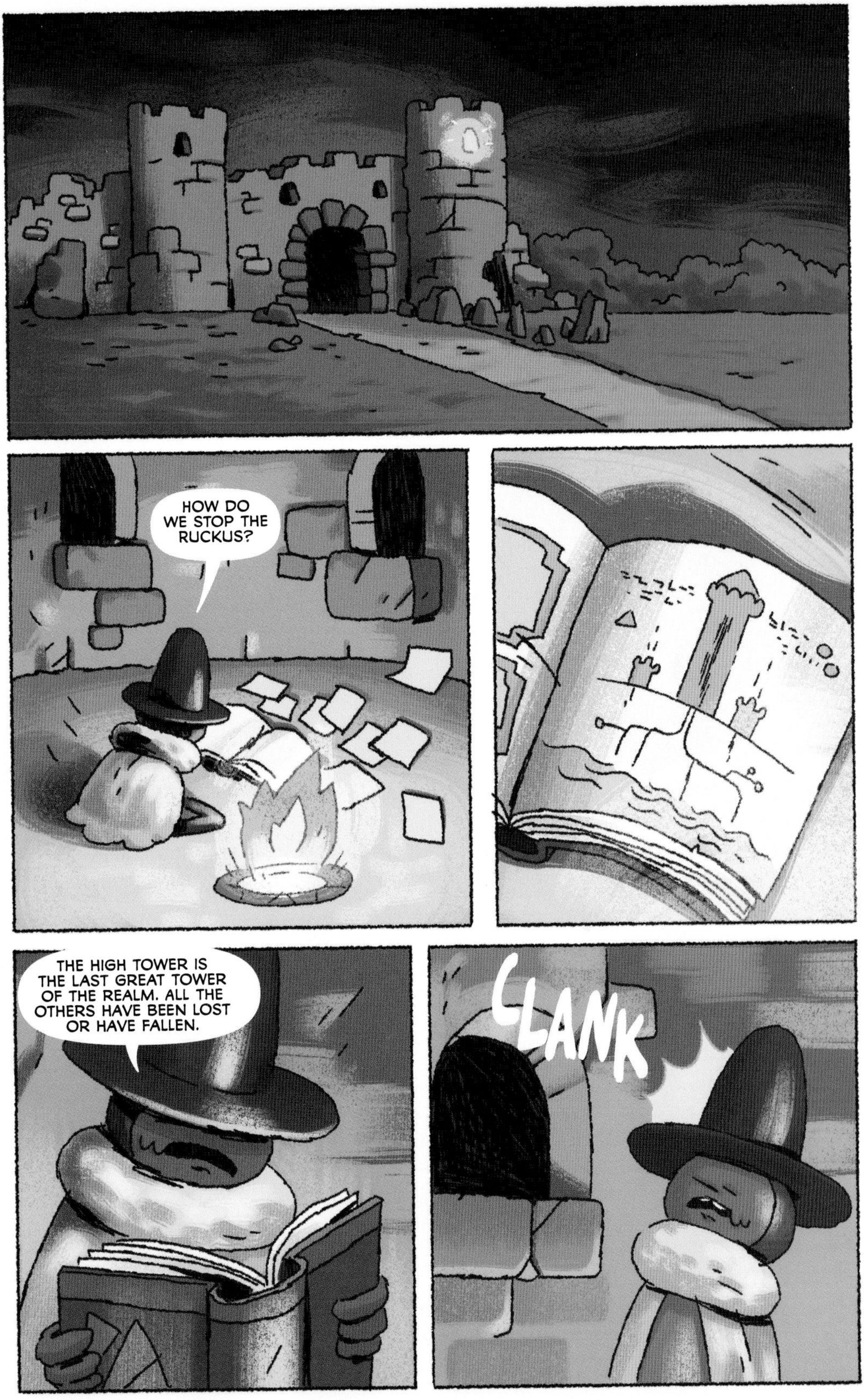
HOW DO WE STOP THE RUCKUS?
THE HIGH TOWER IS THE LAST GREAT TOWER OF THE REALM. ALL THE OTHERS HAVE BEEN LOST OR HAVE FALLEN.
CLANK

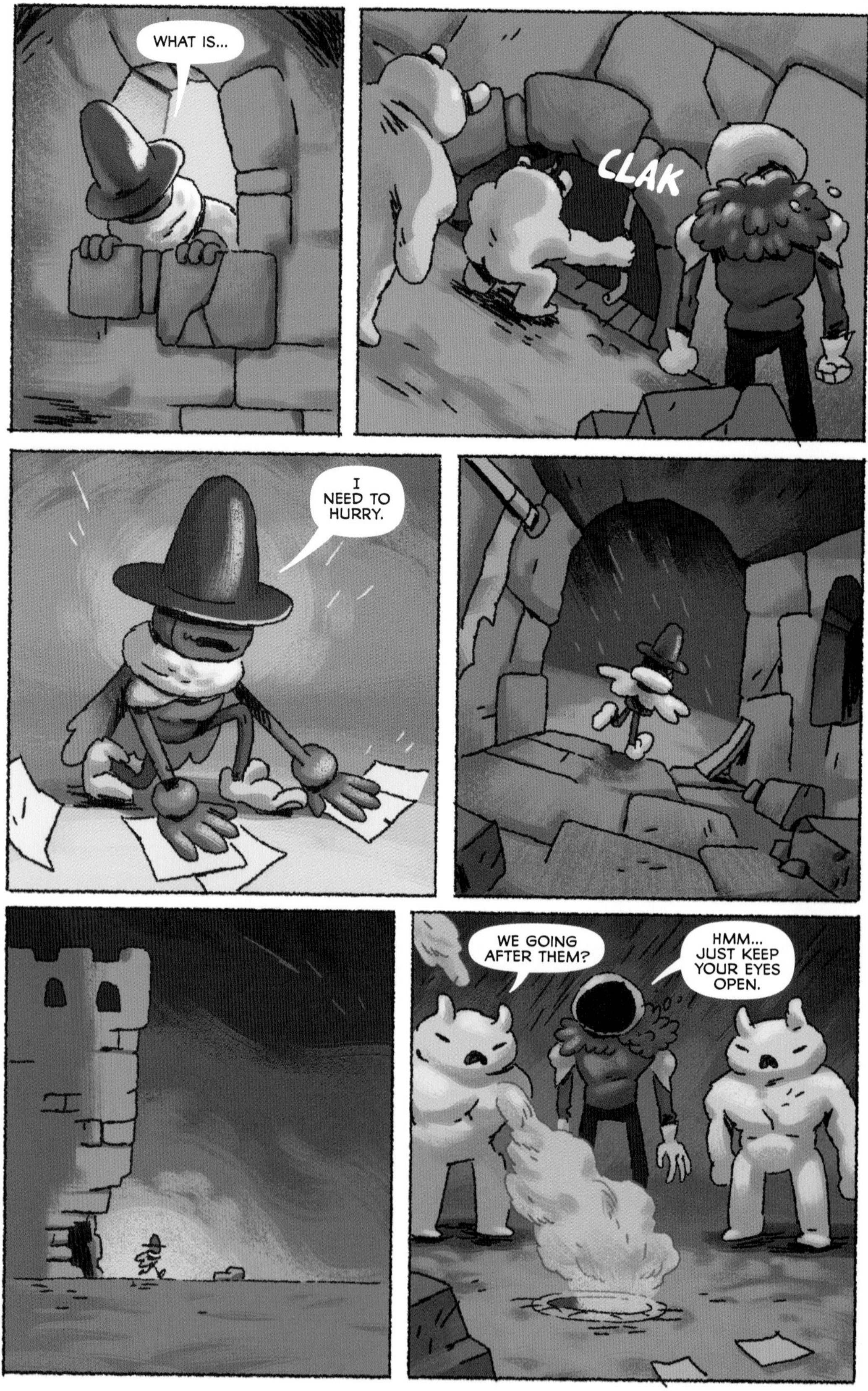
WHAT IS...
CLAK
I NEED TO HURRY.
WE GOING AFTER THEM?
HMM... JUST KEEP YOUR EYES OPEN.

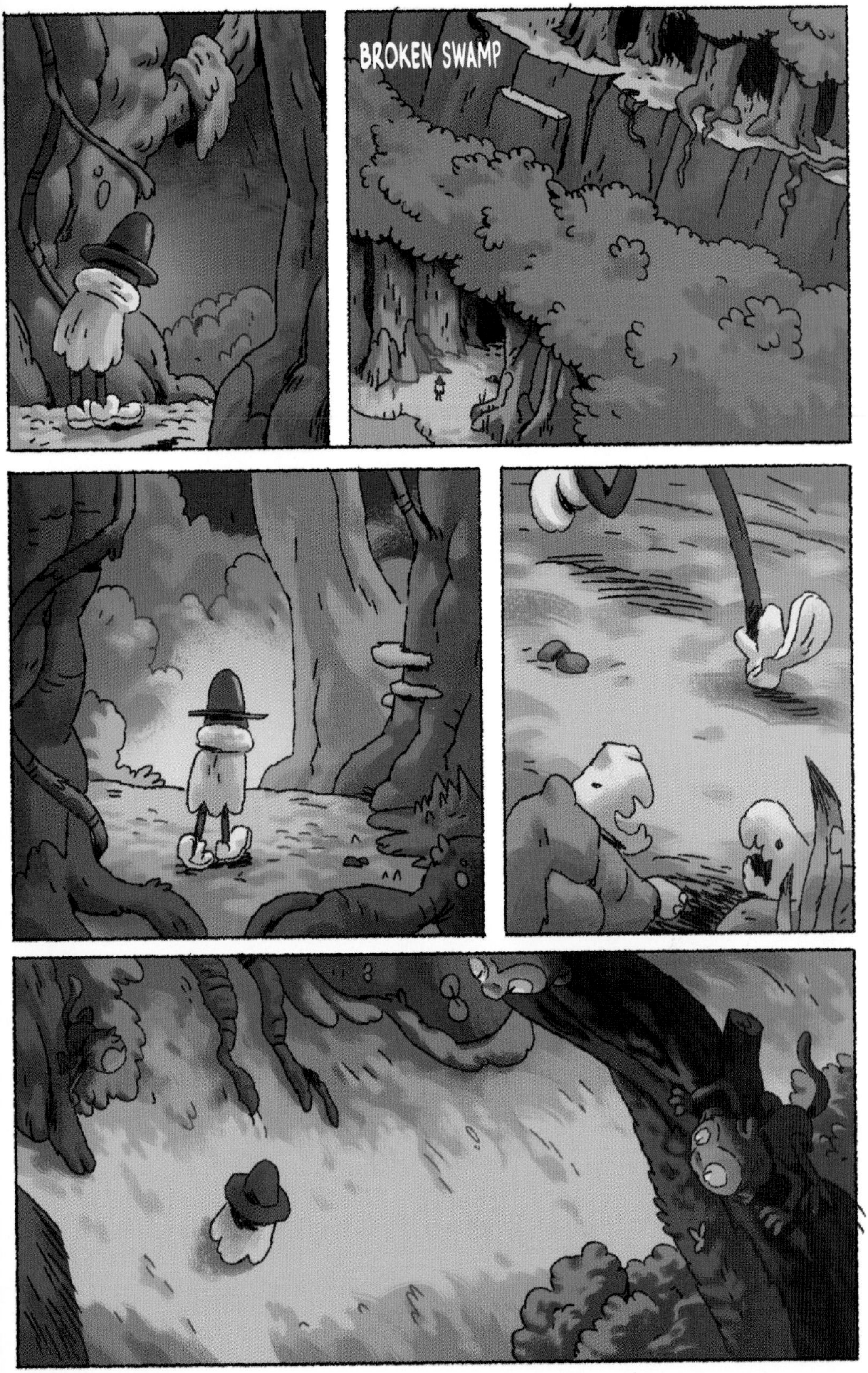
BROKEN SWAMP

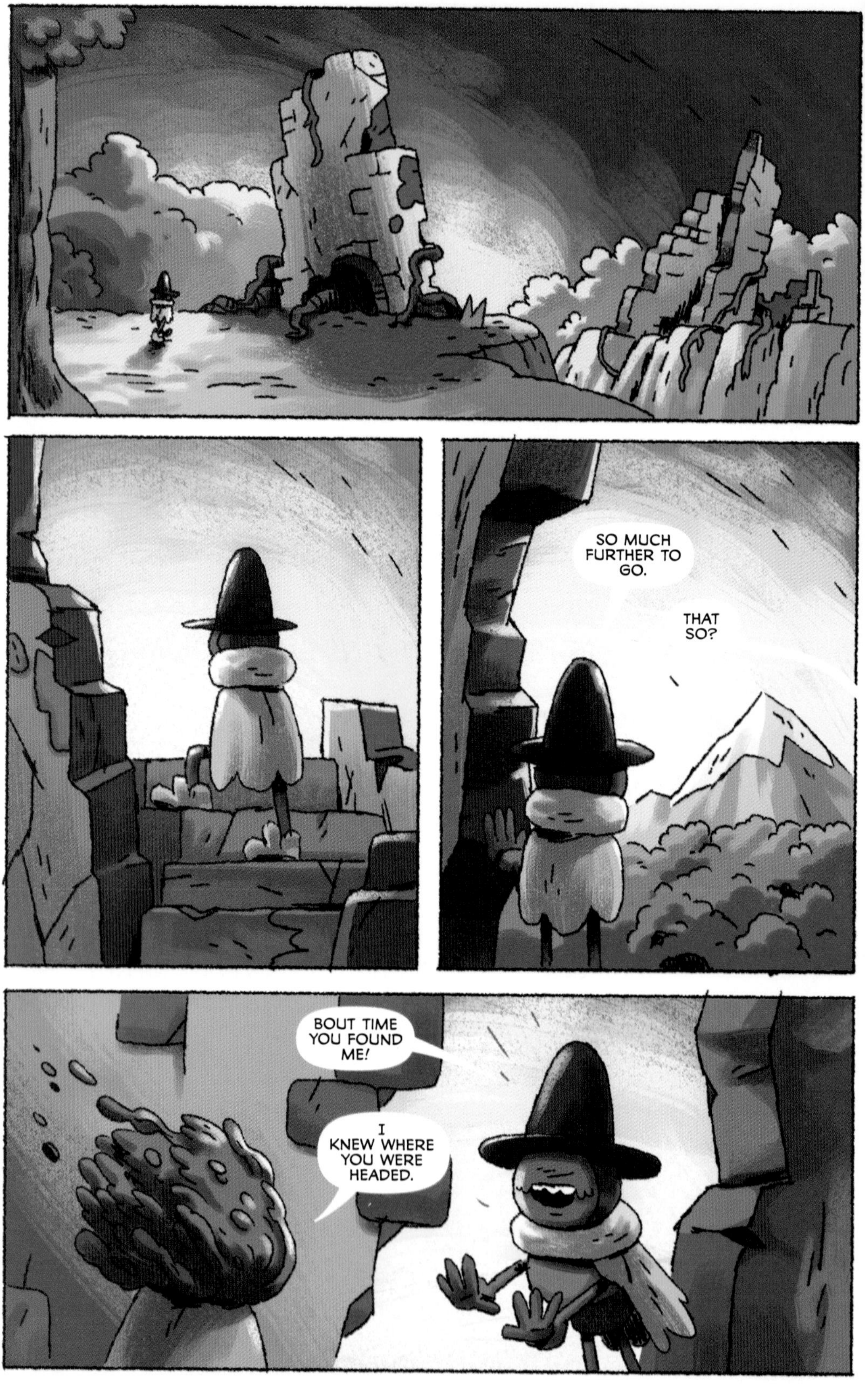
SO MUCH FURTHER TO GO.
THAT SO?
BOUT TIME YOU FOUND ME!
I KNEW WHERE YOU WERE HEADED.

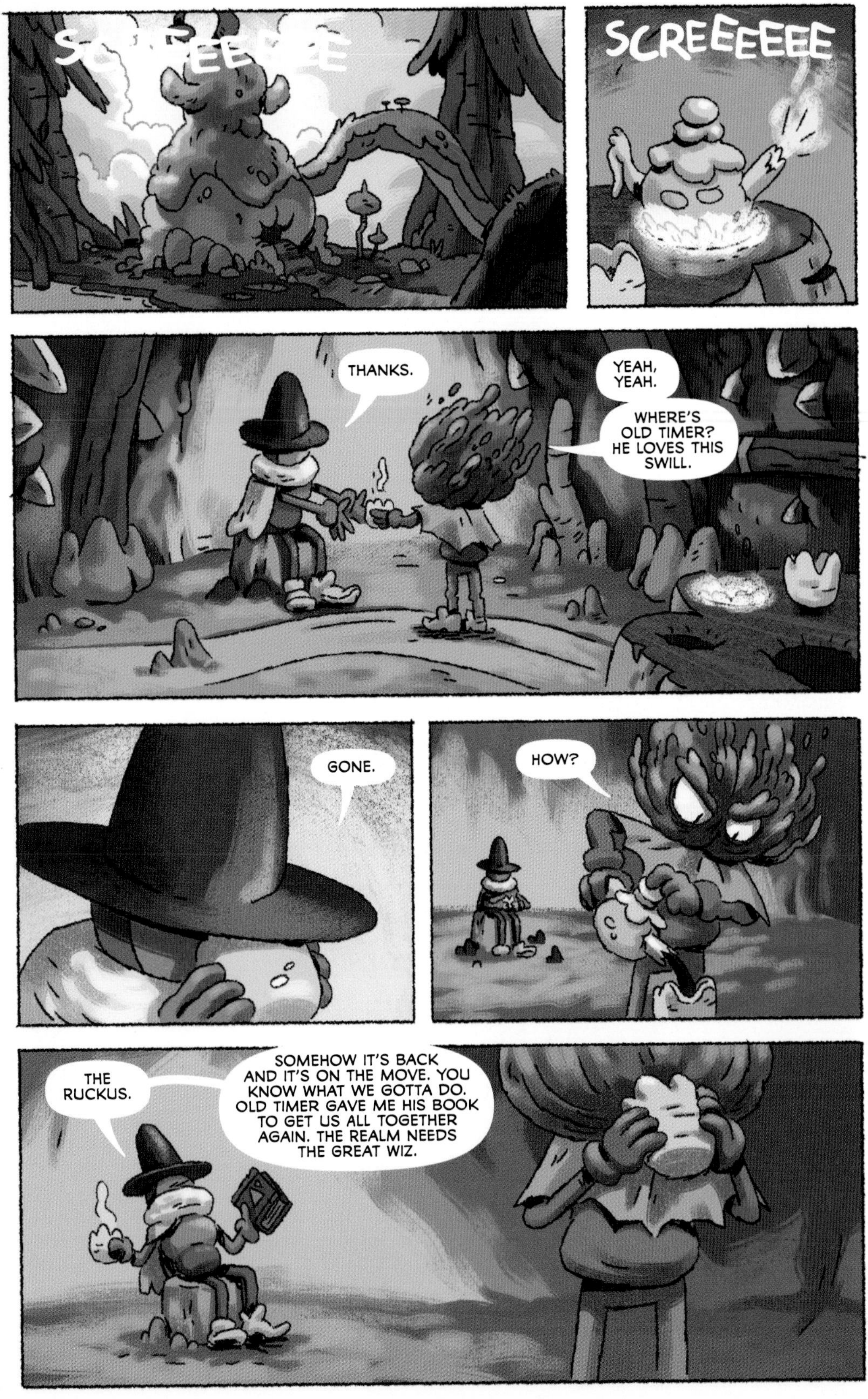
SCREEEEEE
SCREEEEEEE
THANKS.
YEAH, YEAH.
WHERE'S OLD TIMER? HE LOVES THIS SWILL.
GONE.
HOW?
THE RUCKUS.
SOMEHOW IT'S BACK AND IT'S ON THE MOVE. YOU KNOW WHAT WE GOTTA DO. OLD TIMER GAVE ME HIS BOOK TO GET US ALL TOGETHER AGAIN. THE REALM NEEDS THE GREAT WIZ.

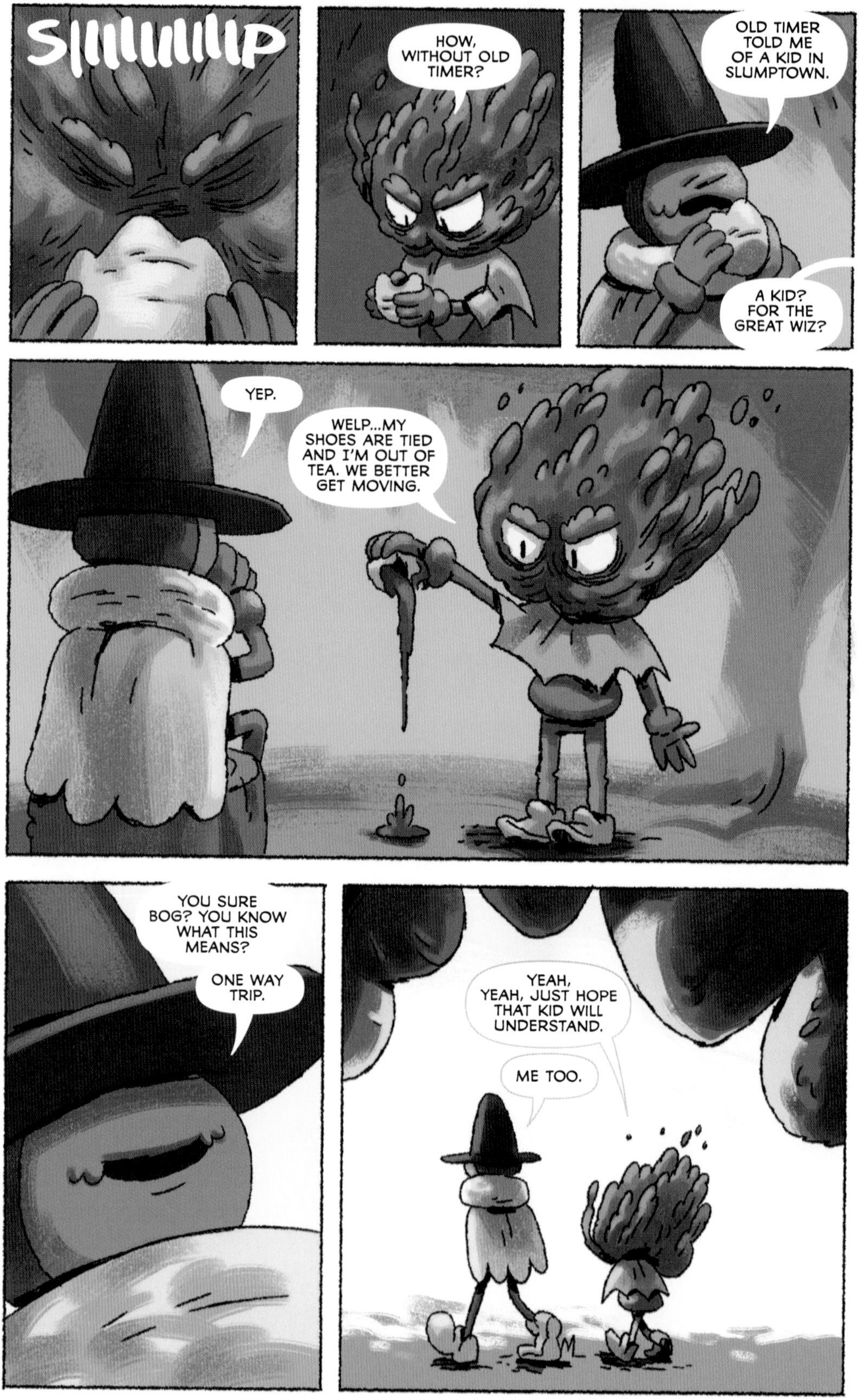

SIIIIIIIP
HOW, WITHOUT OLD TIMER?
OLD TIMER TOLD ME OF A KID IN SLUMPTOWN.
A KID? FOR THE GREAT WIZ?
YEP.
WELP...MY SHOES ARE TIED AND I'M OUT OF TEA. WE BETTER GET MOVING.
YOU SURE BOG? YOU KNOW WHAT THIS MEANS?
ONE WAY TRIP.
YEAH, YEAH, JUST HOPE THAT KID WILL UNDERSTAND.
ME TOO.

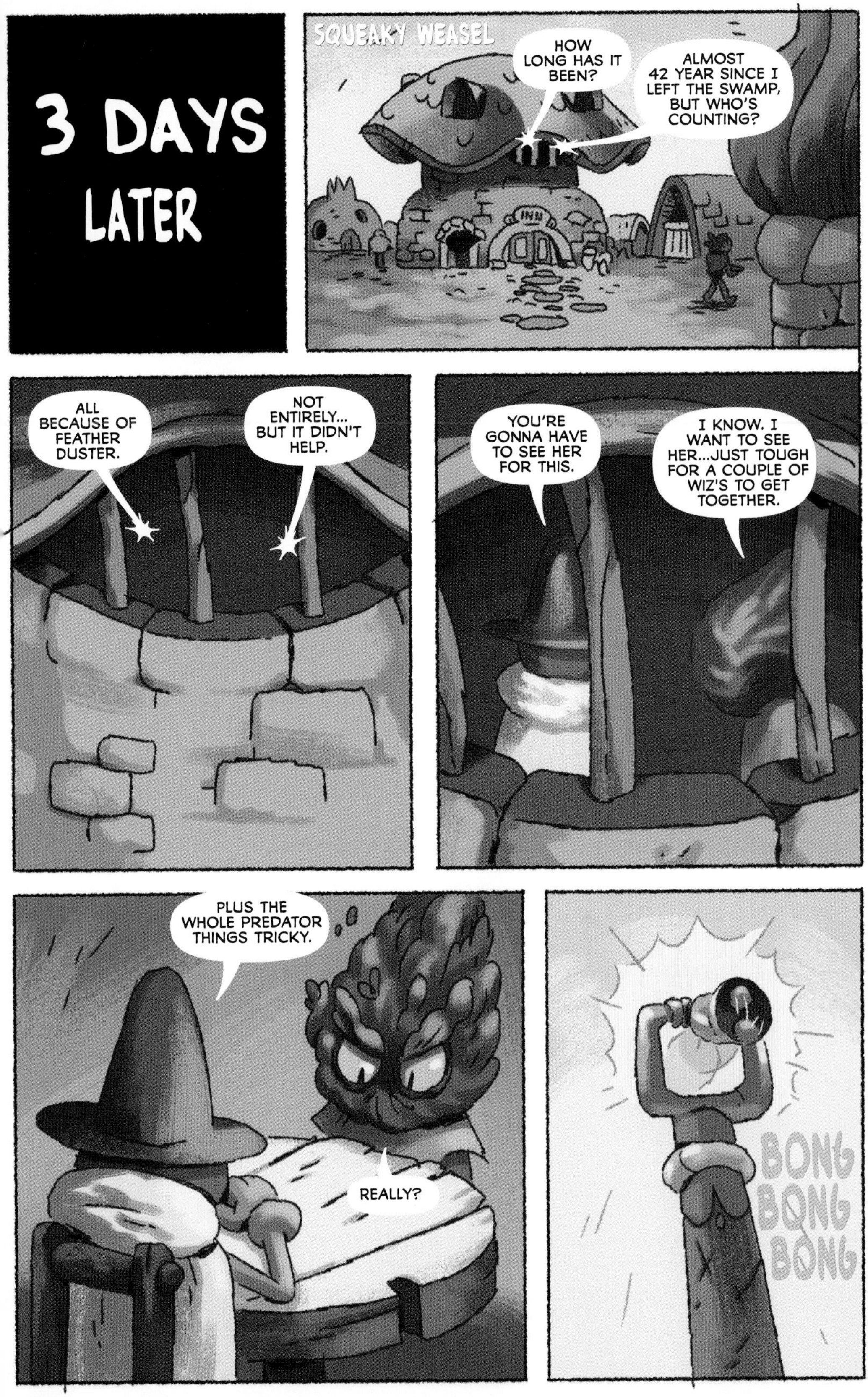
3 DAYS LATER
SQUEAKY WEASEL
HOW LONG HAS IT BEEN?
ALMOST 42 YEAR SINCE I LEFT THE SWAMP, BUT WHO'S COUNTING?
INN
ALL BECAUSE OF FEATHER DUSTER.
NOT ENTIRELY... BUT IT DIDN'T HELP.
YOU'RE GONNA HAVE TO SEE HER FOR THIS.
I KNOW. I WANT TO SEE HER...JUST TOUGH FOR A COUPLE OF WIZ'S TO GET TOGETHER.
PLUS THE WHOLE PREDATOR THINGS TRICKY.
REALLY?
BONG BONG BONG

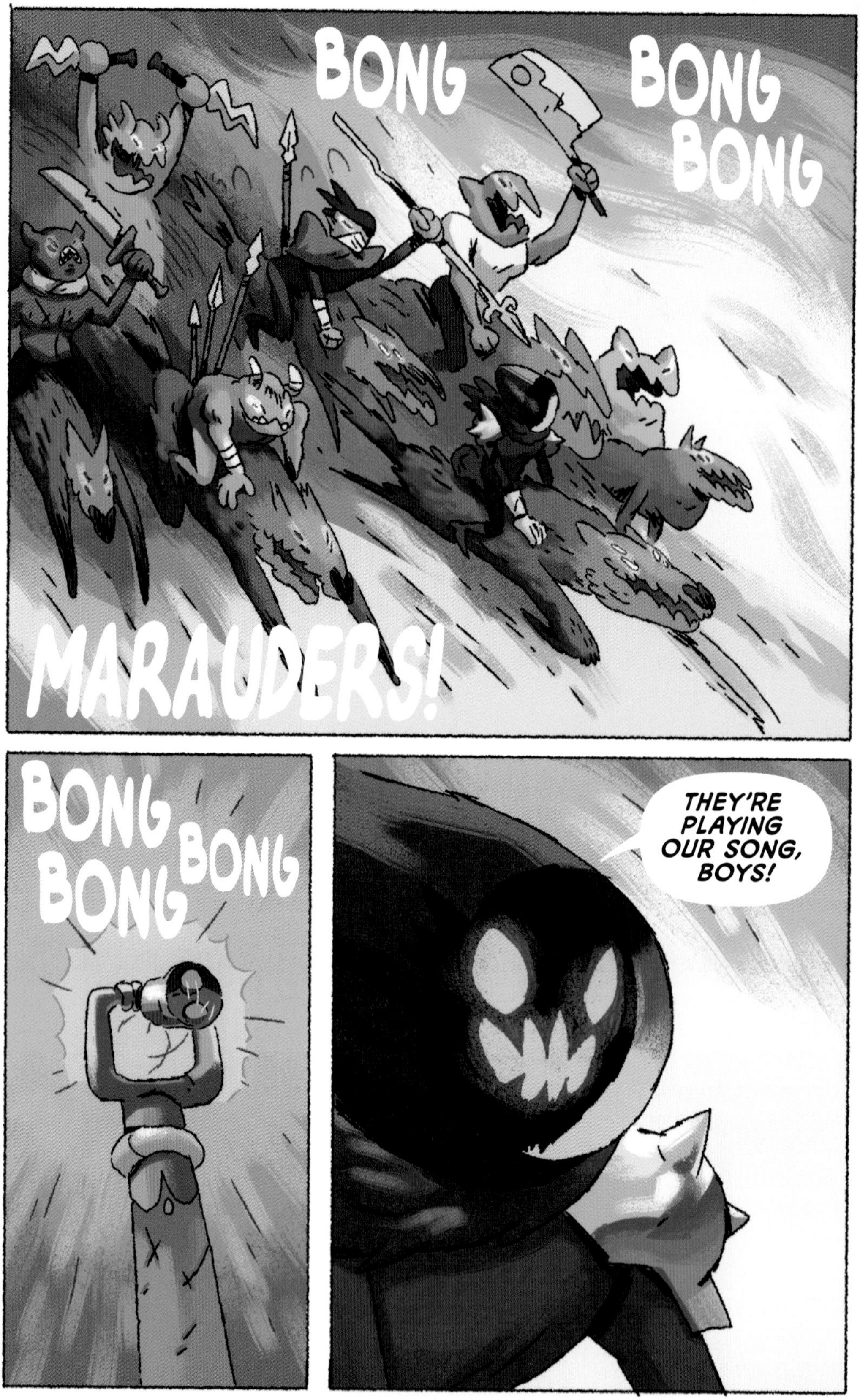
BONG
BONG
BONG
MARAUDERS!
BONG
BONG
BONG
THEY'RE PLAYING OUR SONG, BOYS!

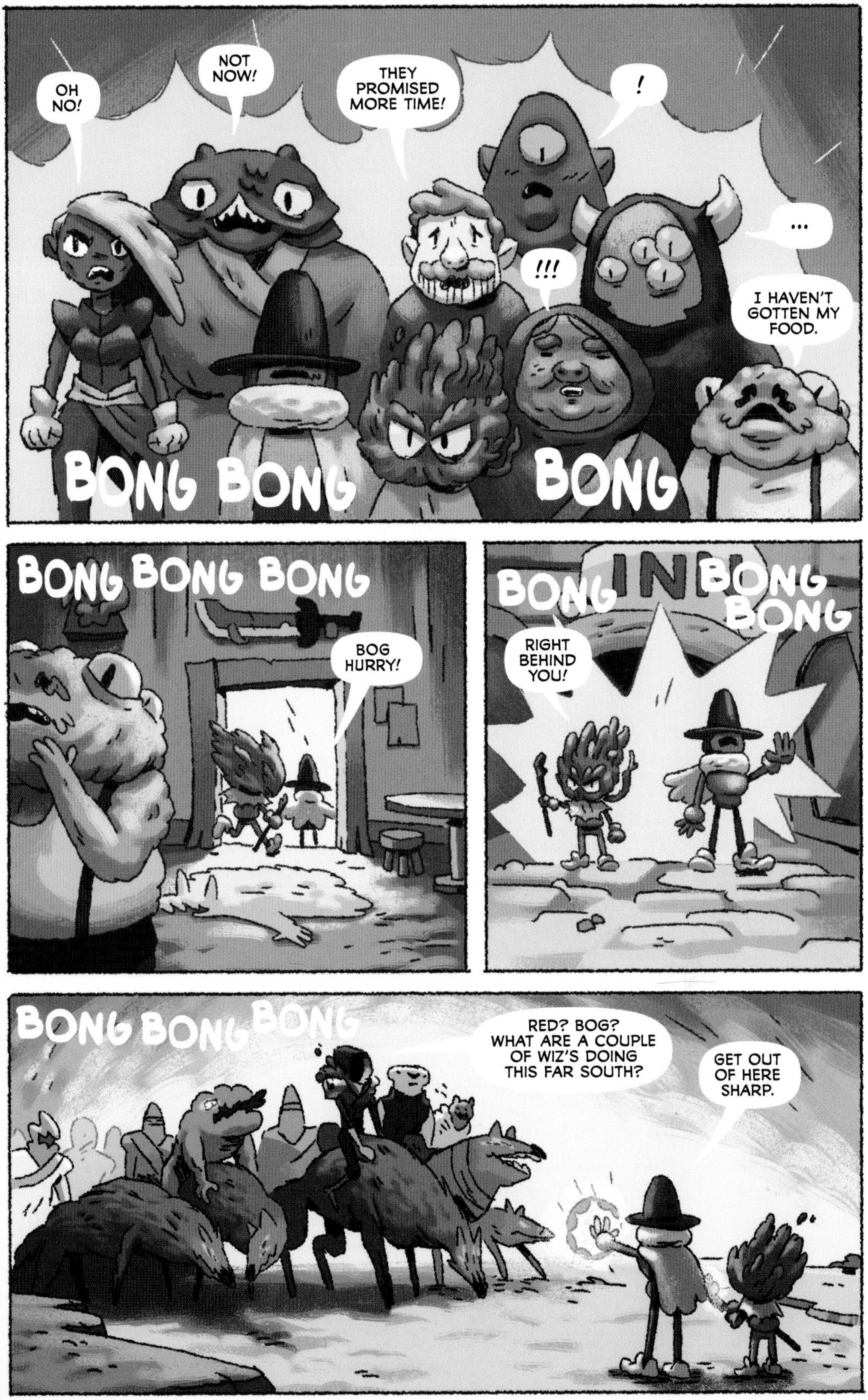
OH NO!
NOT NOW!
THEY PROMISED MORE TIME!
!
...
!!!
I HAVEN'T GOTTEN MY FOOD.
BONG BONG
BONG
BONG BONG BONG
BOG HURRY!
BONG
BONG
BONG
RIGHT BEHIND YOU!
BONG BONG BONG
RED? BOG? WHAT ARE A COUPLE OF WIZ'S DOING THIS FAR SOUTH?
GET OUT OF HERE SHARP.

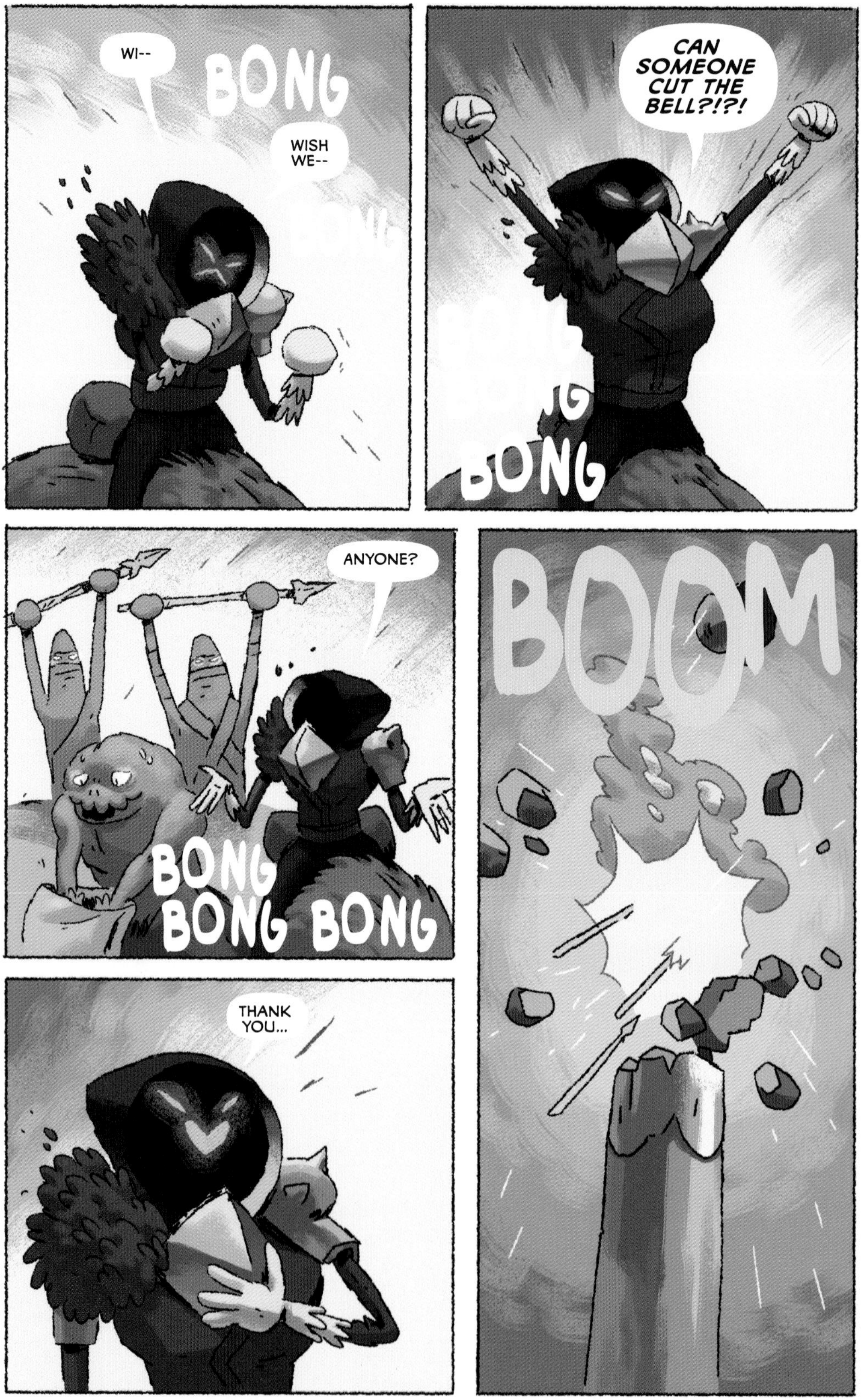
WI--
BONG
WISH WE--
BONG
CAN SOMEONE CUT THE BELL?!?!
BONG
BONG
BONG
ANYONE?
BONG
BONG BONG
BOOM
THANK YOU...

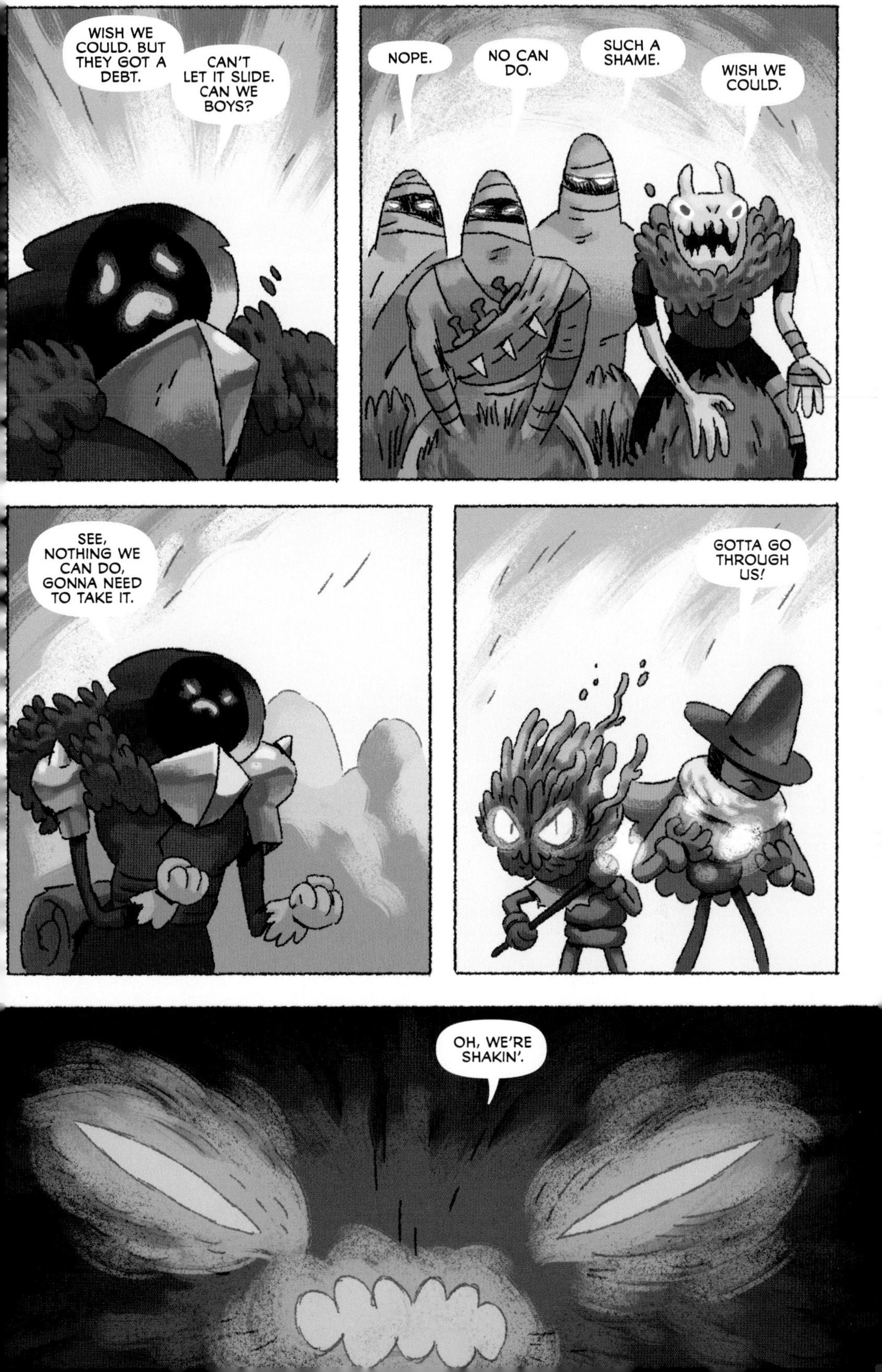
WISH WE COULD. BUT THEY GOT A DEBT.
CAN'T LET IT SLIDE. CAN WE BOYS?
NOPE.
NO CAN DO.
SUCH A SHAME.
WISH WE COULD.
SEE, NOTHING WE CAN DO, GONNA NEED TO TAKE IT.
GOTTA GO THROUGH US!
OH, WE'RE SHAKIN'.

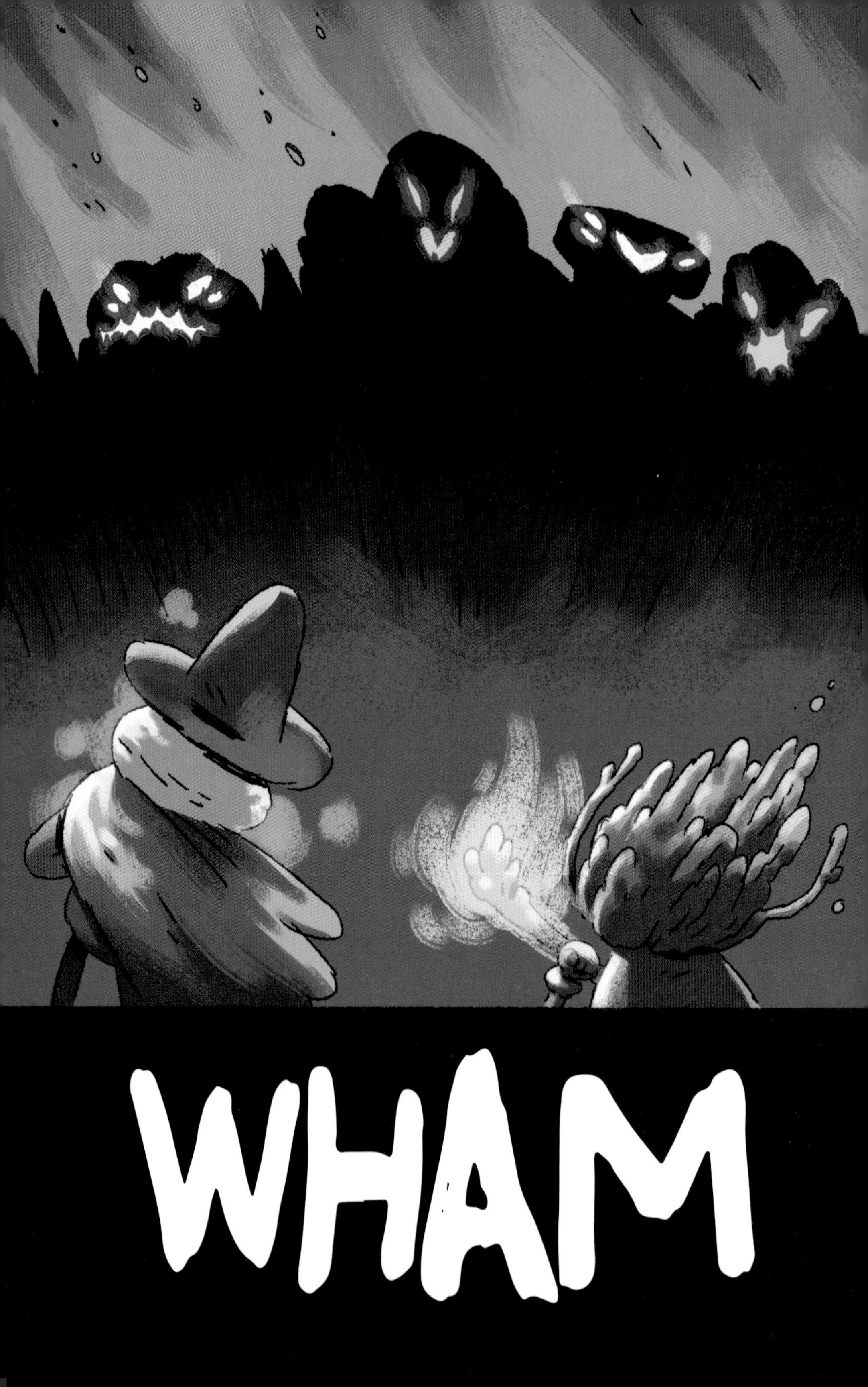
WHAM

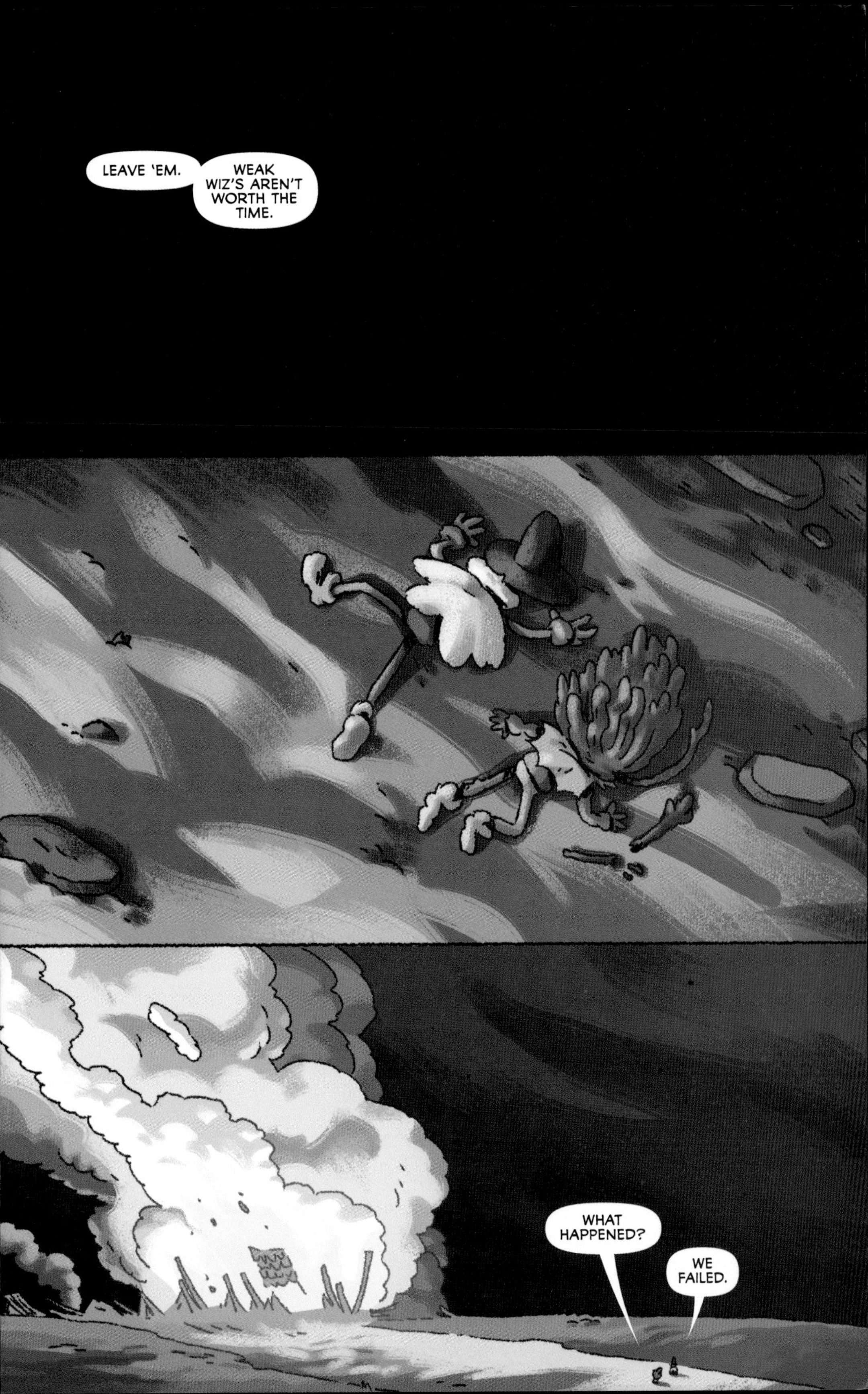
LEAVE 'EM.
WEAK WIZ'S AREN'T WORTH THE TIME.
WHAT HAPPENED?
WE FAILED.

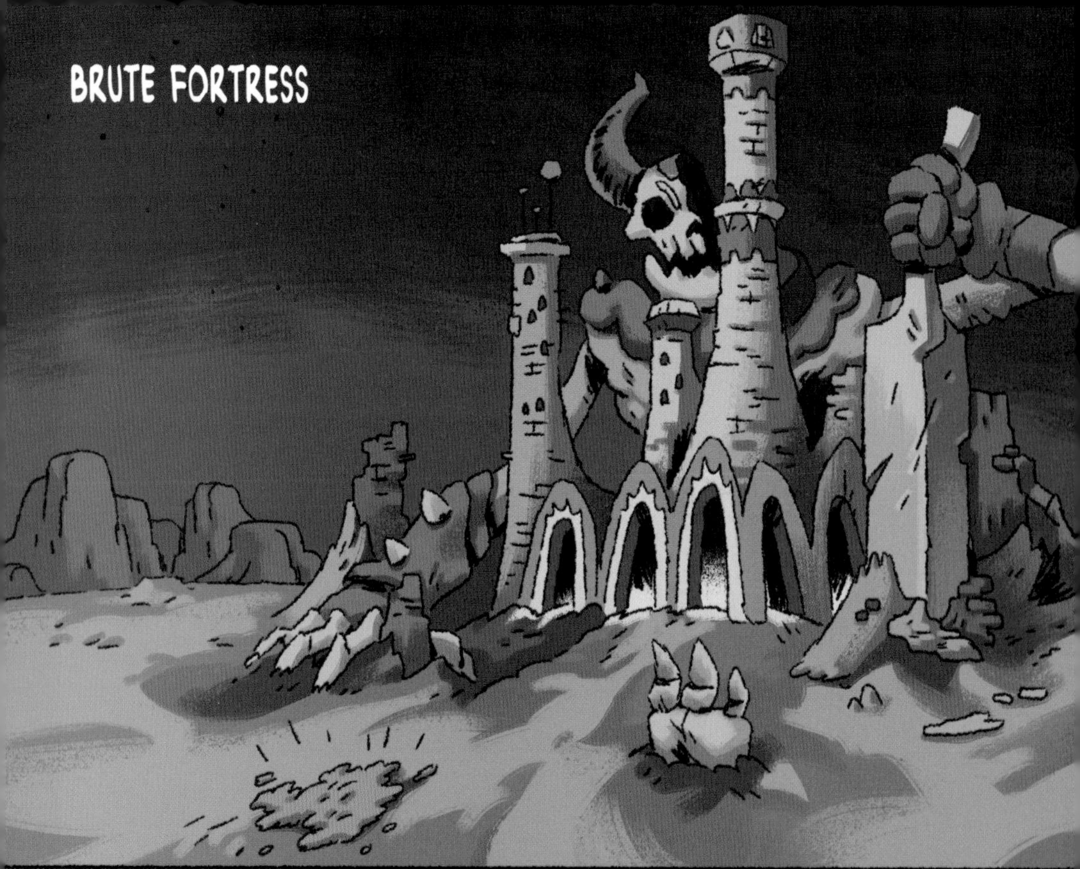
BRUTE FORTRESS

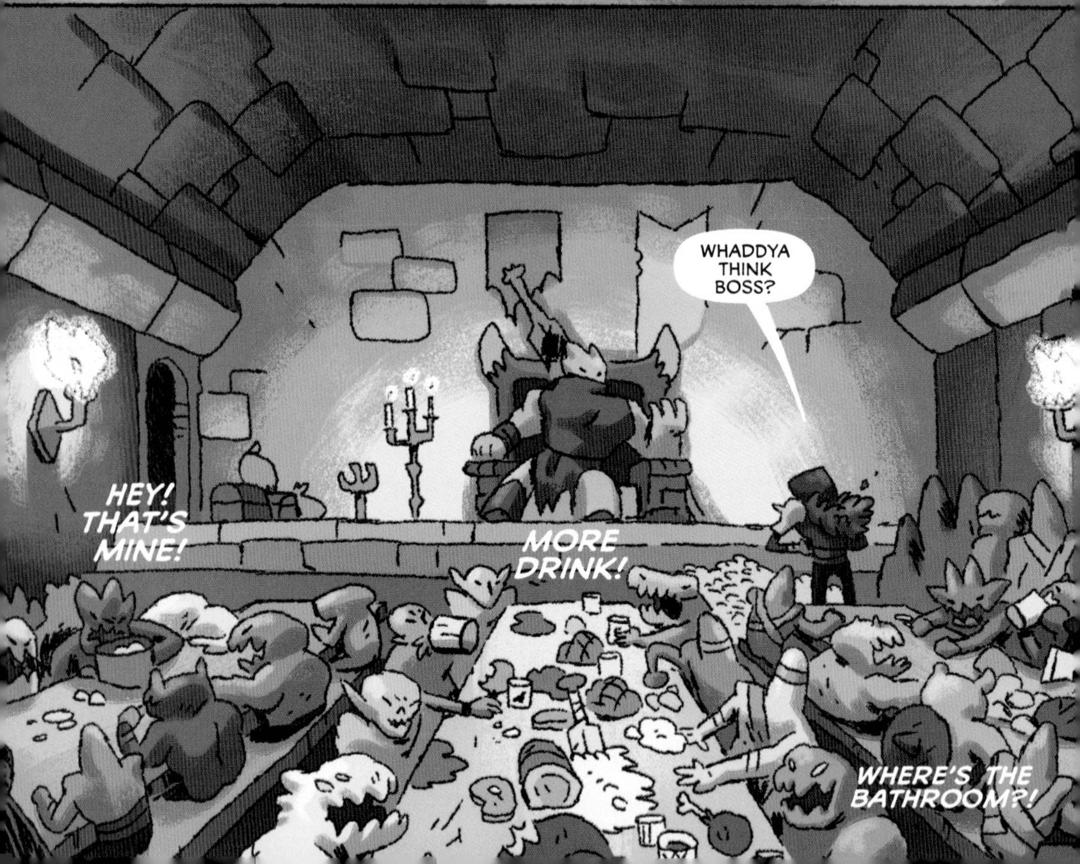
WHADDYA THINK BOSS?
HEY! THAT'S MINE!
MORE DRINK!
WHERE'S THE BATHROOM?!

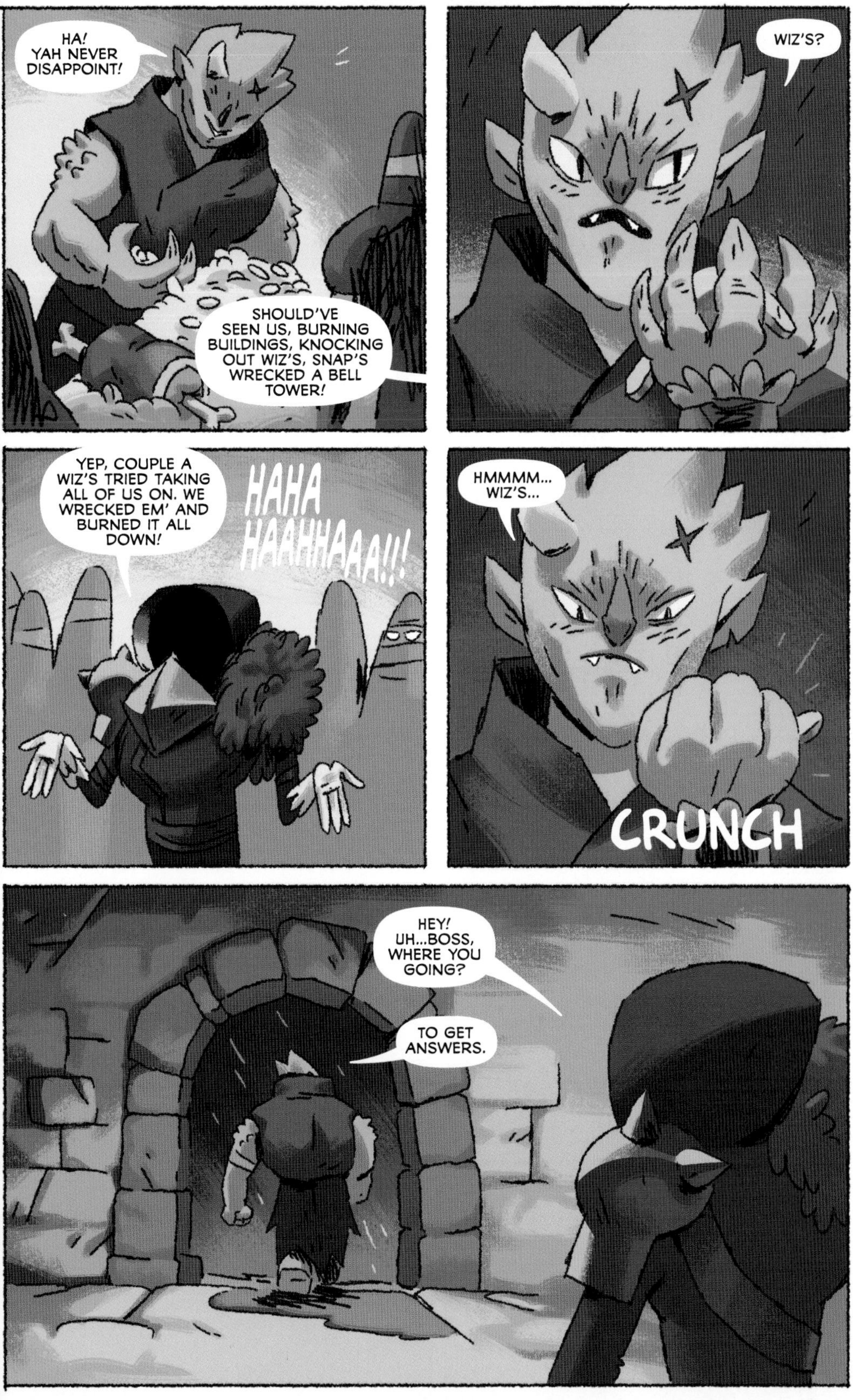
HA! YAH NEVER DISAPPOINT!
SHOULD'VE SEEN US, BURNING BUILDINGS, KNOCKING OUT WIZ'S, SNAP'S WRECKED A BELL TOWER!
WIZ'S?
YEP, COUPLE A WIZ'S TRIED TAKING ALL OF US ON. WE WRECKED EM' AND BURNED IT ALL DOWN!
HAHA HAAHHAAA!!!
HMMMM... WIZ'S...
CRUNCH
HEY! UH...BOSS, WHERE YOU GOING?
TO GET ANSWERS.

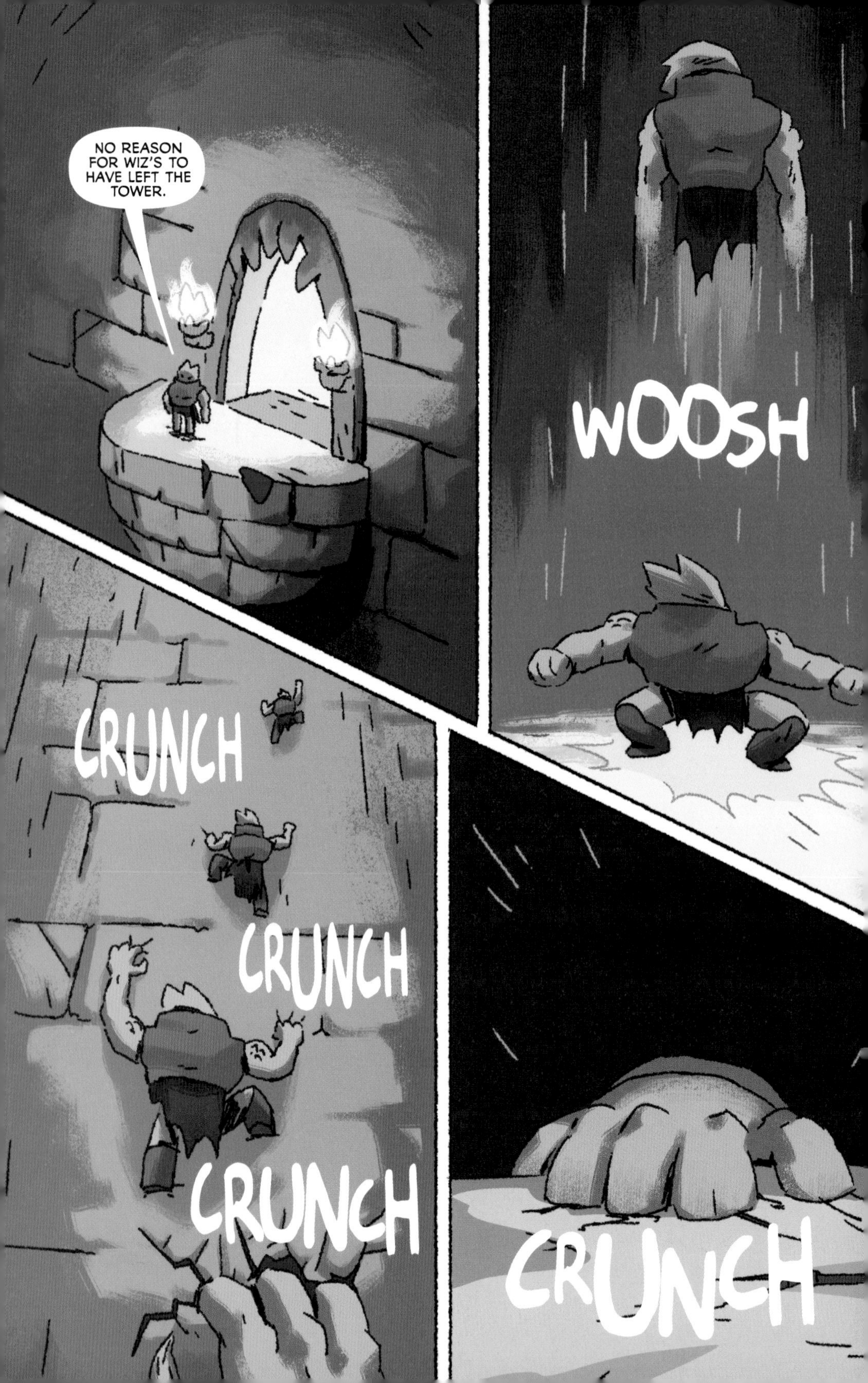
NO REASON FOR WIZ'S TO HAVE LEFT THE TOWER.
WOOSH
CRUNCH
CRUNCH
CRUNCH
CRUNCH

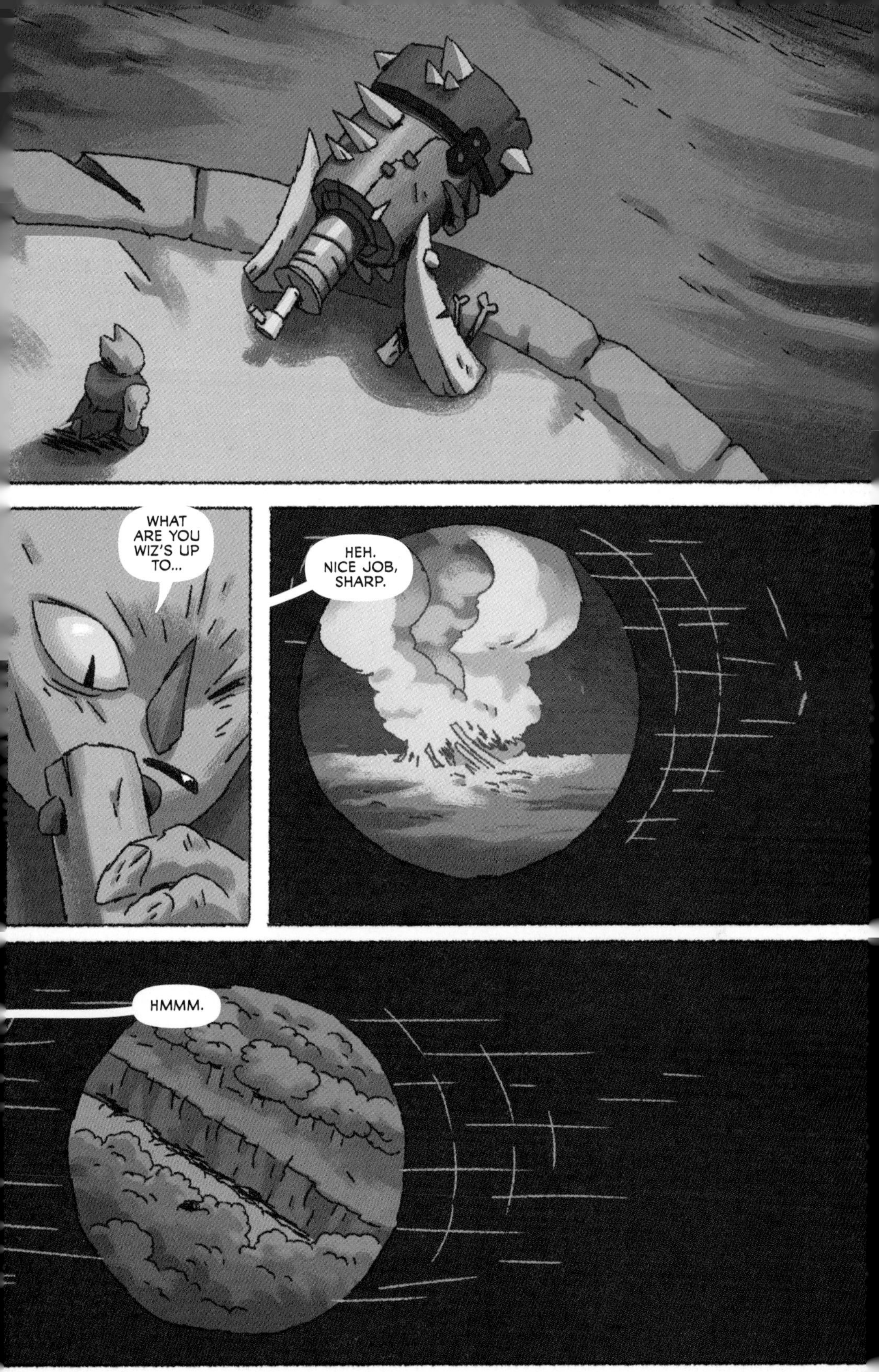
WHAT ARE YOU WIZ'S UP TO...
HEH. NICE JOB, SHARP.
HMMM.

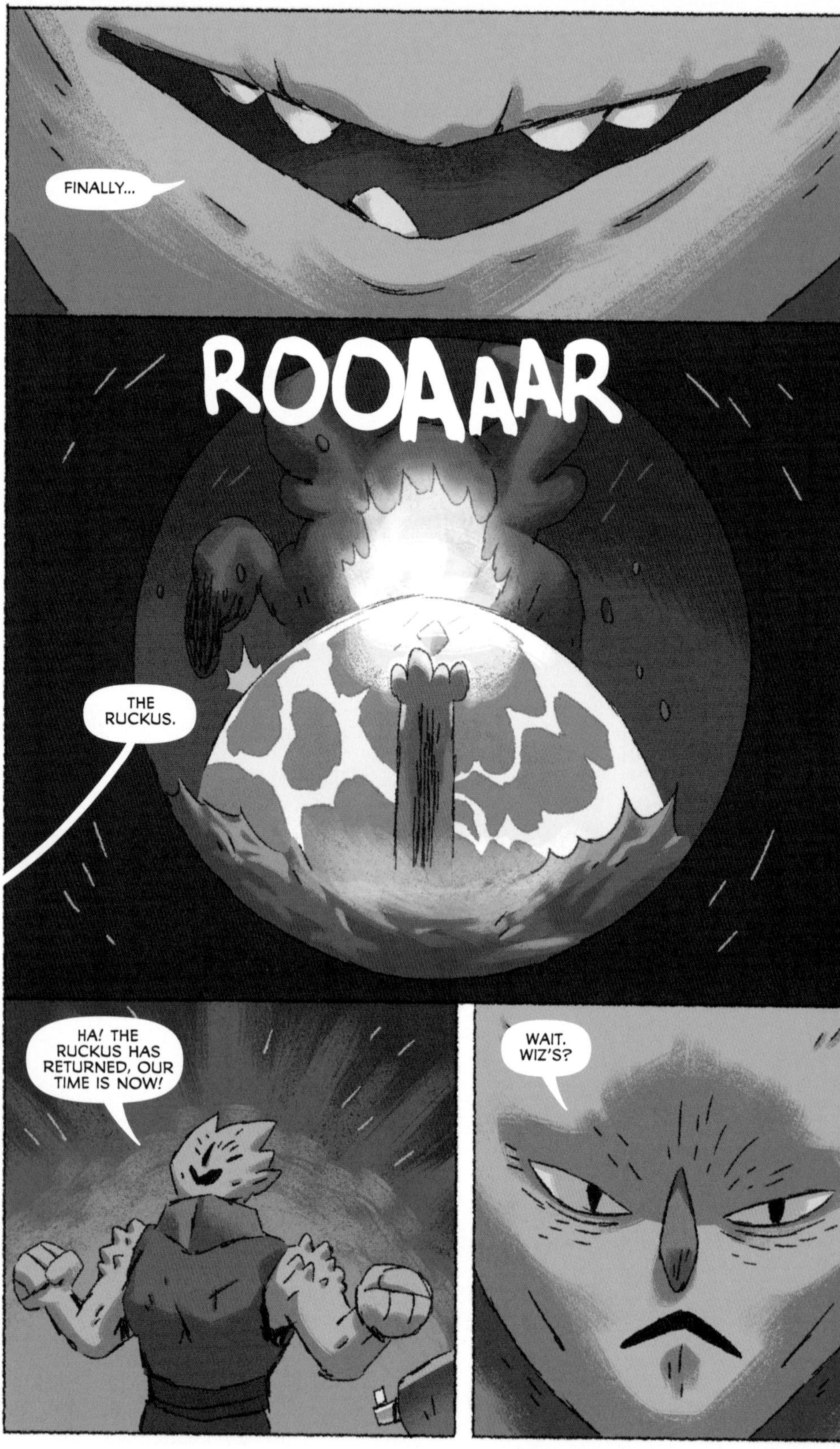
FINALLY...
ROOAAAR
THE RUCKUS.
HA! THE RUCKUS HAS RETURNED, OUR TIME IS NOW!
WAIT. WIZ'S?

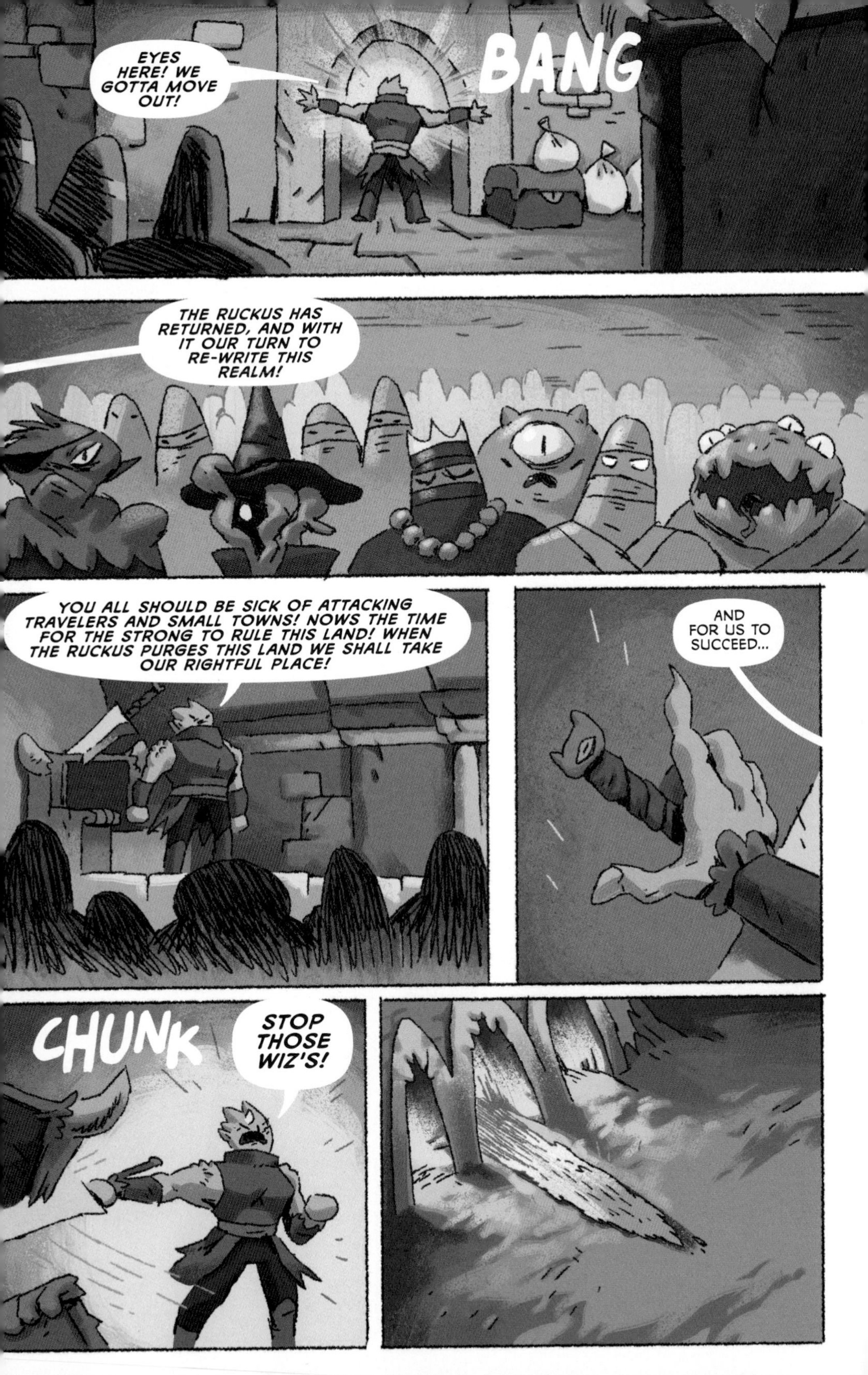
EYES HERE! WE GOTTA MOVE OUT!
BANG
THE RUCKUS HAS RETURNED, AND WITH IT OUR TURN TO RE-WRITE THIS REALM!
YOU ALL SHOULD BE SICK OF ATTACKING TRAVELERS AND SMALL TOWNS! NOWS THE TIME FOR THE STRONG TO RULE THIS LAND! WHEN THE RUCKUS PURGES THIS LAND WE SHALL TAKE OUR RIGHTFUL PLACE!
AND FOR US TO SUCCEED...
CHUNK
STOP THOSE WIZ'S!

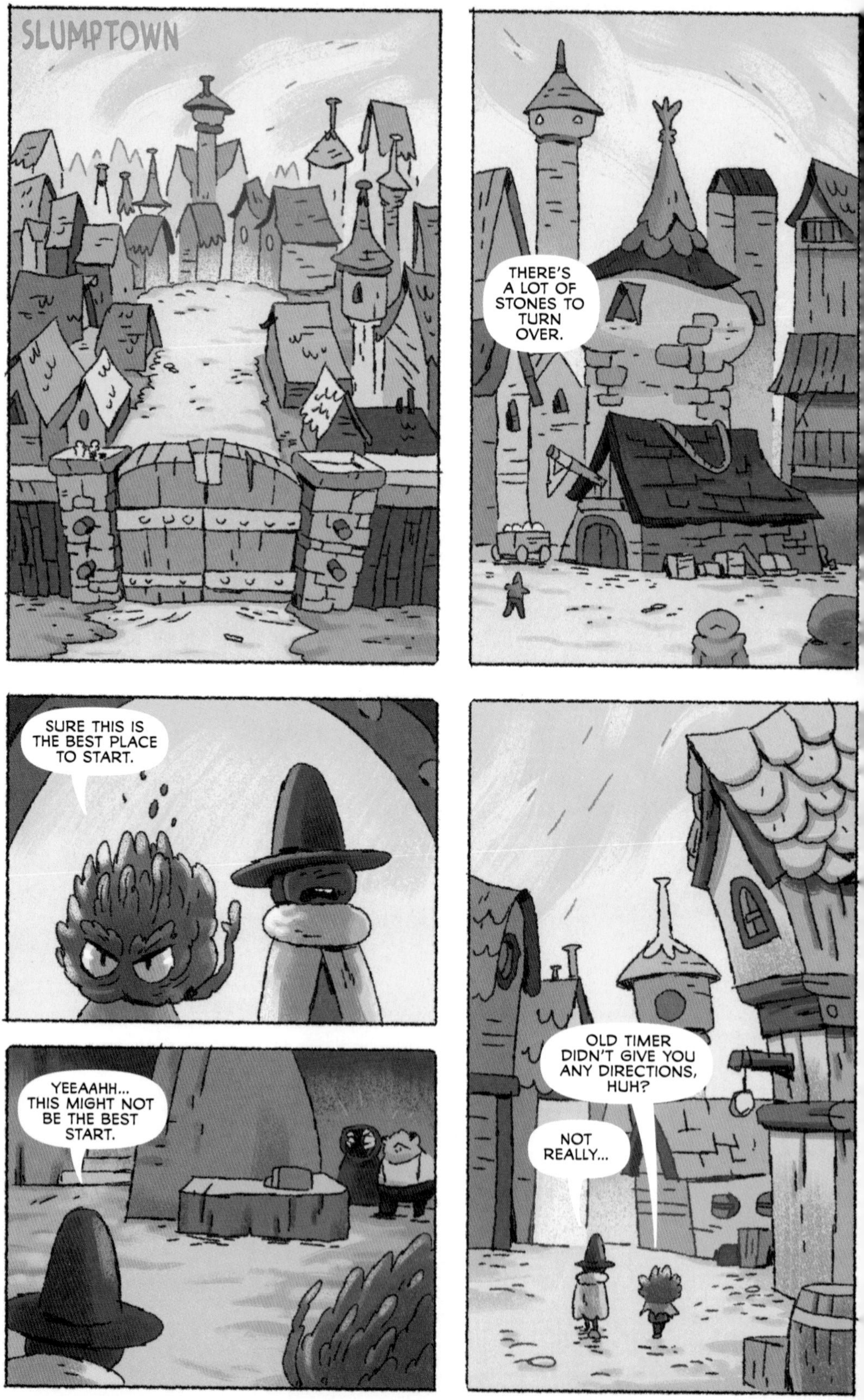
SLUMPTOWN
THERE'S A LOT OF STONES TO TURN OVER.
SURE THIS IS THE BEST PLACE TO START.
YEEAAHH... THIS MIGHT NOT BE THE BEST START.
OLD TIMER DIDN'T GIVE YOU ANY DIRECTIONS, HUH?
NOT REALLY...

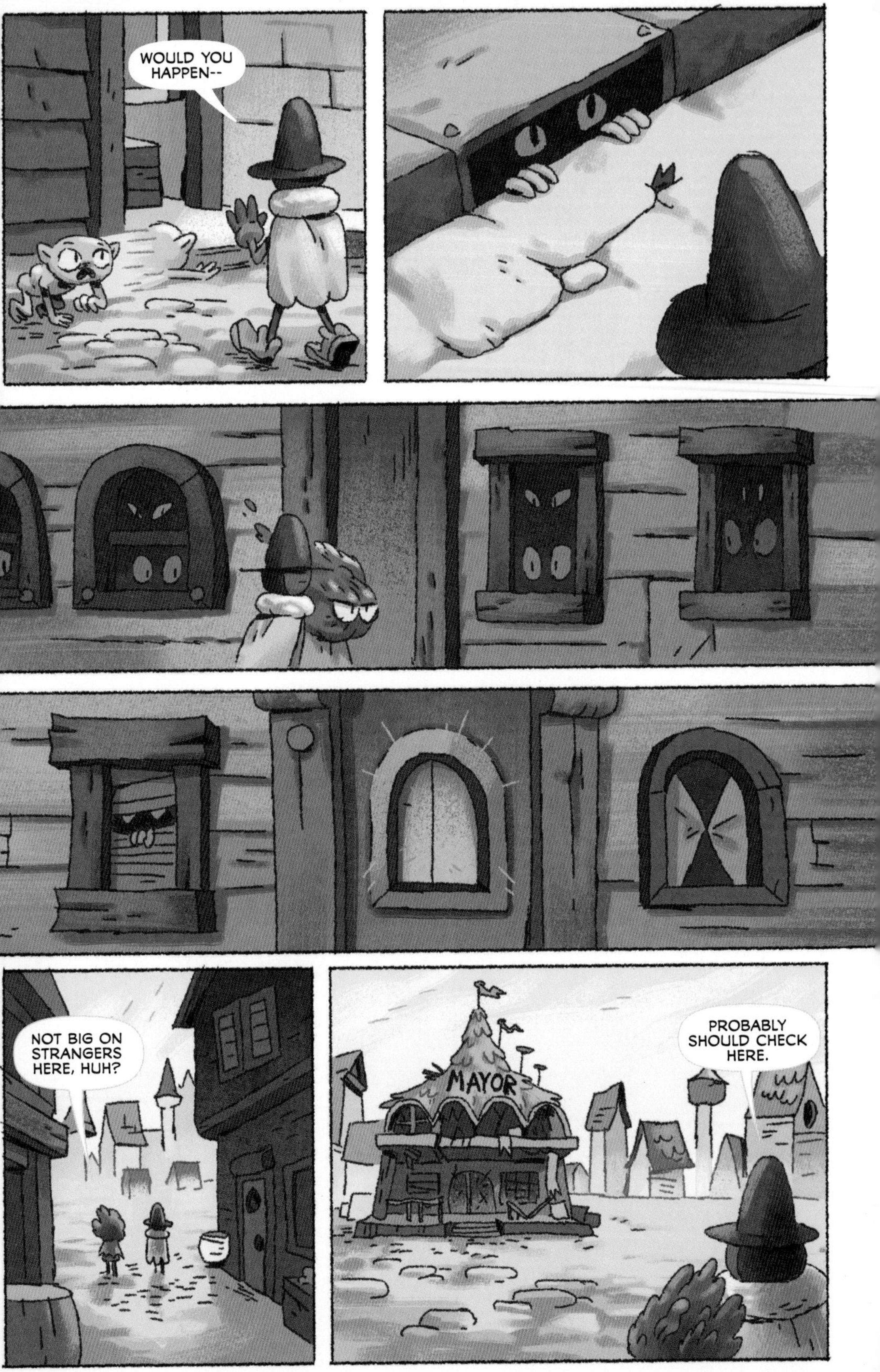
WOULD YOU HAPPEN--
NOT BIG ON STRANGERS HERE, HUH?
MAYOR
PROBABLY SHOULD CHECK HERE.

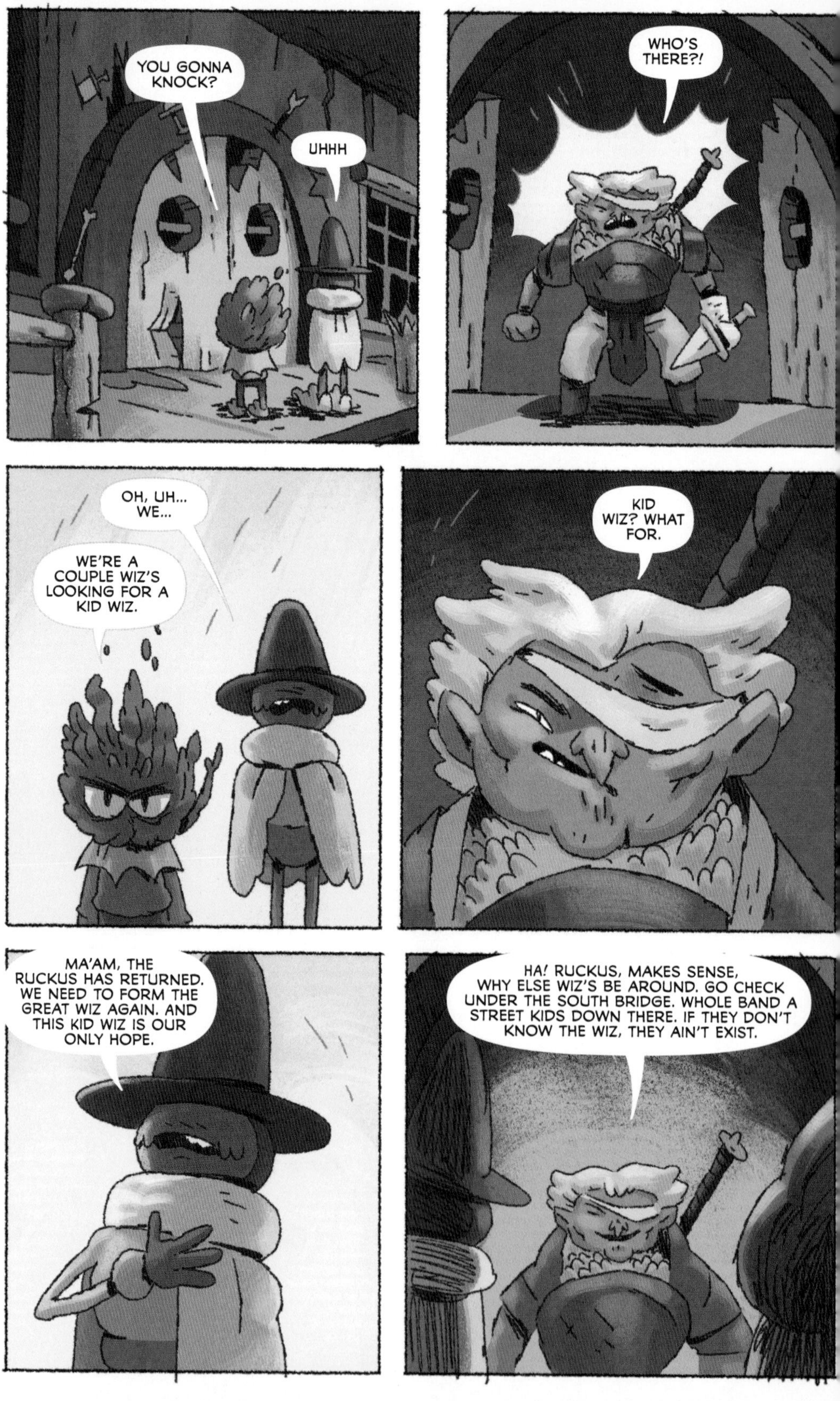
YOU GONNA KNOCK?
UHHH
WHO'S THERE?!
OH, UH... WE...
WE'RE A COUPLE WIZ'S LOOKING FOR A KID WIZ.
KID WIZ? WHAT FOR.
MA'AM, THE RUCKUS HAS RETURNED. WE NEED TO FORM THE GREAT WIZ AGAIN. AND THIS KID WIZ IS OUR ONLY HOPE.
HA! RUCKUS, MAKES SENSE, WHY ELSE WIZ'S BE AROUND. GO CHECK UNDER THE SOUTH BRIDGE. WHOLE BAND A STREET KIDS DOWN THERE. IF THEY DON'T KNOW THE WIZ, THEY AIN'T EXIST.

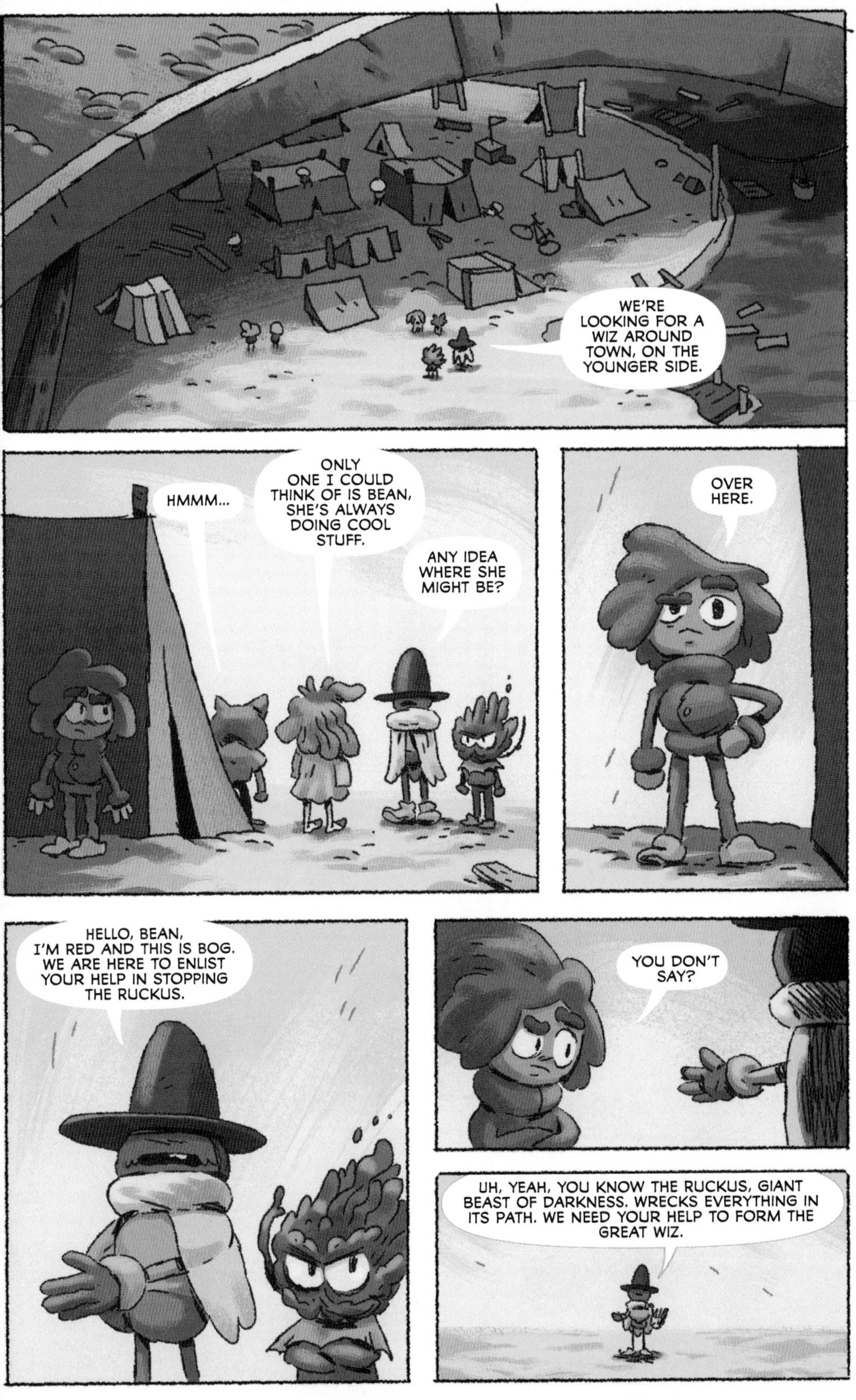
WE'RE LOOKING FOR A WIZ AROUND TOWN, ON THE YOUNGER SIDE.
HMMM...
ONLY ONE I COULD THINK OF IS BEAN, SHE'S ALWAYS DOING COOL STUFF.
ANY IDEA WHERE SHE MIGHT BE?
OVER HERE.
HELLO, BEAN, I'M RED AND THIS IS BOG. WE ARE HERE TO ENLIST YOUR HELP IN STOPPING THE RUCKUS.
YOU DON'T SAY?
UH, YEAH, YOU KNOW THE RUCKUS, GIANT BEAST OF DARKNESS. WRECKS EVERYTHING IN ITS PATH. WE NEED YOUR HELP TO FORM THE GREAT WIZ.

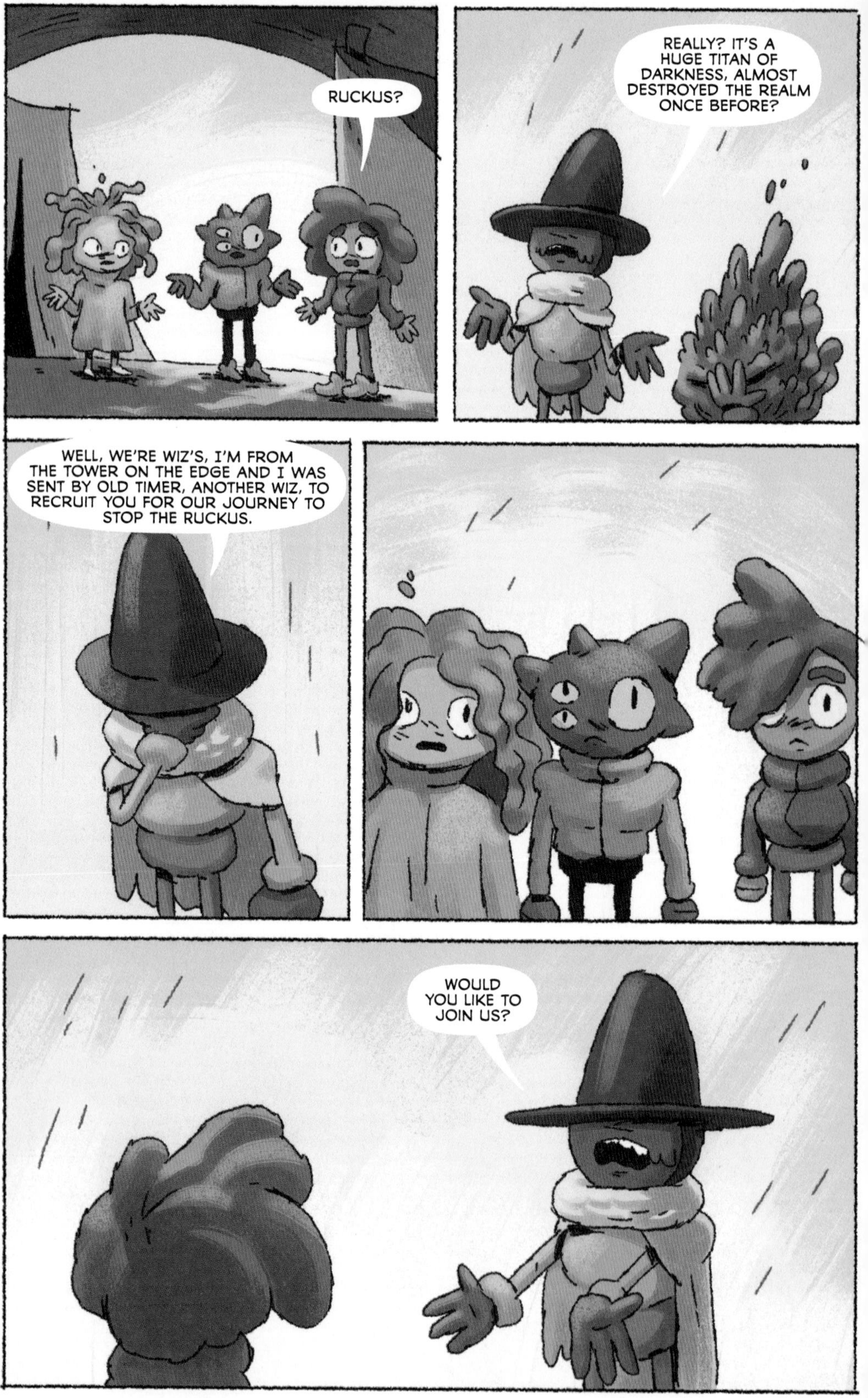
RUCKUS?
REALLY? IT'S A HUGE TITAN OF DARKNESS, ALMOST DESTROYED THE REALM ONCE BEFORE?
WELL, WE'RE WIZ'S, I'M FROM THE TOWER ON THE EDGE AND I WAS SENT BY OLD TIMER, ANOTHER WIZ, TO RECRUIT YOU FOR OUR JOURNEY TO STOP THE RUCKUS.
WOULD YOU LIKE TO JOIN US?

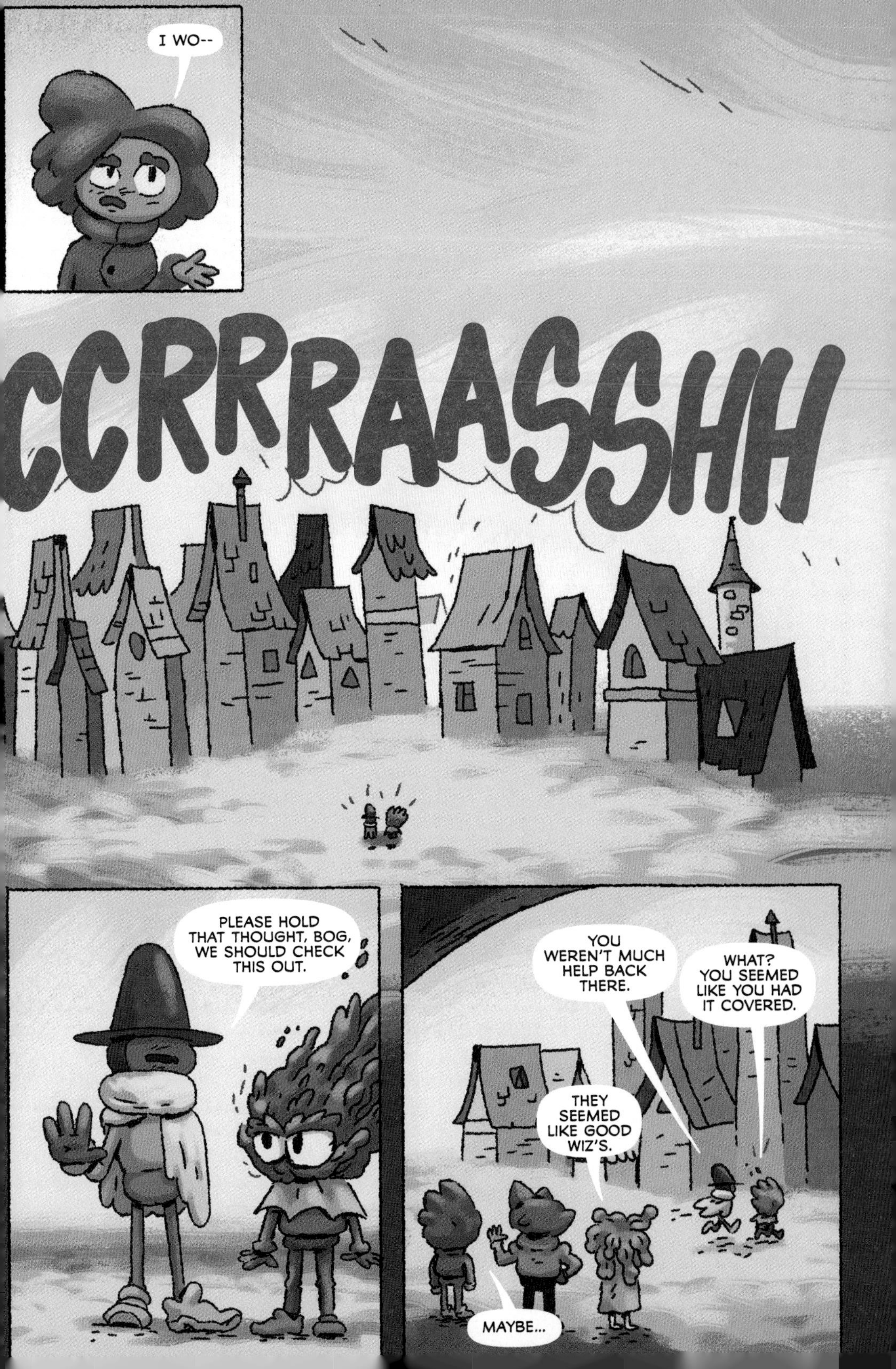
I WO--
CCRRRAASSHH
PLEASE HOLD THAT THOUGHT, BOG, WE SHOULD CHECK THIS OUT.
YOU WEREN'T MUCH HELP BACK THERE.
WHAT? YOU SEEMED LIKE YOU HAD IT COVERED.
THEY SEEMED LIKE GOOD WIZ'S.
MAYBE...

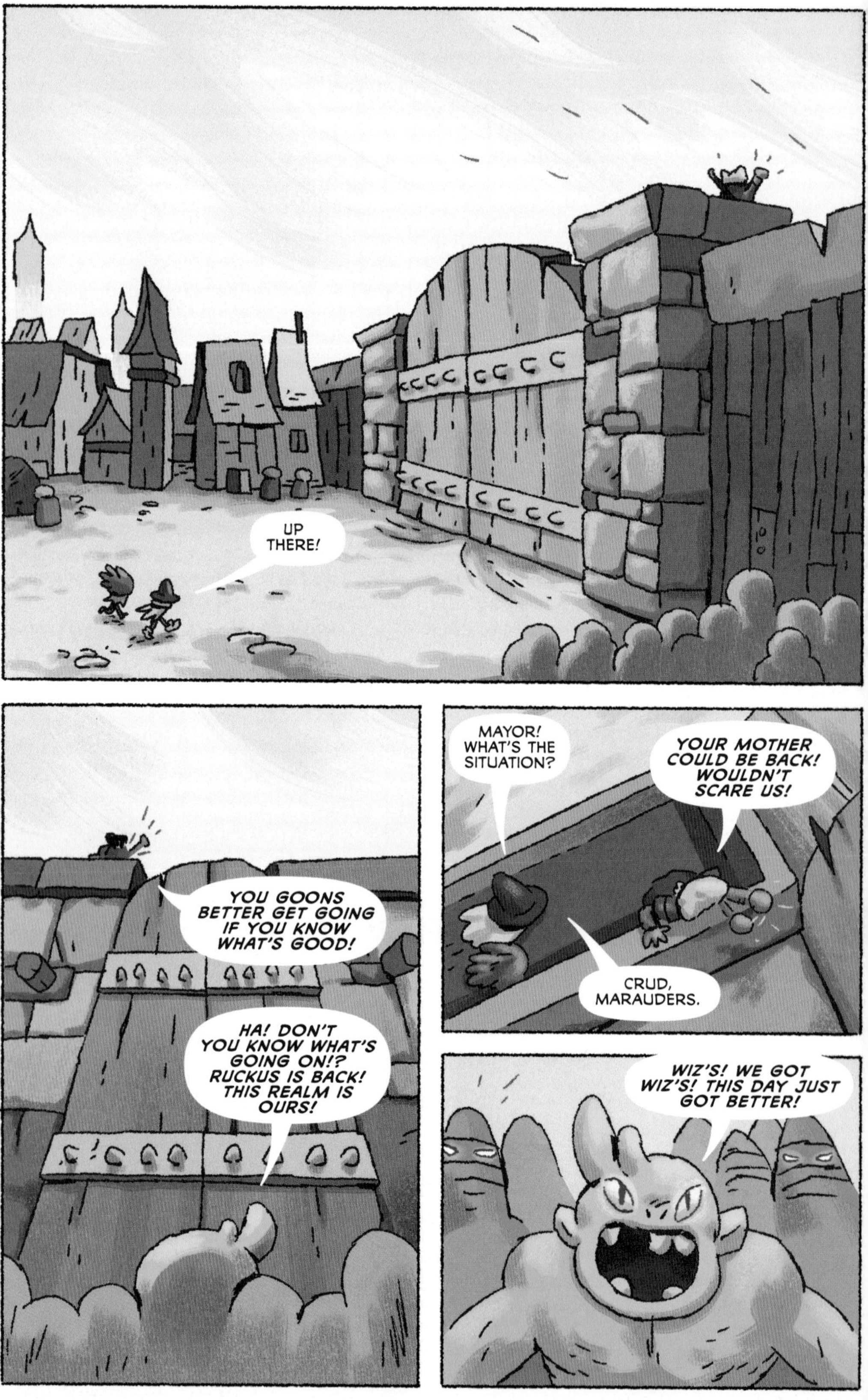
UP THERE!
YOU GOONS BETTER GET GOING IF YOU KNOW WHAT'S GOOD!
HA! DON'T YOU KNOW WHAT'S GOING ON!? RUCKUS IS BACK! THIS REALM IS OURS!
MAYOR! WHAT'S THE SITUATION?
YOUR MOTHER COULD BE BACK! WOULDN'T SCARE US!
CRUD, MARAUDERS.
WIZ'S! WE GOT WIZ'S! THIS DAY JUST GOT BETTER!

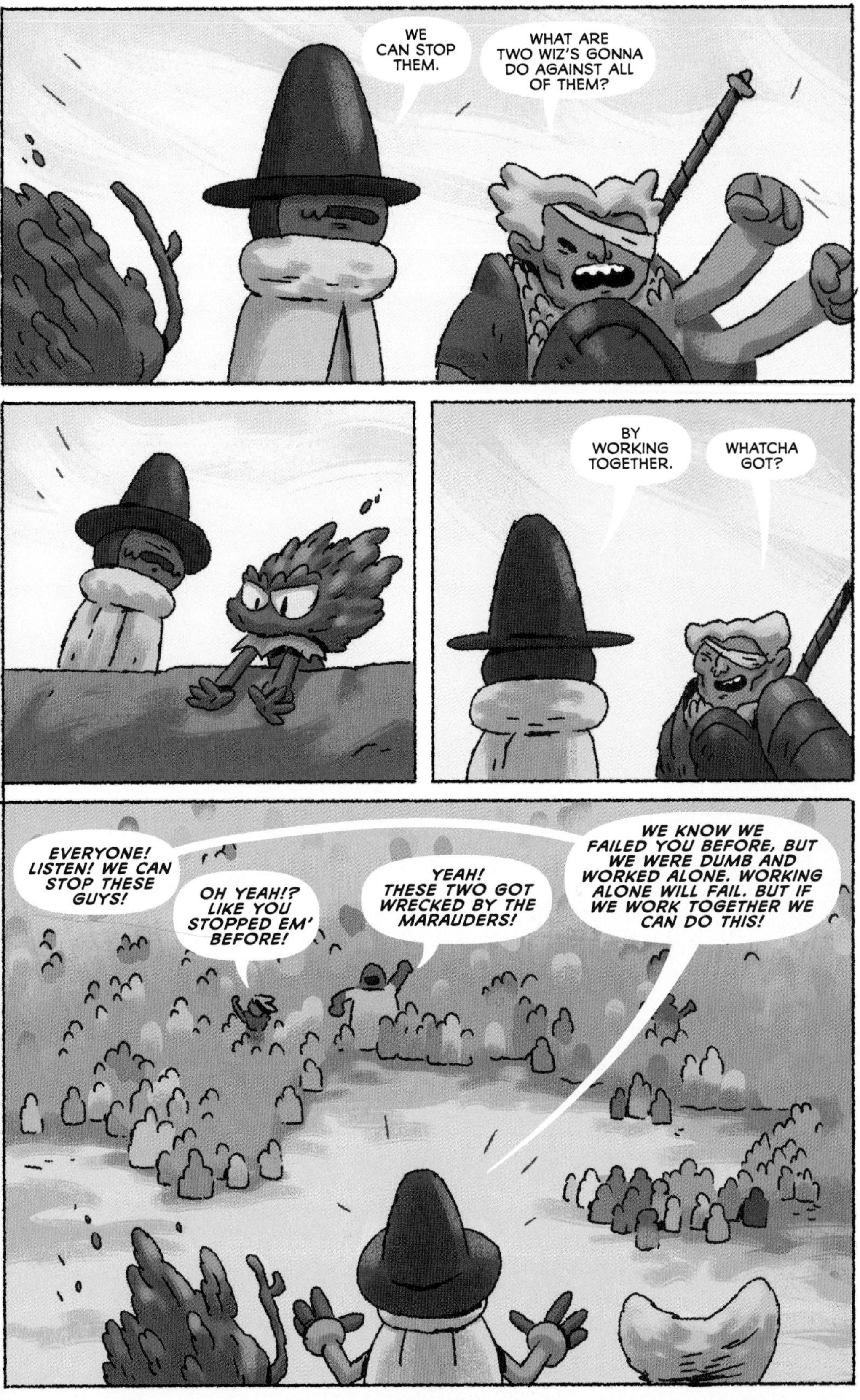
WE CAN STOP THEM.
WHAT ARE TWO WIZ'S GONNA DO AGAINST ALL OF THEM?
BY WORKING TOGETHER.
WHATCHA GOT?
EVERYONE! LISTEN! WE CAN STOP THESE GUYS!
OH YEAH!? LIKE YOU STOPPED EM' BEFORE!
YEAH! THESE TWO GOT WRECKED BY THE MARAUDERS!
WE KNOW WE FAILED YOU BEFORE, BUT WE WERE DUMB AND WORKED ALONE. WORKING ALONE WILL FAIL. BUT IF WE WORK TOGETHER WE CAN DO THIS!

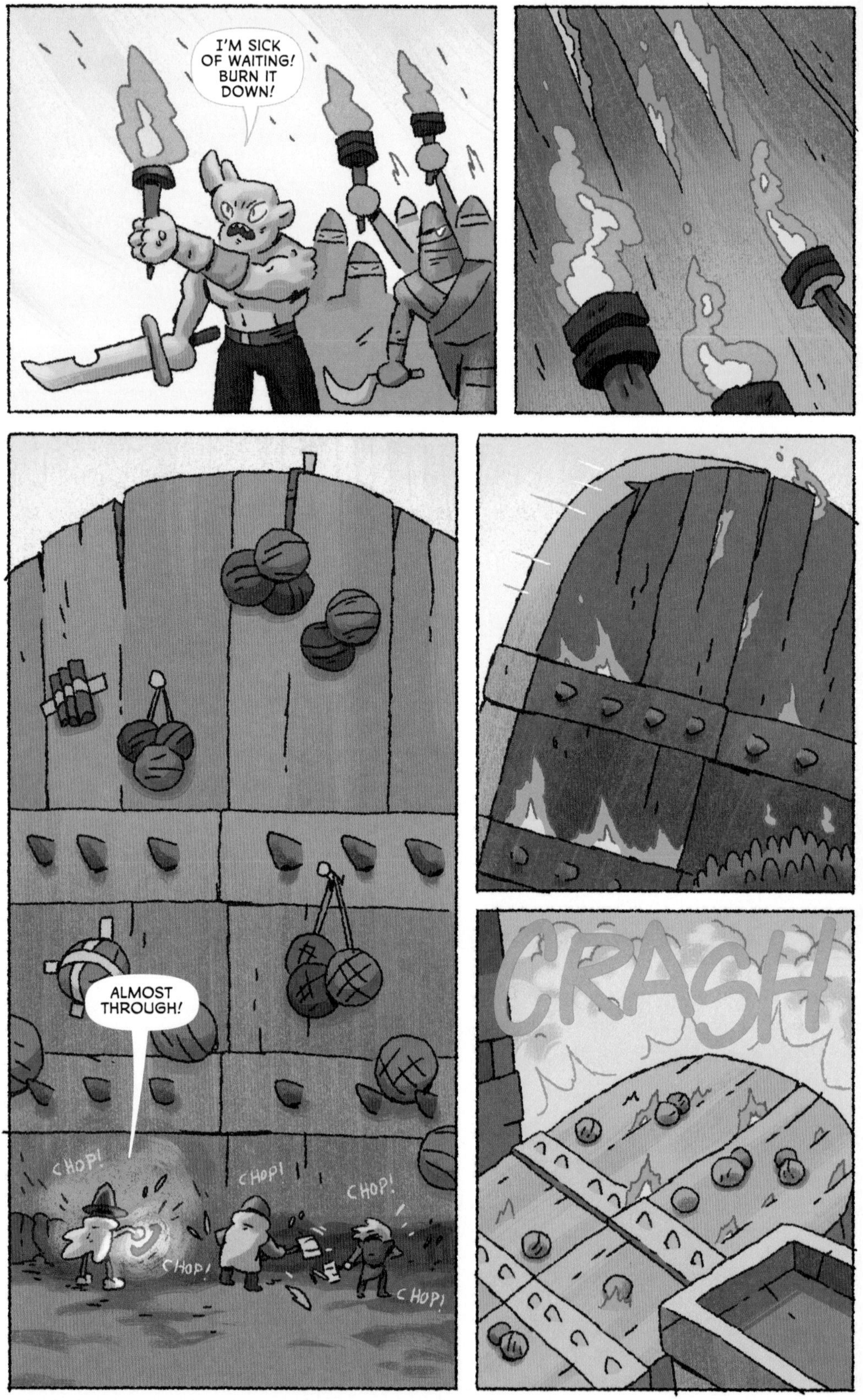
I'M SICK OF WAITING! BURN IT DOWN!
ALMOST THROUGH!
CHOP!
CHOP!
CHOP!
CHOP!
CHOP!
CRASH

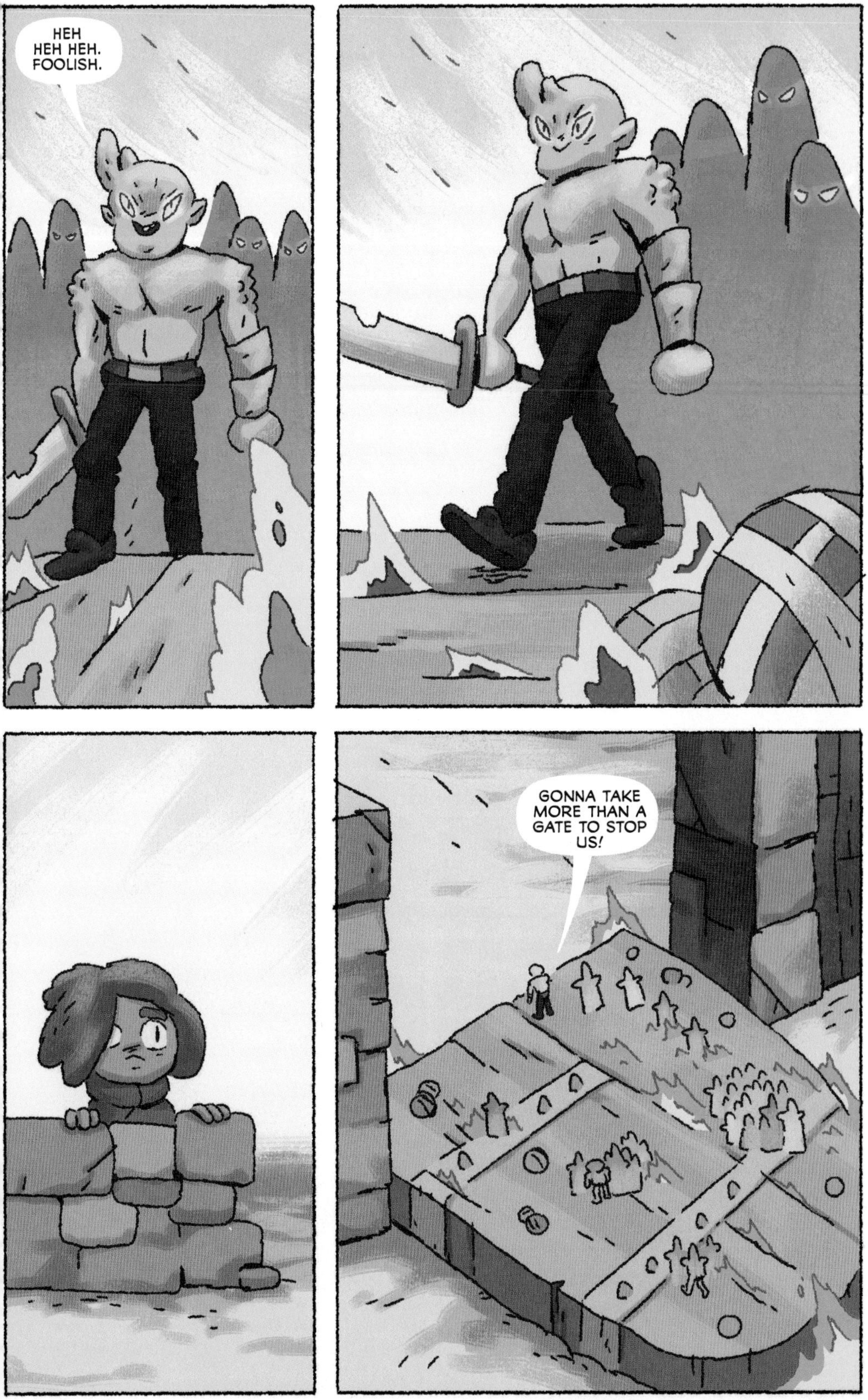
HEH HEH HEH. FOOLISH.
GONNA TAKE MORE THAN A GATE TO STOP US!

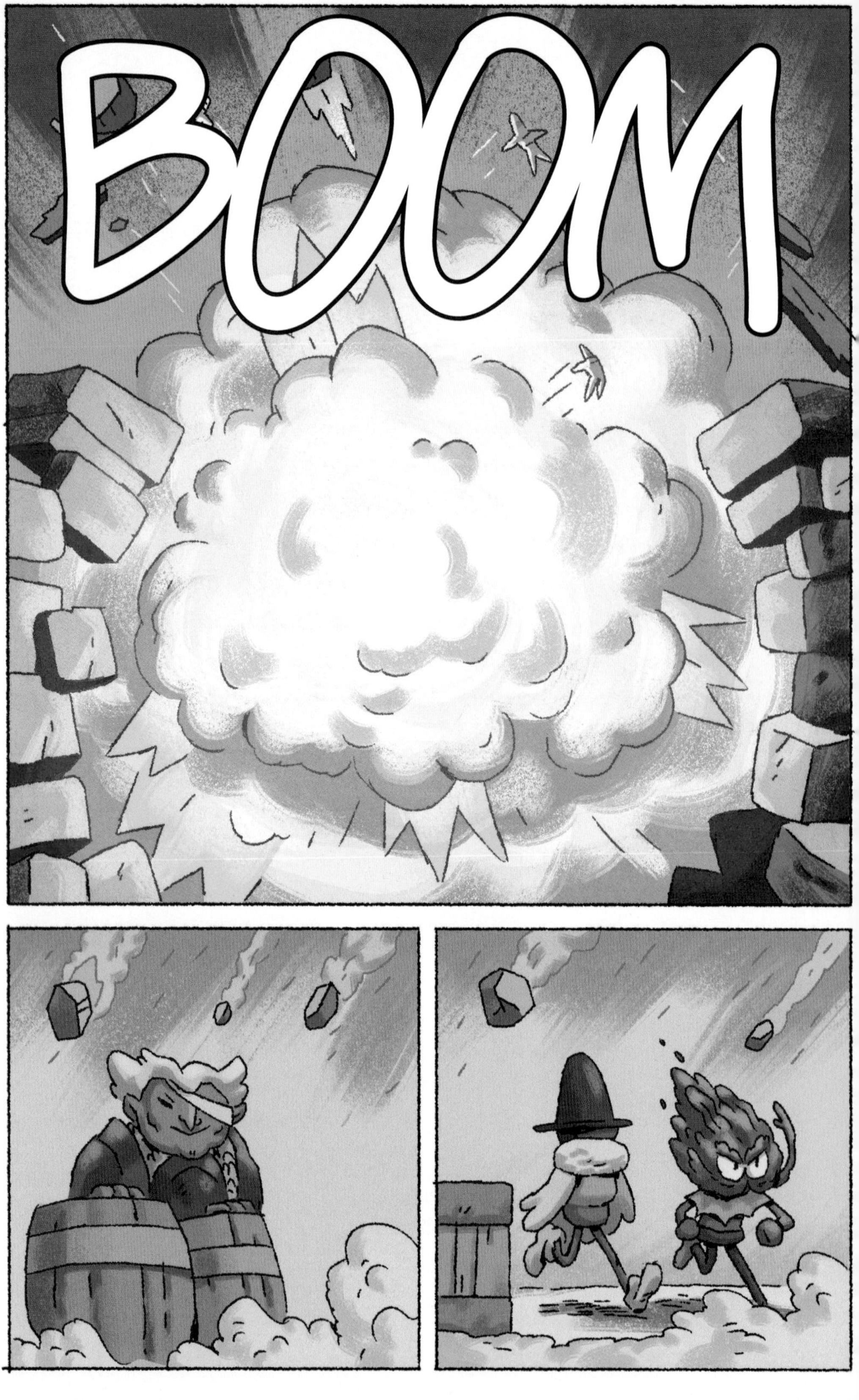
BOOM

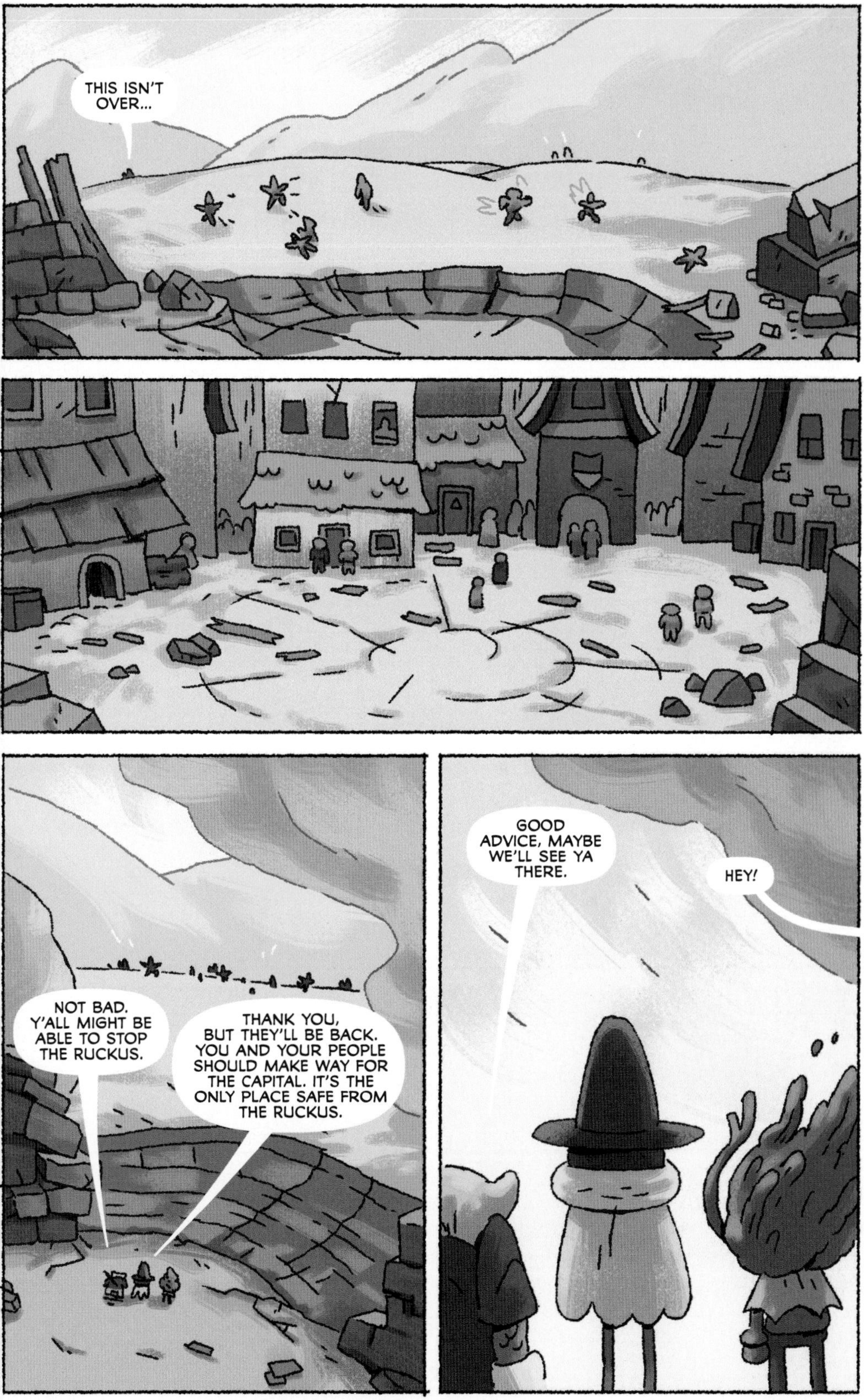
THIS ISN'T OVER...
NOT BAD. Y'ALL MIGHT BE ABLE TO STOP THE RUCKUS.
THANK YOU, BUT THEY'LL BE BACK. YOU AND YOUR PEOPLE SHOULD MAKE WAY FOR THE CAPITAL. IT'S THE ONLY PLACE SAFE FROM THE RUCKUS.
GOOD ADVICE, MAYBE WE'LL SEE YA THERE.
HEY!

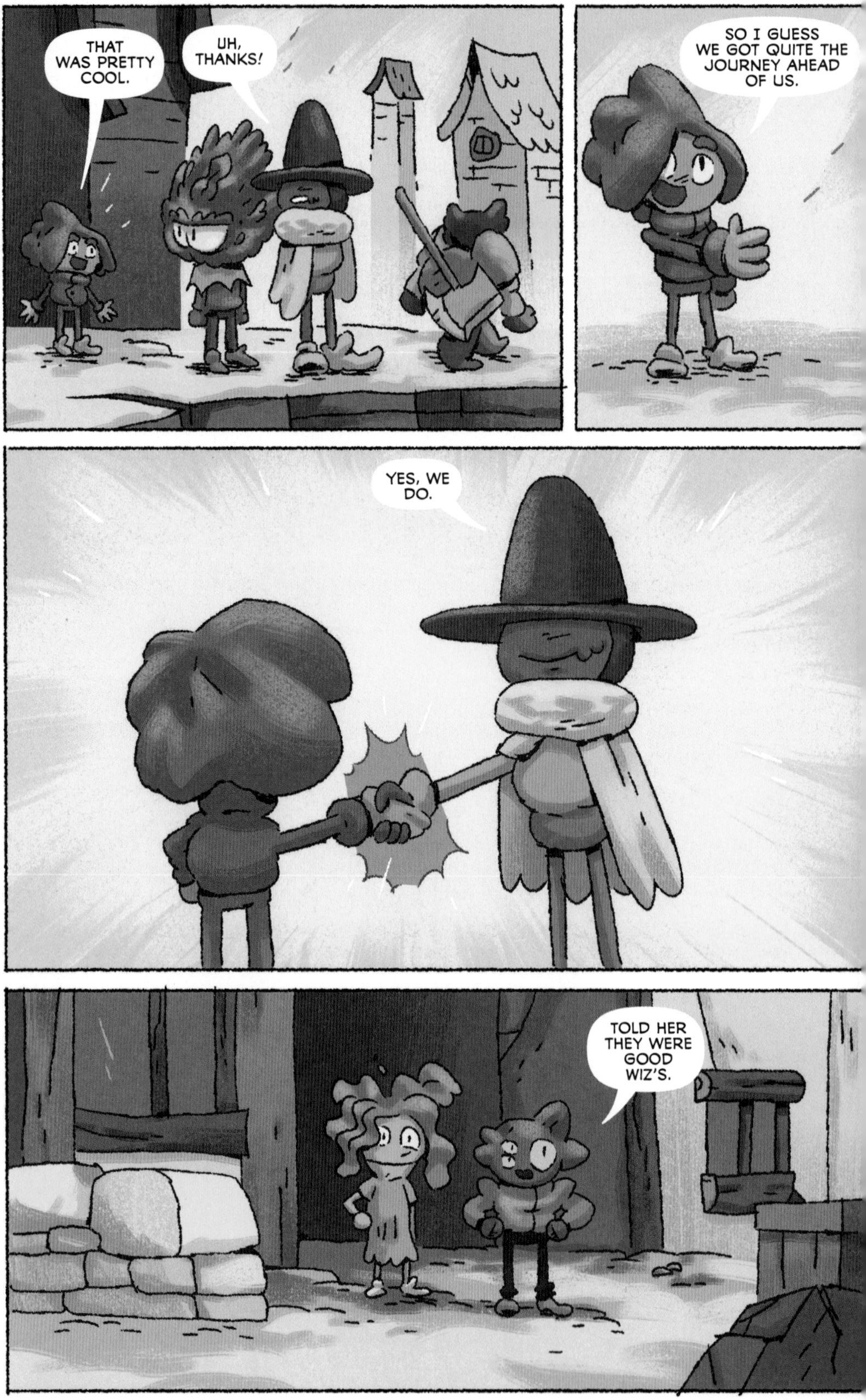
THAT WAS PRETTY COOL.
UH, THANKS!
SO I GUESS WE GOT QUITE THE JOURNEY AHEAD OF US.
YES, WE DO.
TOLD HER THEY WERE GOOD WIZ'S.

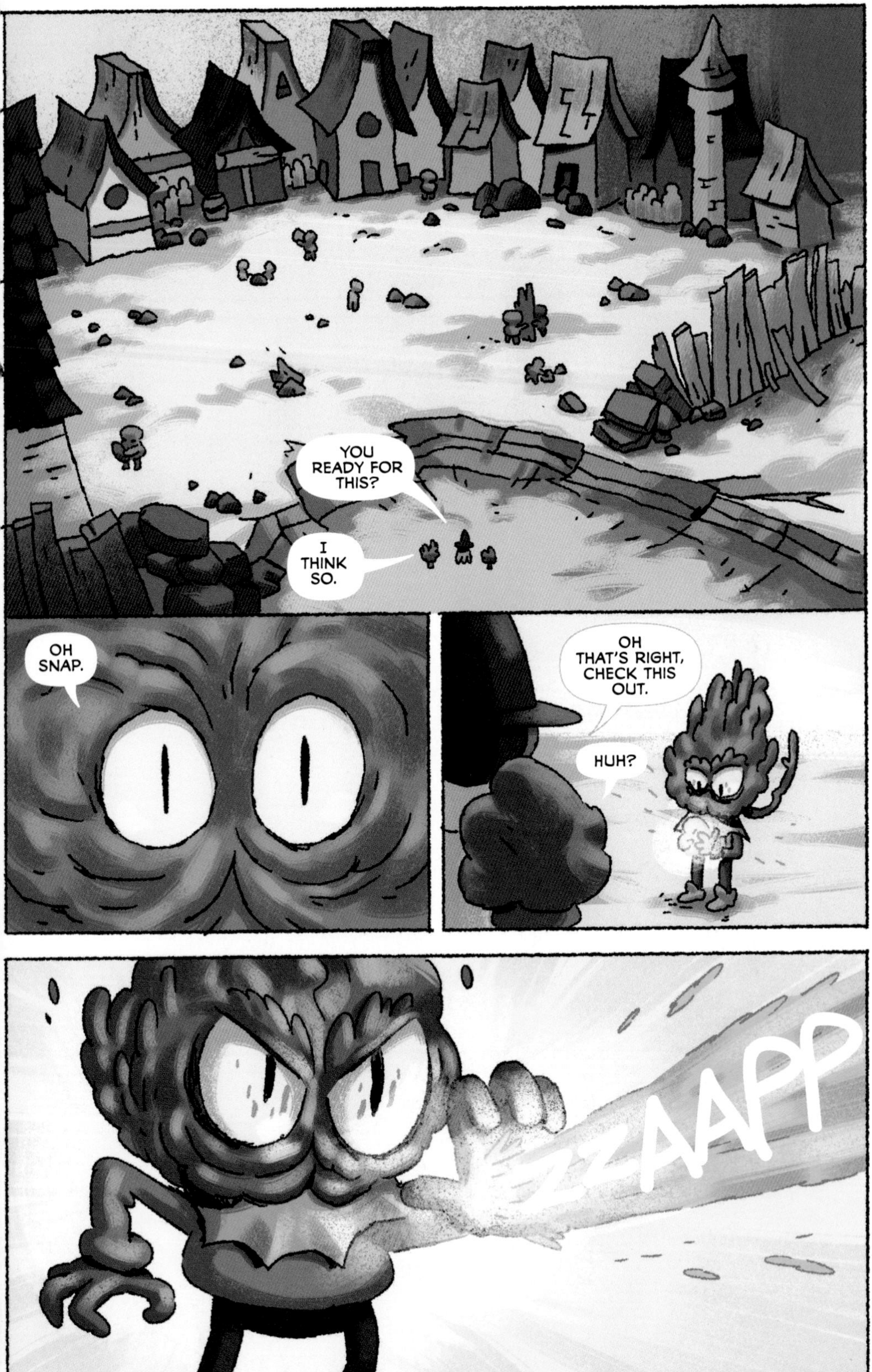
YOU READY FOR THIS?
I THINK SO.
OH SNAP.
OH THAT'S RIGHT, CHECK THIS OUT.
HUH?
ZZAAPP

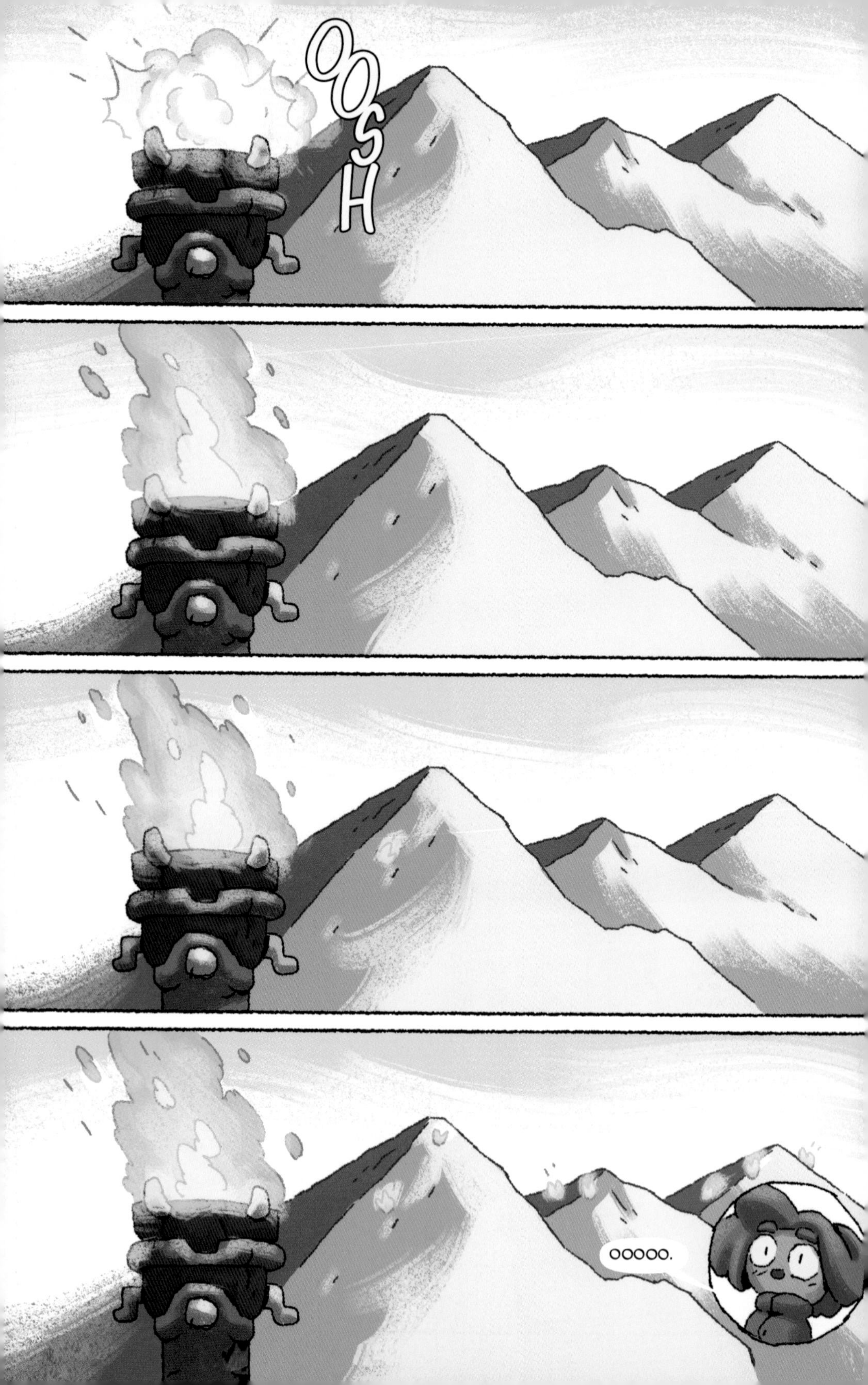
OOSH
OOOOO.

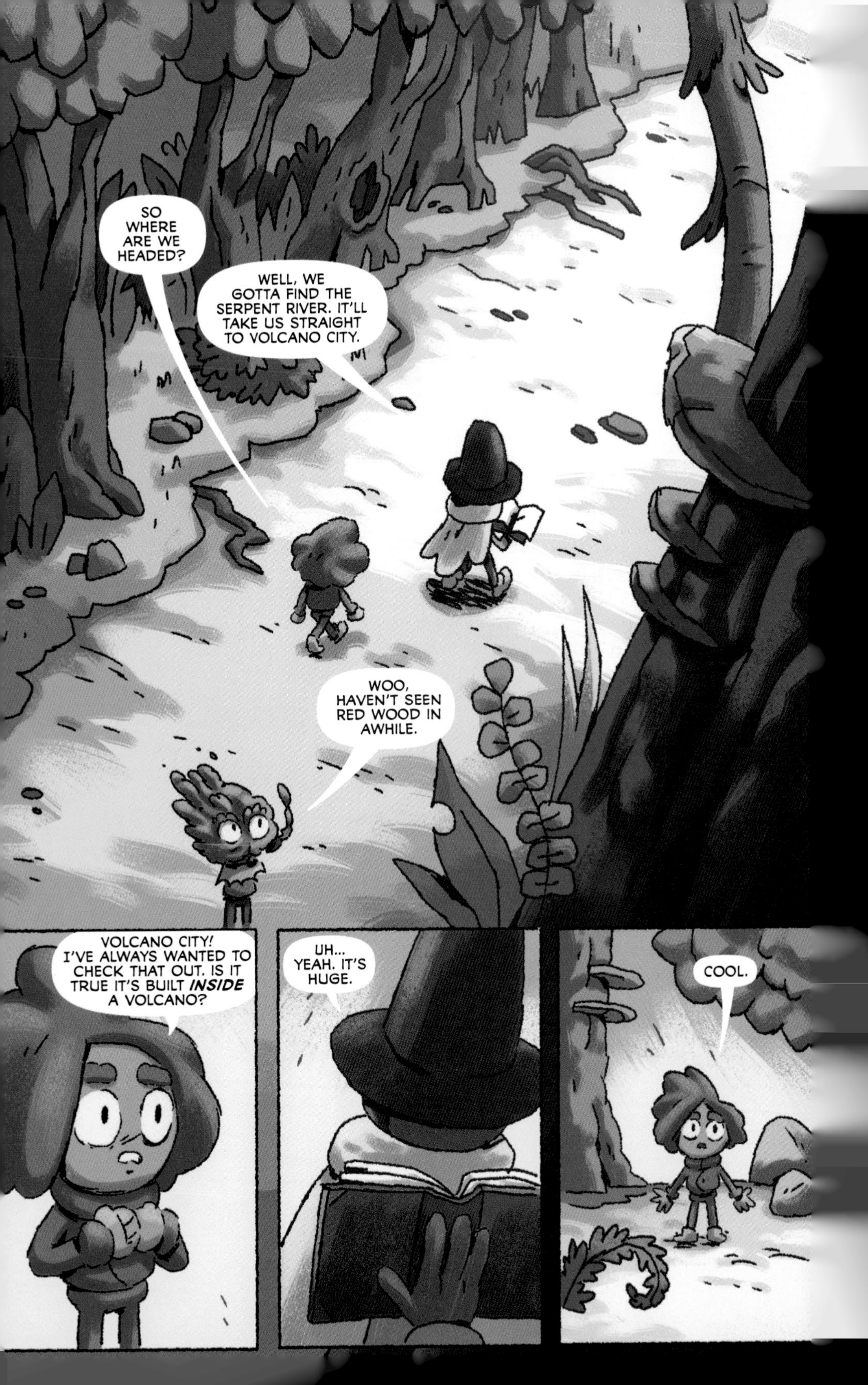
SO WHERE ARE WE HEADED?
WELL, WE GOTTA FIND THE SERPENT RIVER. IT'LL TAKE US STRAIGHT TO VOLCANO CITY.
WOO, HAVEN'T SEEN RED WOOD IN AWHILE.
VOLCANO CITY! I'VE ALWAYS WANTED TO CHECK THAT OUT. IS IT TRUE IT'S BUILT *INSIDE* A VOLCANO?
UH... YEAH. IT'S HUGE.
COOL.

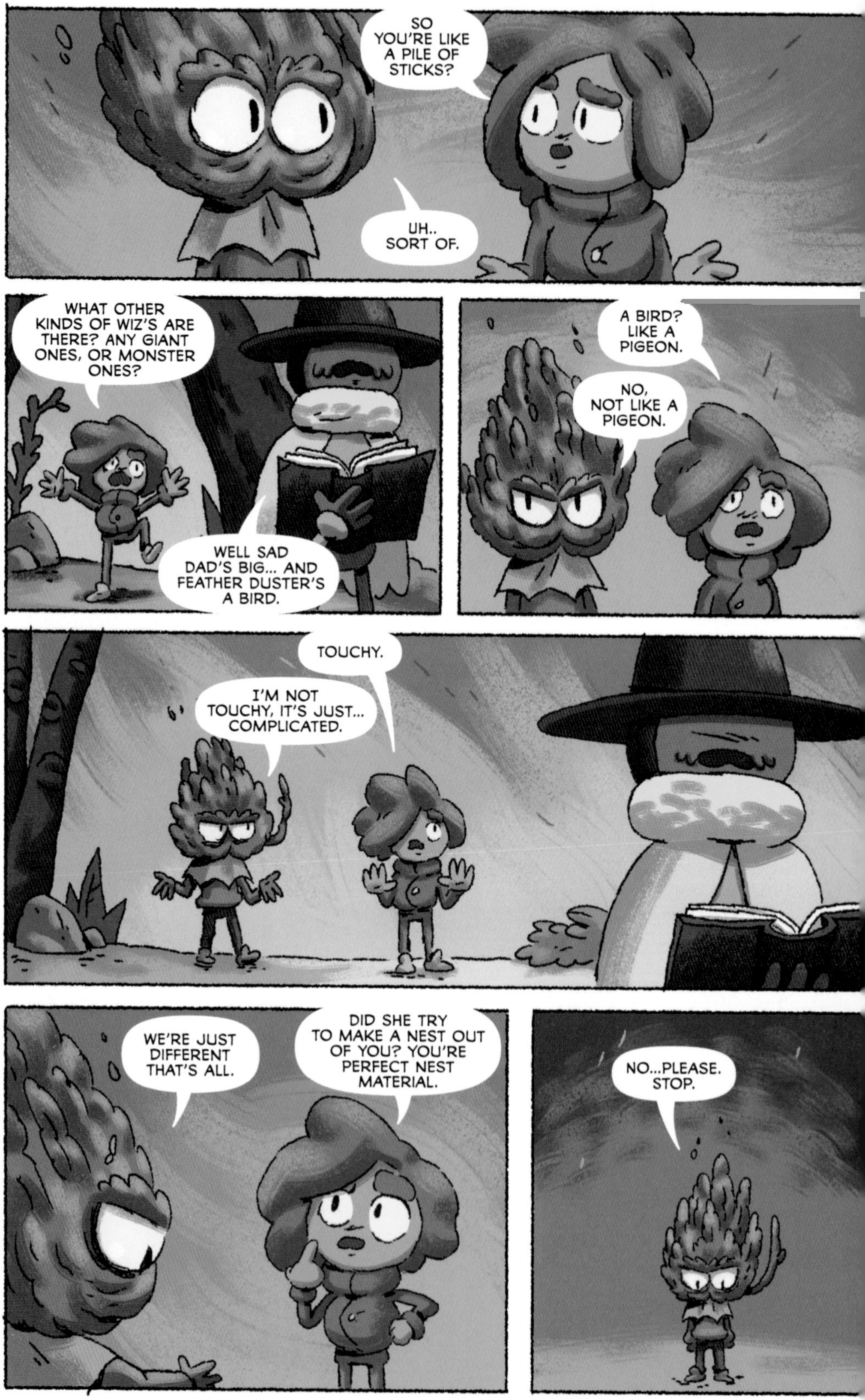
SO YOU'RE LIKE A PILE OF STICKS?
UH.. SORT OF.
WHAT OTHER KINDS OF WIZ'S ARE THERE? ANY GIANT ONES, OR MONSTER ONES?
WELL SAD DAD'S BIG... AND FEATHER DUSTER'S A BIRD.
A BIRD? LIKE A PIGEON.
NO, NOT LIKE A PIGEON.
TOUCHY.
I'M NOT TOUCHY, IT'S JUST... COMPLICATED.
WE'RE JUST DIFFERENT THAT'S ALL.
DID SHE TRY TO MAKE A NEST OUT OF YOU? YOU'RE PERFECT NEST MATERIAL.
NO...PLEASE. STOP.

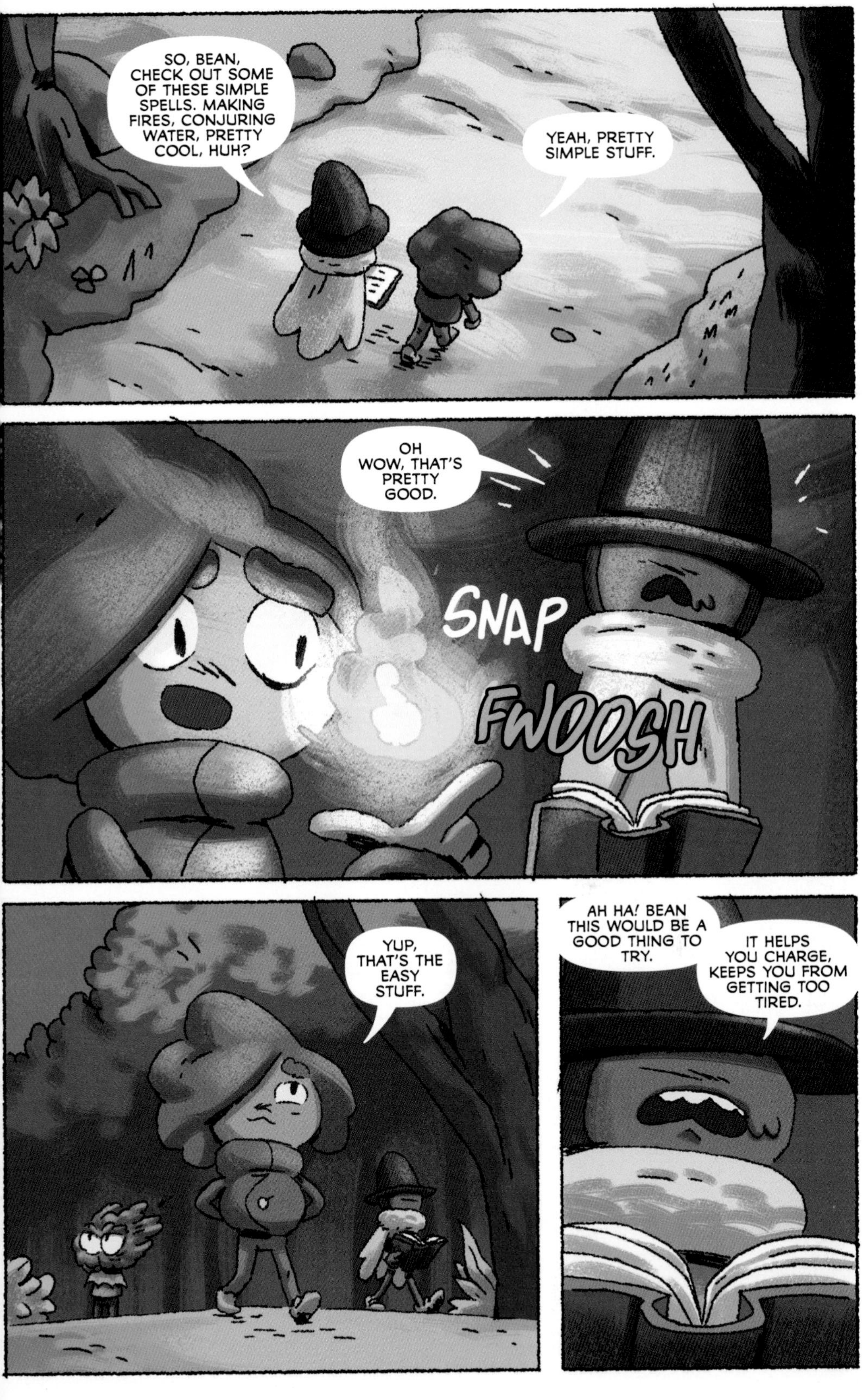
SO, BEAN, CHECK OUT SOME OF THESE SIMPLE SPELLS. MAKING FIRES, CONJURING WATER, PRETTY COOL, HUH?
YEAH, PRETTY SIMPLE STUFF.
OH WOW, THAT'S PRETTY GOOD.
SNAP
FWOOSH
YUP, THAT'S THE EASY STUFF.
AH HA! BEAN THIS WOULD BE A GOOD THING TO TRY.
IT HELPS YOU CHARGE, KEEPS YOU FROM GETTING TOO TIRED.

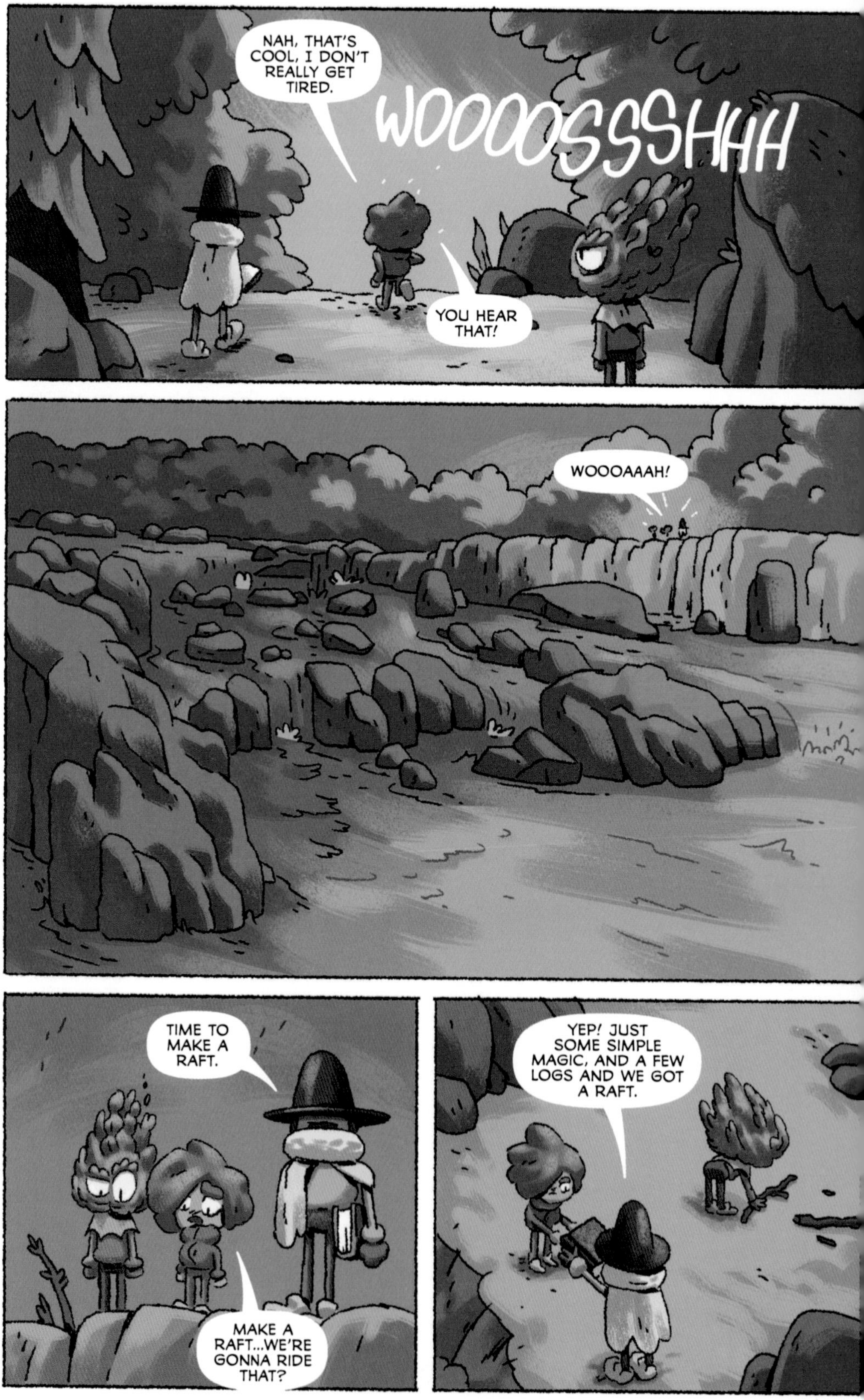
NAH, THAT'S COOL, I DON'T REALLY GET TIRED.
WOOOOSSSHHH
YOU HEAR THAT!
WOOOAAAH!
TIME TO MAKE A RAFT.
MAKE A RAFT...WE'RE GONNA RIDE THAT?
YEP! JUST SOME SIMPLE MAGIC, AND A FEW LOGS AND WE GOT A RAFT.

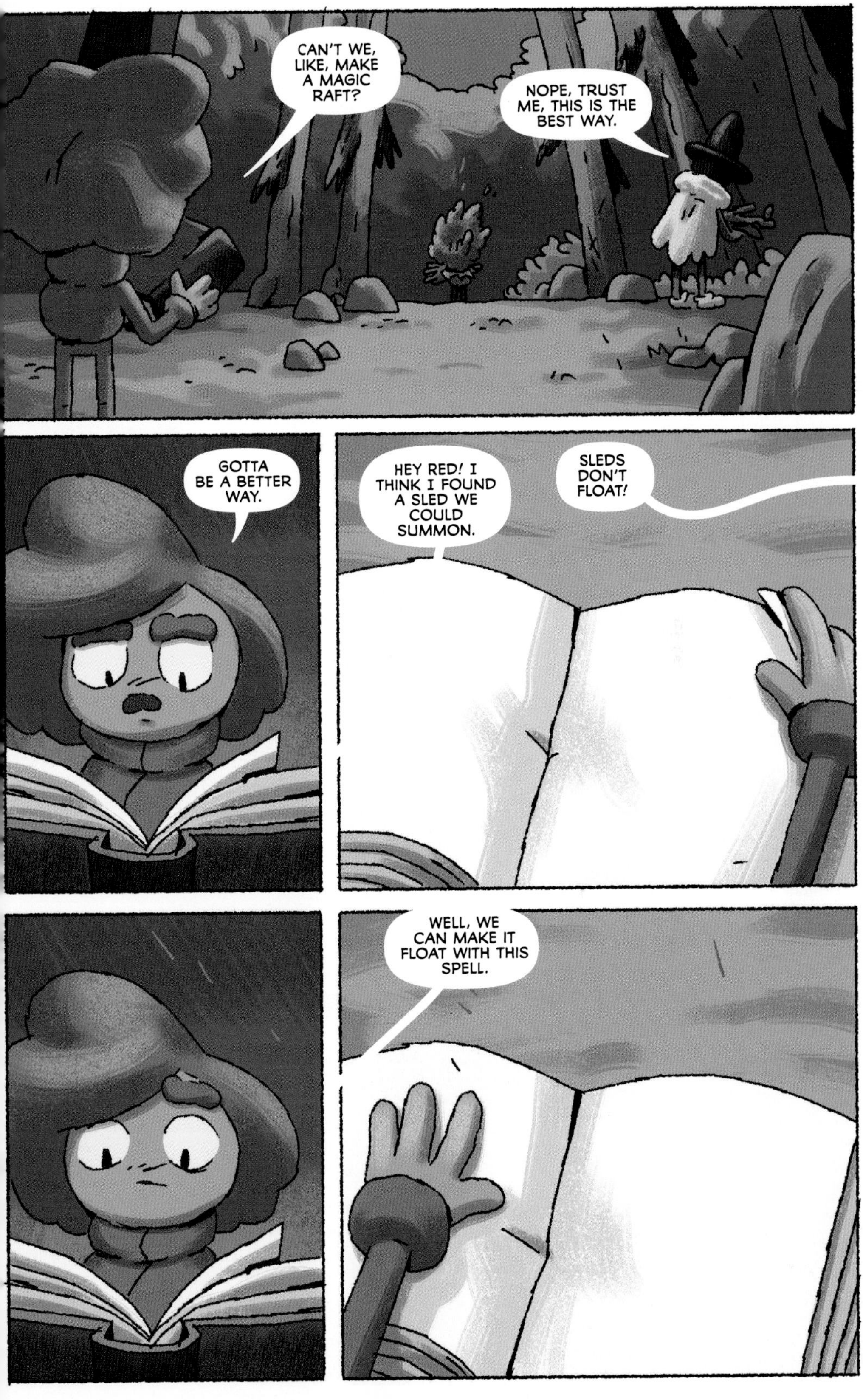
CAN'T WE, LIKE, MAKE A MAGIC RAFT?
NOPE, TRUST ME, THIS IS THE BEST WAY.
GOTTA BE A BETTER WAY.
HEY RED! I THINK I FOUND A SLED WE COULD SUMMON.
SLEDS DON'T FLOAT!
WELL, WE CAN MAKE IT FLOAT WITH THIS SPELL.

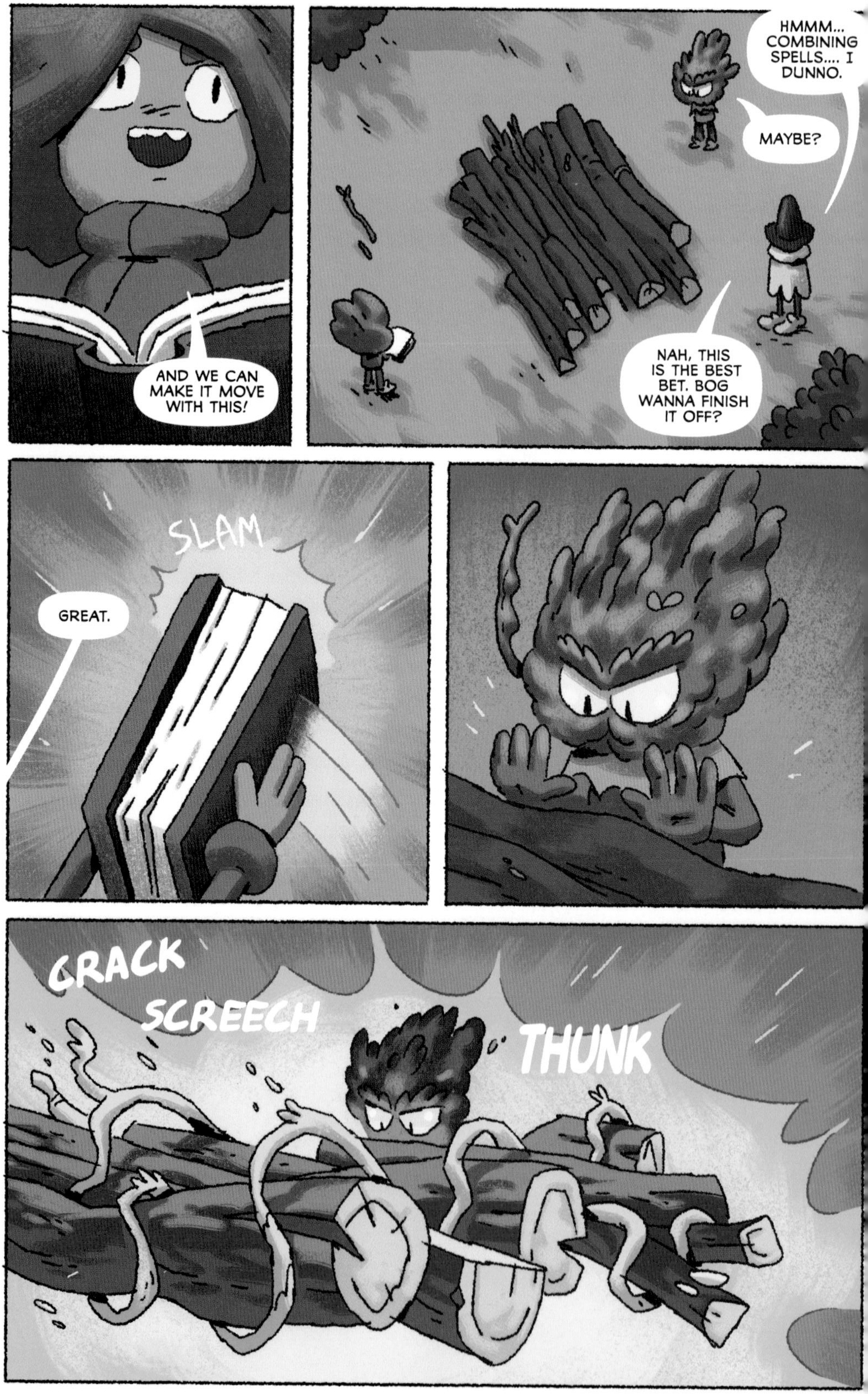
AND WE CAN MAKE IT MOVE WITH THIS!
HMMM... COMBINING SPELLS.... I DUNNO.
MAYBE?
NAH, THIS IS THE BEST BET. BOG WANNA FINISH IT OFF?
SLAM
GREAT.
CRACK
SCREECH
THUNK

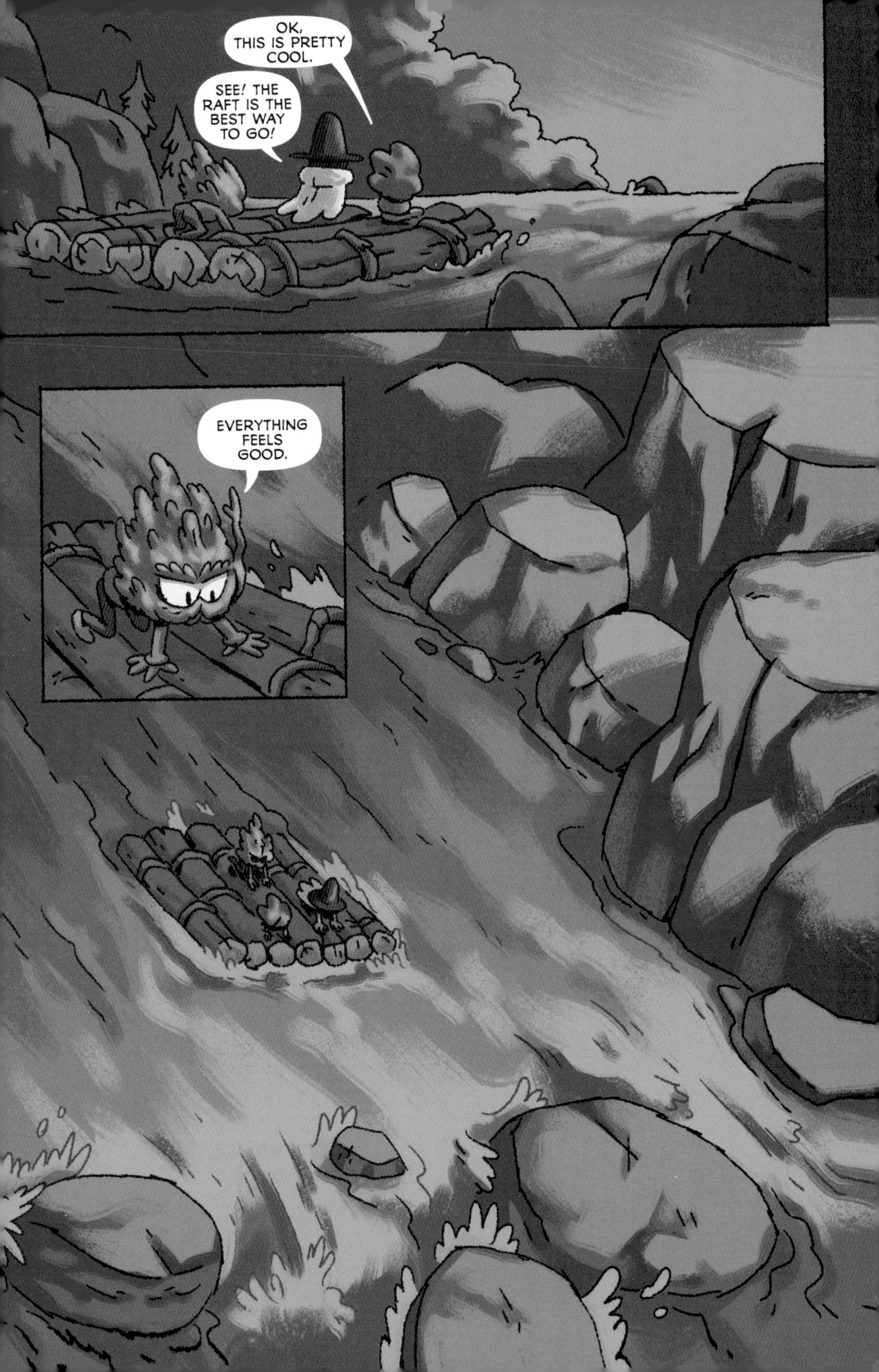
SEE! THE RAFT IS THE BEST WAY TO GO!
OK, THIS IS PRETTY COOL.
EVERYTHING FEELS GOOD.

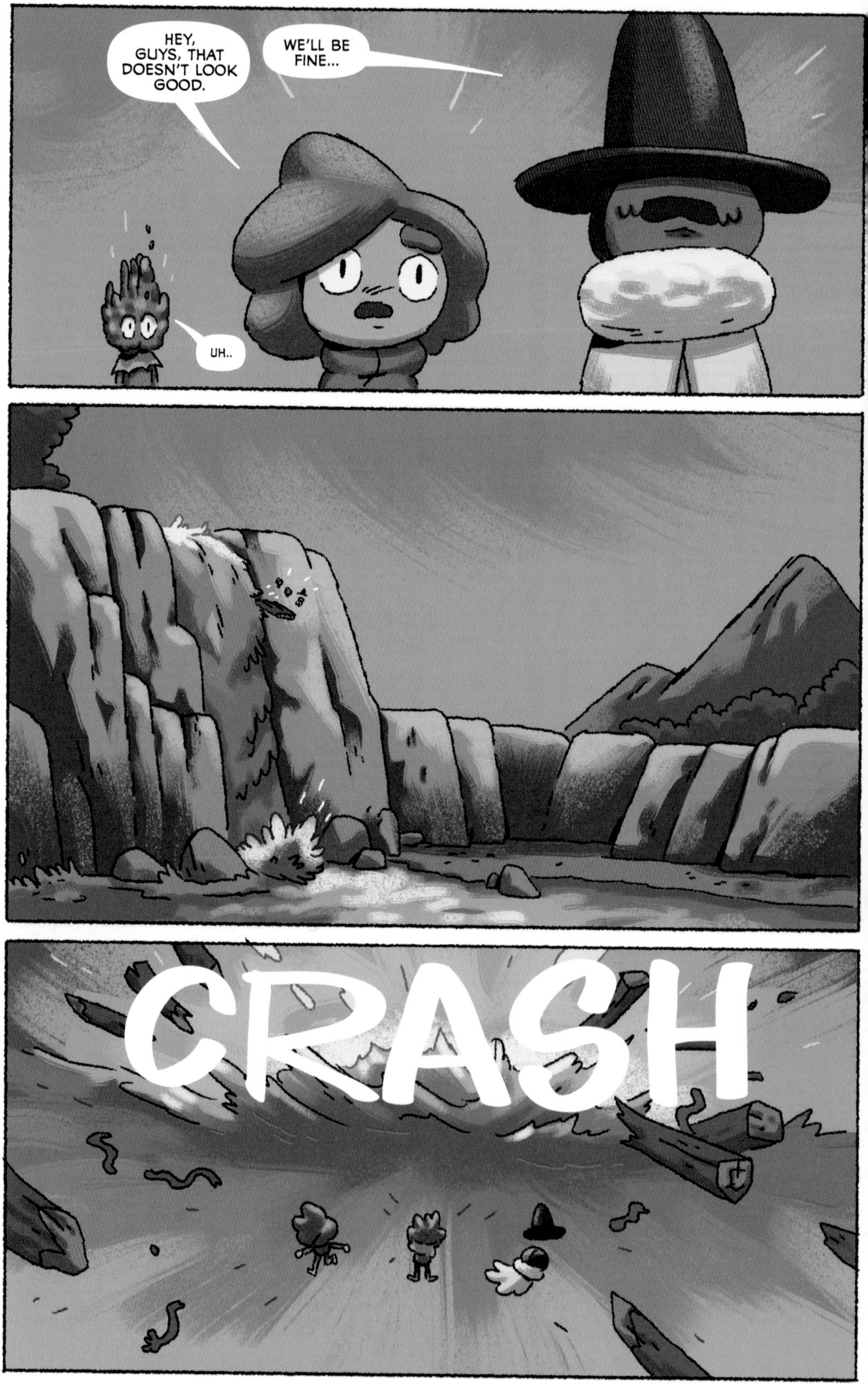
HEY, GUYS, THAT DOESN'T LOOK GOOD.
WE'LL BE FINE...
UH..
CRASH

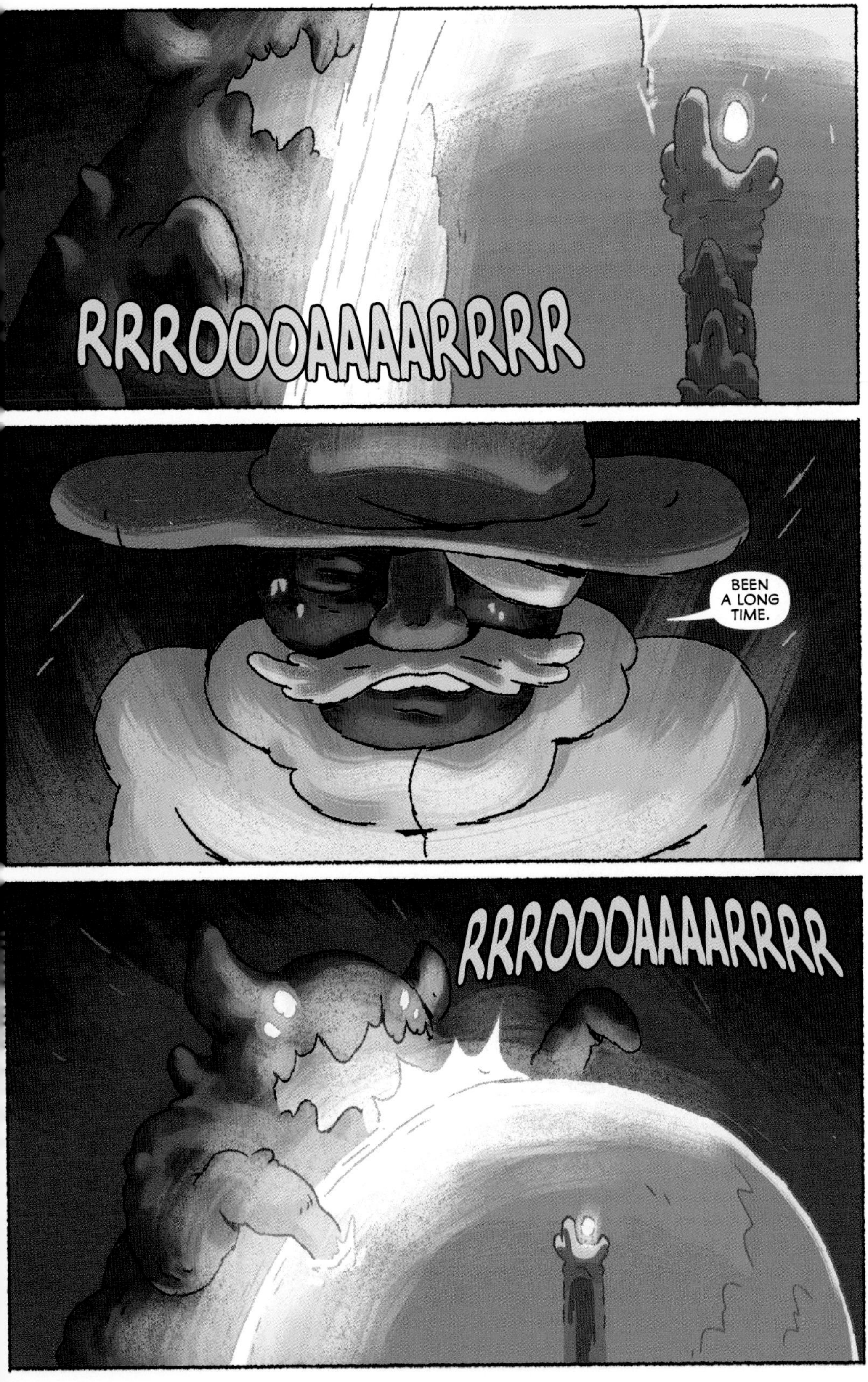
RRROOOAAAARRRR
BEEN A LONG TIME.
RRROOOAAAARRRR

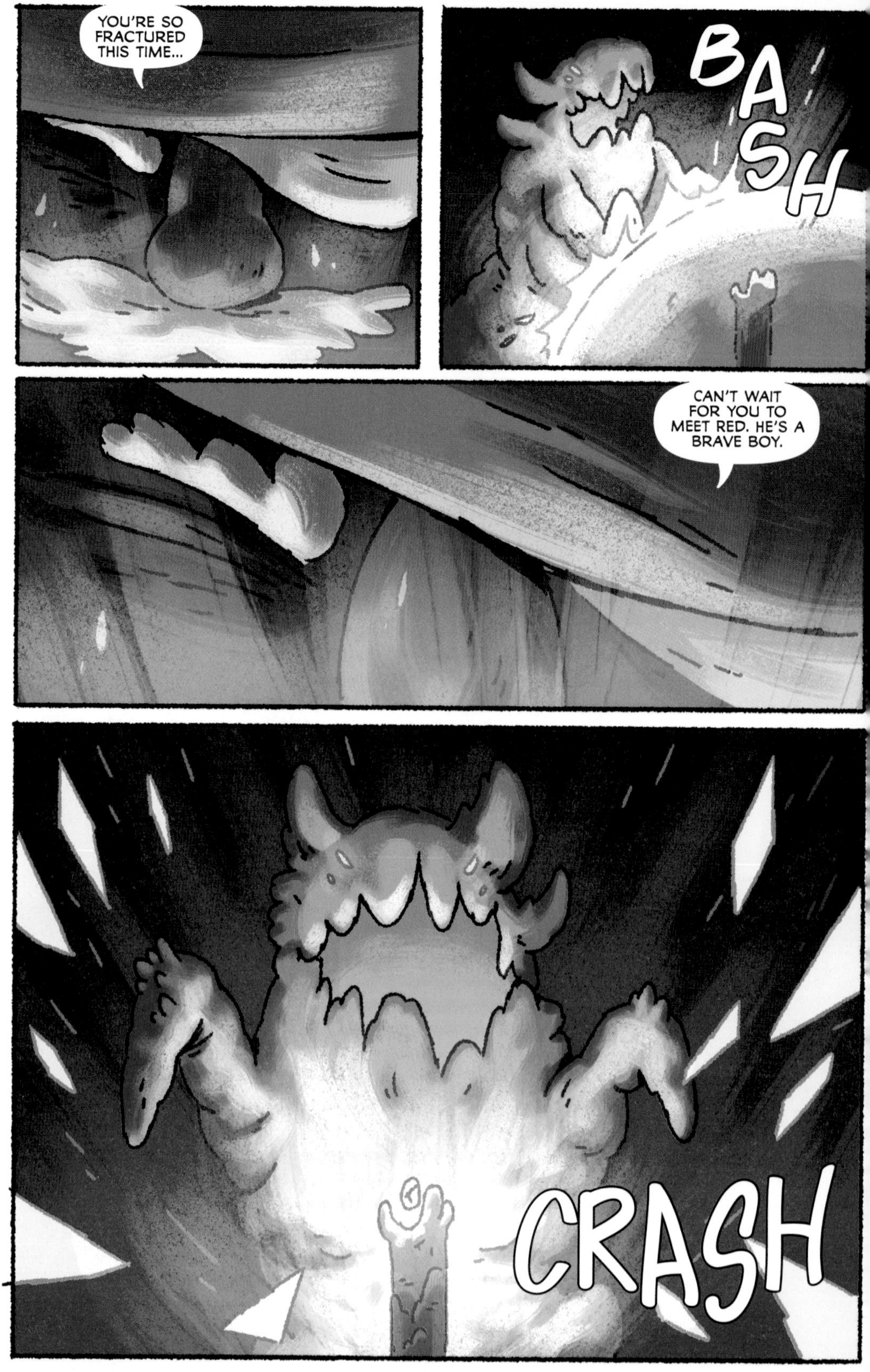
YOU'RE SO FRACTURED THIS TIME...
BASH
CAN'T WAIT FOR YOU TO MEET RED. HE'S A BRAVE BOY.
CRASH

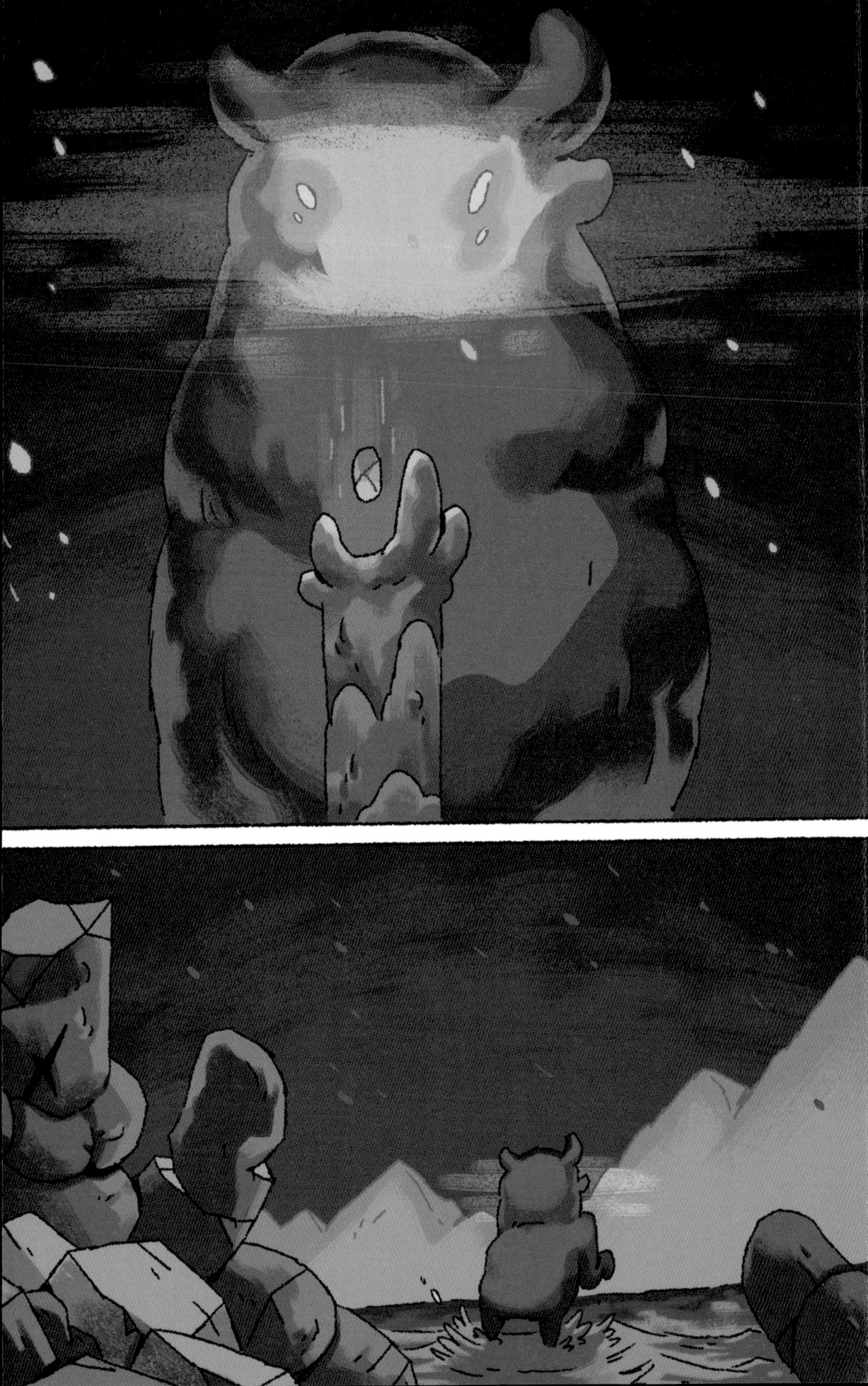

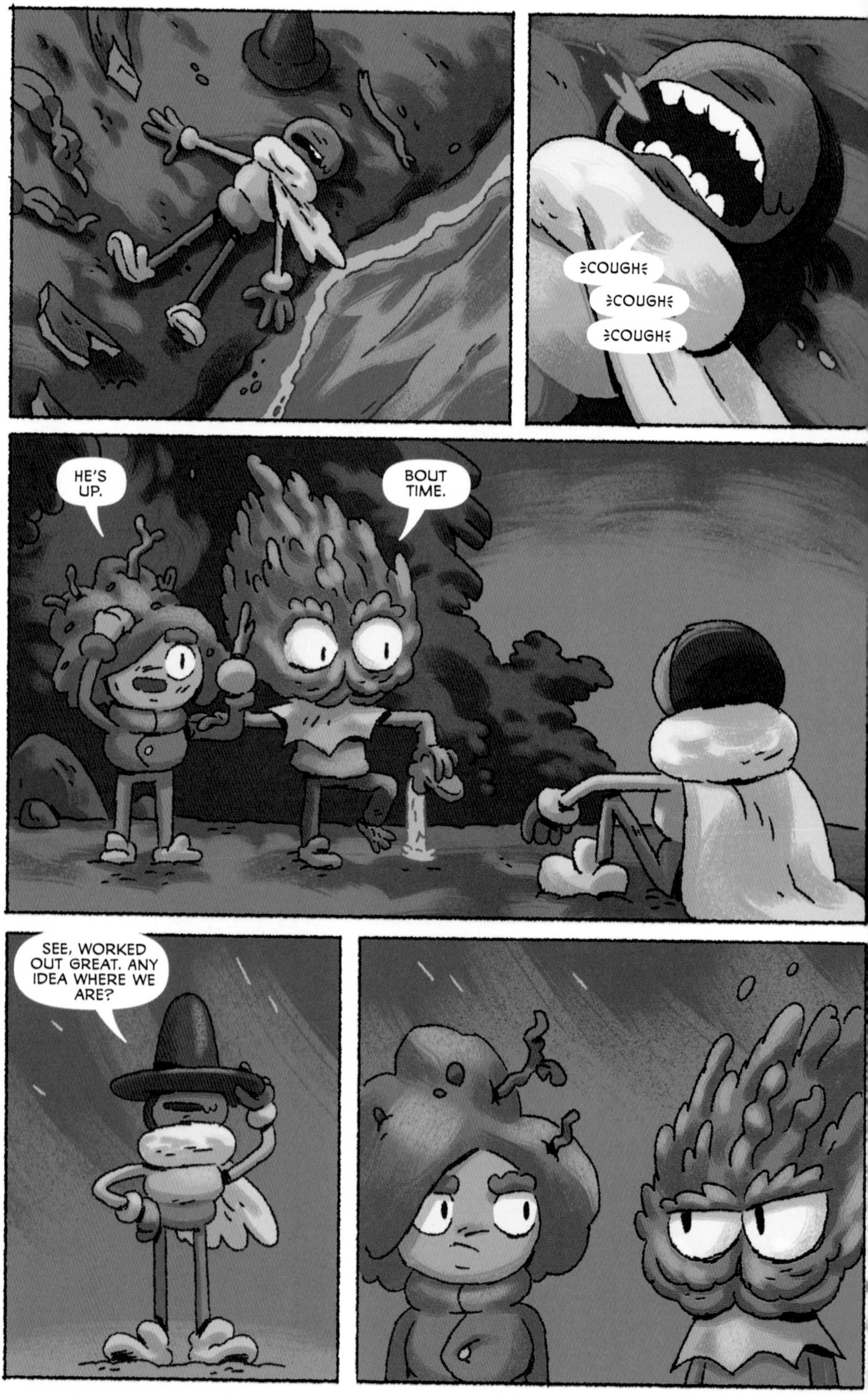
COUGH
COUGH
COUGH
HE'S UP.
BOUT TIME.
SEE, WORKED OUT GREAT. ANY IDEA WHERE WE ARE?

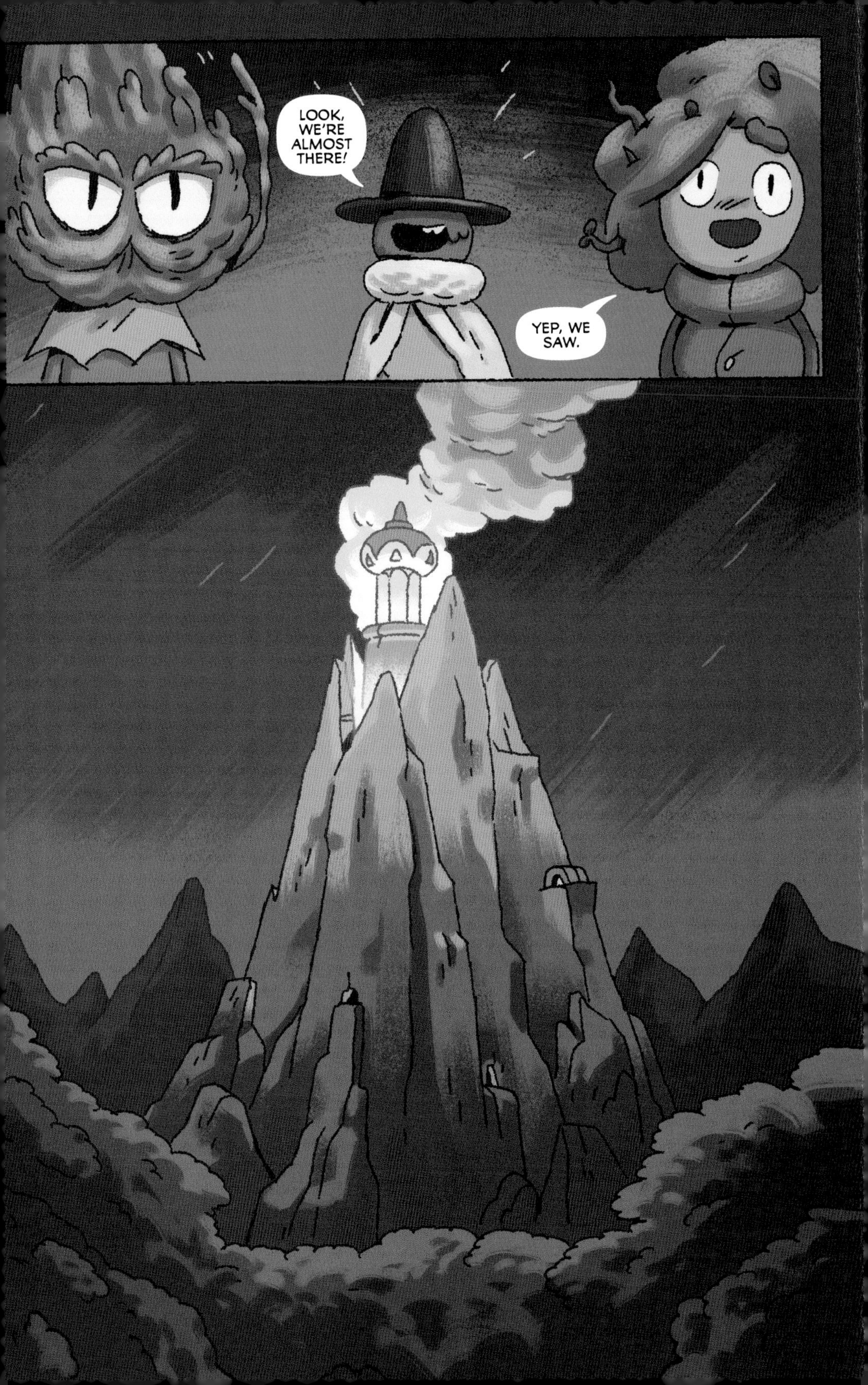
LOOK, WE'RE ALMOST THERE!
YEP, WE SAW.

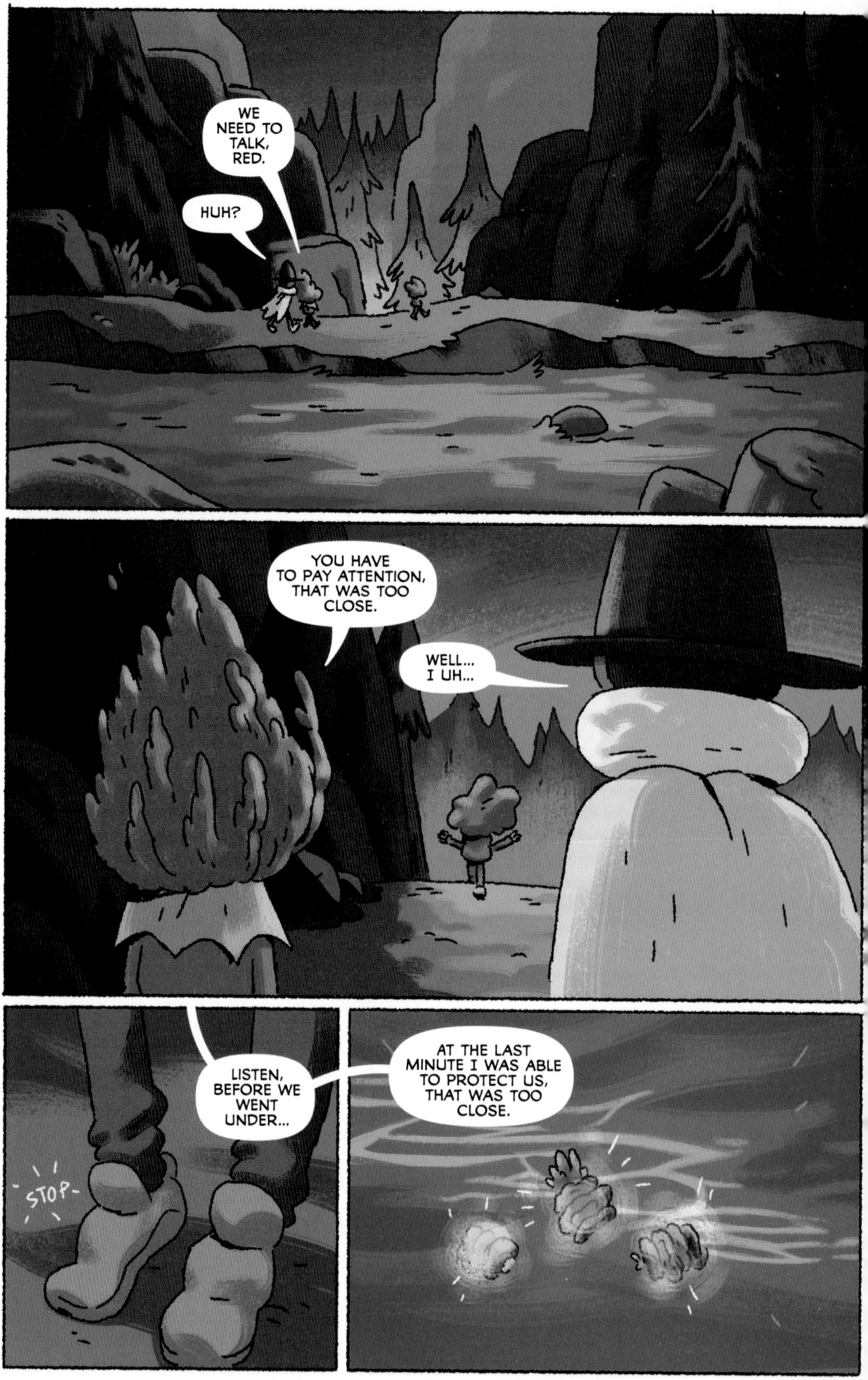
WE NEED TO TALK, RED.
HUH?
YOU HAVE TO PAY ATTENTION, THAT WAS TOO CLOSE.
WELL... I UH...
STOP
LISTEN, BEFORE WE WENT UNDER...
AT THE LAST MINUTE I WAS ABLE TO PROTECT US, THAT WAS TOO CLOSE.

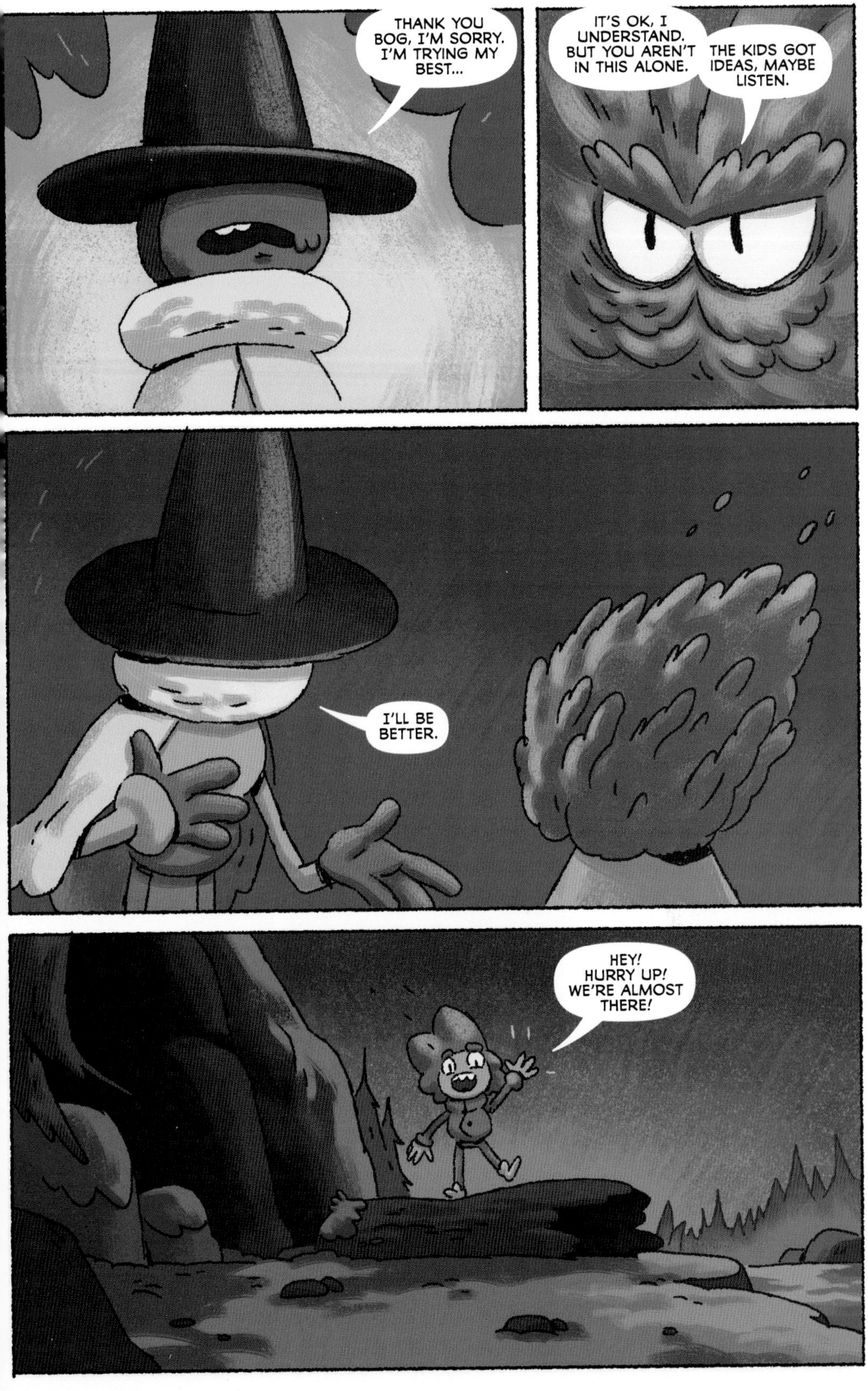
THANK YOU BOG, I'M SORRY. I'M TRYING MY BEST...
IT'S OK, I UNDERSTAND. BUT YOU AREN'T IN THIS ALONE.
THE KIDS GOT IDEAS, MAYBE LISTEN.
I'LL BE BETTER.
HEY! HURRY UP! WE'RE ALMOST THERE!

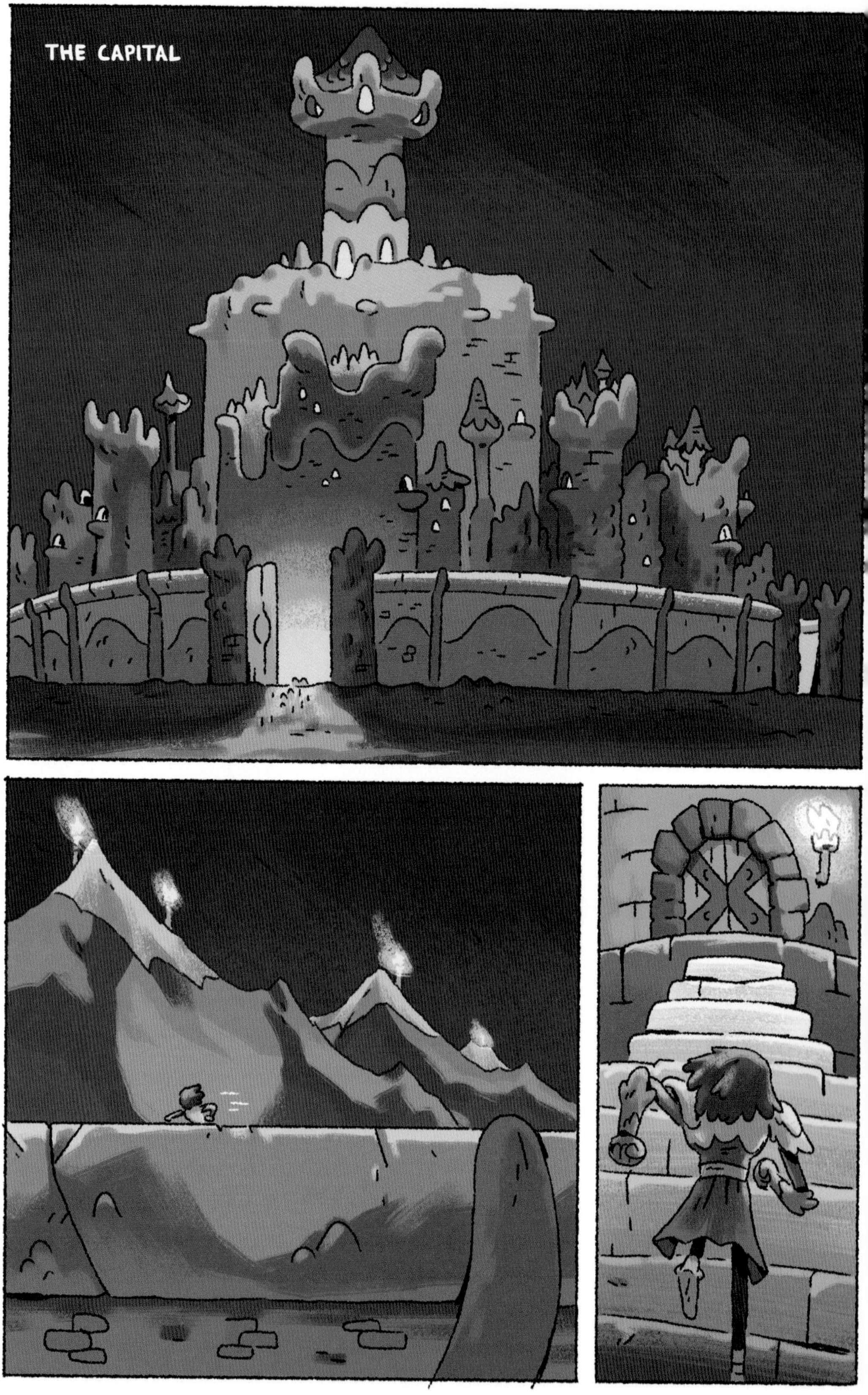
THE CAPITAL

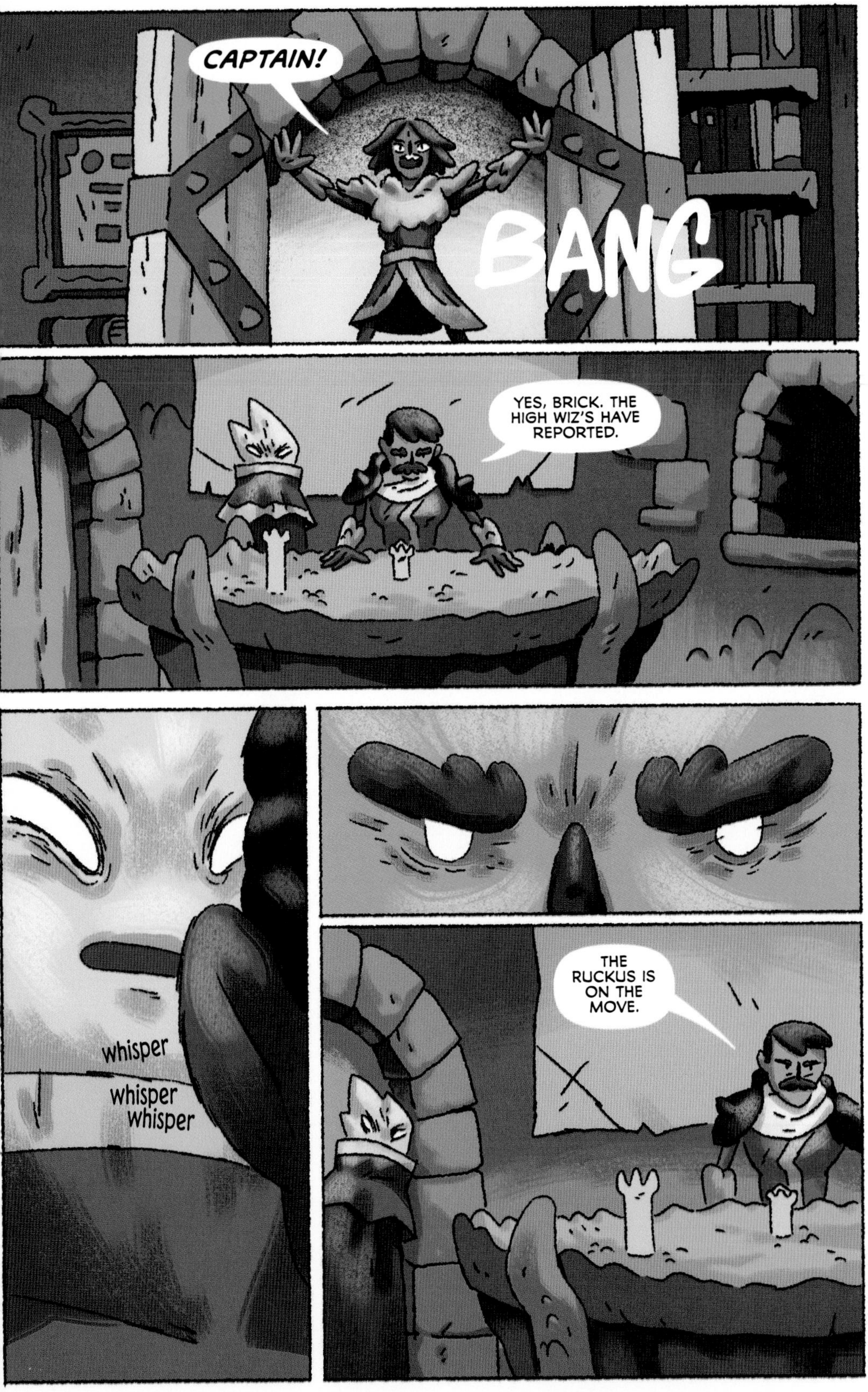
CAPTAIN!
BANG
YES, BRICK. THE HIGH WIZ'S HAVE REPORTED.
whisper
whisper
whisper
THE RUCKUS IS ON THE MOVE.

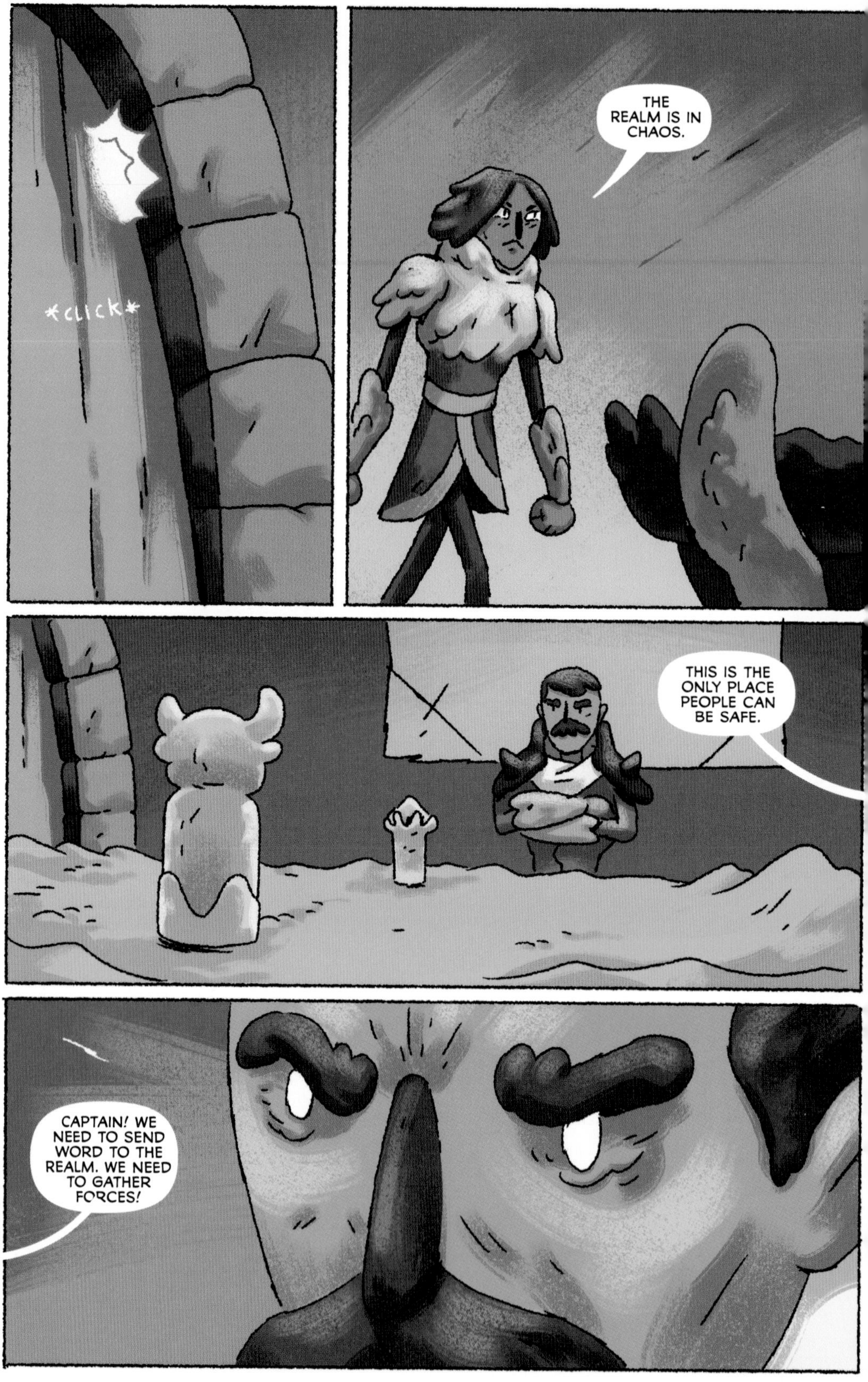
click
THE REALM IS IN CHAOS.
THIS IS THE ONLY PLACE PEOPLE CAN BE SAFE.
CAPTAIN! WE NEED TO SEND WORD TO THE REALM. WE NEED TO GATHER FORCES!

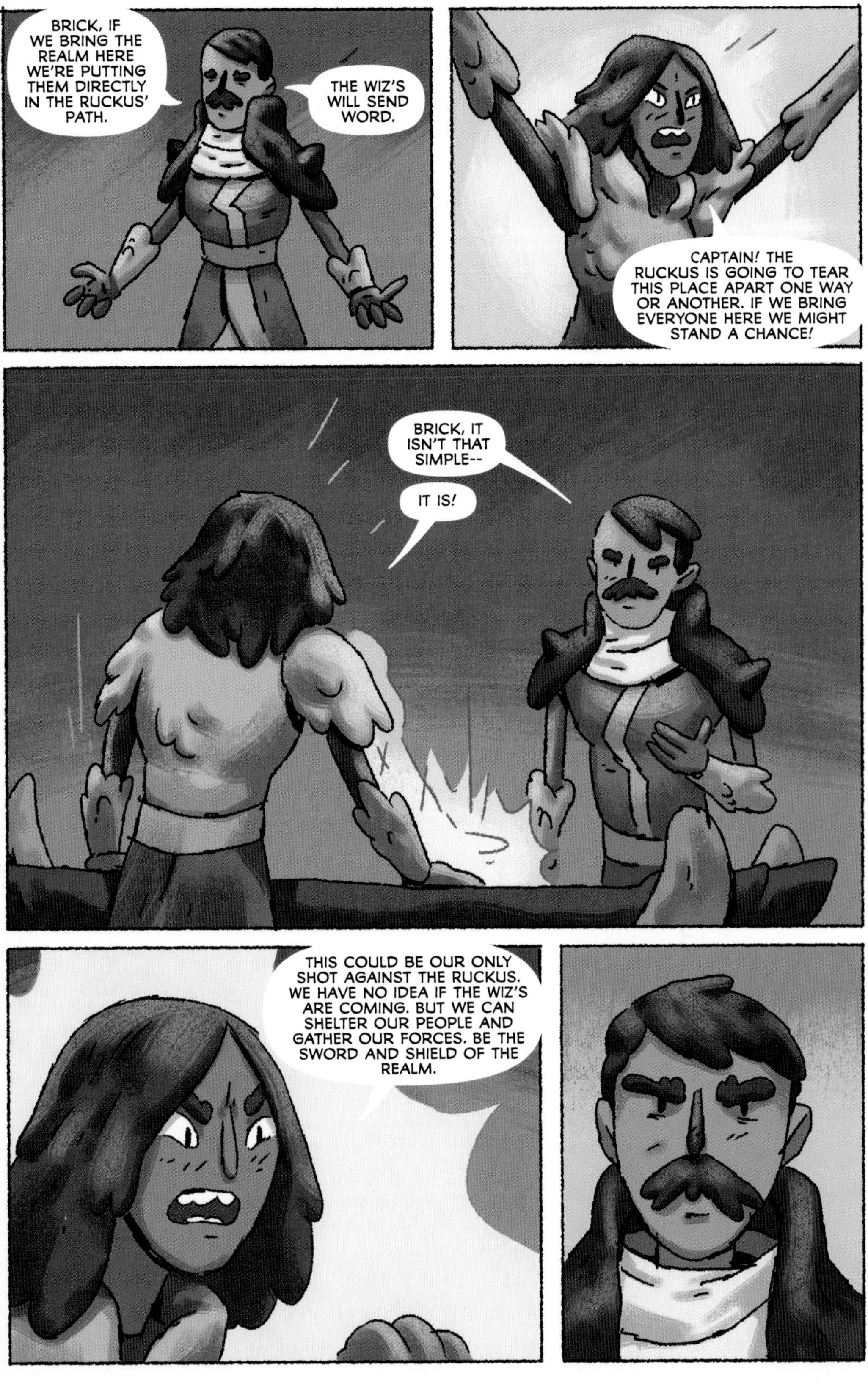
BRICK, IF WE BRING THE REALM HERE WE'RE PUTTING THEM DIRECTLY IN THE RUCKUS' PATH.
THE WIZ'S WILL SEND WORD.
CAPTAIN! THE RUCKUS IS GOING TO TEAR THIS PLACE APART ONE WAY OR ANOTHER. IF WE BRING EVERYONE HERE WE MIGHT STAND A CHANCE!
BRICK, IT ISN'T THAT SIMPLE--
IT IS!
THIS COULD BE OUR ONLY SHOT AGAINST THE RUCKUS. WE HAVE NO IDEA IF THE WIZ'S ARE COMING. BUT WE CAN SHELTER OUR PEOPLE AND GATHER OUR FORCES. BE THE SWORD AND SHIELD OF THE REALM.

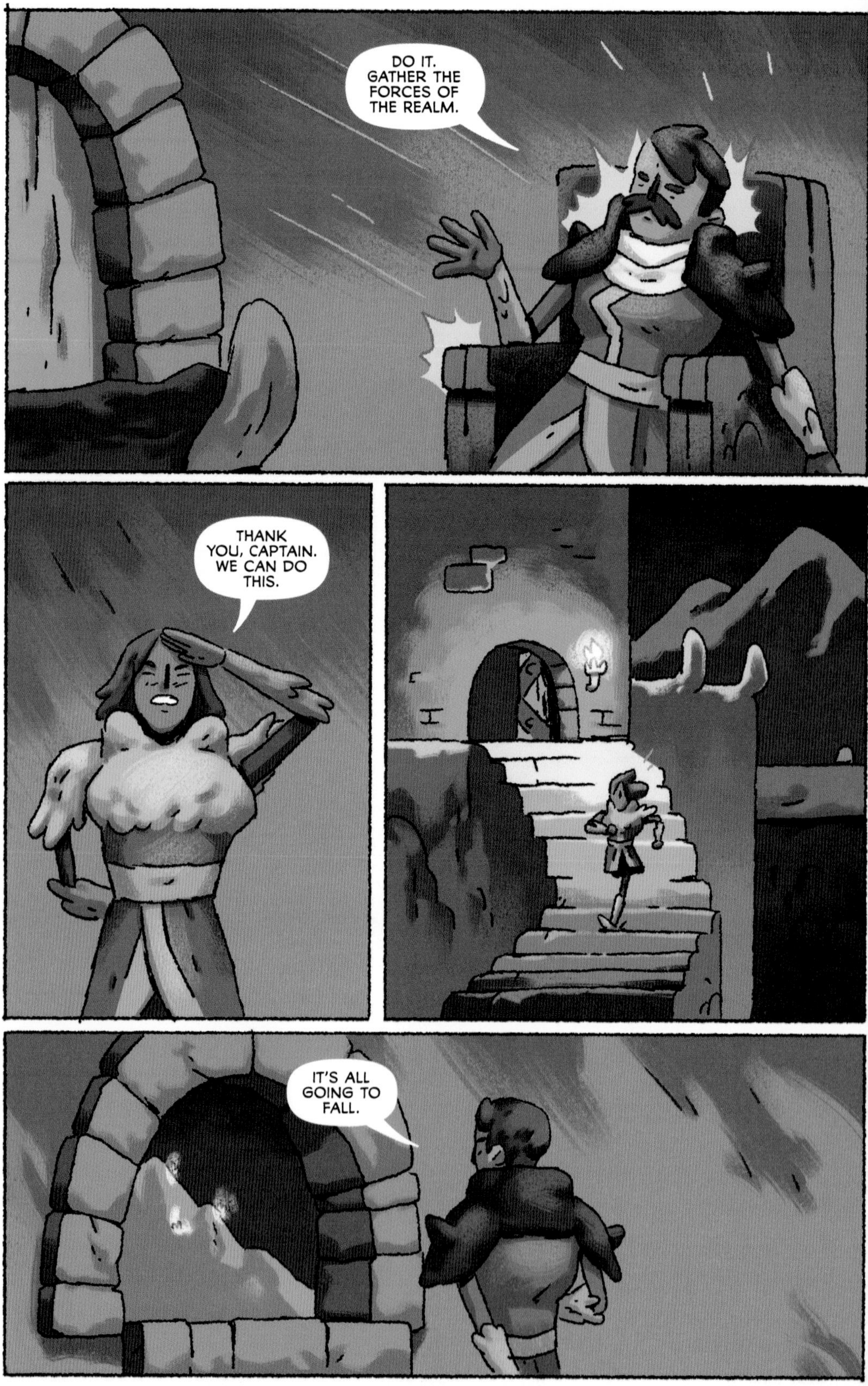
DO IT. GATHER THE FORCES OF THE REALM.
THANK YOU, CAPTAIN. WE CAN DO THIS.
IT'S ALL GOING TO FALL.

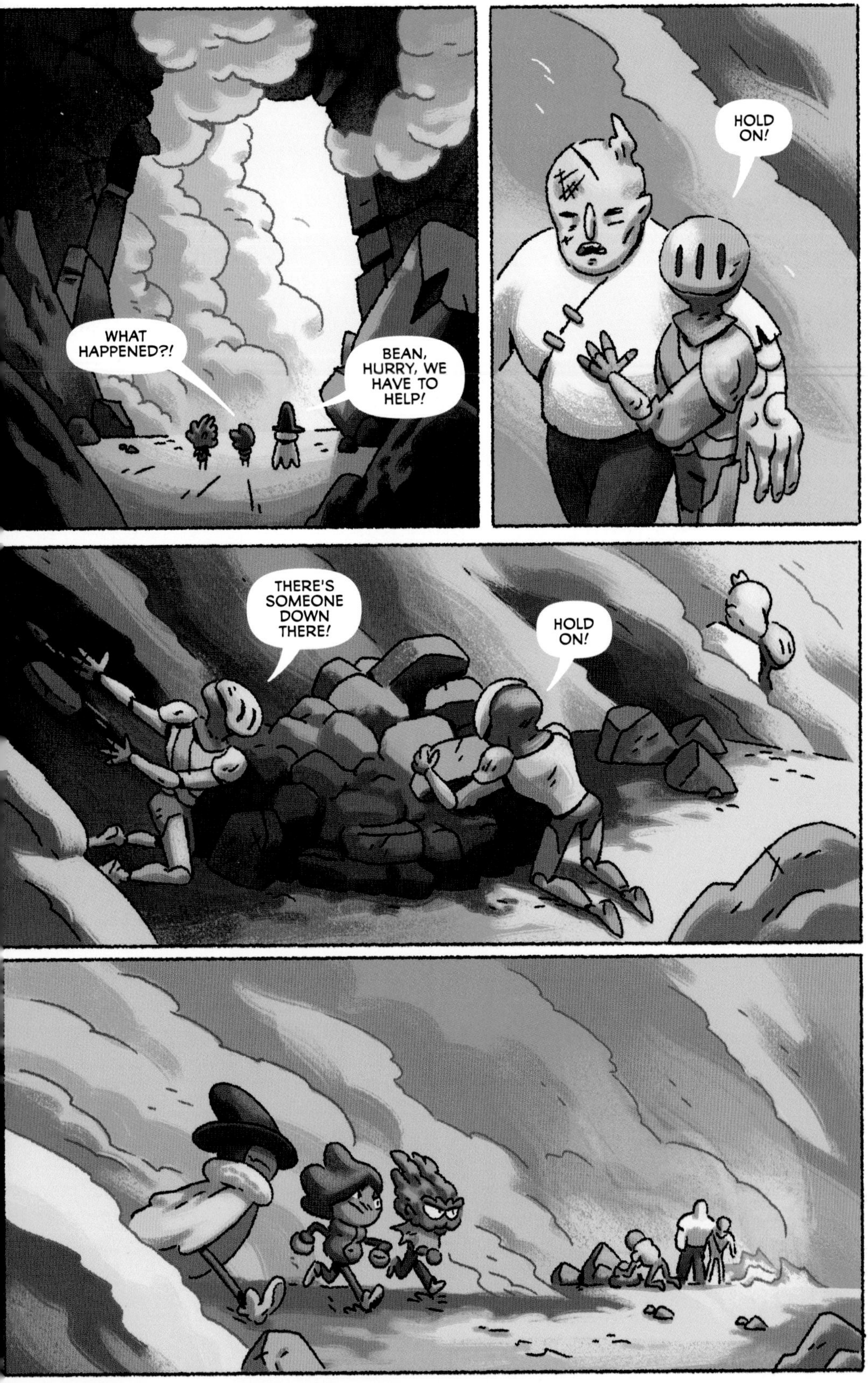
WHAT HAPPENED?!
BEAN, HURRY, WE HAVE TO HELP!
HOLD ON!
THERE'S SOMEONE DOWN THERE!
HOLD ON!

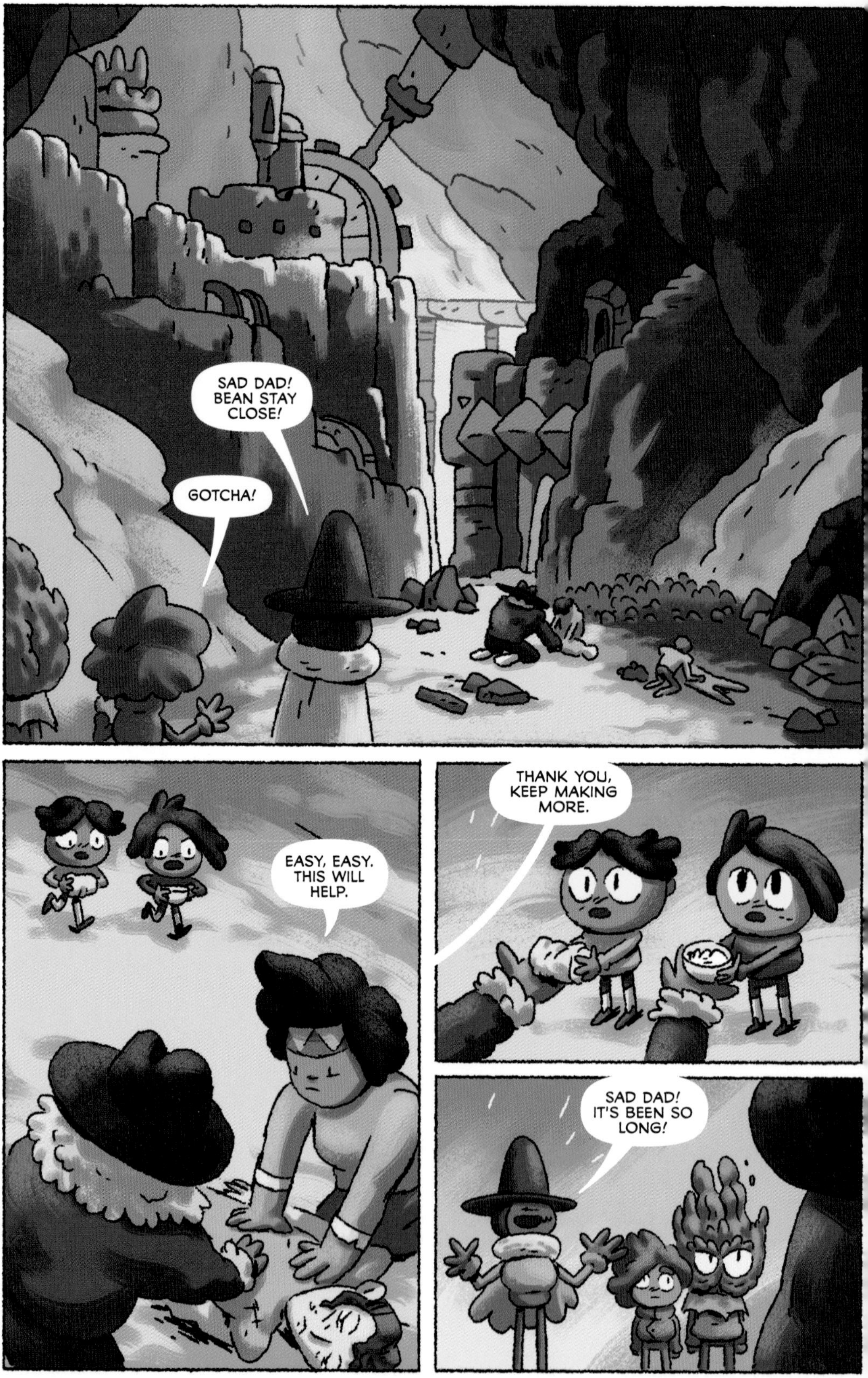

SAD DAD! BEAN STAY CLOSE!
GOTCHA!
EASY, EASY. THIS WILL HELP.
THANK YOU, KEEP MAKING MORE.
SAD DAD! IT'S BEEN SO LONG!

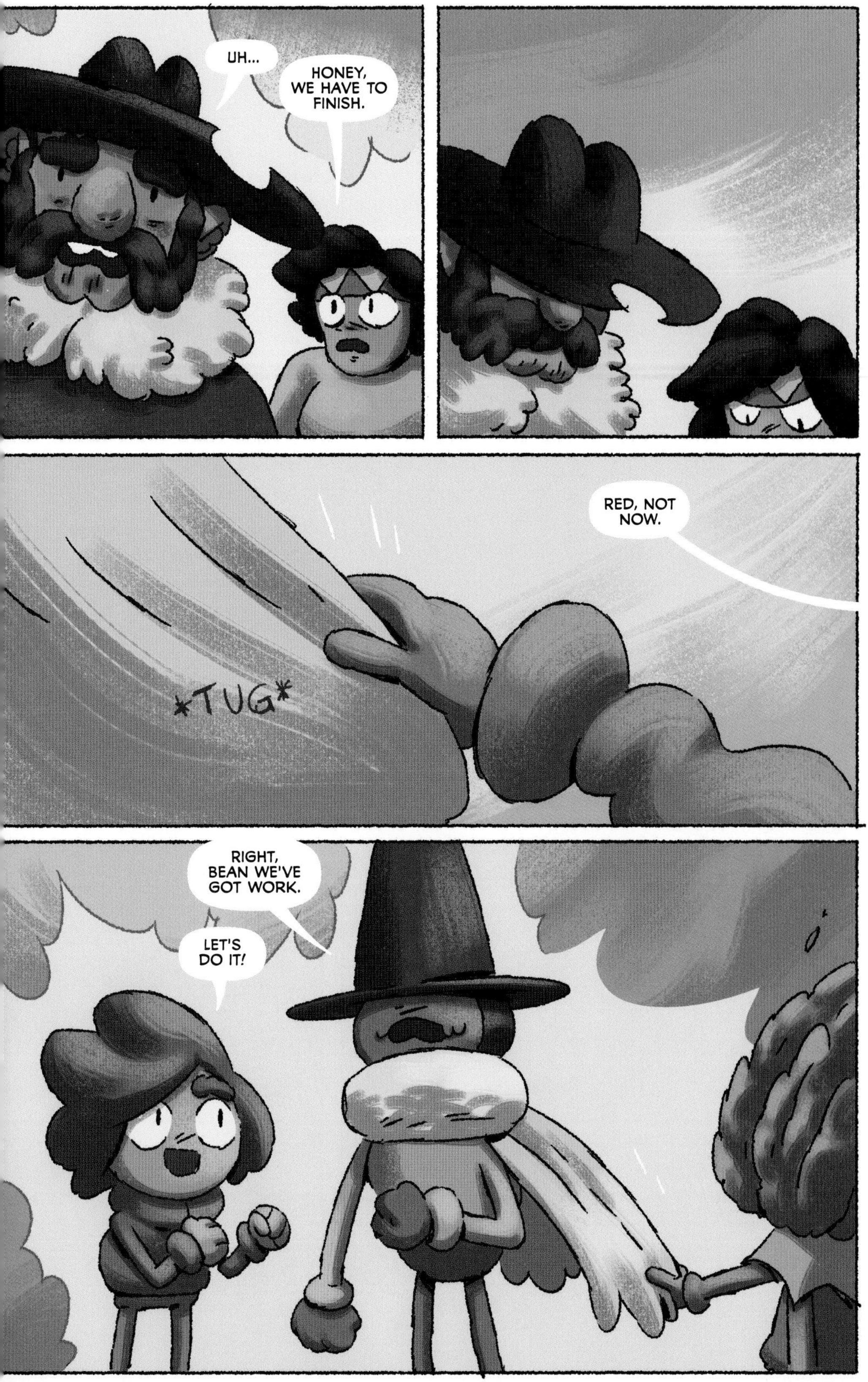
UH...
HONEY, WE HAVE TO FINISH.
RED, NOT NOW.
TUG
RIGHT, BEAN WE'VE GOT WORK.
LET'S DO IT!

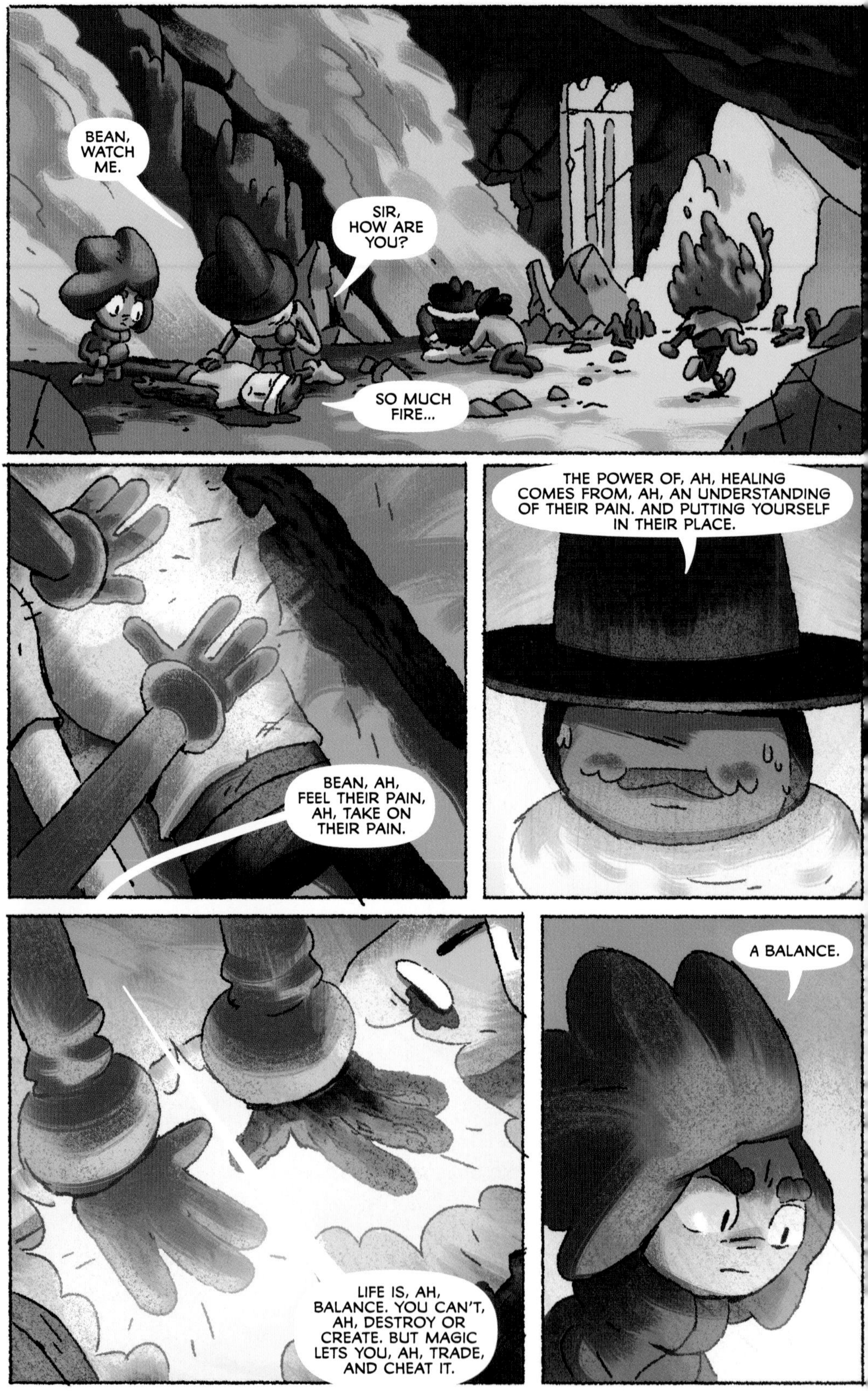
BEAN, WATCH ME.
SIR, HOW ARE YOU?
SO MUCH FIRE...
THE POWER OF, AH, HEALING COMES FROM, AH, AN UNDERSTANDING OF THEIR PAIN. AND PUTTING YOURSELF IN THEIR PLACE.
BEAN, AH, FEEL THEIR PAIN, AH, TAKE ON THEIR PAIN.
LIFE IS, AH, BALANCE. YOU CAN'T, AH, DESTROY OR CREATE. BUT MAGIC LETS YOU, AH, TRADE, AND CHEAT IT.
A BALANCE.

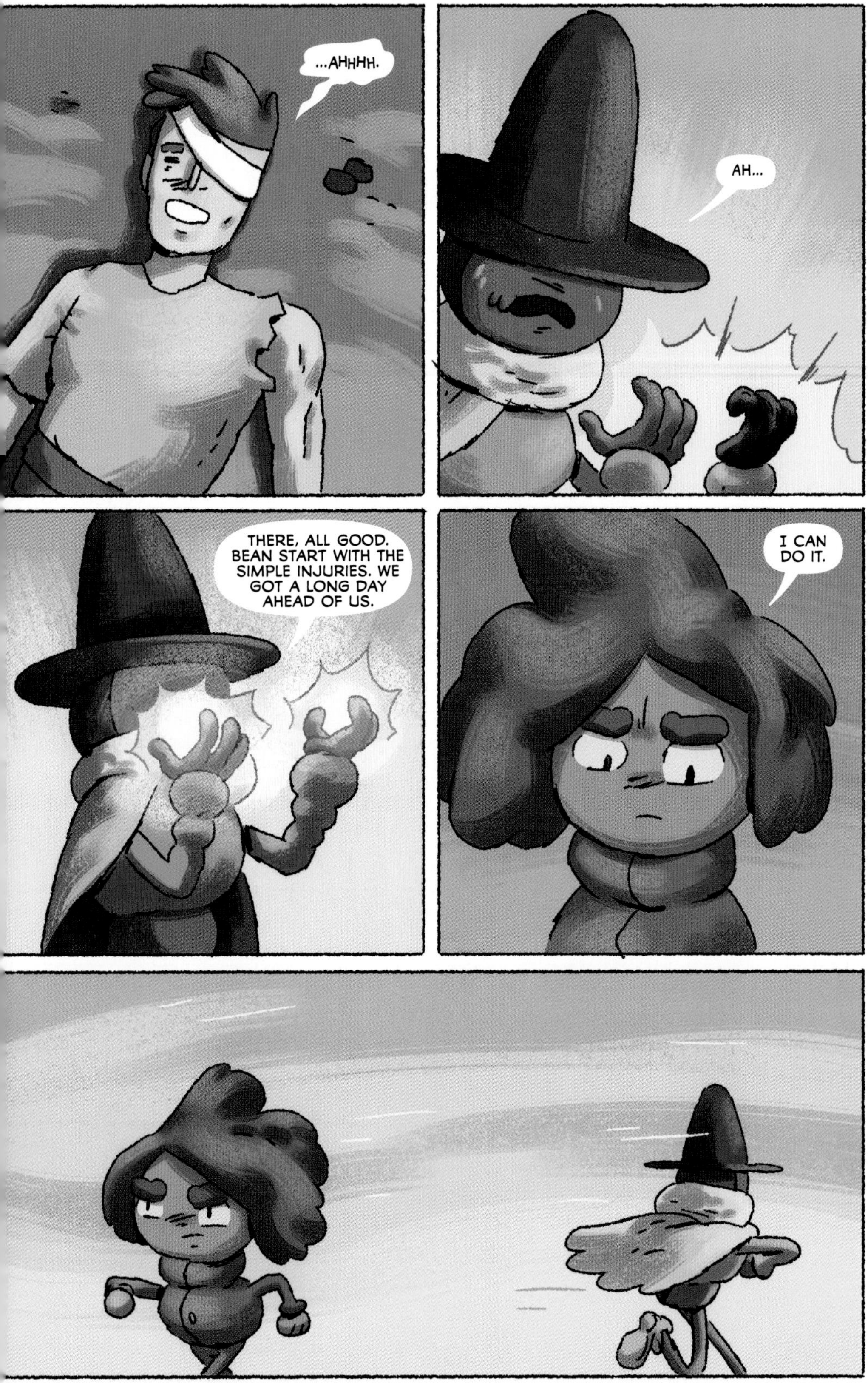
...AHHHH.
AH...
THERE, ALL GOOD. BEAN START WITH THE SIMPLE INJURIES. WE GOT A LONG DAY AHEAD OF US.
I CAN DO IT.

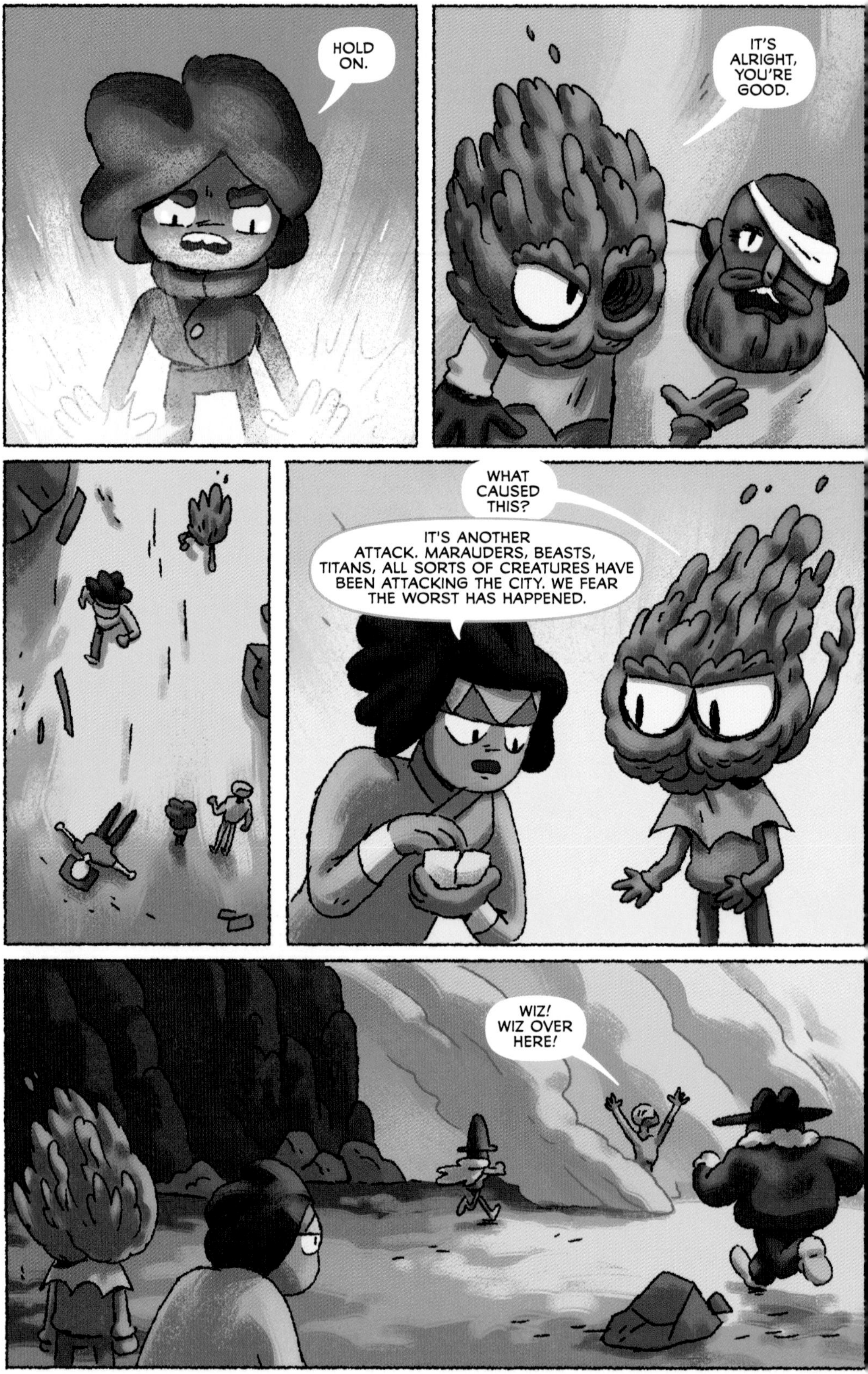
HOLD ON.
IT'S ALRIGHT, YOU'RE GOOD.
WHAT CAUSED THIS?
IT'S ANOTHER ATTACK. MARAUDERS, BEASTS, TITANS, ALL SORTS OF CREATURES HAVE BEEN ATTACKING THE CITY. WE FEAR THE WORST HAS HAPPENED.
WIZ! WIZ OVER HERE!

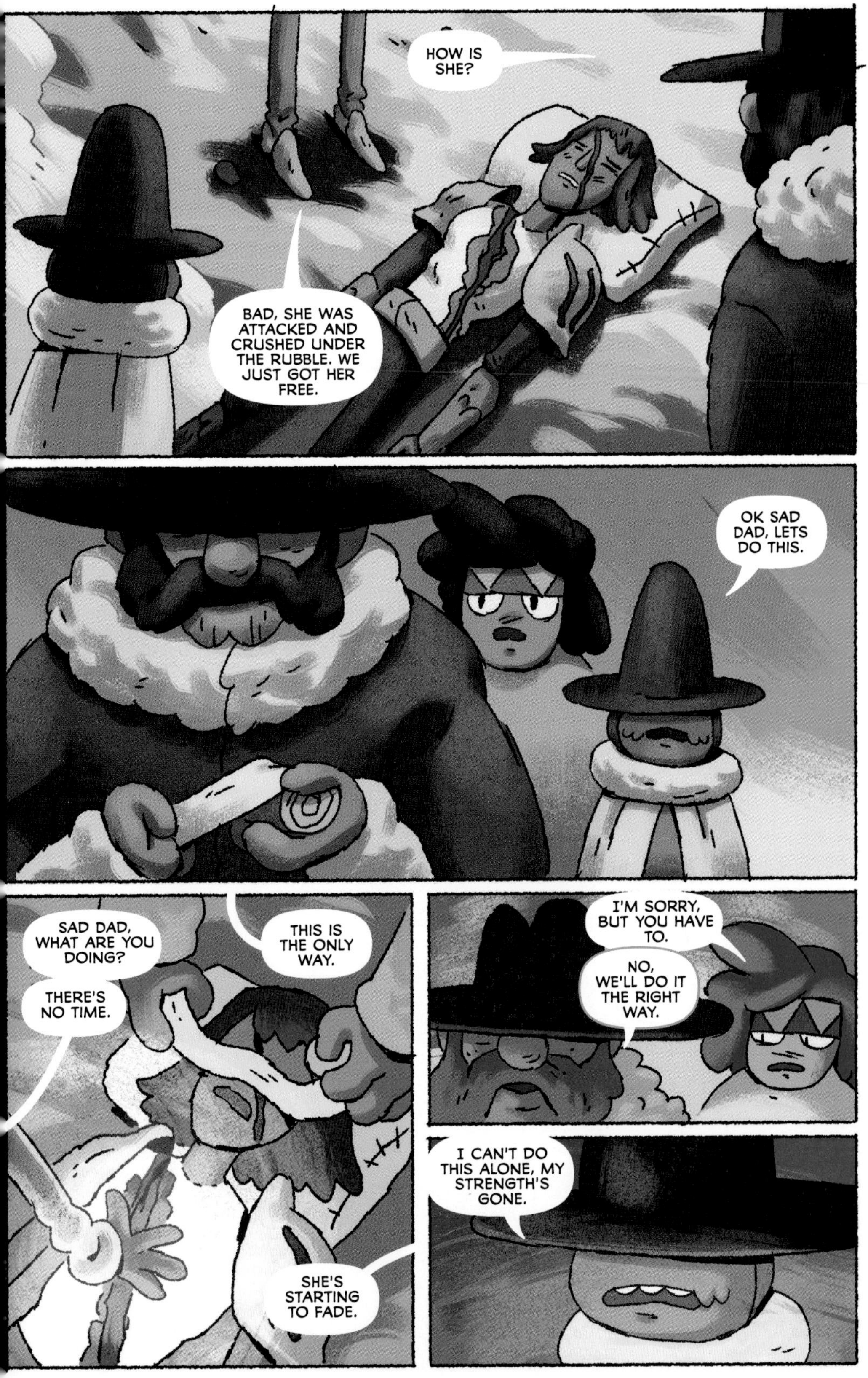
HOW IS SHE?
BAD, SHE WAS ATTACKED AND CRUSHED UNDER THE RUBBLE. WE JUST GOT HER FREE.
OK SAD DAD, LETS DO THIS.
SAD DAD, WHAT ARE YOU DOING?
THERE'S NO TIME.
THIS IS THE ONLY WAY.
SHE'S STARTING TO FADE.
I'M SORRY, BUT YOU HAVE TO.
NO, WE'LL DO IT THE RIGHT WAY.
I CAN'T DO THIS ALONE, MY STRENGTH'S GONE.

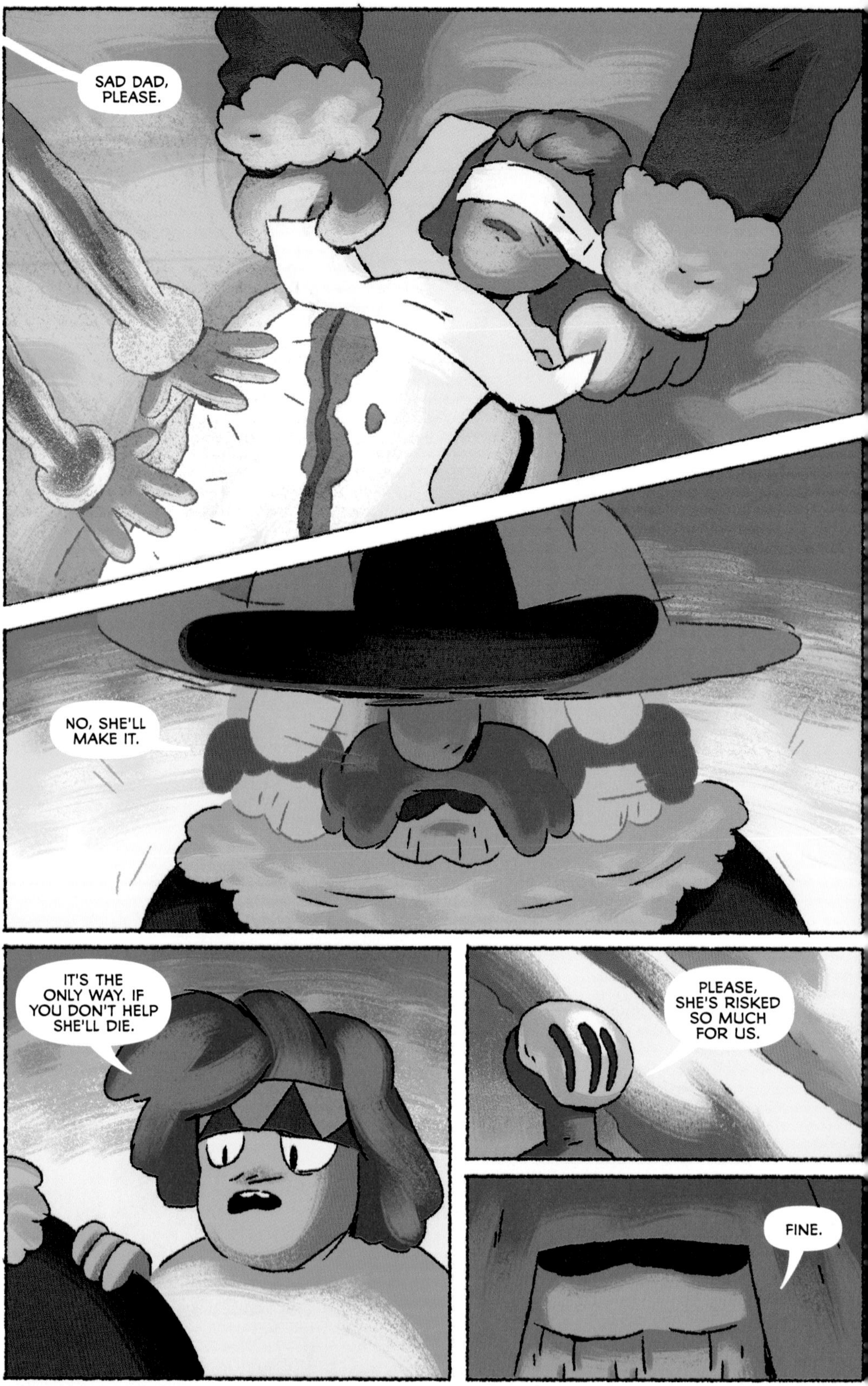
SAD DAD, PLEASE.
NO, SHE'LL MAKE IT.
IT'S THE ONLY WAY. IF YOU DON'T HELP SHE'LL DIE.
PLEASE, SHE'S RISKED SO MUCH FOR US.
FINE.

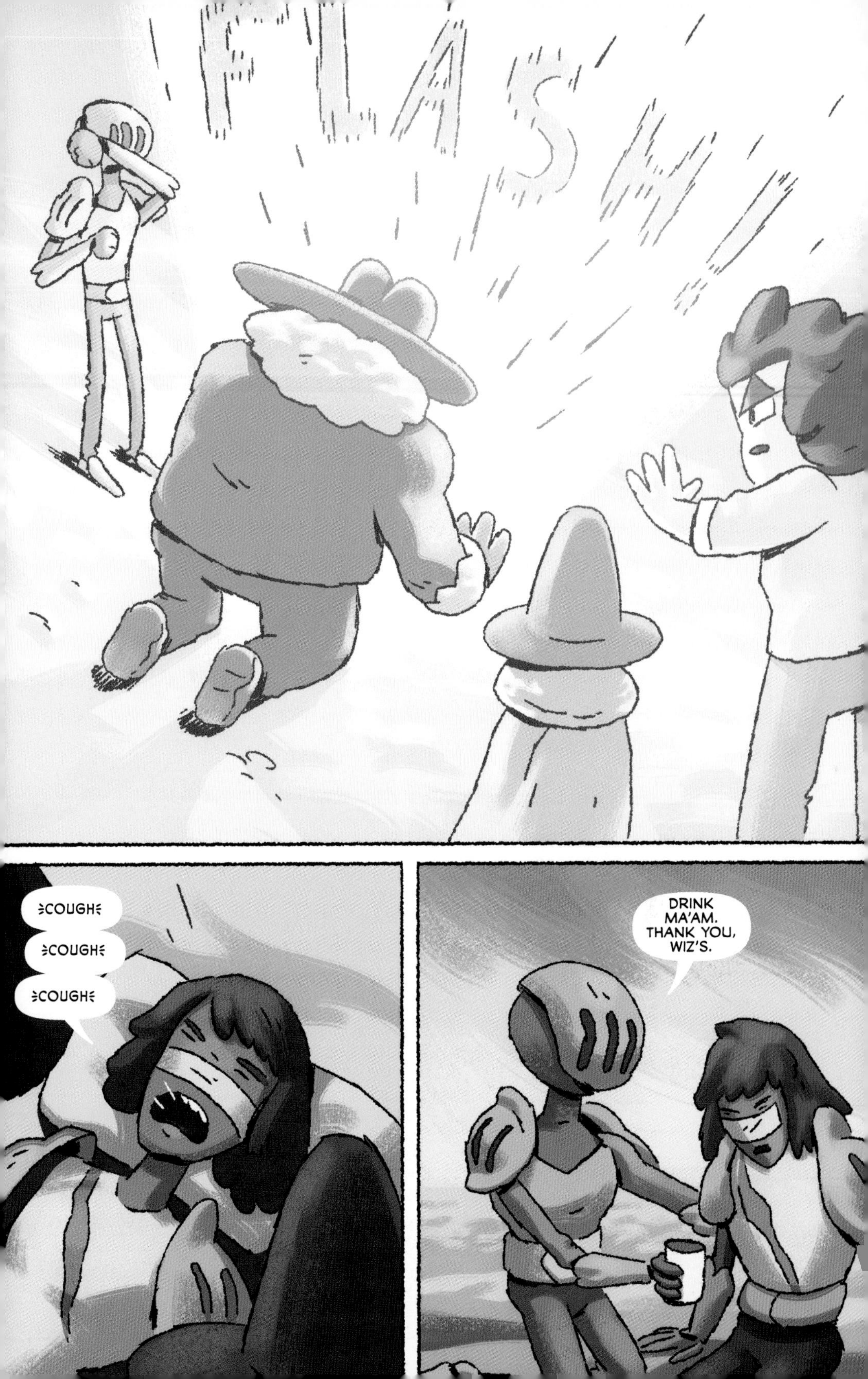
FLASH!
COUGH
COUGH
COUGH
DRINK MA'AM.
THANK YOU, WIZ'S.

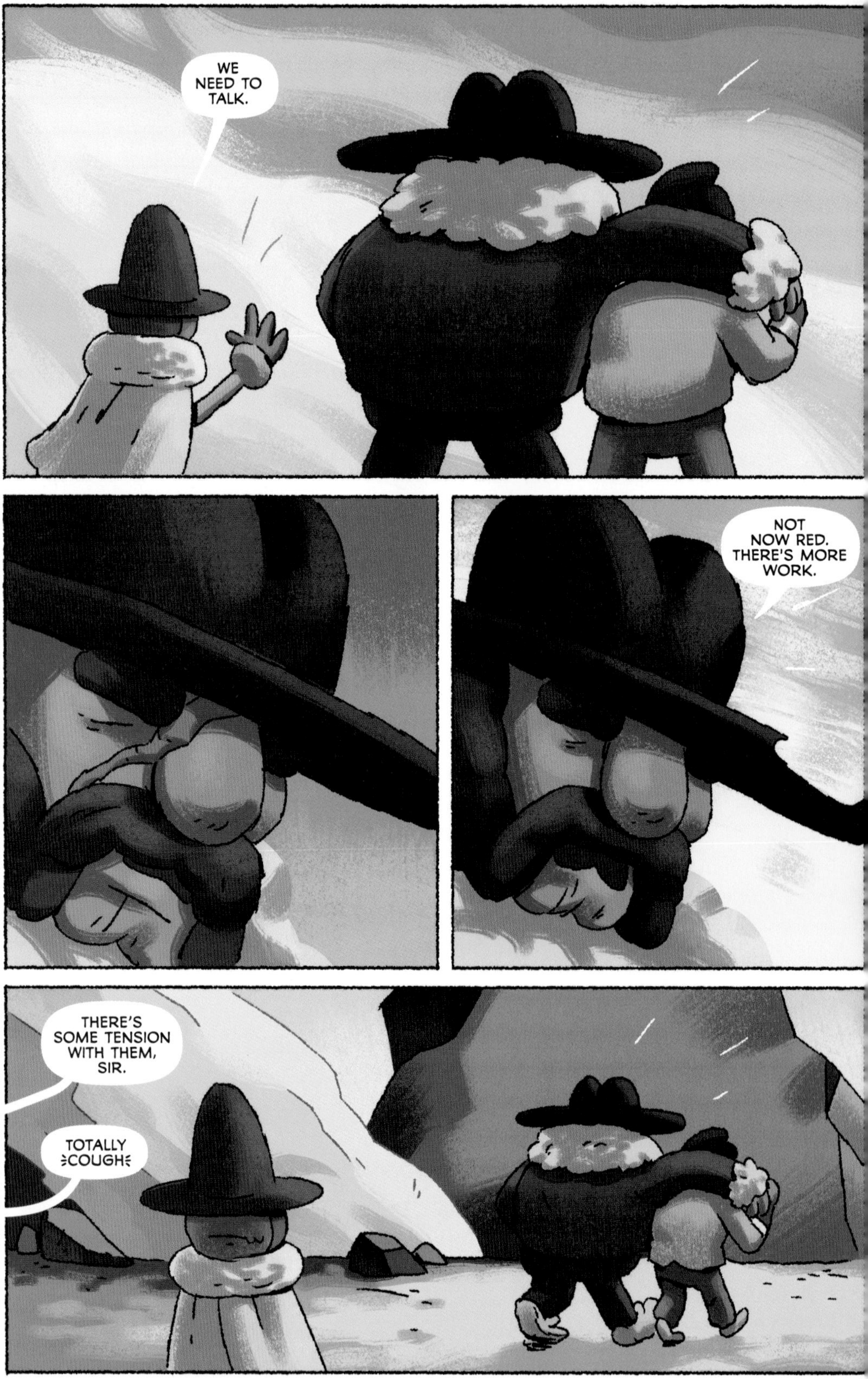
WE NEED TO TALK.
NOT NOW RED. THERE'S MORE WORK.
THERE'S SOME TENSION WITH THEM, SIR.
TOTALLY ≶COUGH≶

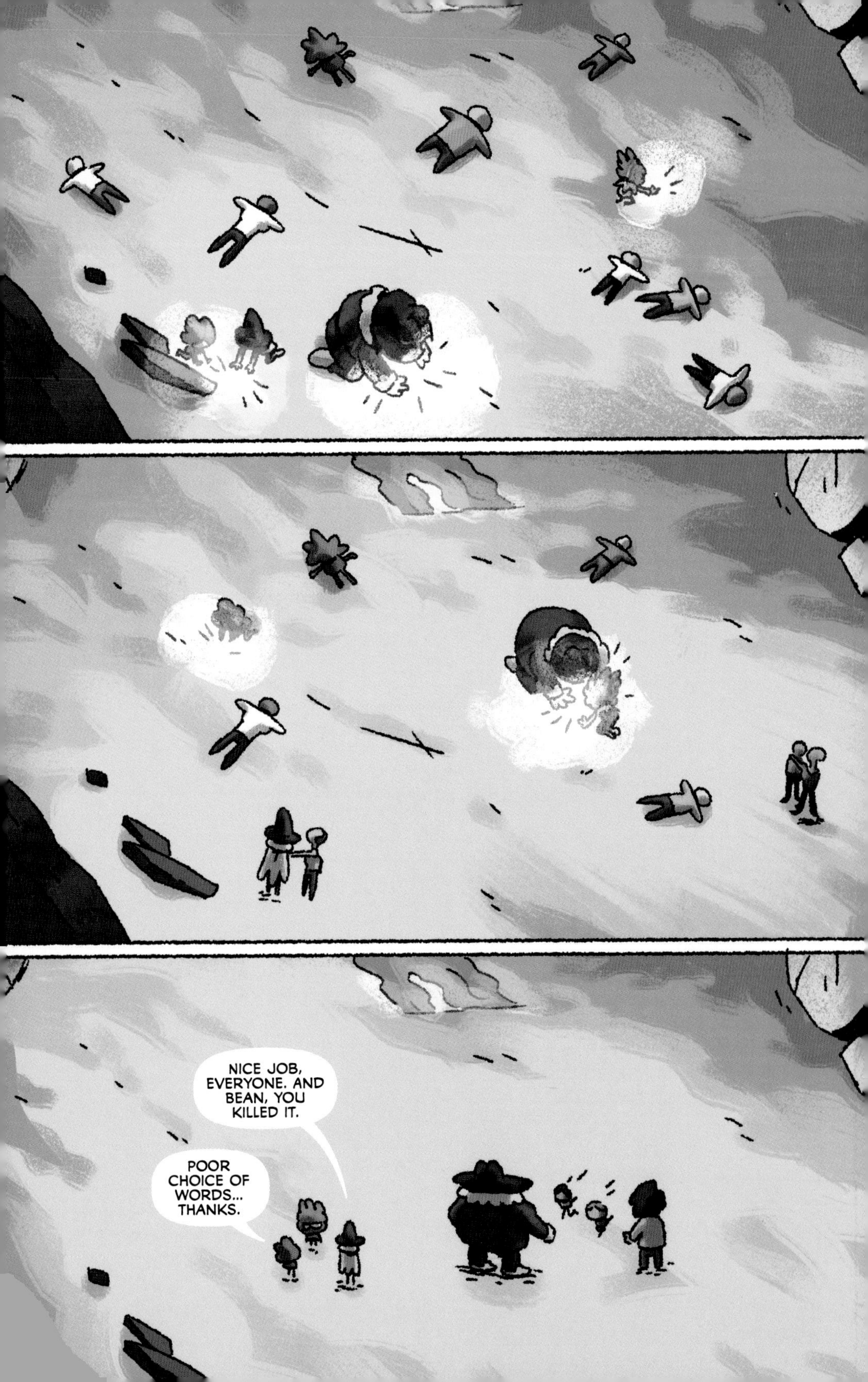
NICE JOB, EVERYONE. AND BEAN, YOU KILLED IT.
POOR CHOICE OF WORDS... THANKS.

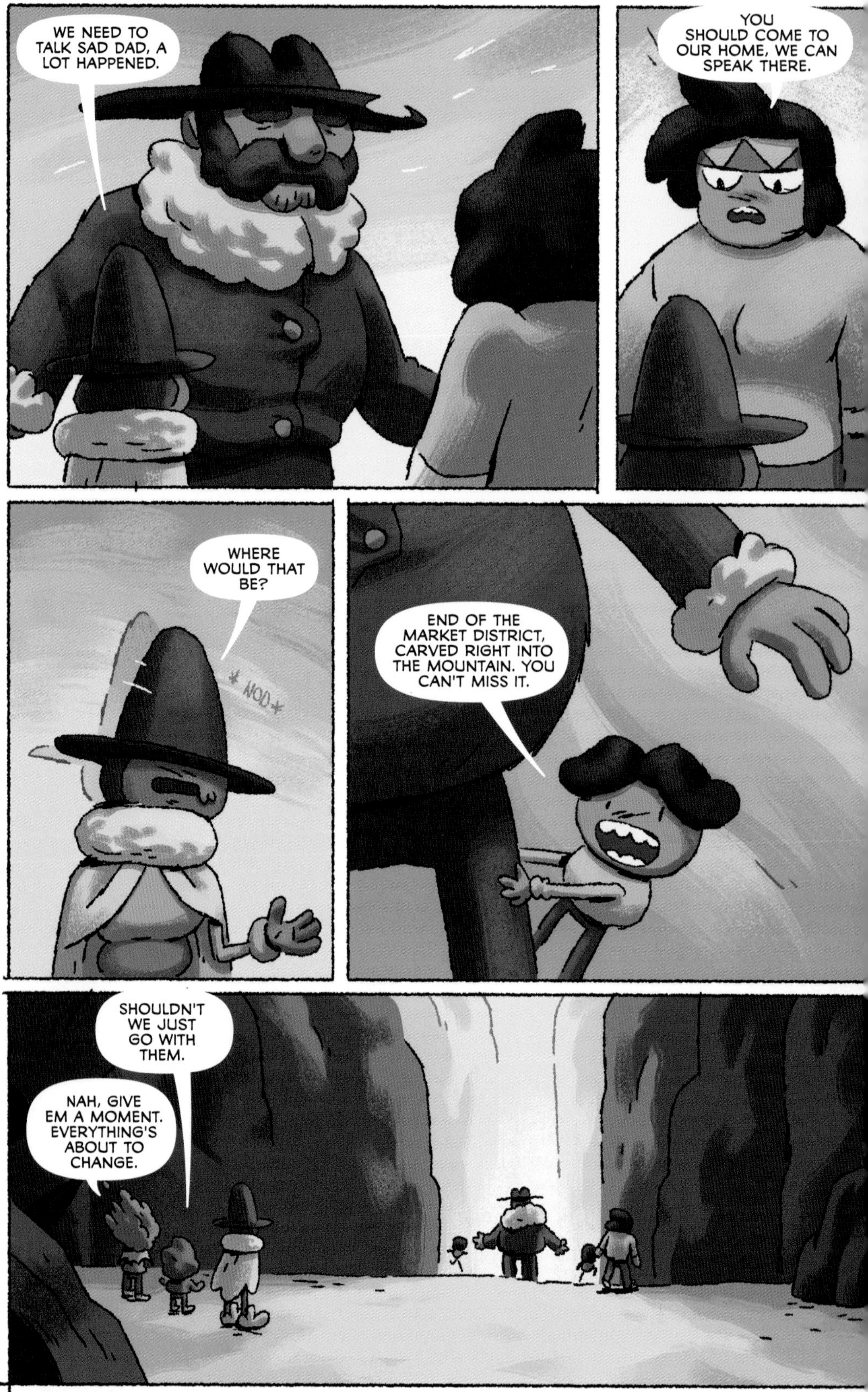
WE NEED TO TALK SAD DAD, A LOT HAPPENED.
YOU SHOULD COME TO OUR HOME, WE CAN SPEAK THERE.
WHERE WOULD THAT BE?
NOD
END OF THE MARKET DISTRICT, CARVED RIGHT INTO THE MOUNTAIN. YOU CAN'T MISS IT.
SHOULDN'T WE JUST GO WITH THEM.
NAH, GIVE EM A MOMENT. EVERYTHING'S ABOUT TO CHANGE.

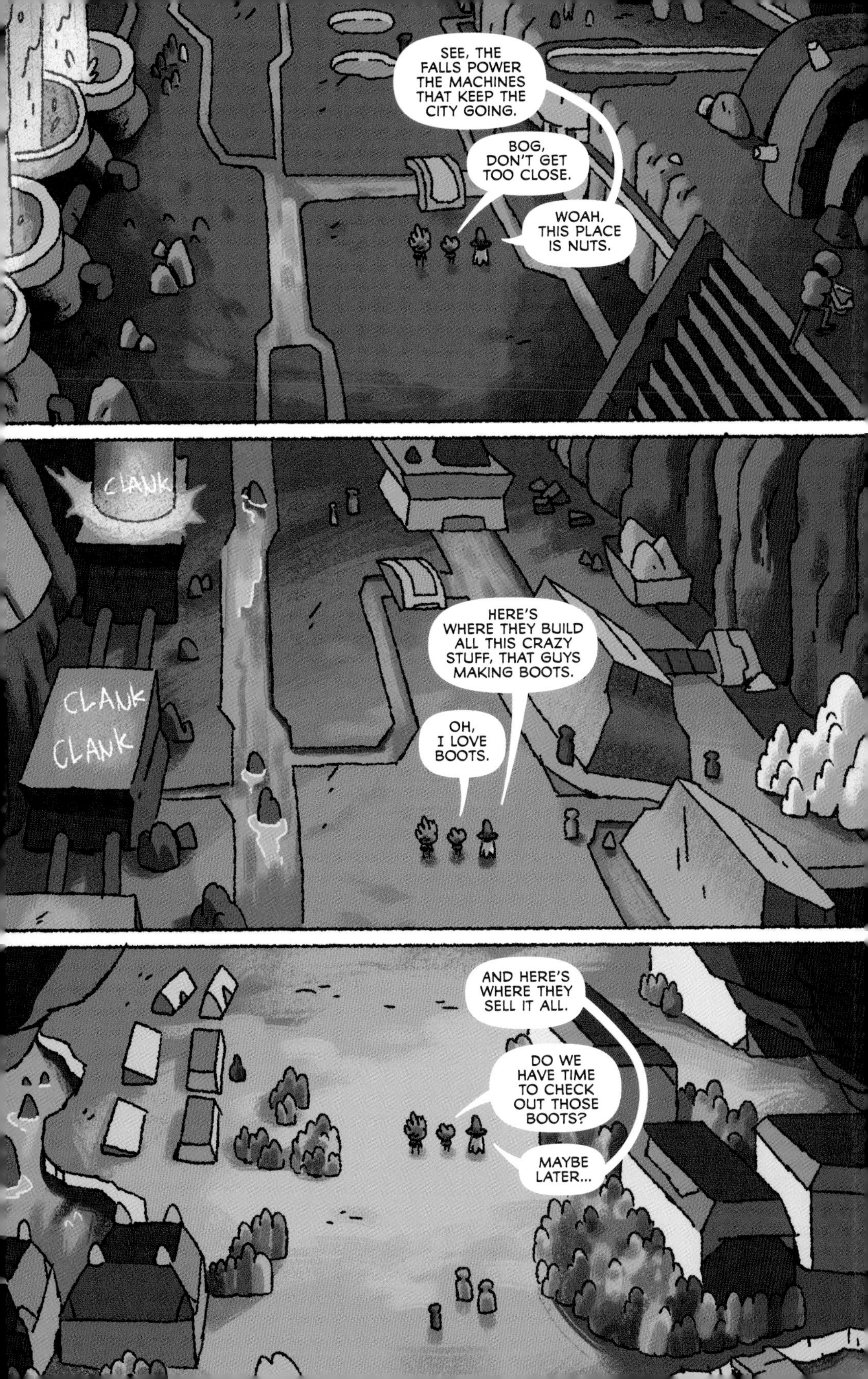
SEE, THE FALLS POWER THE MACHINES THAT KEEP THE CITY GOING.
BOG, DON'T GET TOO CLOSE.
WOAH, THIS PLACE IS NUTS.
CLANK
CLANK CLANK
HERE'S WHERE THEY BUILD ALL THIS CRAZY STUFF, THAT GUYS MAKING BOOTS.
OH, I LOVE BOOTS.
AND HERE'S WHERE THEY SELL IT ALL.
DO WE HAVE TIME TO CHECK OUT THOSE BOOTS?
MAYBE LATER...

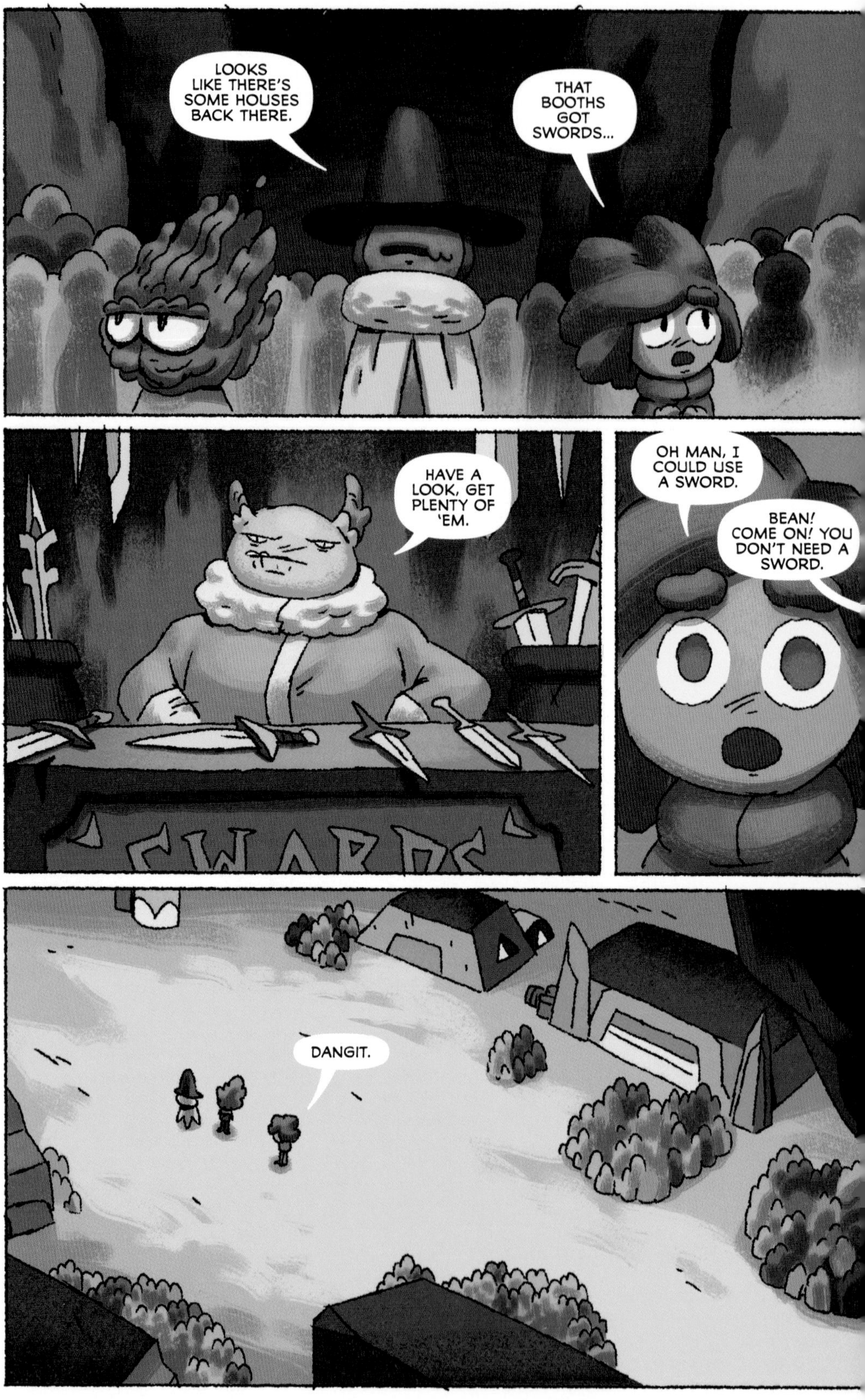
LOOKS LIKE THERE'S SOME HOUSES BACK THERE.
THAT BOOTHS GOT SWORDS...
HAVE A LOOK, GET PLENTY OF 'EM.
OH MAN, I COULD USE A SWORD.
BEAN! COME ON! YOU DON'T NEED A SWORD.
DANGIT.

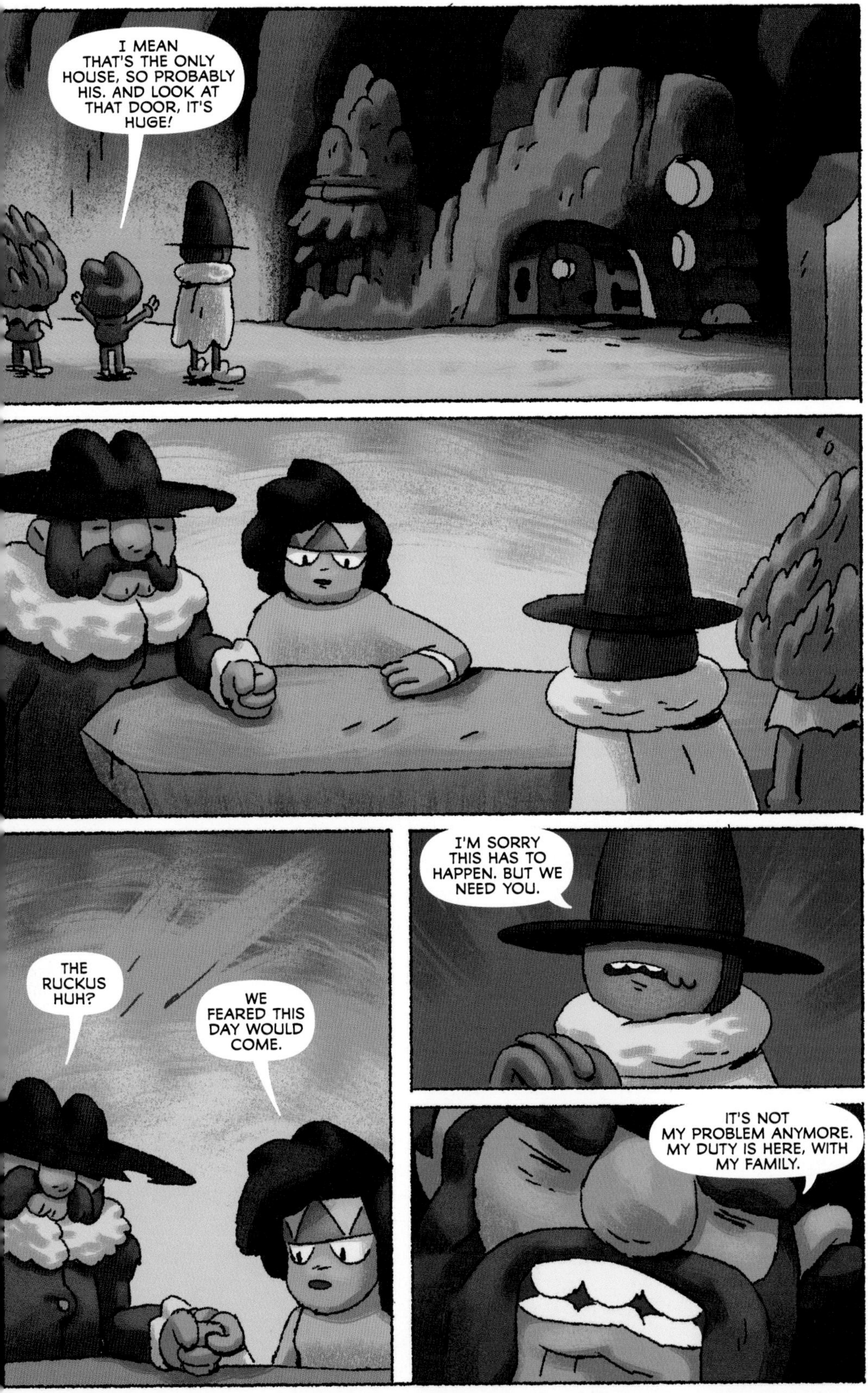
I MEAN THAT'S THE ONLY HOUSE, SO PROBABLY HIS. AND LOOK AT THAT DOOR, IT'S HUGE!
THE RUCKUS HUH?
WE FEARED THIS DAY WOULD COME.
I'M SORRY THIS HAS TO HAPPEN. BUT WE NEED YOU.
IT'S NOT MY PROBLEM ANYMORE. MY DUTY IS HERE, WITH MY FAMILY.

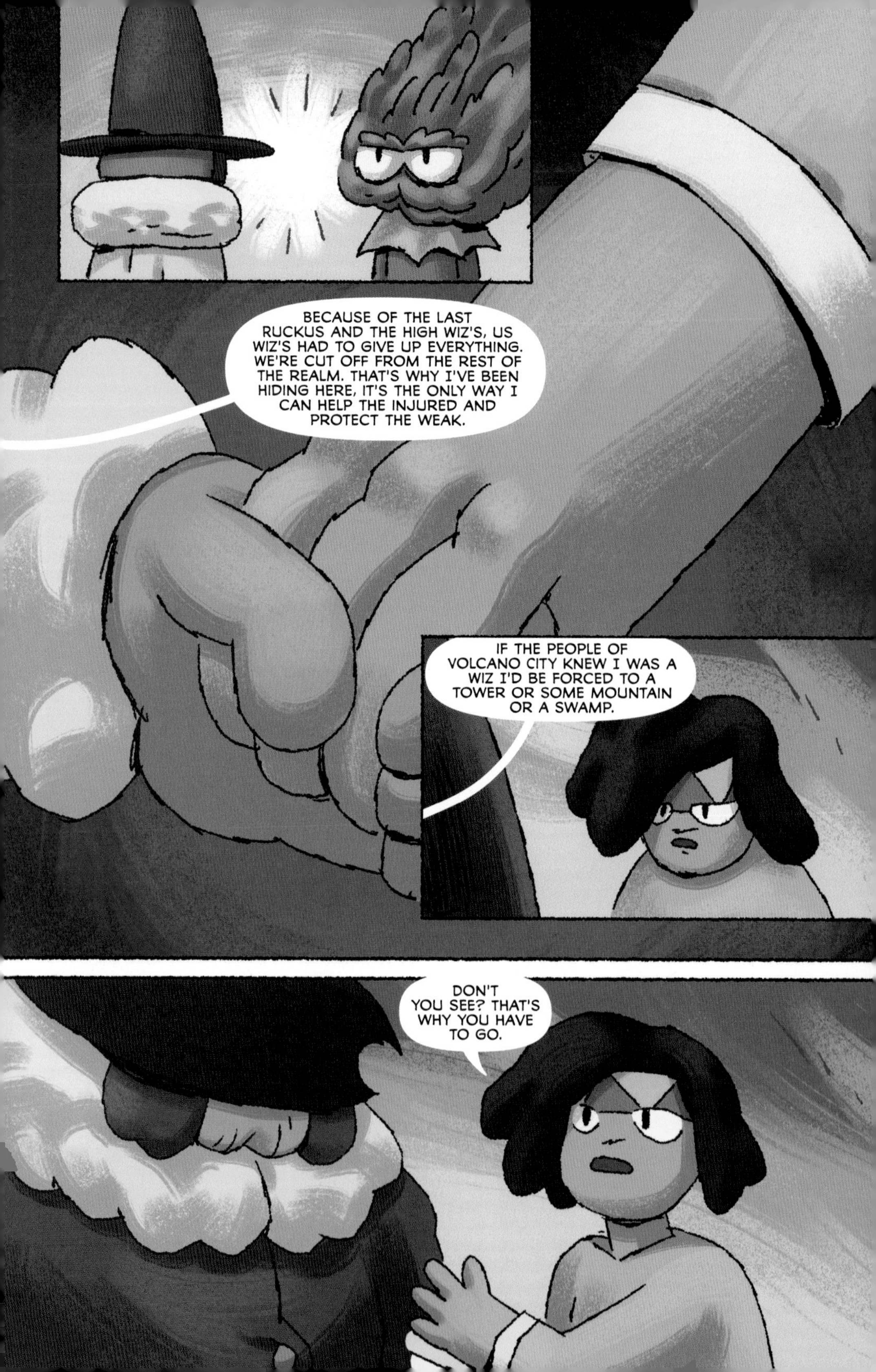
BECAUSE OF THE LAST RUCKUS AND THE HIGH WIZ'S, US WIZ'S HAD TO GIVE UP EVERYTHING. WE'RE CUT OFF FROM THE REST OF THE REALM. THAT'S WHY I'VE BEEN HIDING HERE, IT'S THE ONLY WAY I CAN HELP THE INJURED AND PROTECT THE WEAK.
IF THE PEOPLE OF VOLCANO CITY KNEW I WAS A WIZ I'D BE FORCED TO A TOWER OR SOME MOUNTAIN OR A SWAMP.
DON'T YOU SEE? THAT'S WHY YOU HAVE TO GO.

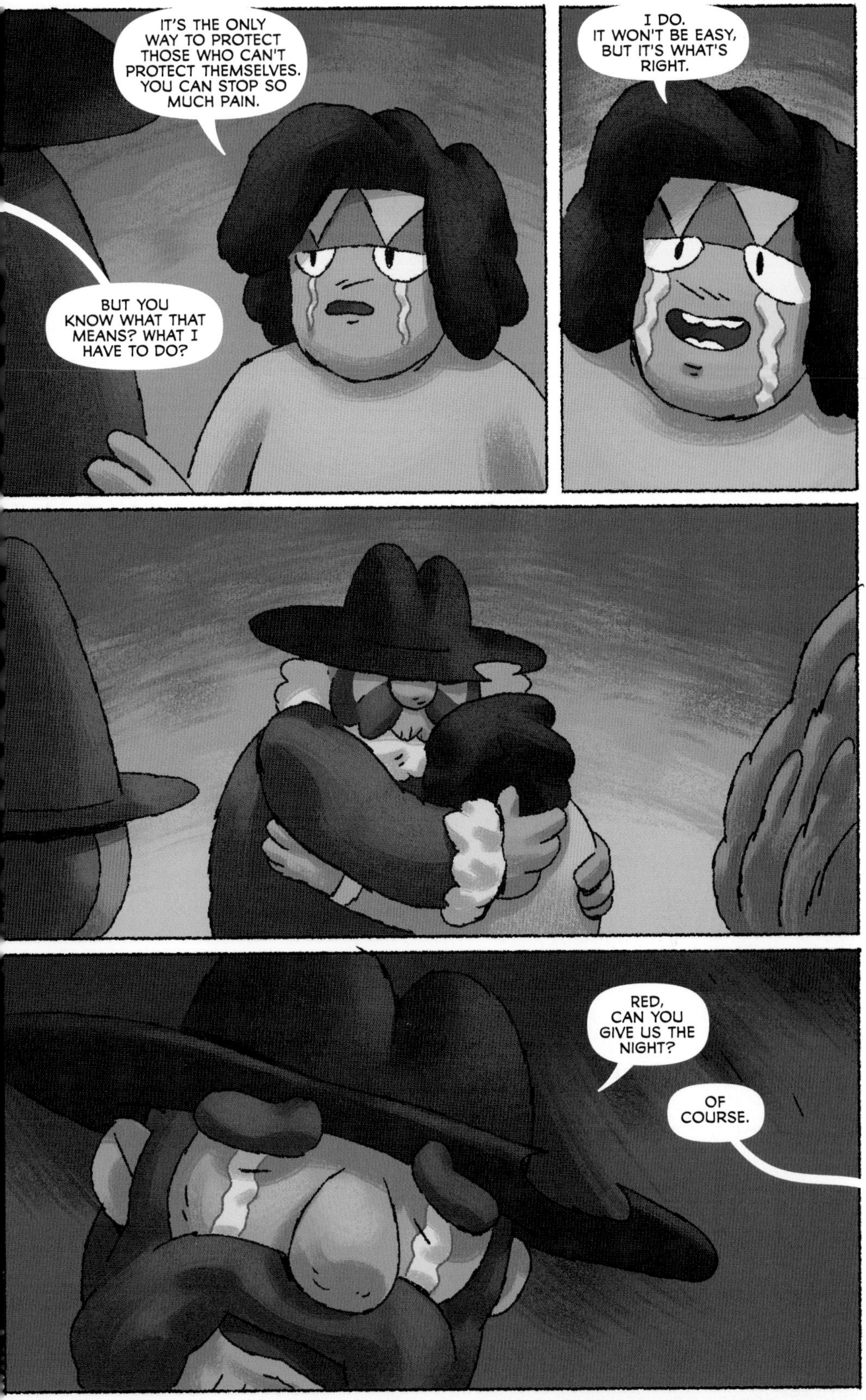
IT'S THE ONLY WAY TO PROTECT THOSE WHO CAN'T PROTECT THEMSELVES. YOU CAN STOP SO MUCH PAIN.
BUT YOU KNOW WHAT THAT MEANS? WHAT I HAVE TO DO?
I DO. IT WON'T BE EASY, BUT IT'S WHAT'S RIGHT.
RED, CAN YOU GIVE US THE NIGHT?
OF COURSE.

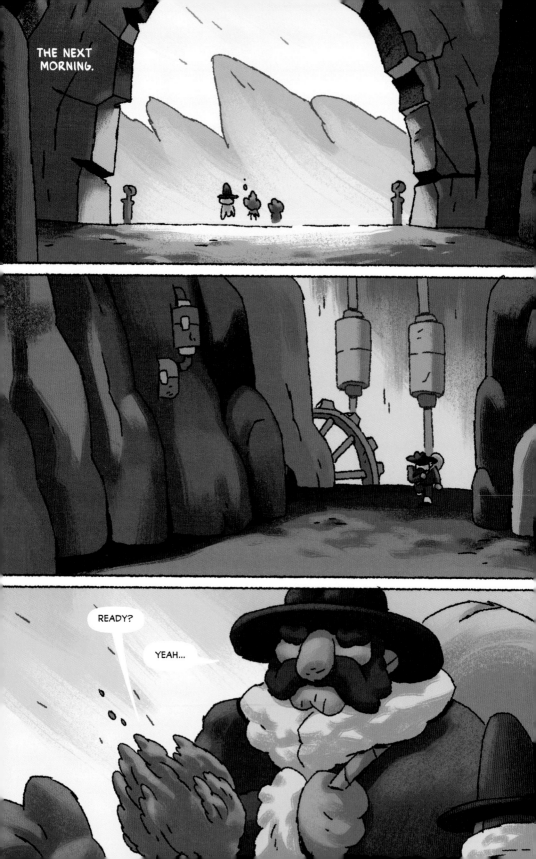

THE NEXT MORNING.

READY?

YEAH...

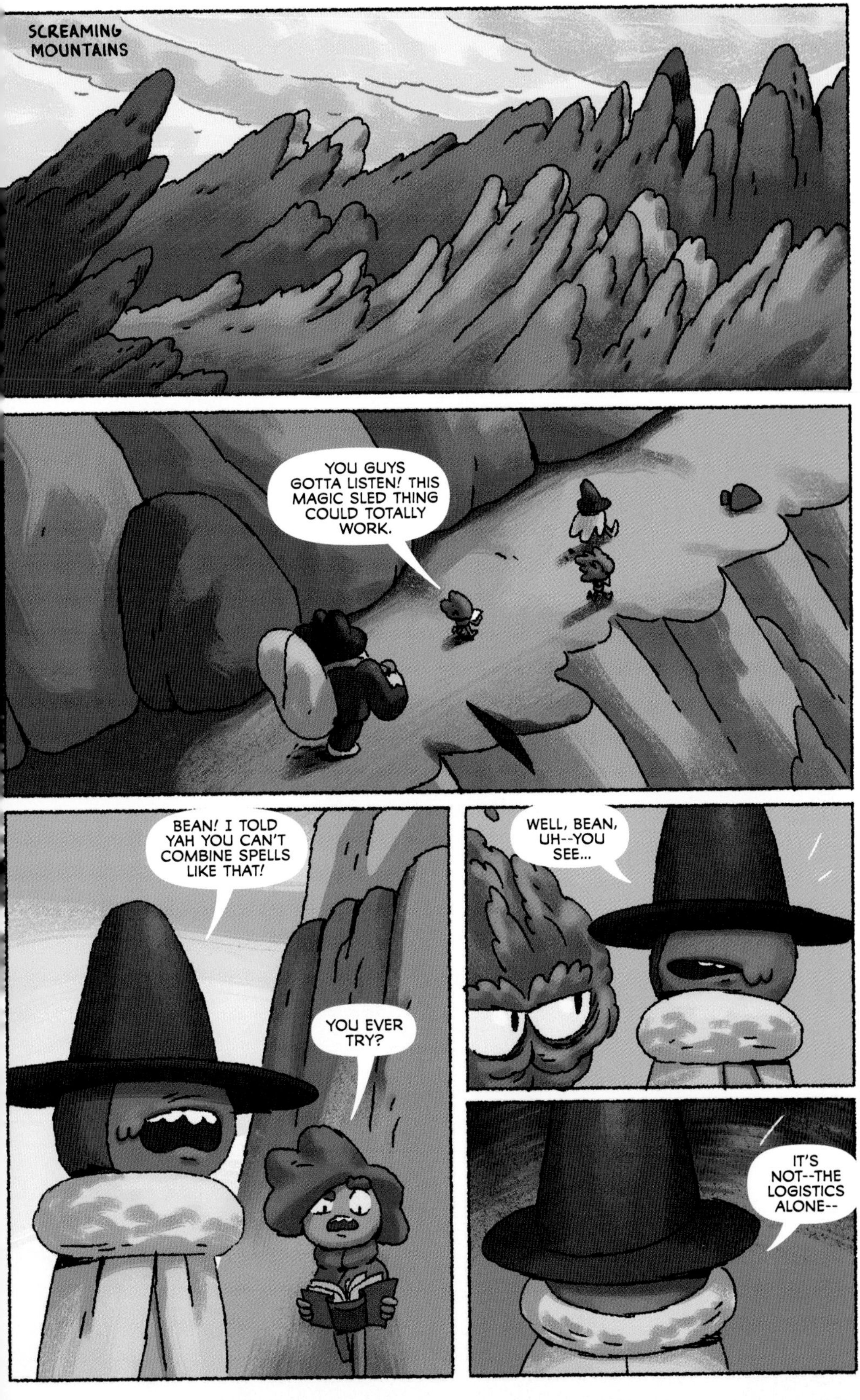
SCREAMING MOUNTAINS
YOU GUYS GOTTA LISTEN! THIS MAGIC SLED THING COULD TOTALLY WORK.
BEAN! I TOLD YAH YOU CAN'T COMBINE SPELLS LIKE THAT!
YOU EVER TRY?
WELL, BEAN, UH--YOU SEE...
IT'S NOT--THE LOGISTICS ALONE--

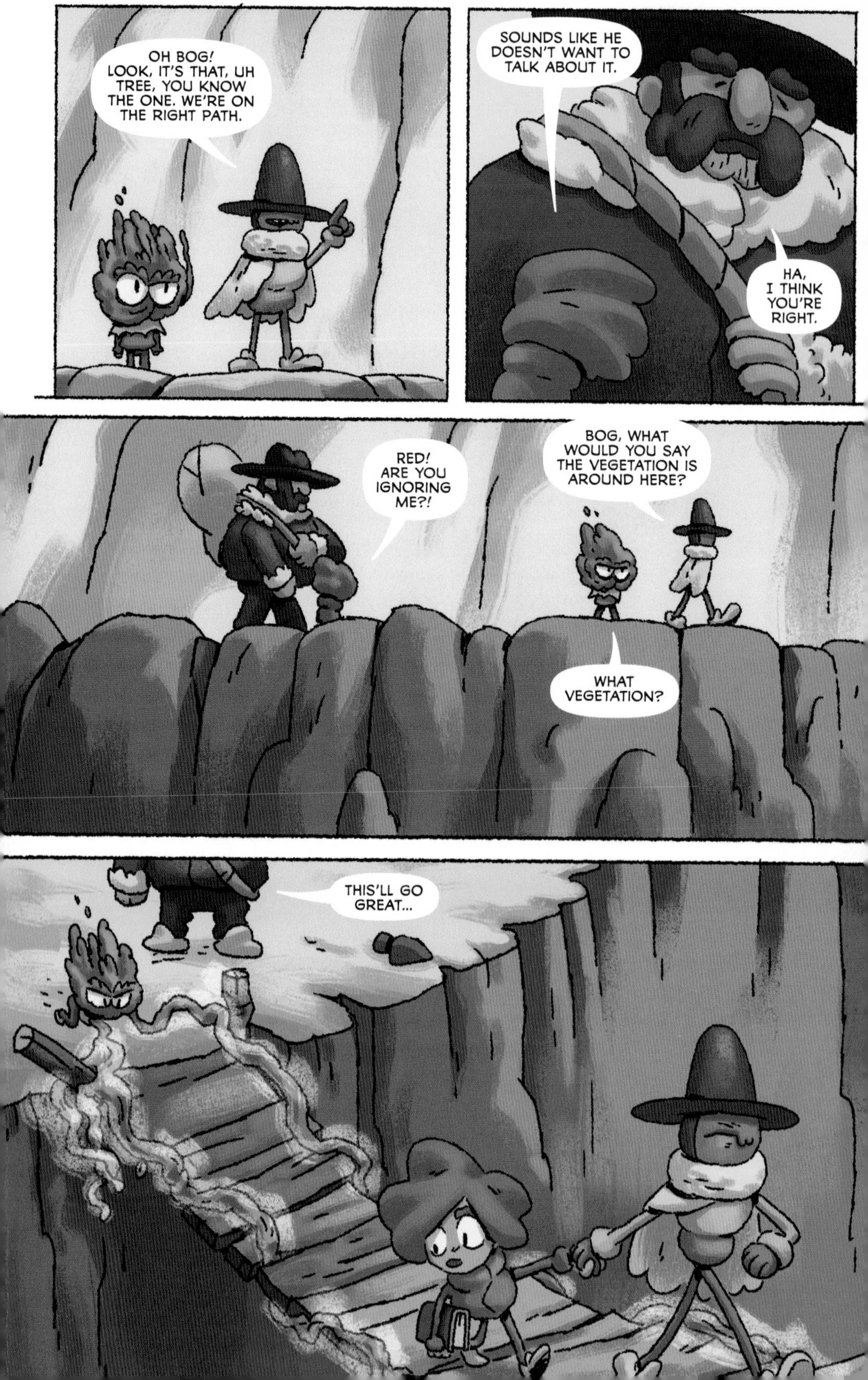
OH BOG! LOOK, IT'S THAT, UH TREE, YOU KNOW THE ONE. WE'RE ON THE RIGHT PATH.
SOUNDS LIKE HE DOESN'T WANT TO TALK ABOUT IT.
HA, I THINK YOU'RE RIGHT.
RED! ARE YOU IGNORING ME?!
BOG, WHAT WOULD YOU SAY THE VEGETATION IS AROUND HERE?
WHAT VEGETATION?
THIS'LL GO GREAT...

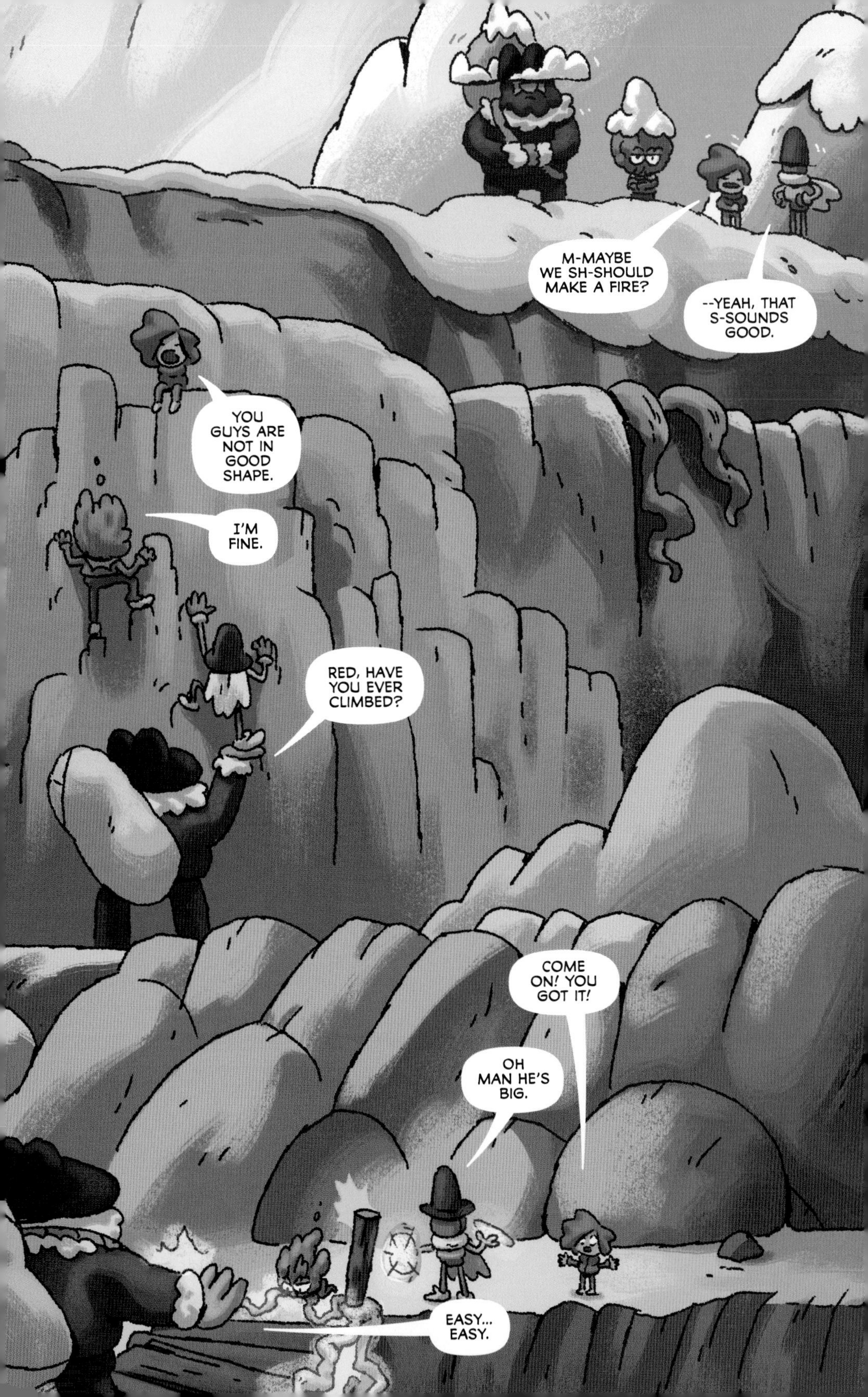
M-MAYBE WE SH-SHOULD MAKE A FIRE?
--YEAH, THAT S-SOUNDS GOOD.
YOU GUYS ARE NOT IN GOOD SHAPE.
I'M FINE.
RED, HAVE YOU EVER CLIMBED?
COME ON! YOU GOT IT!
OH MAN HE'S BIG.
EASY... EASY.

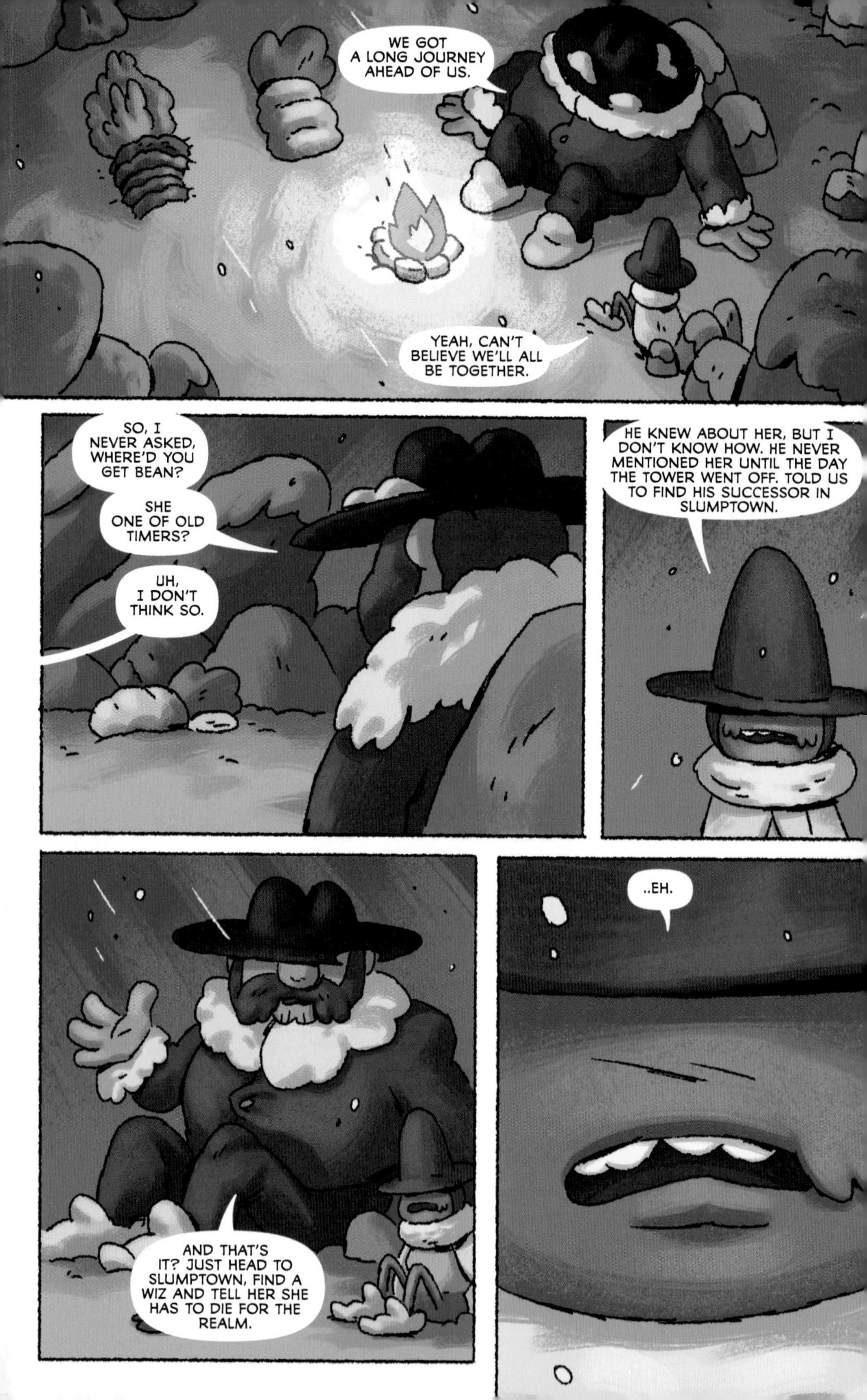
WE GOT A LONG JOURNEY AHEAD OF US.
YEAH, CAN'T BELIEVE WE'LL ALL BE TOGETHER.
SO, I NEVER ASKED, WHERE'D YOU GET BEAN?
SHE ONE OF OLD TIMERS?
UH, I DON'T THINK SO.
HE KNEW ABOUT HER, BUT I DON'T KNOW HOW. HE NEVER MENTIONED HER UNTIL THE DAY THE TOWER WENT OFF. TOLD US TO FIND HIS SUCCESSOR IN SLUMPTOWN.
AND THAT'S IT? JUST HEAD TO SLUMPTOWN, FIND A WIZ AND TELL HER SHE HAS TO DIE FOR THE REALM.
..EH.

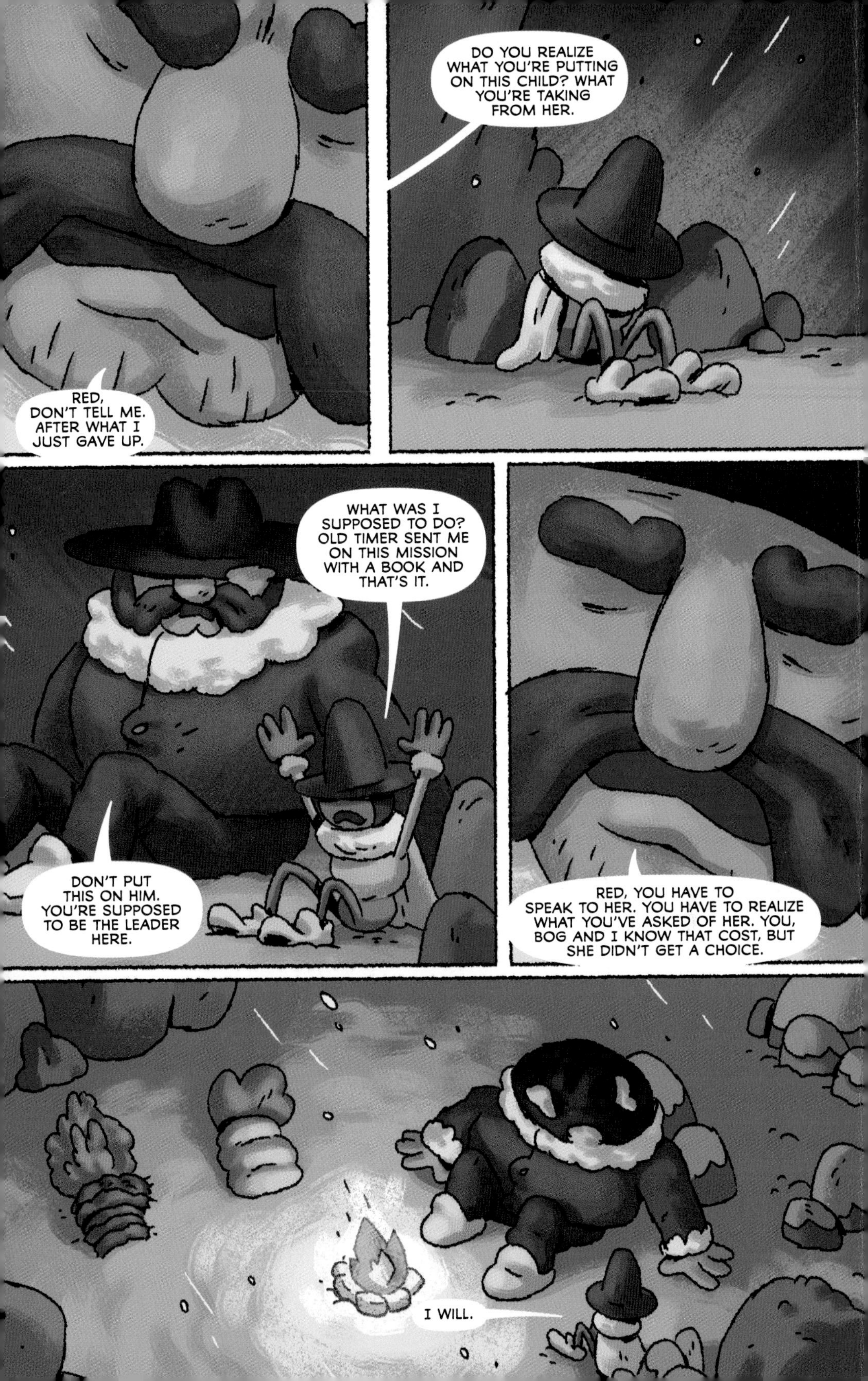
RED, DON'T TELL ME. AFTER WHAT I JUST GAVE UP.
DO YOU REALIZE WHAT YOU'RE PUTTING ON THIS CHILD? WHAT YOU'RE TAKING FROM HER.
WHAT WAS I SUPPOSED TO DO? OLD TIMER SENT ME ON THIS MISSION WITH A BOOK AND THAT'S IT.
DON'T PUT THIS ON HIM. YOU'RE SUPPOSED TO BE THE LEADER HERE.
RED, YOU HAVE TO SPEAK TO HER. YOU HAVE TO REALIZE WHAT YOU'VE ASKED OF HER. YOU, BOG AND I KNOW THAT COST, BUT SHE DIDN'T GET A CHOICE.
I WILL.

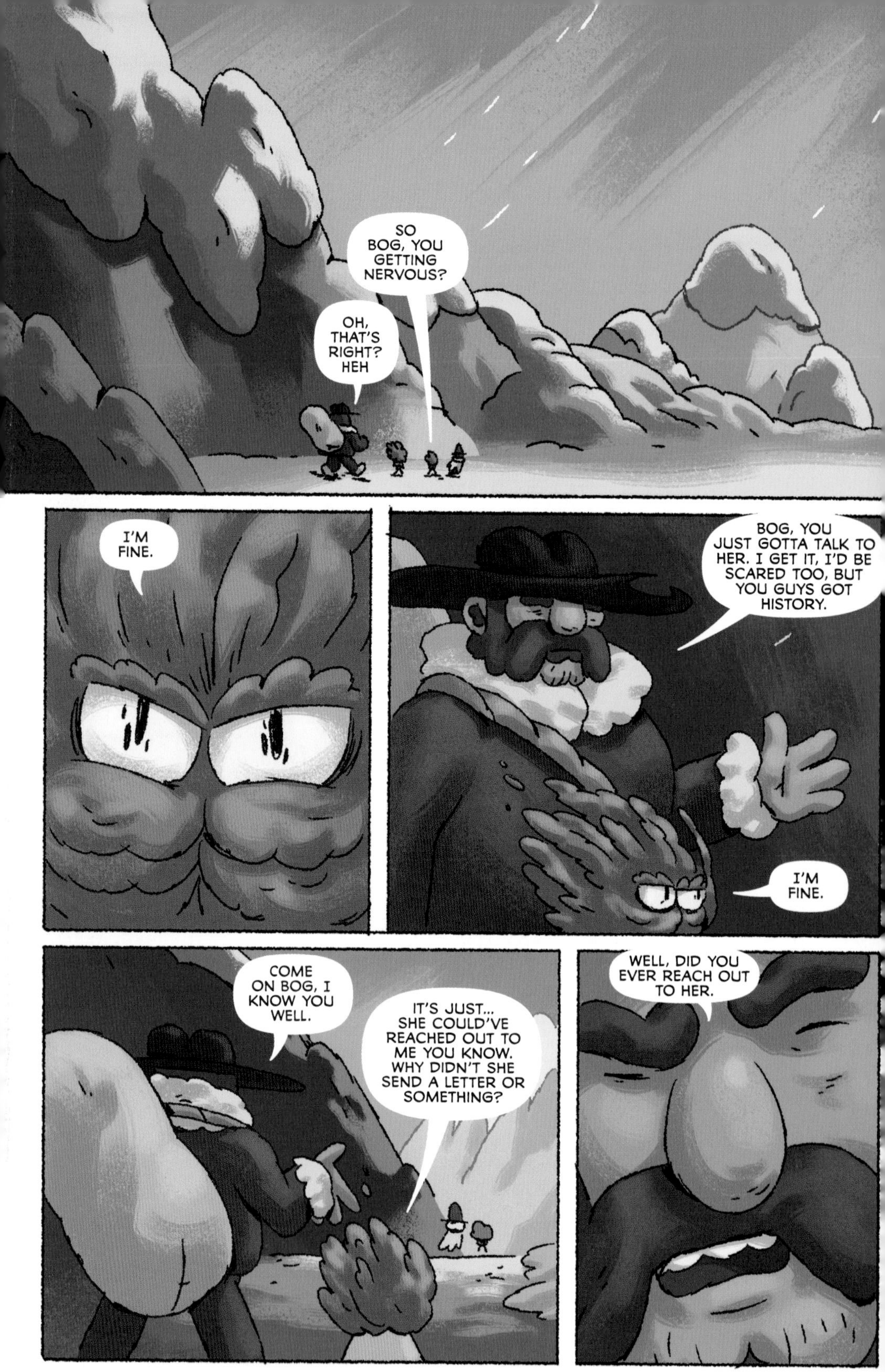
SO BOG, YOU GETTING NERVOUS?
OH, THAT'S RIGHT? HEH
I'M FINE.
BOG, YOU JUST GOTTA TALK TO HER. I GET IT, I'D BE SCARED TOO, BUT YOU GUYS GOT HISTORY.
I'M FINE.
COME ON BOG, I KNOW YOU WELL.
IT'S JUST... SHE COULD'VE REACHED OUT TO ME YOU KNOW. WHY DIDN'T SHE SEND A LETTER OR SOMETHING?
WELL, DID YOU EVER REACH OUT TO HER.

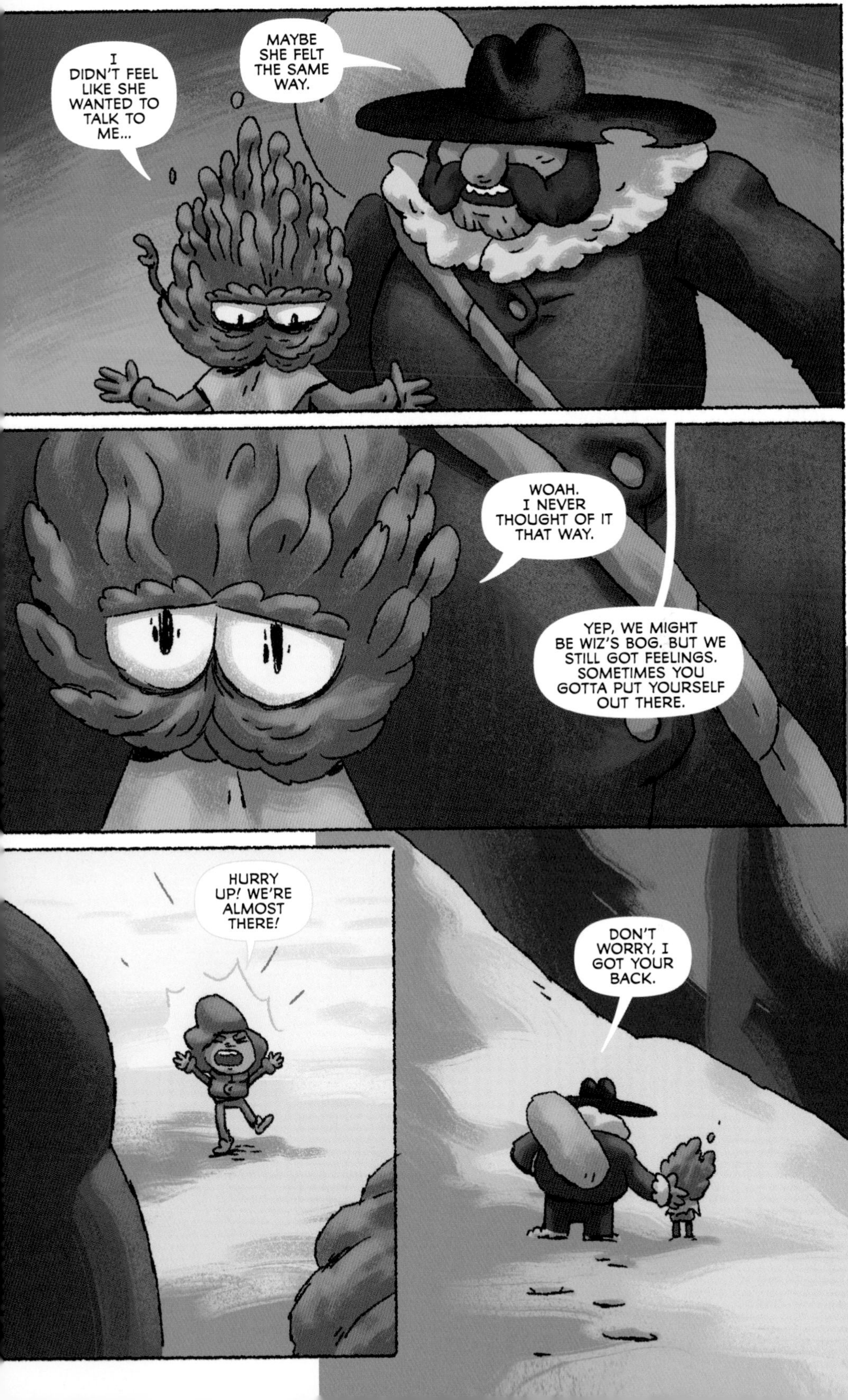
I DIDN'T FEEL LIKE SHE WANTED TO TALK TO ME...
MAYBE SHE FELT THE SAME WAY.
WOAH. I NEVER THOUGHT OF IT THAT WAY.
YEP, WE MIGHT BE WIZ'S BOG. BUT WE STILL GOT FEELINGS. SOMETIMES YOU GOTTA PUT YOURSELF OUT THERE.
HURRY UP! WE'RE ALMOST THERE!
DON'T WORRY, I GOT YOUR BACK.

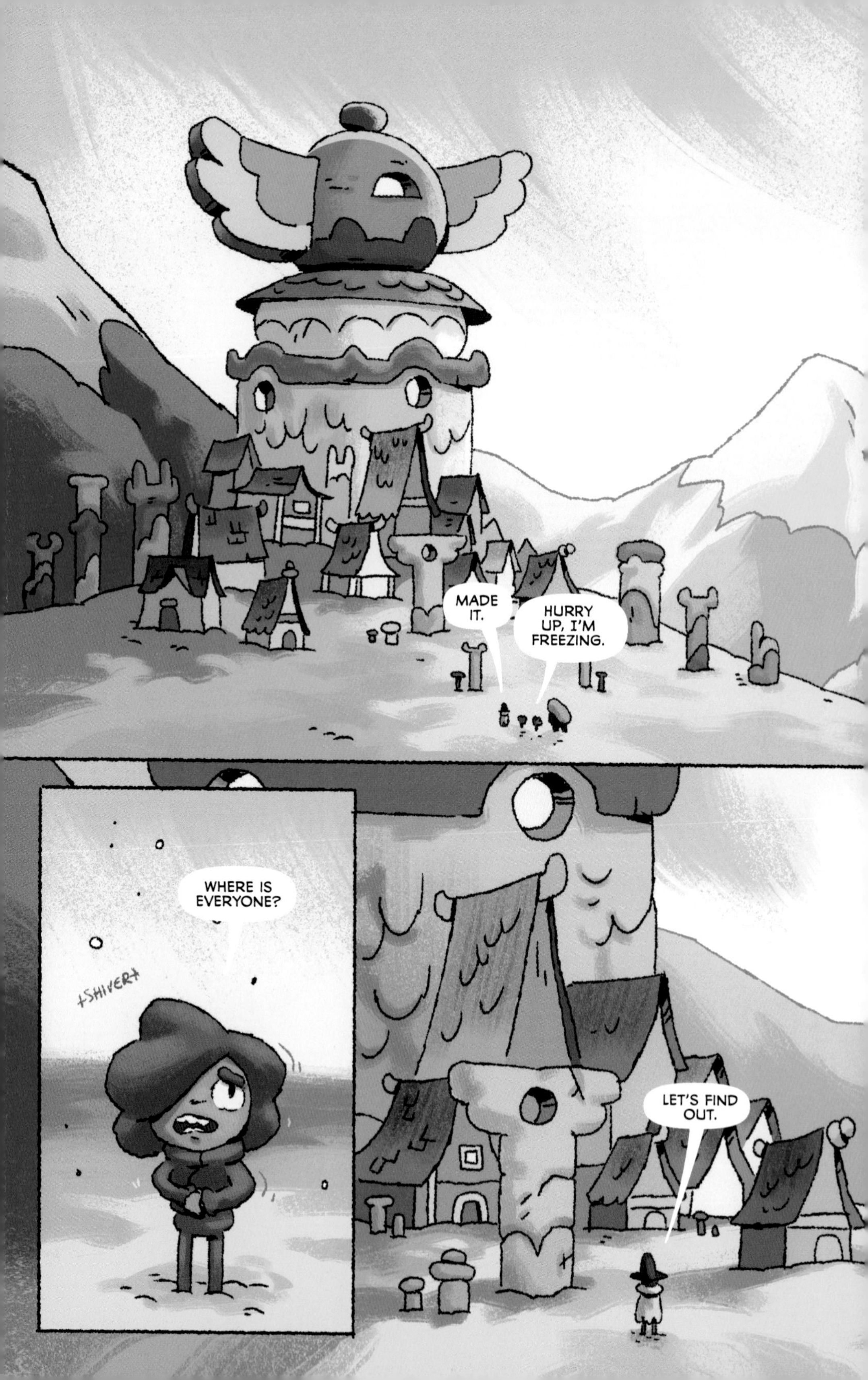
MADE IT.
HURRY UP, I'M FREEZING.
WHERE IS EVERYONE?
SHIVER
LET'S FIND OUT.

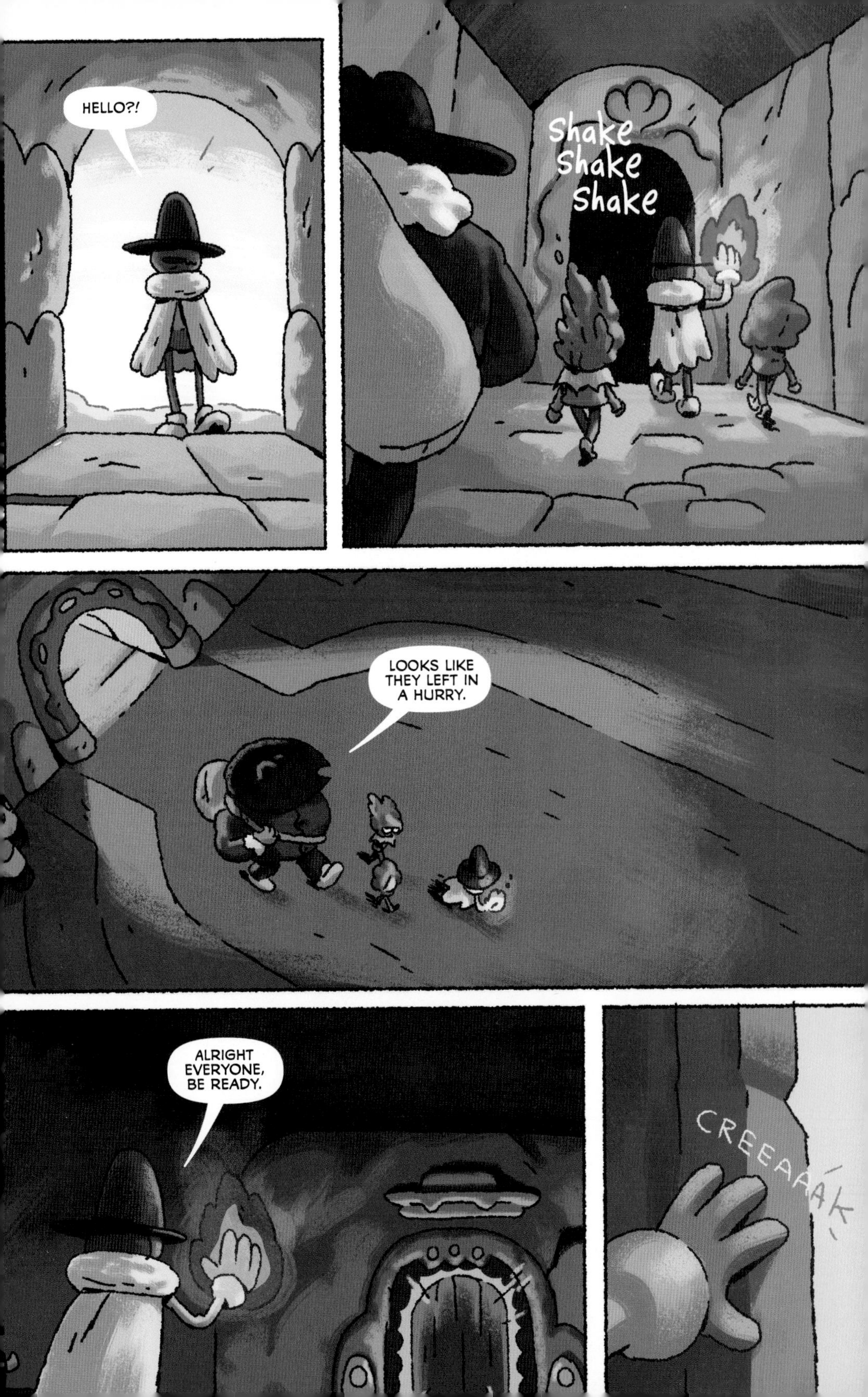
HELLO?!
Shake
Shake
Shake
LOOKS LIKE THEY LEFT IN A HURRY.
ALRIGHT EVERYONE, BE READY.
CREEAAAAK

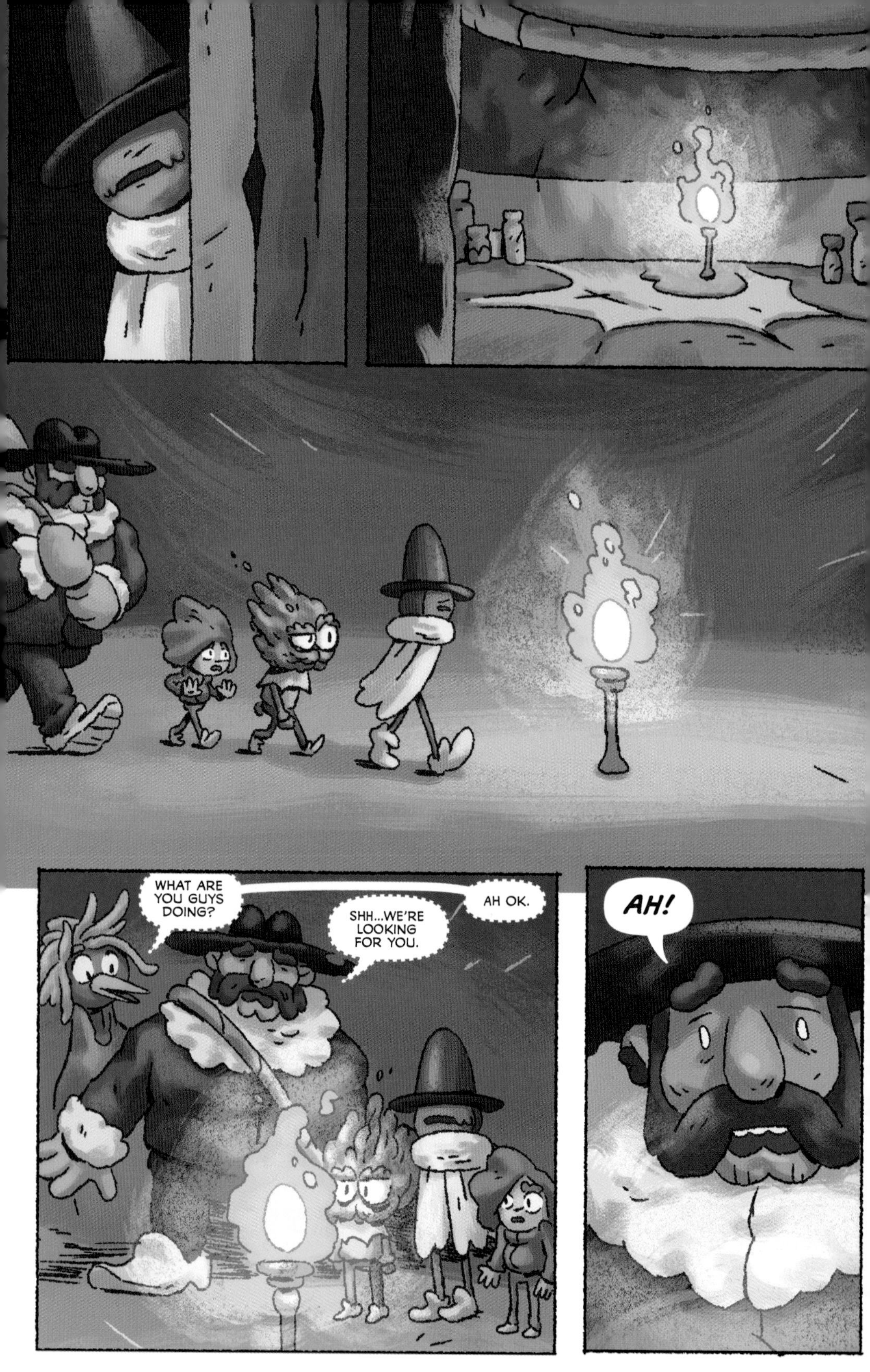
WHAT ARE YOU GUYS DOING?
SHH...WE'RE LOOKING FOR YOU.
AH OK.
AH!

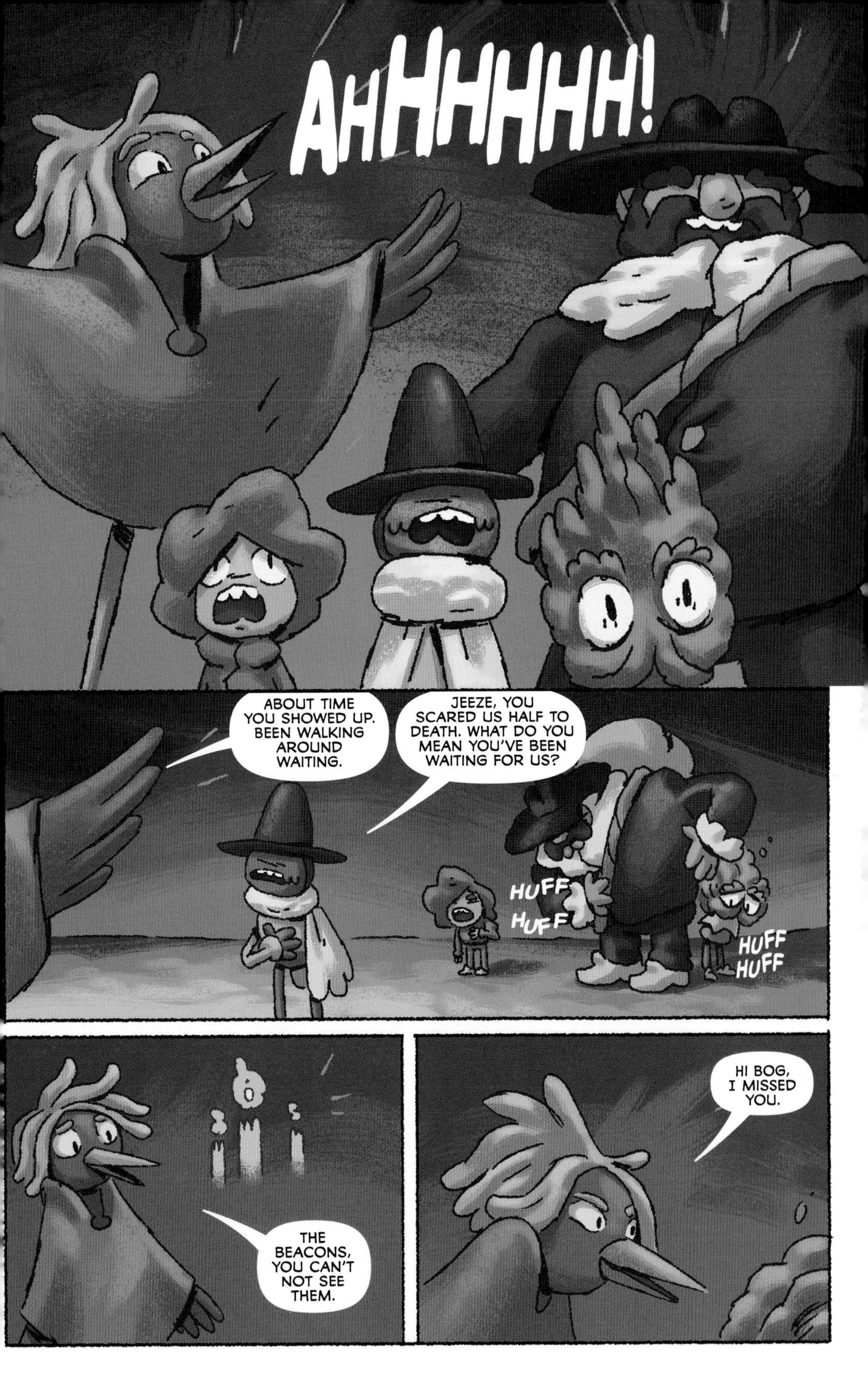
AHHHHHH!
ABOUT TIME YOU SHOWED UP. BEEN WALKING AROUND WAITING.
JEEZE, YOU SCARED US HALF TO DEATH. WHAT DO YOU MEAN YOU'VE BEEN WAITING FOR US?
HUFF HUFF
HUFF HUFF
THE BEACONS, YOU CAN'T NOT SEE THEM.
HI BOG, I MISSED YOU.

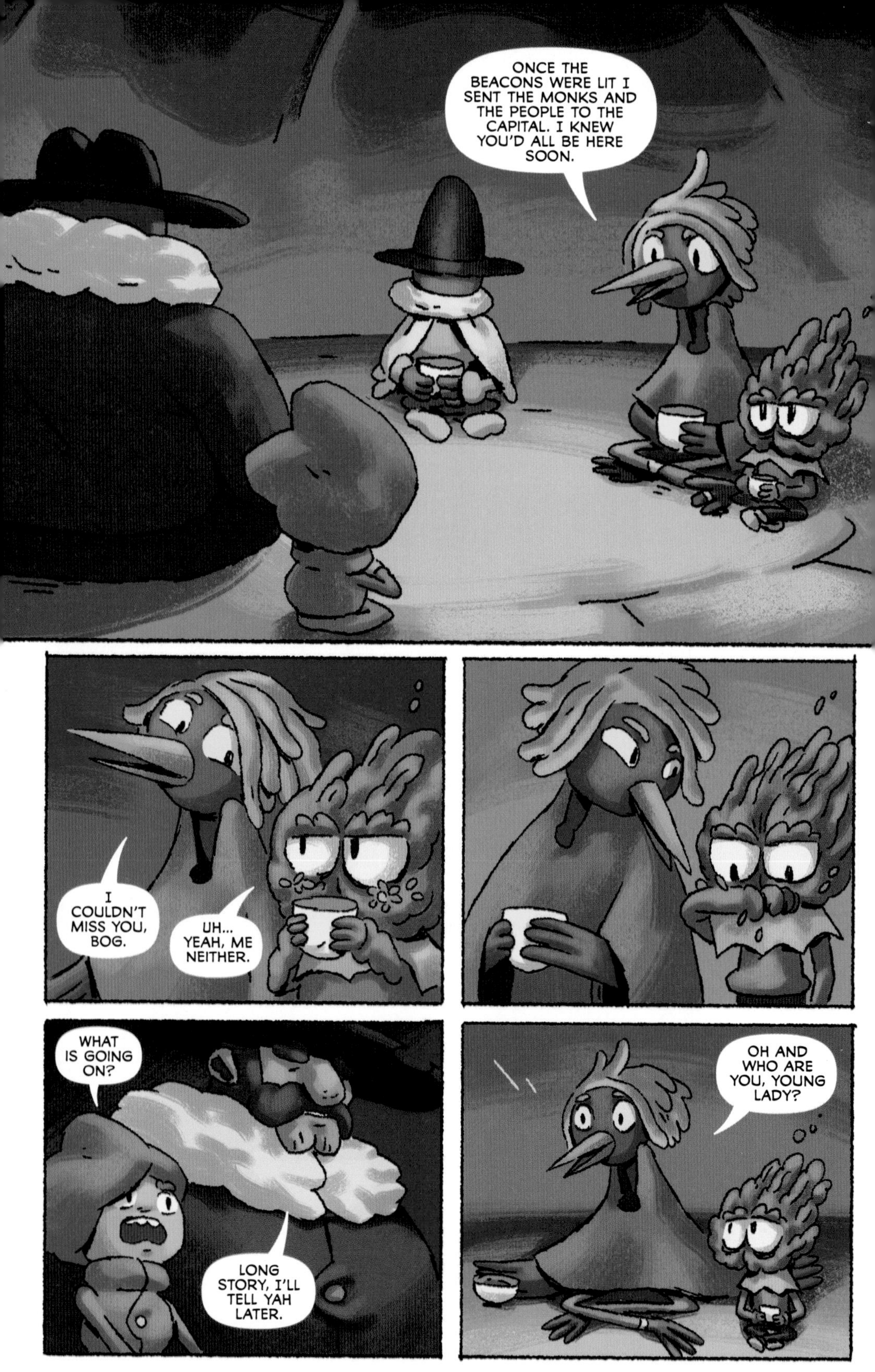
ONCE THE BEACONS WERE LIT I SENT THE MONKS AND THE PEOPLE TO THE CAPITAL. I KNEW YOU'D ALL BE HERE SOON.
I COULDN'T MISS YOU, BOG.
UH... YEAH, ME NEITHER.
WHAT IS GOING ON?
LONG STORY, I'LL TELL YAH LATER.
OH AND WHO ARE YOU, YOUNG LADY?

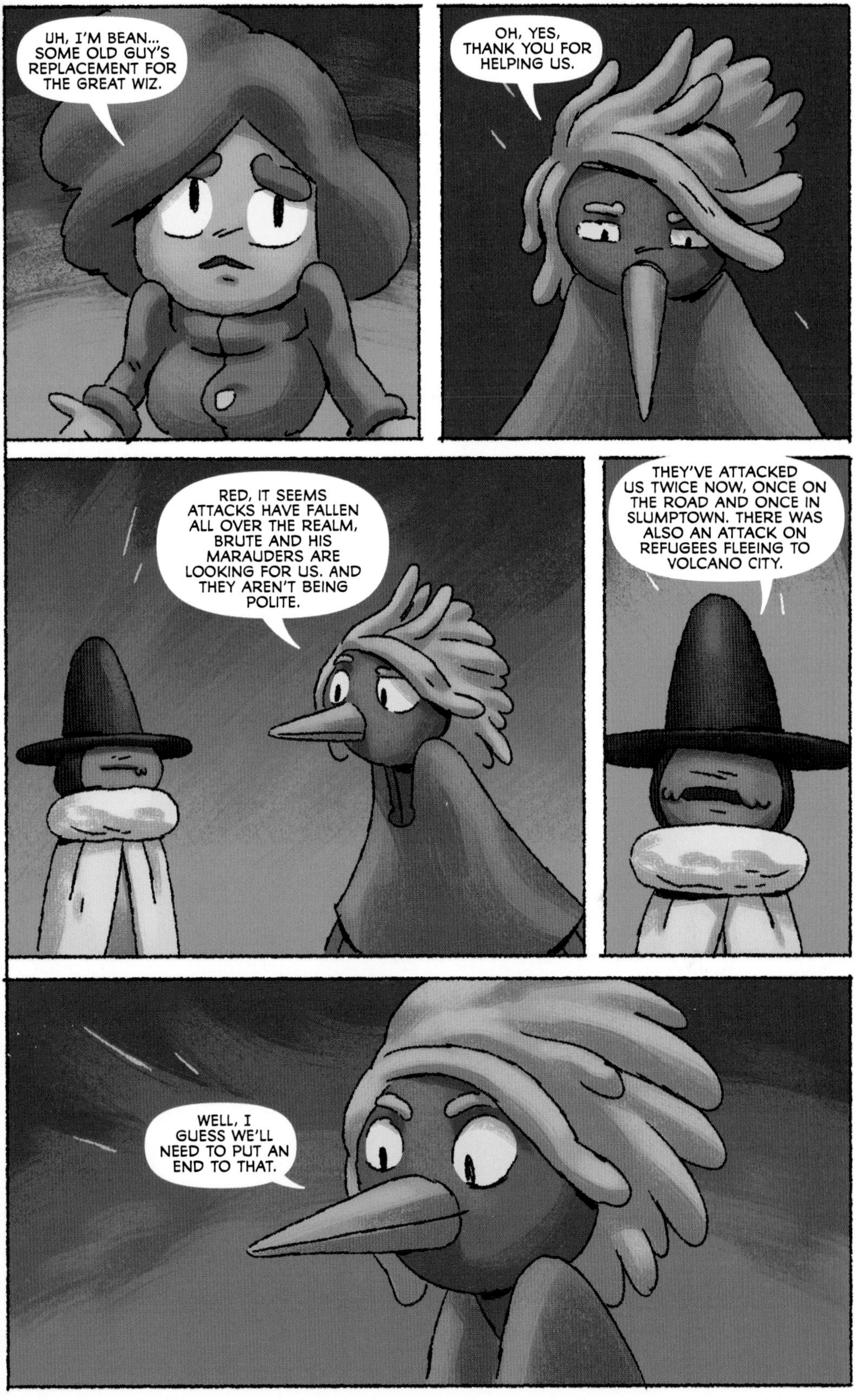
UH, I'M BEAN... SOME OLD GUY'S REPLACEMENT FOR THE GREAT WIZ.
OH, YES, THANK YOU FOR HELPING US.
RED, IT SEEMS ATTACKS HAVE FALLEN ALL OVER THE REALM, BRUTE AND HIS MARAUDERS ARE LOOKING FOR US. AND THEY AREN'T BEING POLITE.
THEY'VE ATTACKED US TWICE NOW, ONCE ON THE ROAD AND ONCE IN SLUMPTOWN. THERE WAS ALSO AN ATTACK ON REFUGEES FLEEING TO VOLCANO CITY.
WELL, I GUESS WE'LL NEED TO PUT AN END TO THAT.

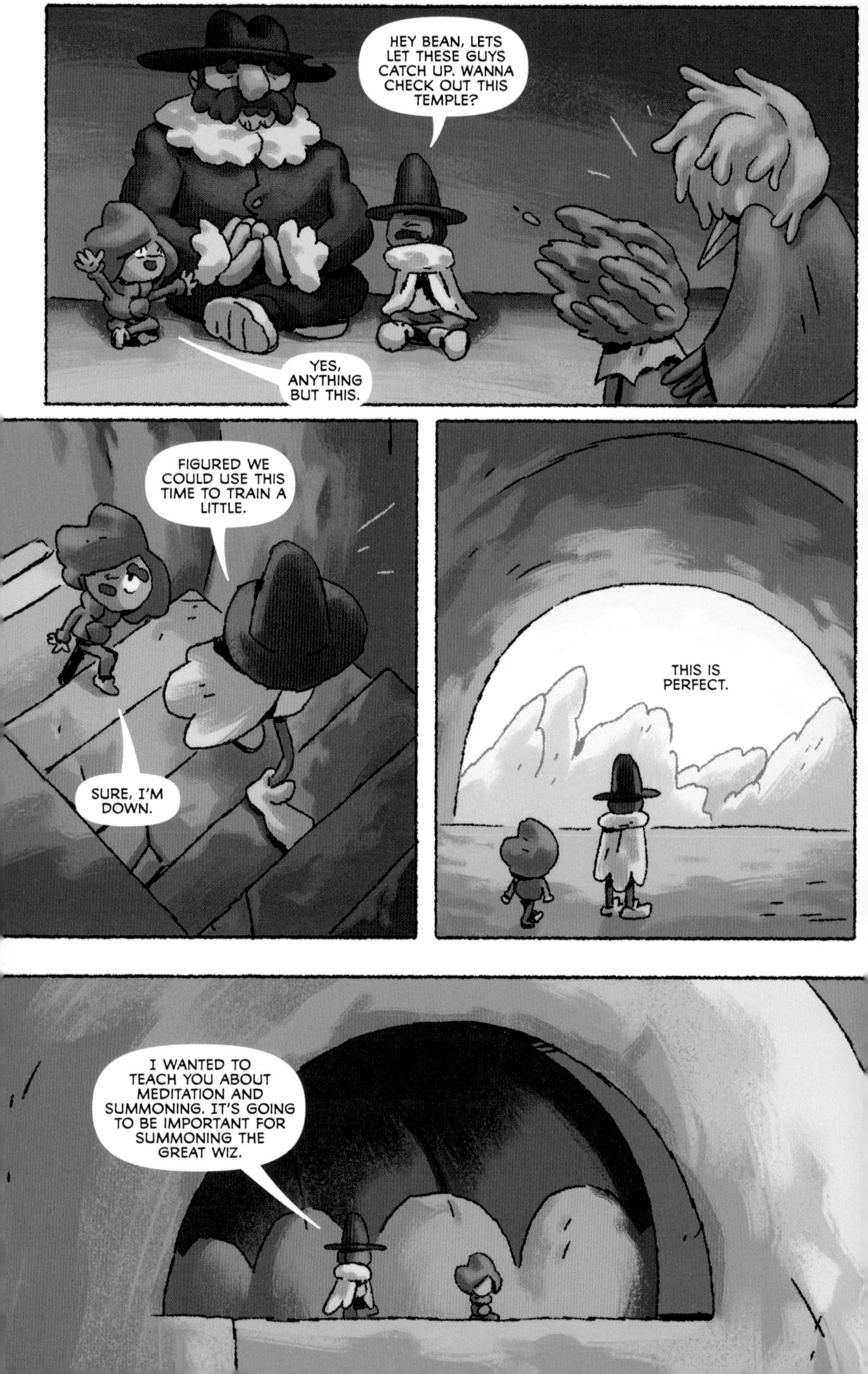
HEY BEAN, LETS LET THESE GUYS CATCH UP. WANNA CHECK OUT THIS TEMPLE?
YES, ANYTHING BUT THIS.
FIGURED WE COULD USE THIS TIME TO TRAIN A LITTLE.
SURE, I'M DOWN.
THIS IS PERFECT.
I WANTED TO TEACH YOU ABOUT MEDITATION AND SUMMONING. IT'S GOING TO BE IMPORTANT FOR SUMMONING THE GREAT WIZ.

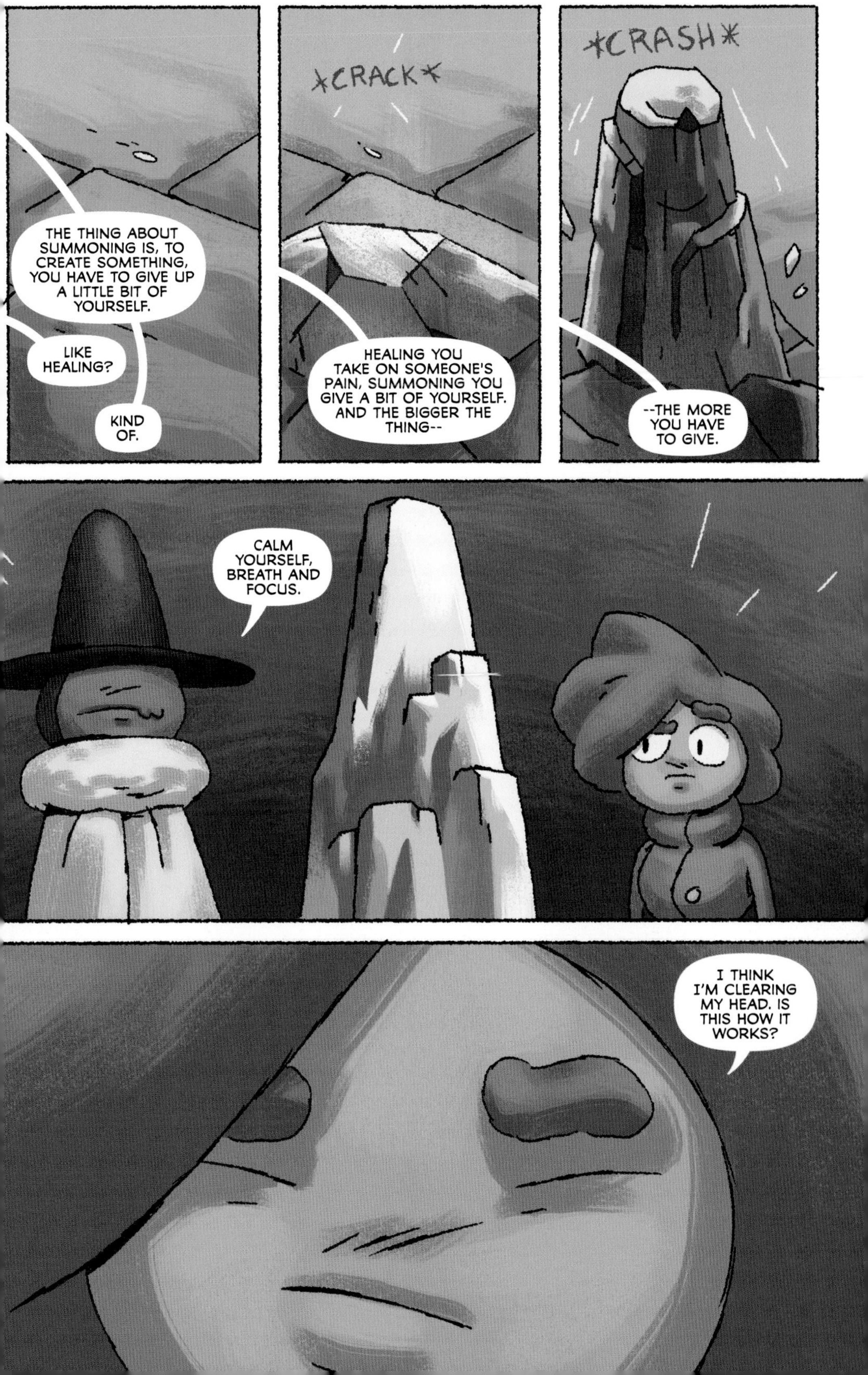
THE THING ABOUT SUMMONING IS, TO CREATE SOMETHING, YOU HAVE TO GIVE UP A LITTLE BIT OF YOURSELF.
LIKE HEALING?
KIND OF.
CRACK
HEALING YOU TAKE ON SOMEONE'S PAIN, SUMMONING YOU GIVE A BIT OF YOURSELF. AND THE BIGGER THE THING--
CRASH
--THE MORE YOU HAVE TO GIVE.
CALM YOURSELF, BREATH AND FOCUS.
I THINK I'M CLEARING MY HEAD. IS THIS HOW IT WORKS?

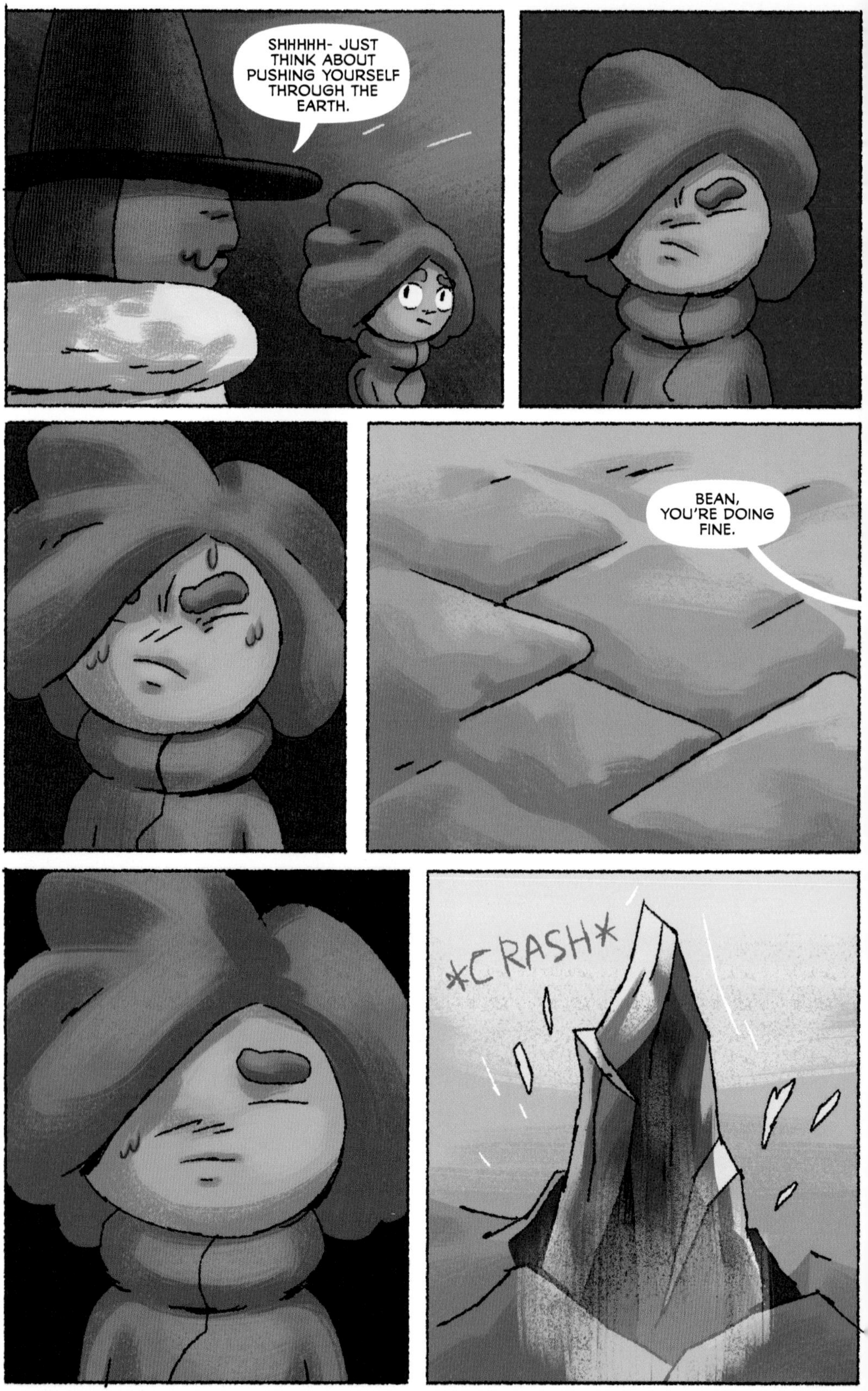
SHHHHH- JUST THINK ABOUT PUSHING YOURSELF THROUGH THE EARTH.
BEAN, YOU'RE DOING FINE.
CRASH

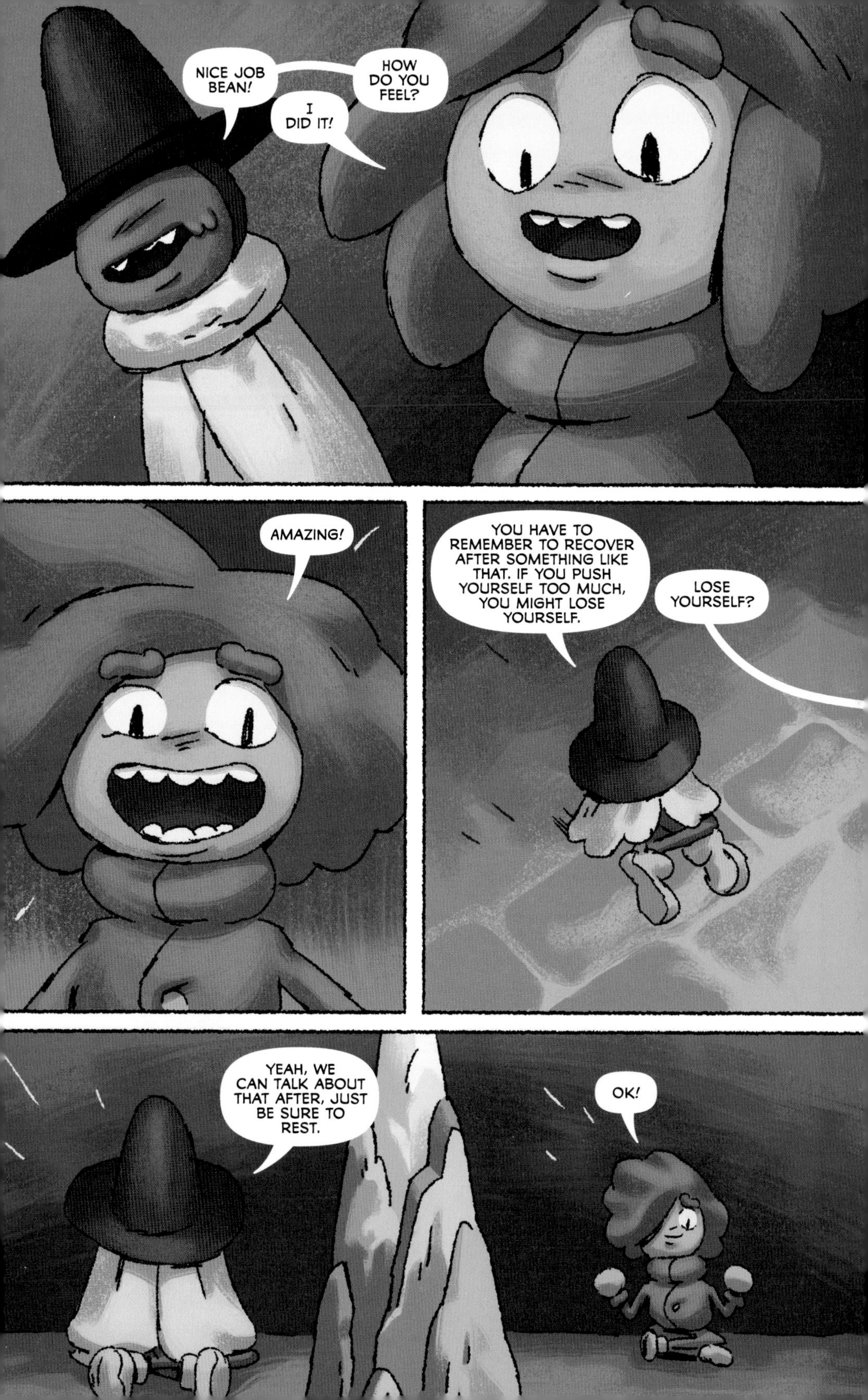
NICE JOB BEAN!
HOW DO YOU FEEL?
I DID IT!
AMAZING!
YOU HAVE TO REMEMBER TO RECOVER AFTER SOMETHING LIKE THAT. IF YOU PUSH YOURSELF TOO MUCH, YOU MIGHT LOSE YOURSELF.
LOSE YOURSELF?
YEAH, WE CAN TALK ABOUT THAT AFTER, JUST BE SURE TO REST.
OK!

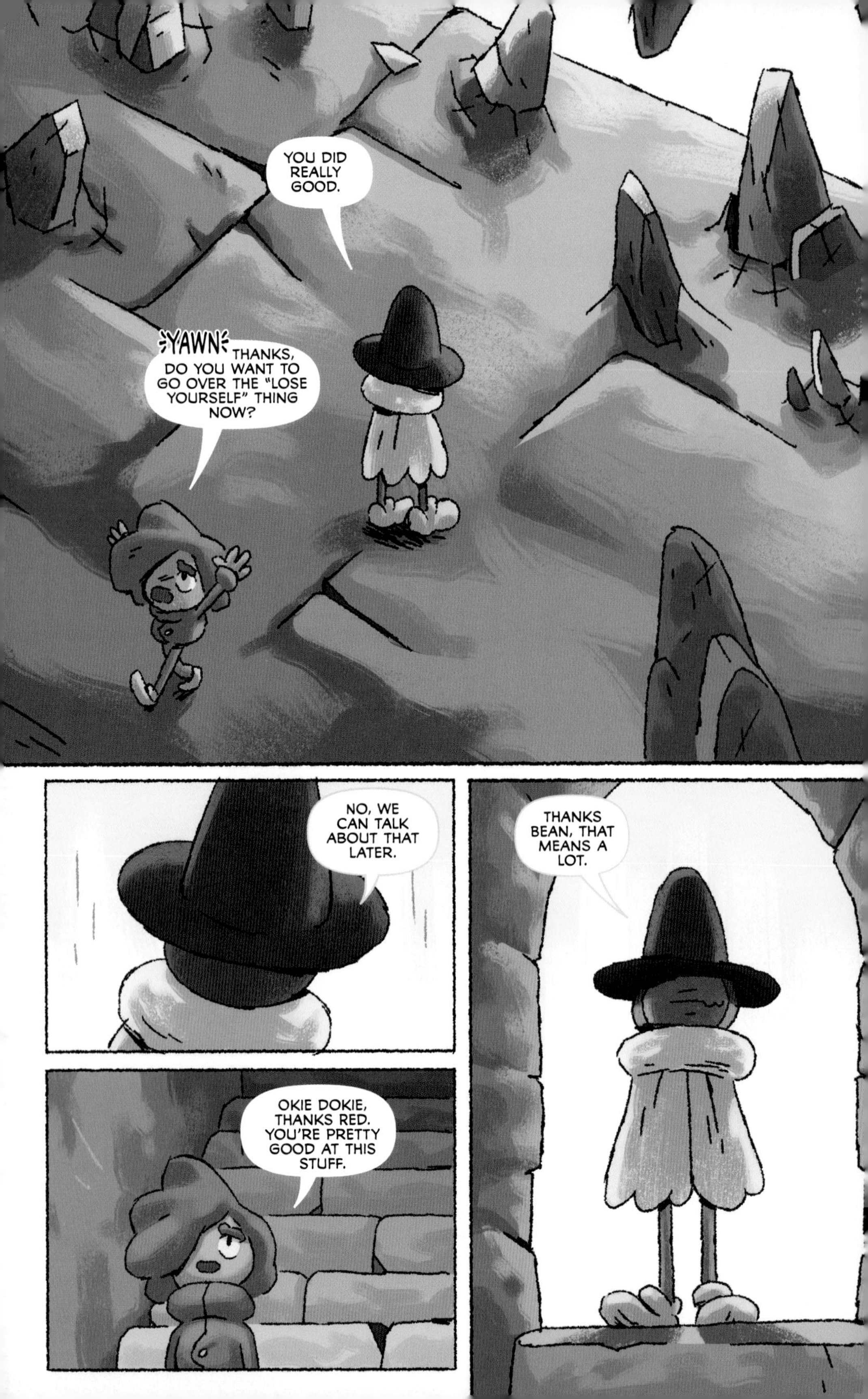
YOU DID REALLY GOOD.
YAWN THANKS, DO YOU WANT TO GO OVER THE "LOSE YOURSELF" THING NOW?
NO, WE CAN TALK ABOUT THAT LATER.
OKIE DOKIE, THANKS RED. YOU'RE PRETTY GOOD AT THIS STUFF.
THANKS BEAN, THAT MEANS A LOT.

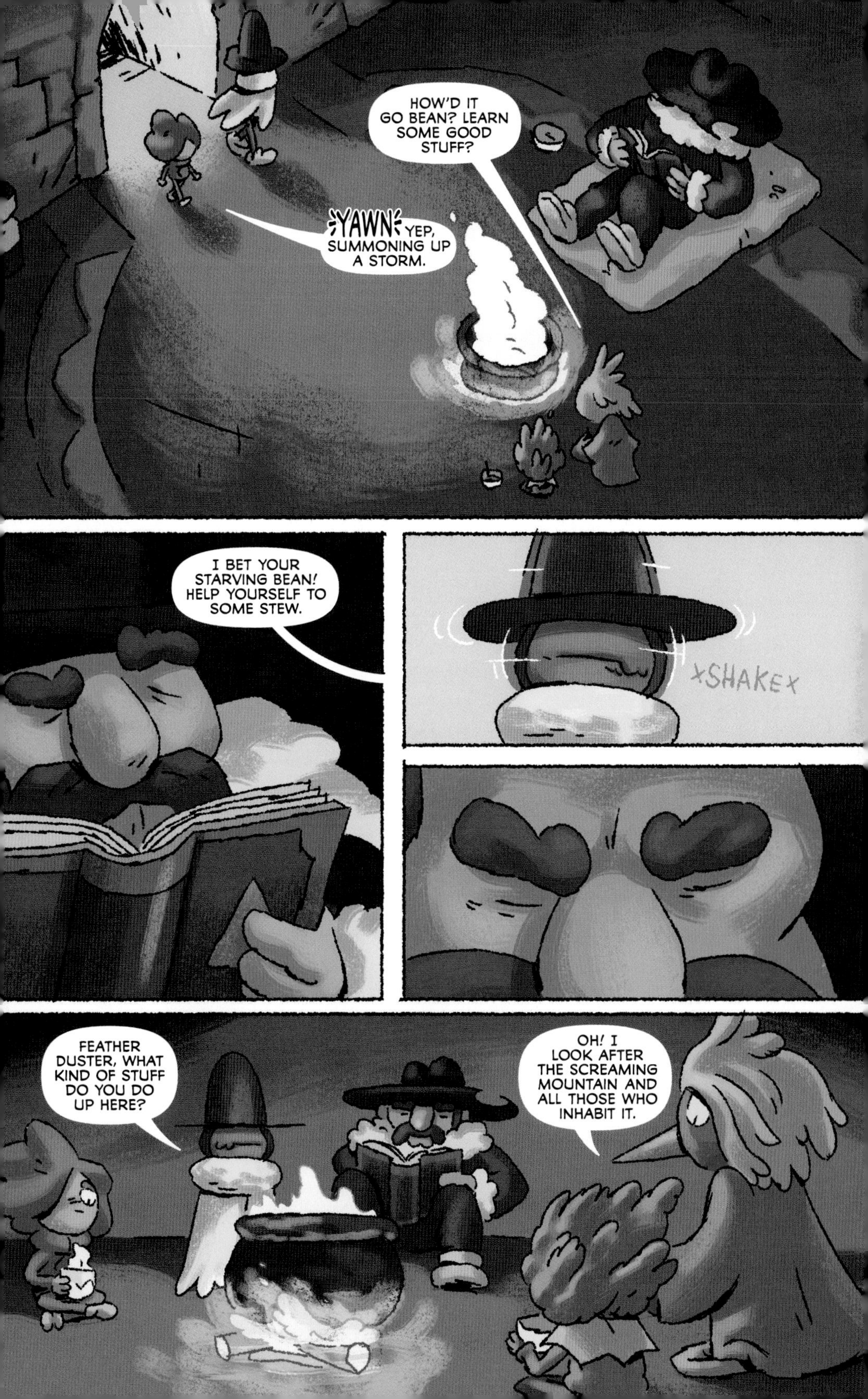

HOW'D IT GO BEAN? LEARN SOME GOOD STUFF?
YAWN YEP, SUMMONING UP A STORM.
I BET YOUR STARVING BEAN! HELP YOURSELF TO SOME STEW.
SHAKE
FEATHER DUSTER, WHAT KIND OF STUFF DO YOU DO UP HERE?
OH! I LOOK AFTER THE SCREAMING MOUNTAIN AND ALL THOSE WHO INHABIT IT.

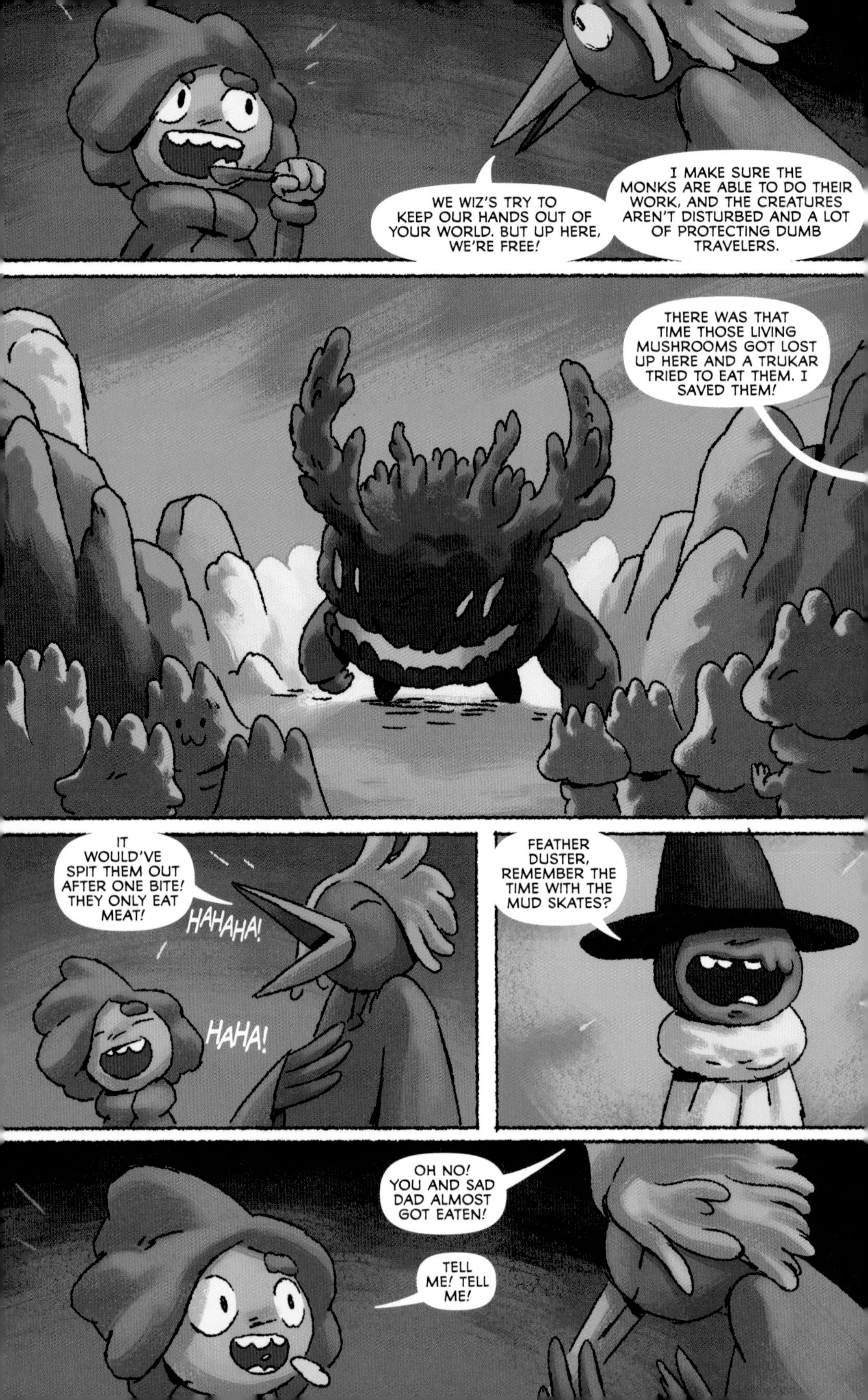
WE WIZ'S TRY TO KEEP OUR HANDS OUT OF YOUR WORLD. BUT UP HERE, WE'RE FREE!
I MAKE SURE THE MONKS ARE ABLE TO DO THEIR WORK, AND THE CREATURES AREN'T DISTURBED AND A LOT OF PROTECTING DUMB TRAVELERS.
THERE WAS THAT TIME THOSE LIVING MUSHROOMS GOT LOST UP HERE AND A TRUKAR TRIED TO EAT THEM. I SAVED THEM!
IT WOULD'VE SPIT THEM OUT AFTER ONE BITE! THEY ONLY EAT MEAT!
HAHAHA!
HAHA!
FEATHER DUSTER, REMEMBER THE TIME WITH THE MUD SKATES?
OH NO! YOU AND SAD DAD ALMOST GOT EATEN!
TELL ME! TELL ME!

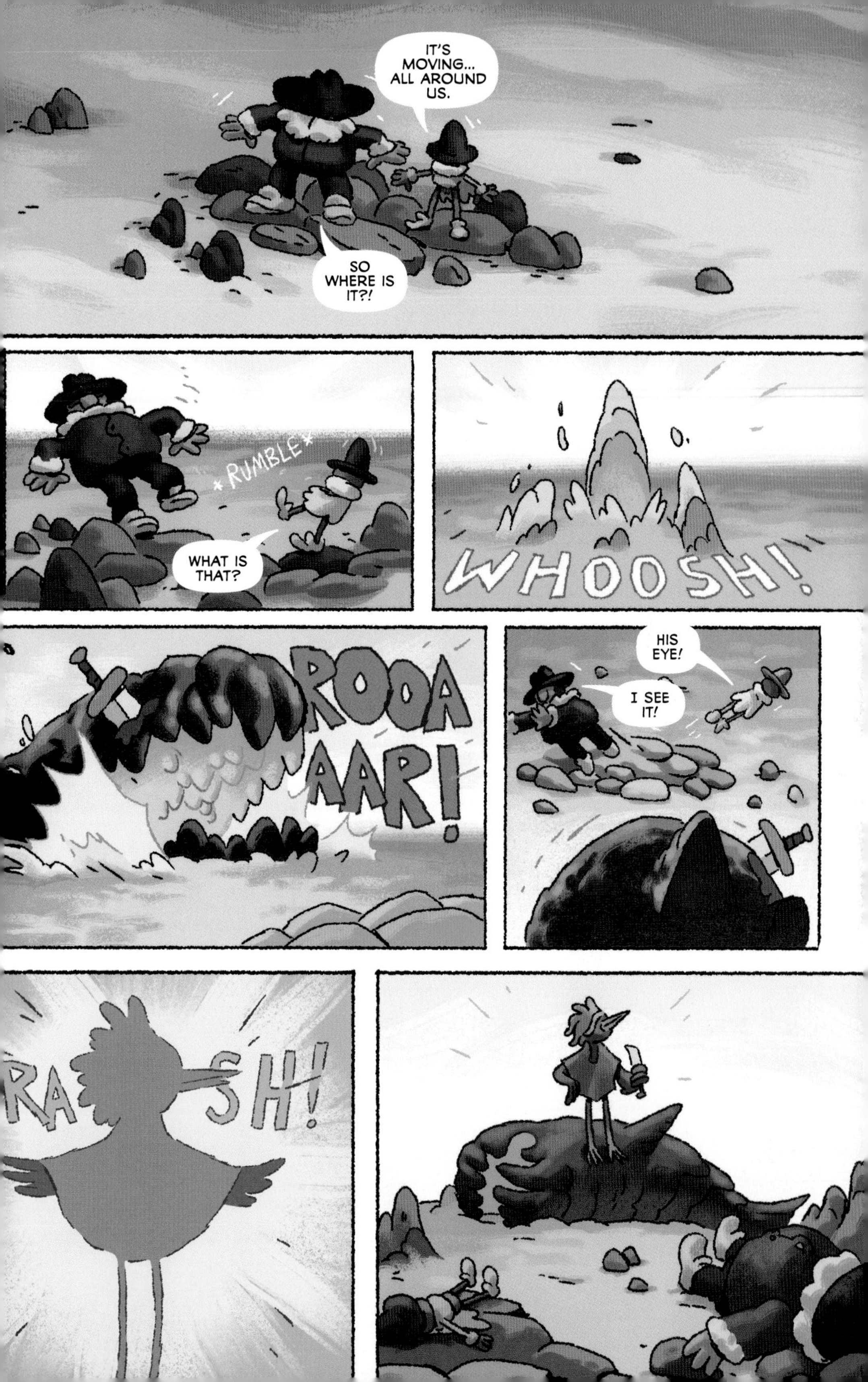

IT'S MOVING... ALL AROUND US.
SO WHERE IS IT?!
RUMBLE
WHAT IS THAT?
WHOOSH!
ROOAAAR!
HIS EYE!
I SEE IT!
RA SH!

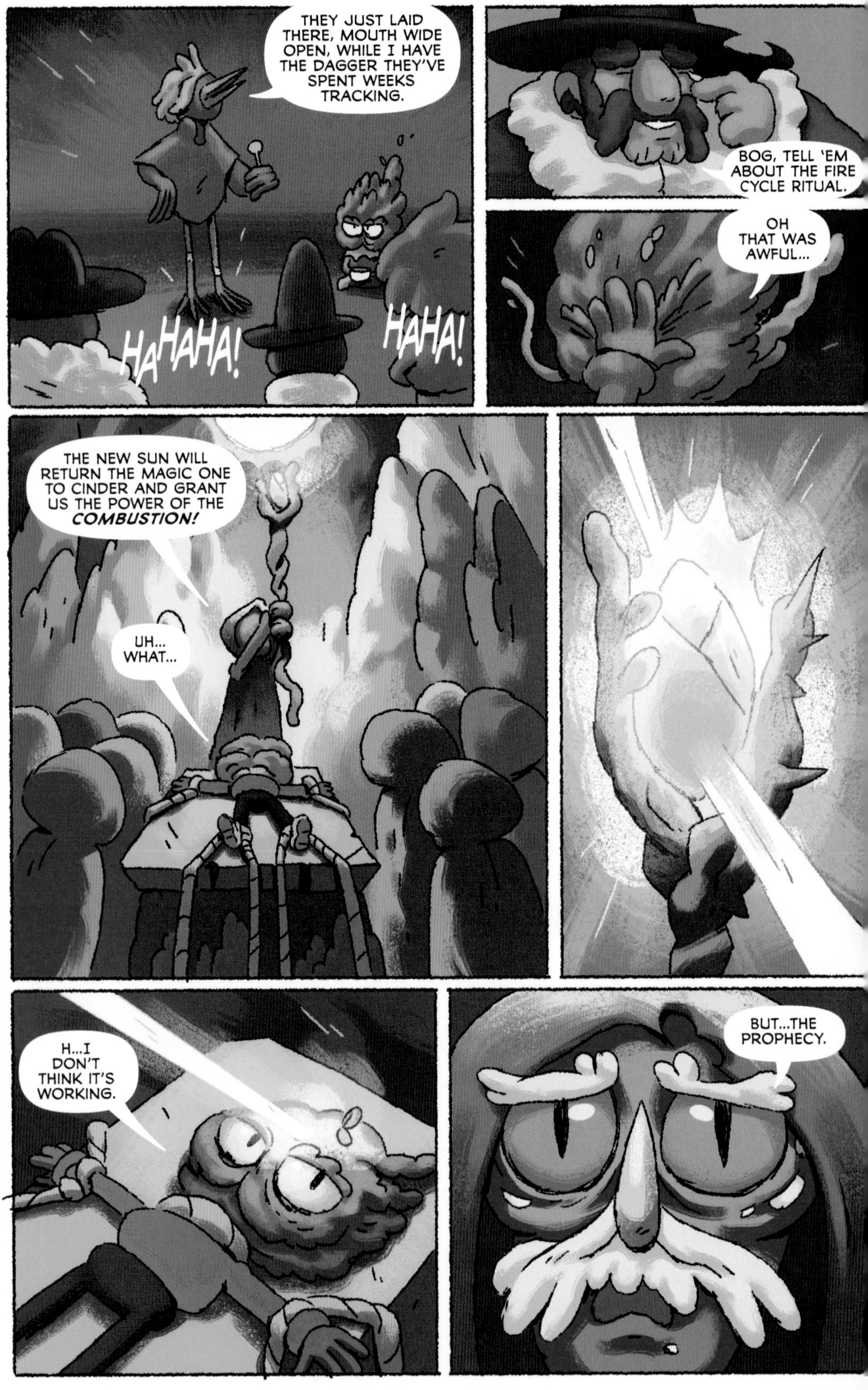

THEY JUST LAID THERE, MOUTH WIDE OPEN, WHILE I HAVE THE DAGGER THEY'VE SPENT WEEKS TRACKING.
HAHAHA!
HAHA!
BOG, TELL 'EM ABOUT THE FIRE CYCLE RITUAL.
OH THAT WAS AWFUL...
THE NEW SUN WILL RETURN THE MAGIC ONE TO CINDER AND GRANT US THE POWER OF THE COMBUSTION!
UH... WHAT...
H...I DON'T THINK IT'S WORKING.
BUT...THE PROPHECY.

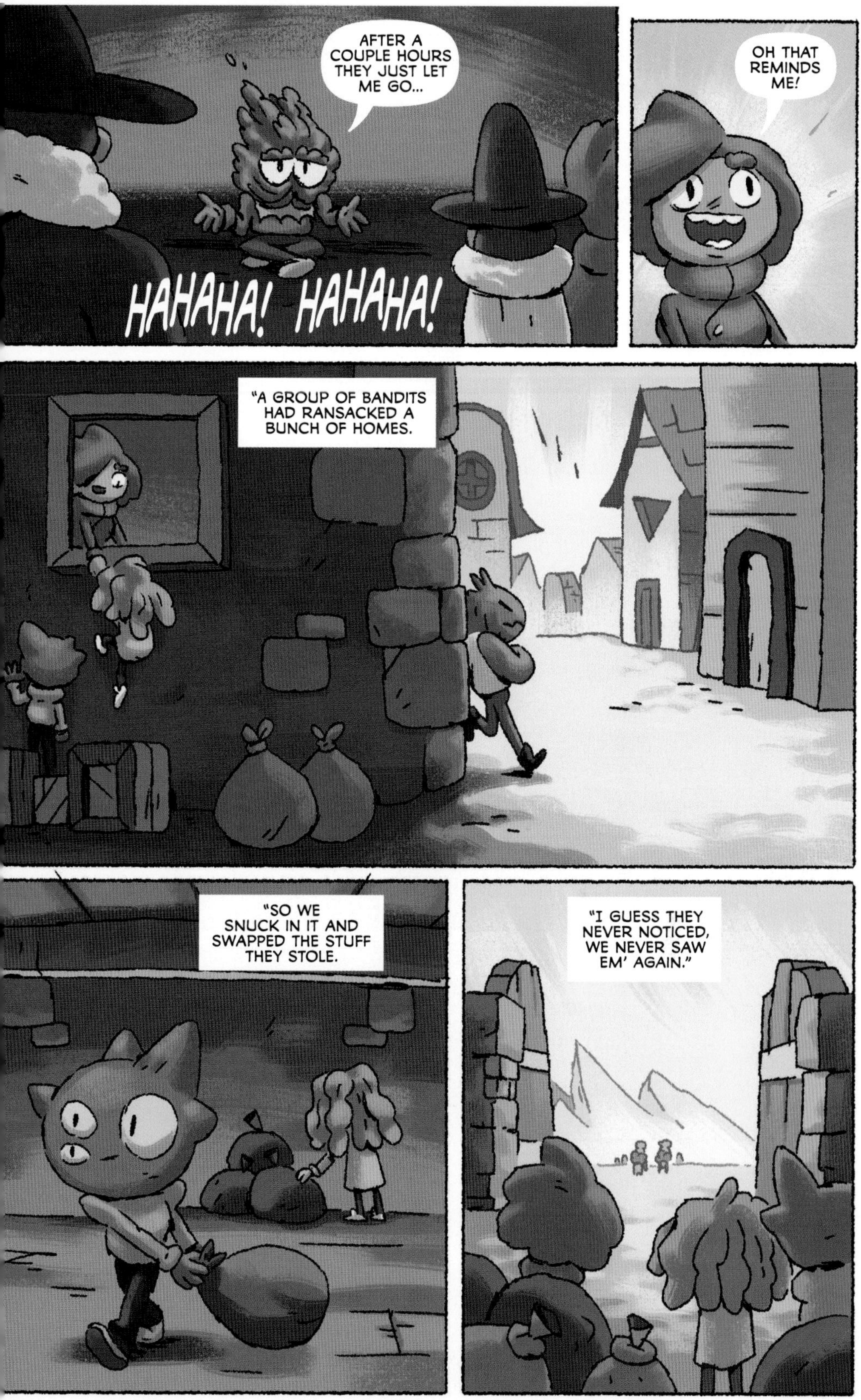
AFTER A COUPLE HOURS THEY JUST LET ME GO...
HAHAHA! HAHAHA!
OH THAT REMINDS ME!
"A GROUP OF BANDITS HAD RANSACKED A BUNCH OF HOMES.
"SO WE SNUCK IN IT AND SWAPPED THE STUFF THEY STOLE.
"I GUESS THEY NEVER NOTICED, WE NEVER SAW EM' AGAIN."

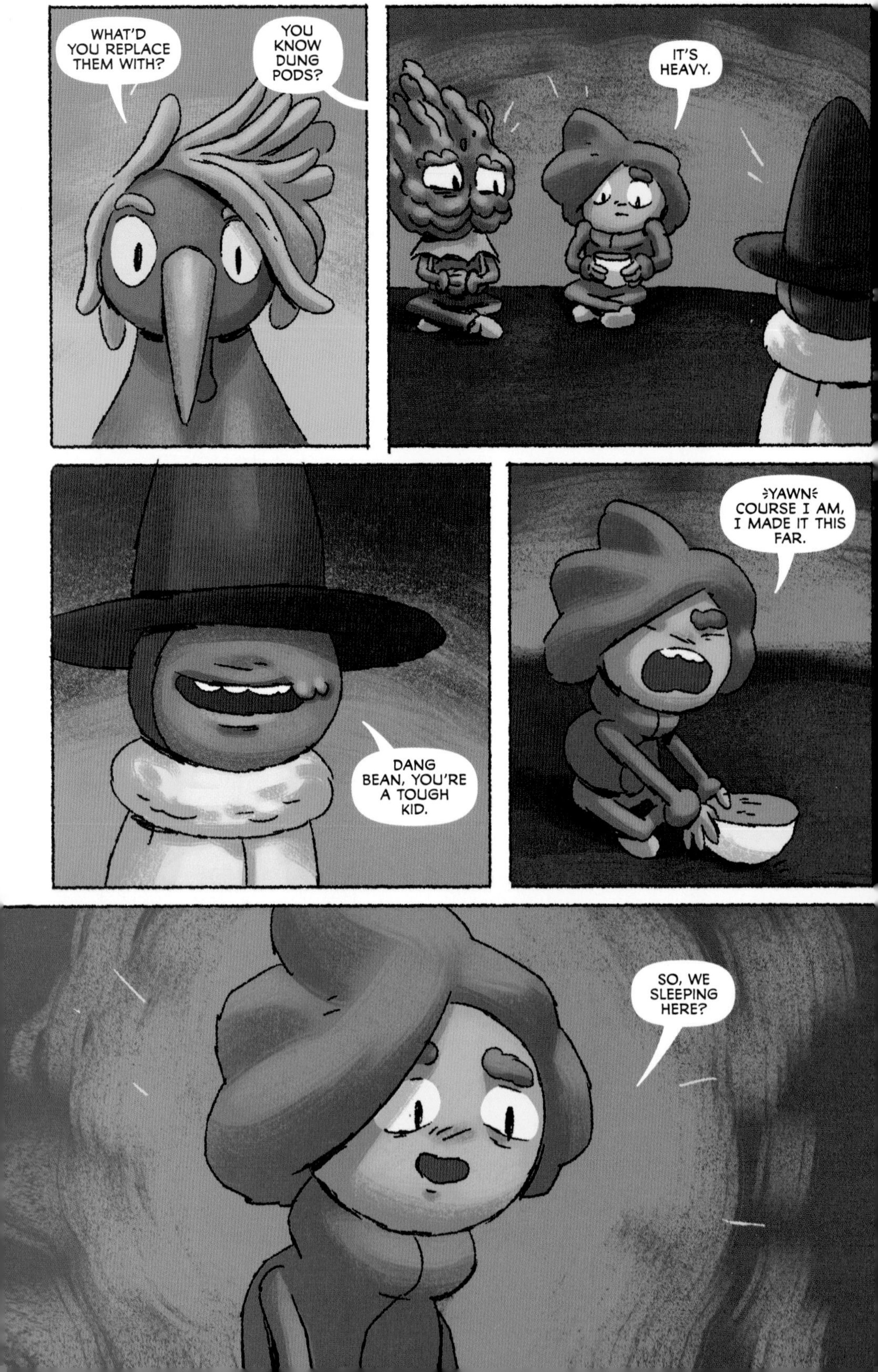
WHAT'D YOU REPLACE THEM WITH?
YOU KNOW DUNG PODS?
IT'S HEAVY.
DANG BEAN, YOU'RE A TOUGH KID.
⪢YAWN⪡ COURSE I AM, I MADE IT THIS FAR.
SO, WE SLEEPING HERE?

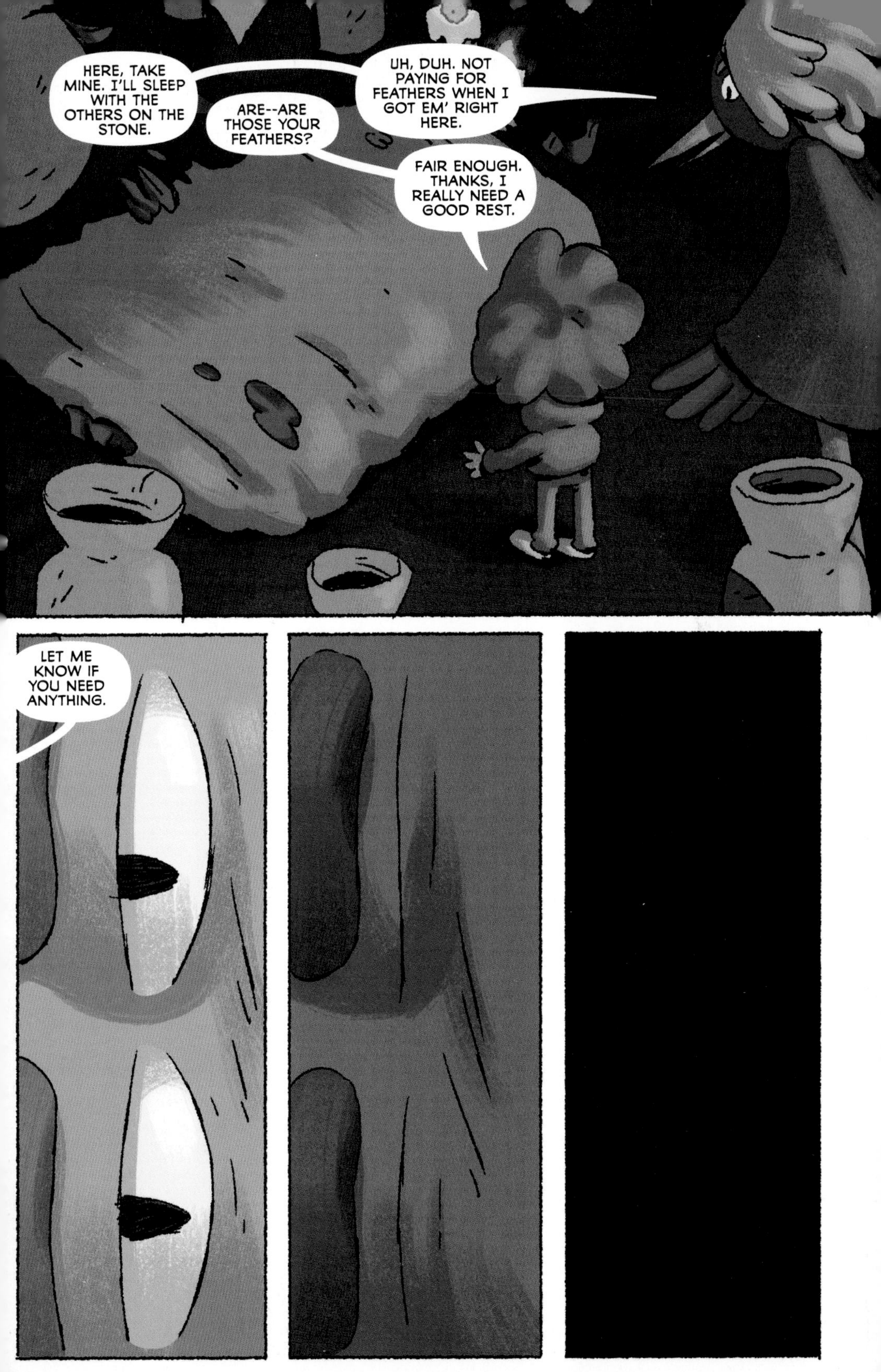
HERE, TAKE MINE. I'LL SLEEP WITH THE OTHERS ON THE STONE.
ARE--ARE THOSE YOUR FEATHERS?
UH, DUH. NOT PAYING FOR FEATHERS WHEN I GOT EM' RIGHT HERE.
FAIR ENOUGH. THANKS, I REALLY NEED A GOOD REST.
LET ME KNOW IF YOU NEED ANYTHING.

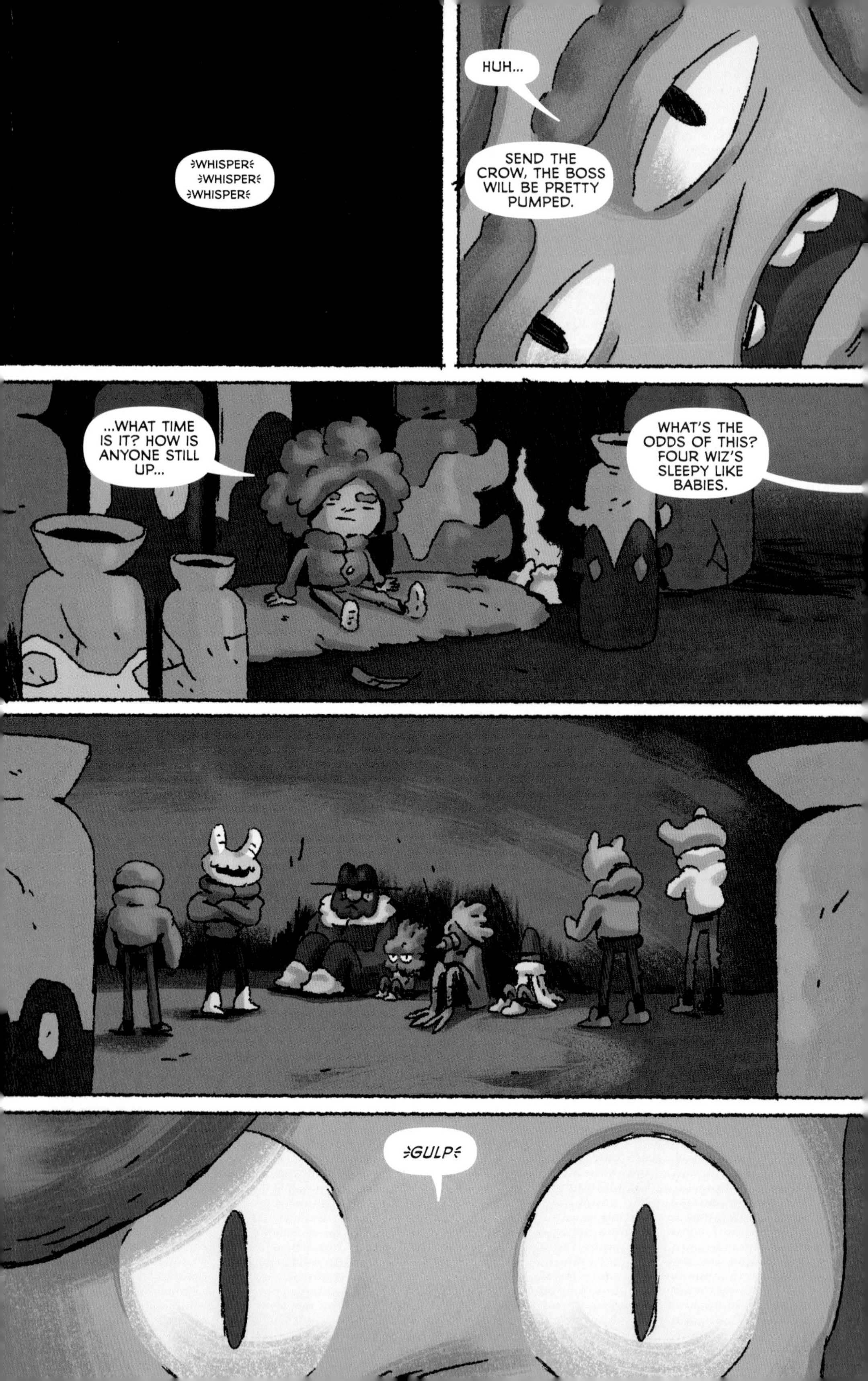

⪢WHISPER⪡ ⪢WHISPER⪡ ⪢WHISPER⪡
HUH...
SEND THE CROW, THE BOSS WILL BE PRETTY PUMPED.
...WHAT TIME IS IT? HOW IS ANYONE STILL UP...
WHAT'S THE ODDS OF THIS? FOUR WIZ'S SLEEPY LIKE BABIES.
⪢GULP⪡

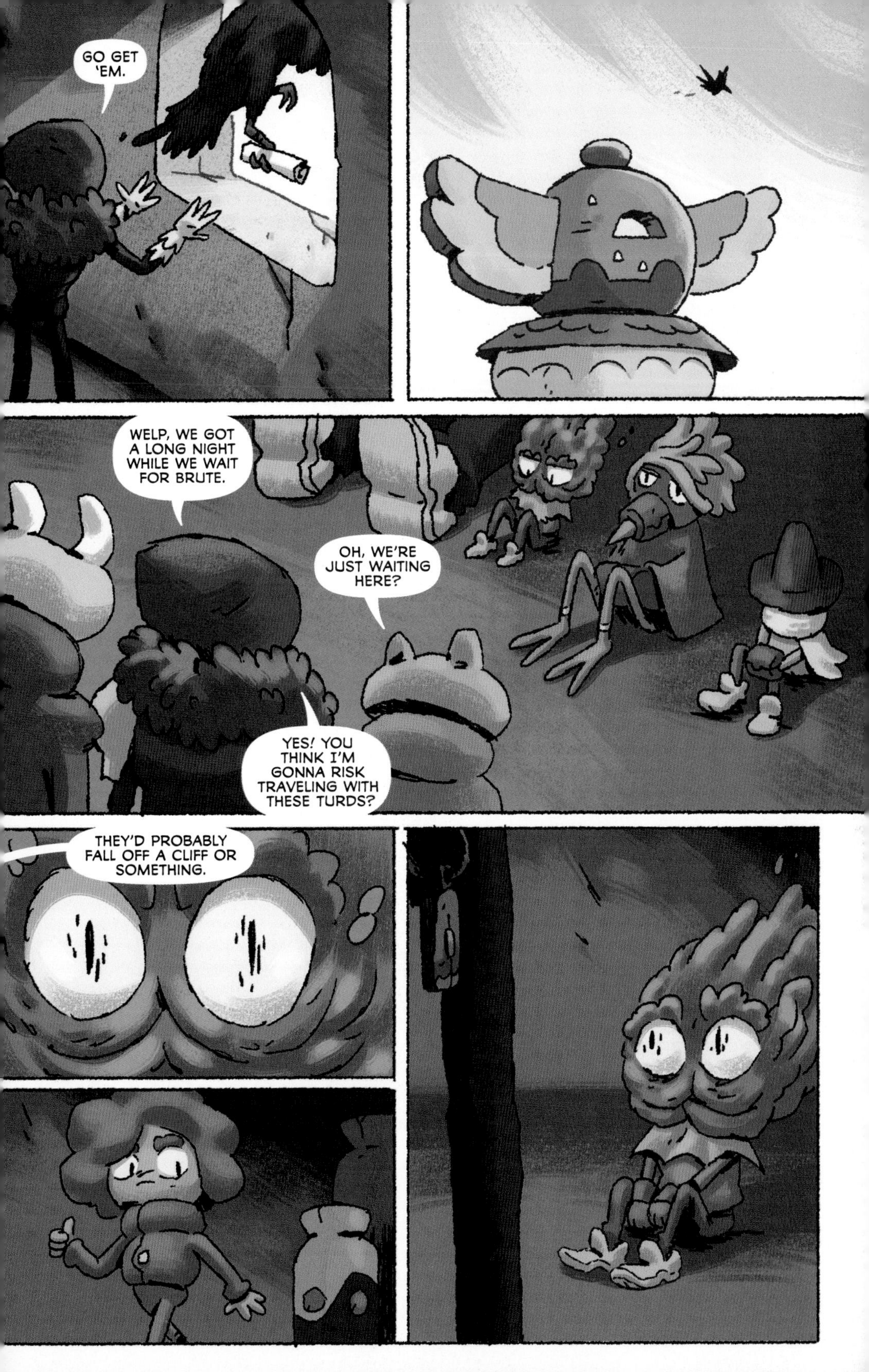
GO GET 'EM.
WELP, WE GOT A LONG NIGHT WHILE WE WAIT FOR BRUTE.
OH, WE'RE JUST WAITING HERE?
YES! YOU THINK I'M GONNA RISK TRAVELING WITH THESE TURDS?
THEY'D PROBABLY FALL OFF A CLIFF OR SOMETHING.

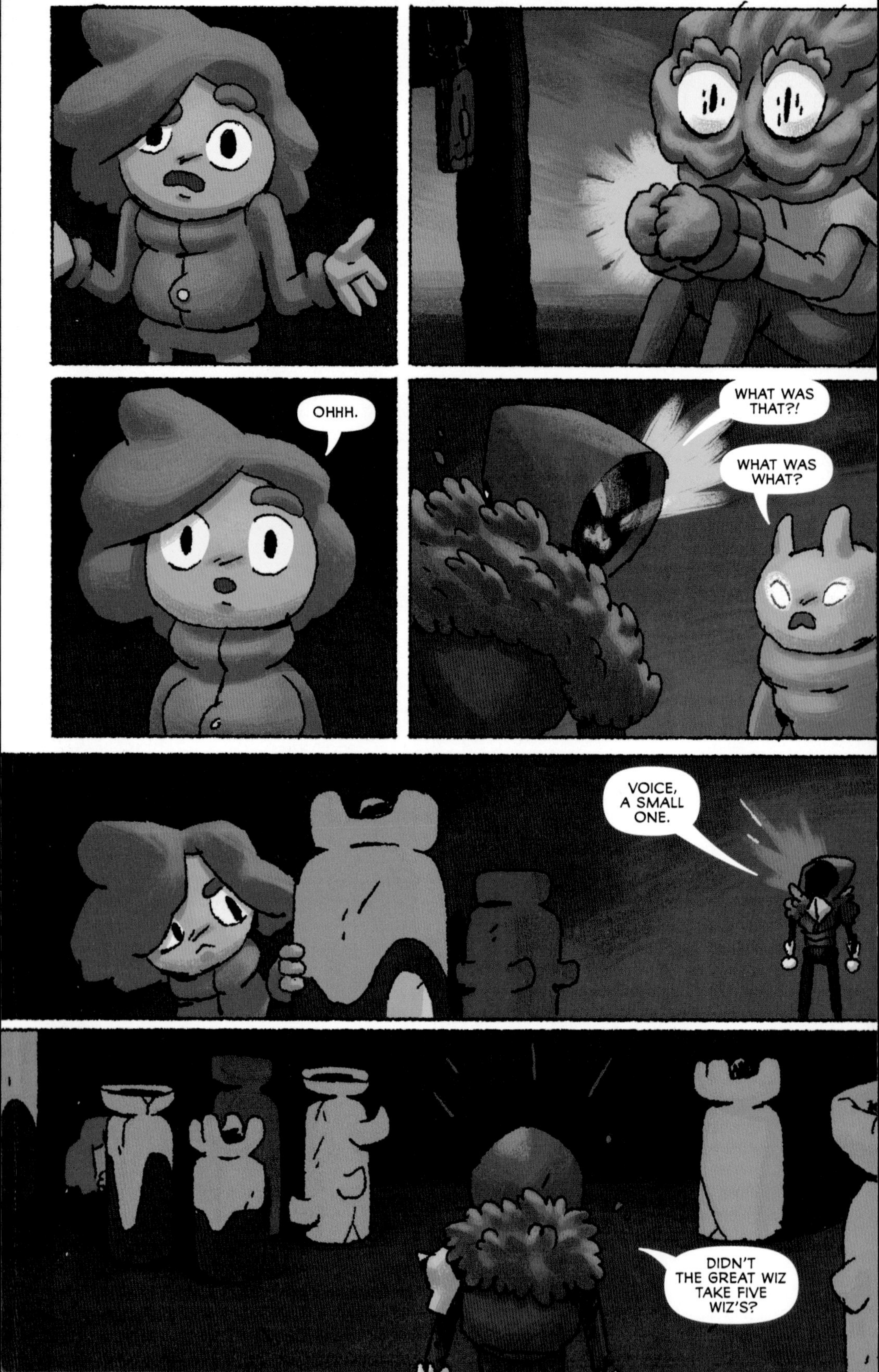
OHHH.
WHAT WAS THAT?!
WHAT WAS WHAT?
VOICE, A SMALL ONE.
DIDN'T THE GREAT WIZ TAKE FIVE WIZ'S?

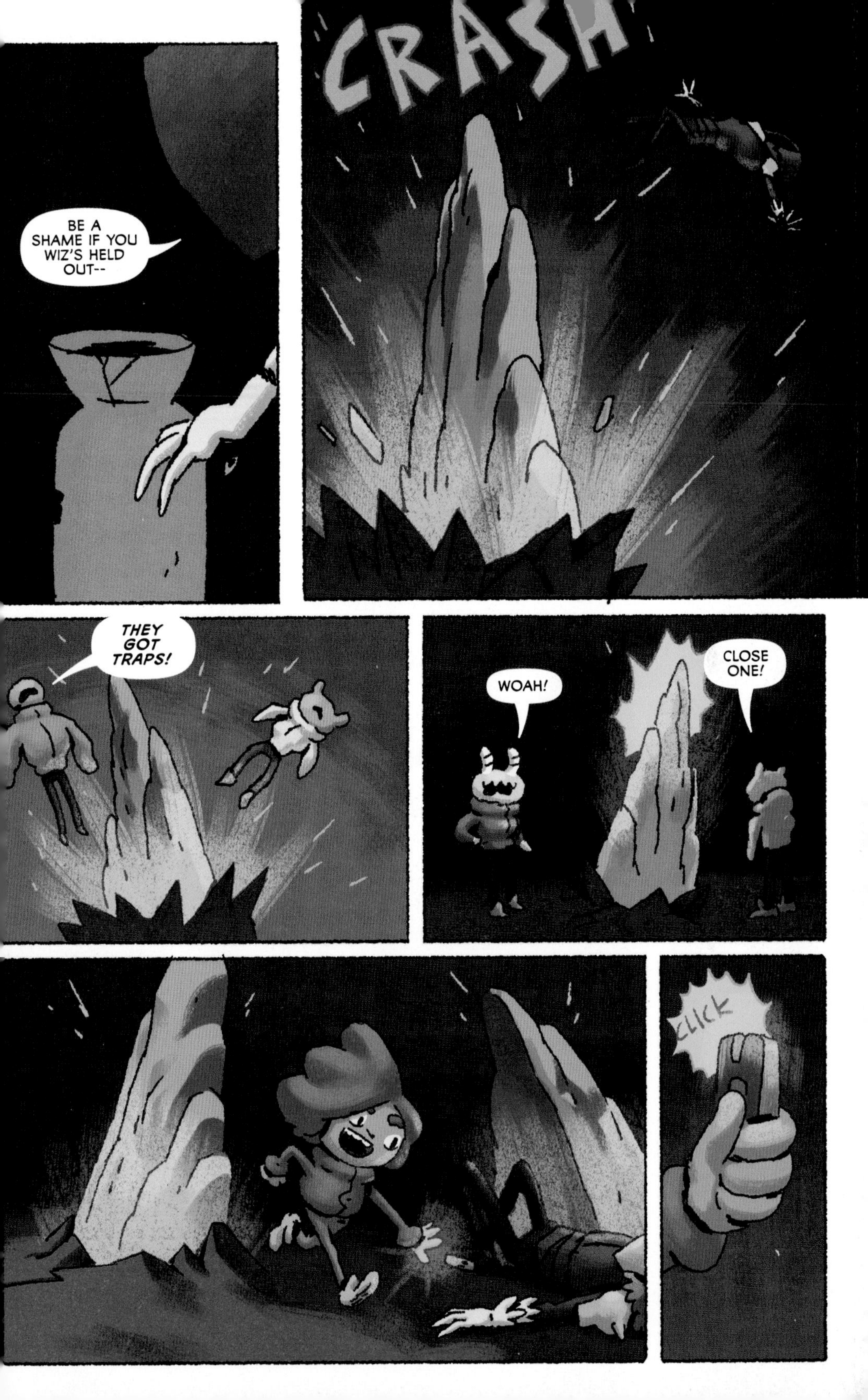
BE A SHAME IF YOU WIZ'S HELD OUT--
CRASH
THEY GOT TRAPS!
WOAH!
CLOSE ONE!
CLICK

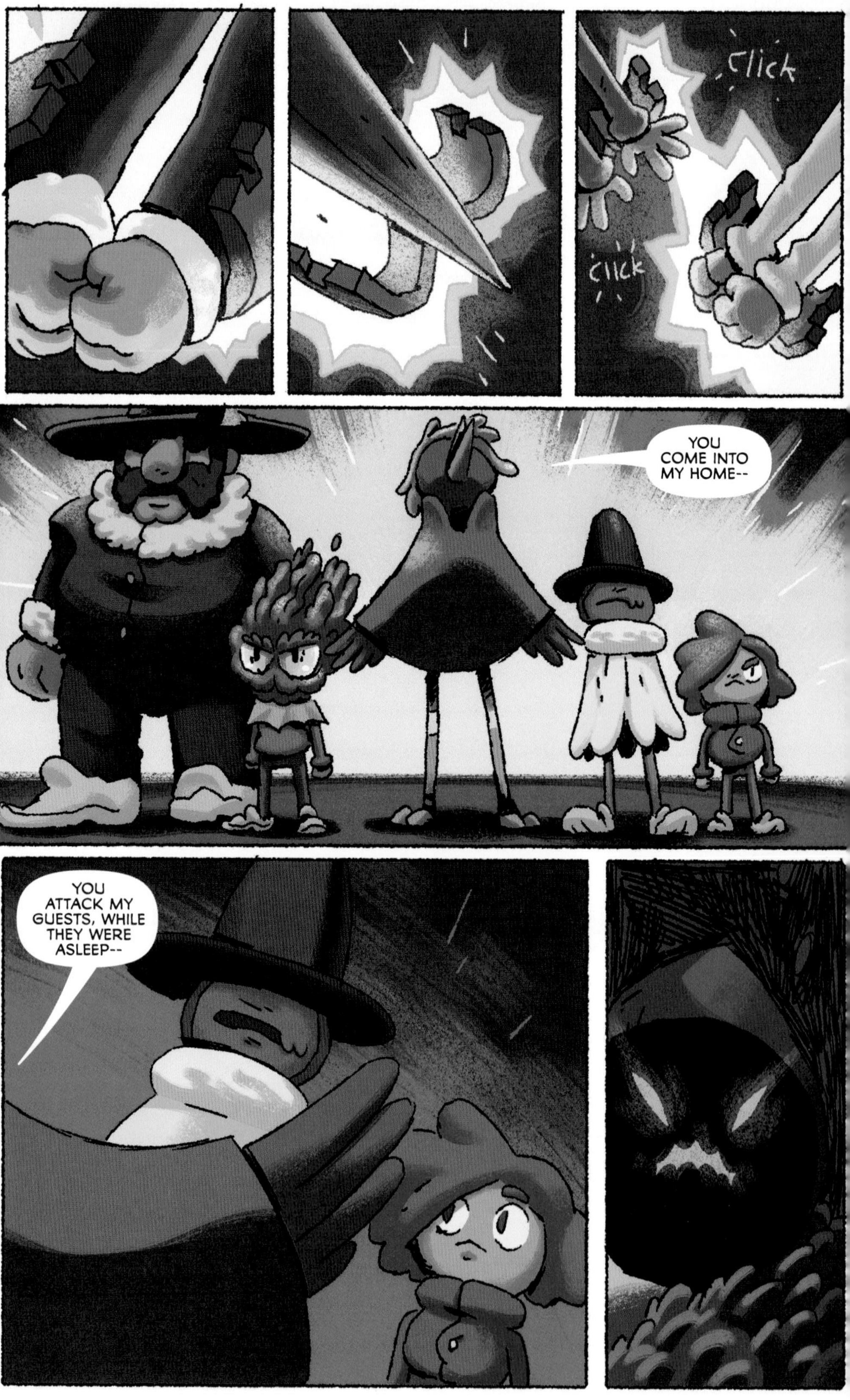
click
click
YOU COME INTO MY HOME--
YOU ATTACK MY GUESTS, WHILE THEY WERE ASLEEP--

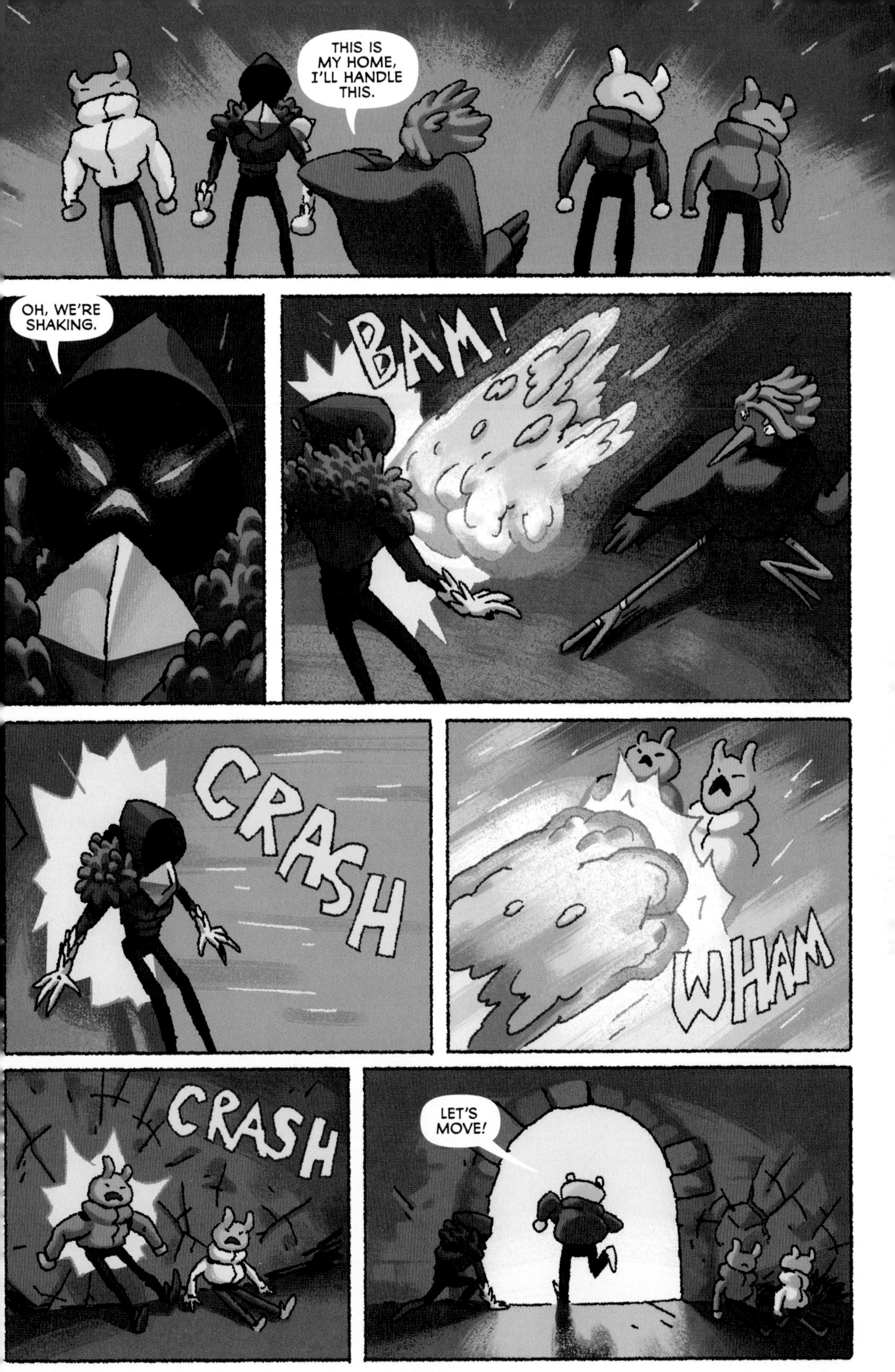
THIS IS MY HOME, I'LL HANDLE THIS.
OH, WE'RE SHAKING.
BAM!
CRASH
WHAM
CRASH
LET'S MOVE!

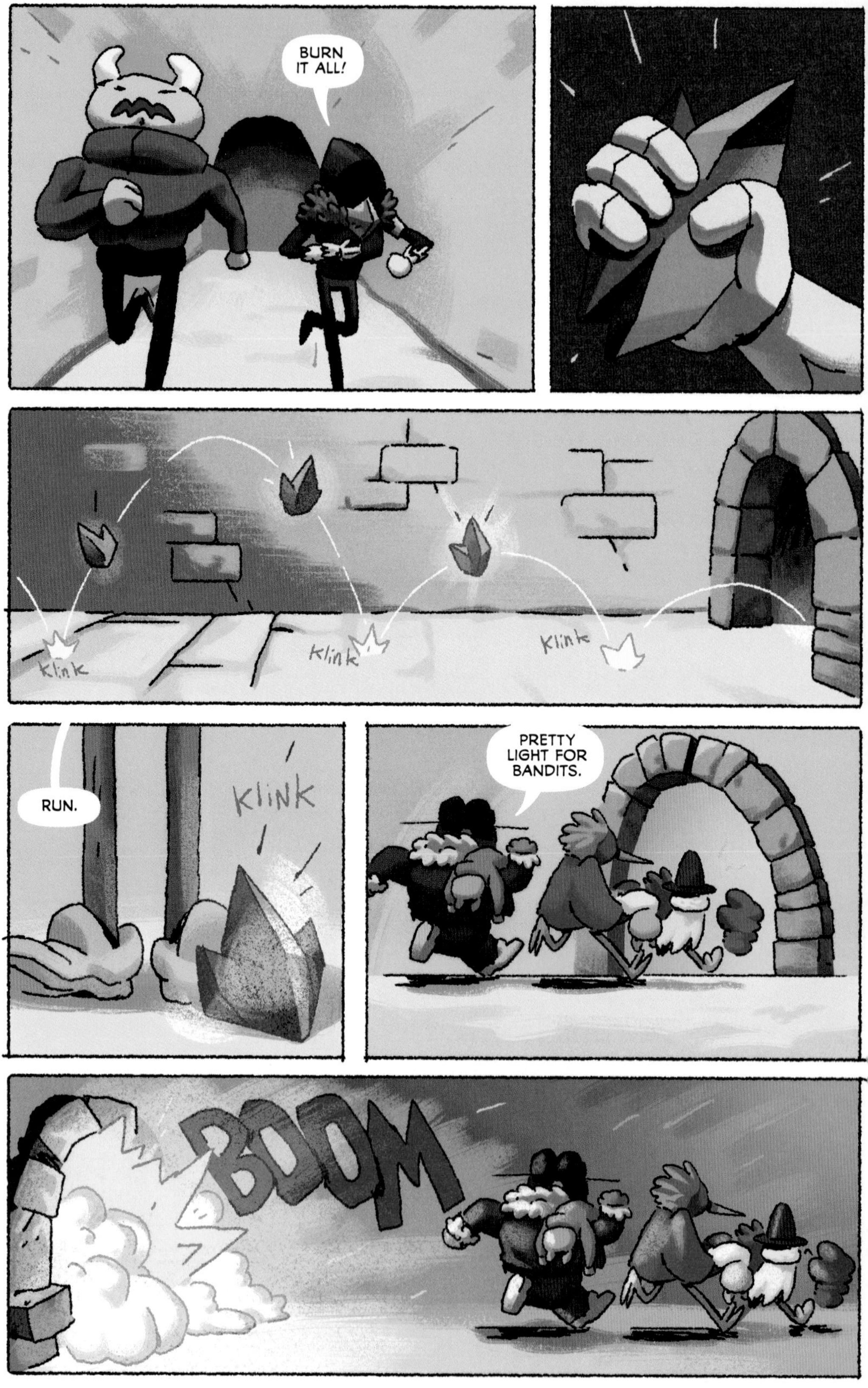
BURN IT ALL!
klink
klink
klink
RUN.
KLINK
PRETTY LIGHT FOR BANDITS.
BOOM

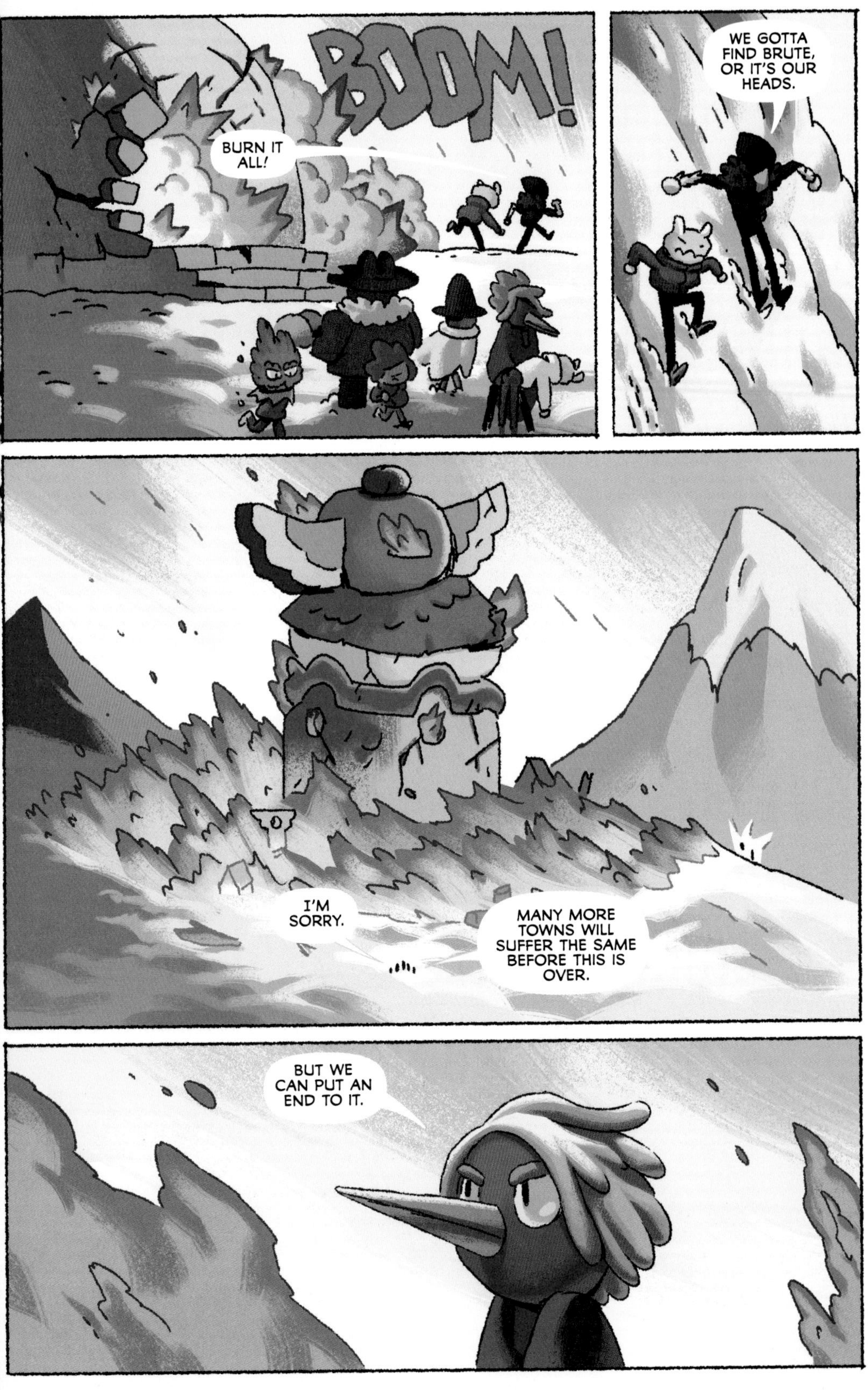
BOOM!
BURN IT ALL!
WE GOTTA FIND BRUTE, OR IT'S OUR HEADS.
I'M SORRY.
MANY MORE TOWNS WILL SUFFER THE SAME BEFORE THIS IS OVER.
BUT WE CAN PUT AN END TO IT.

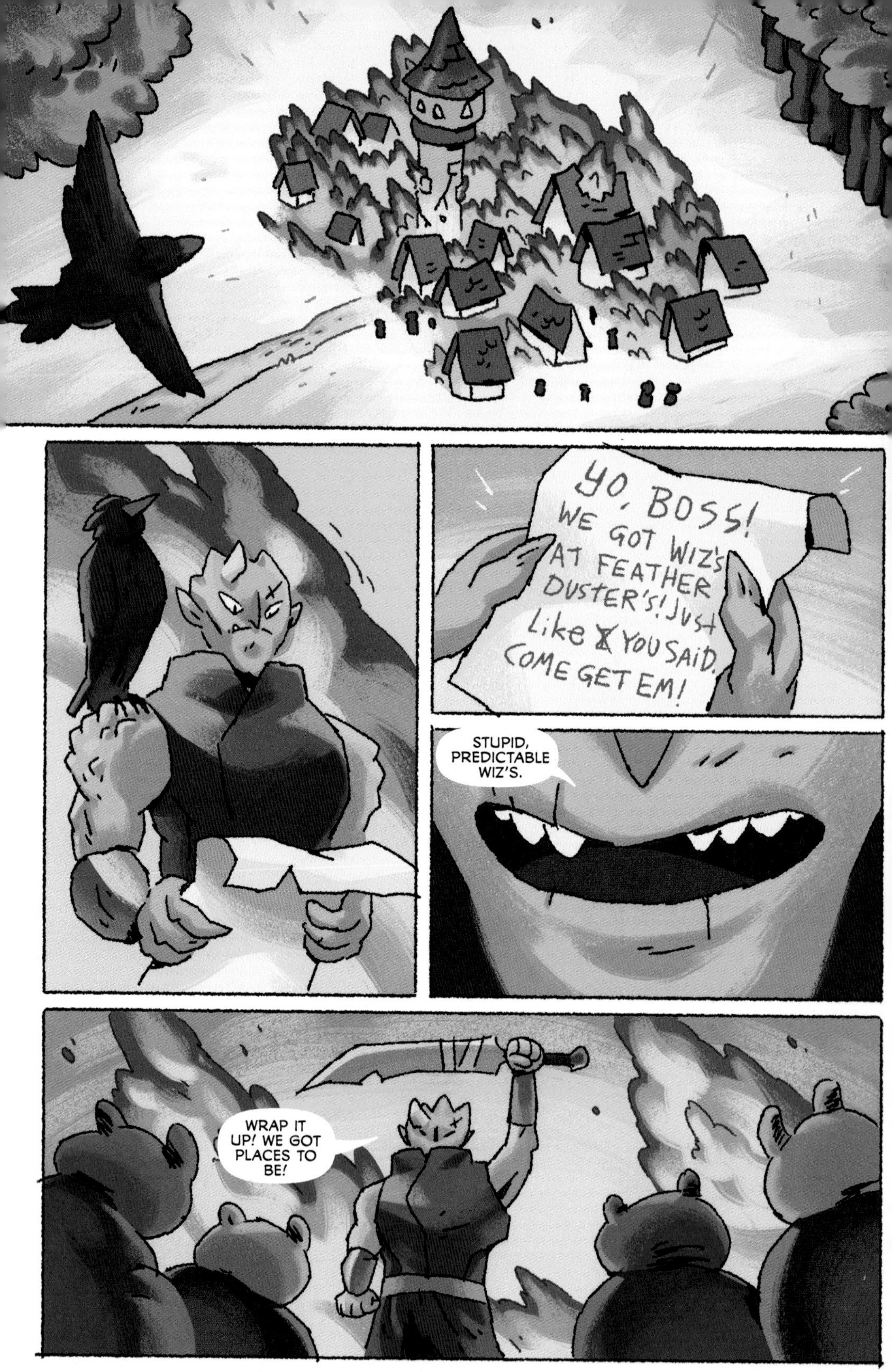
YO, BOSS!
WE GOT WIZ's AT FEATHER DUSTER's! Just Like ~~I~~ YOU SAID. COME GET EM!
STUPID, PREDICTABLE WIZ'S.
WRAP IT UP! WE GOT PLACES TO BE!

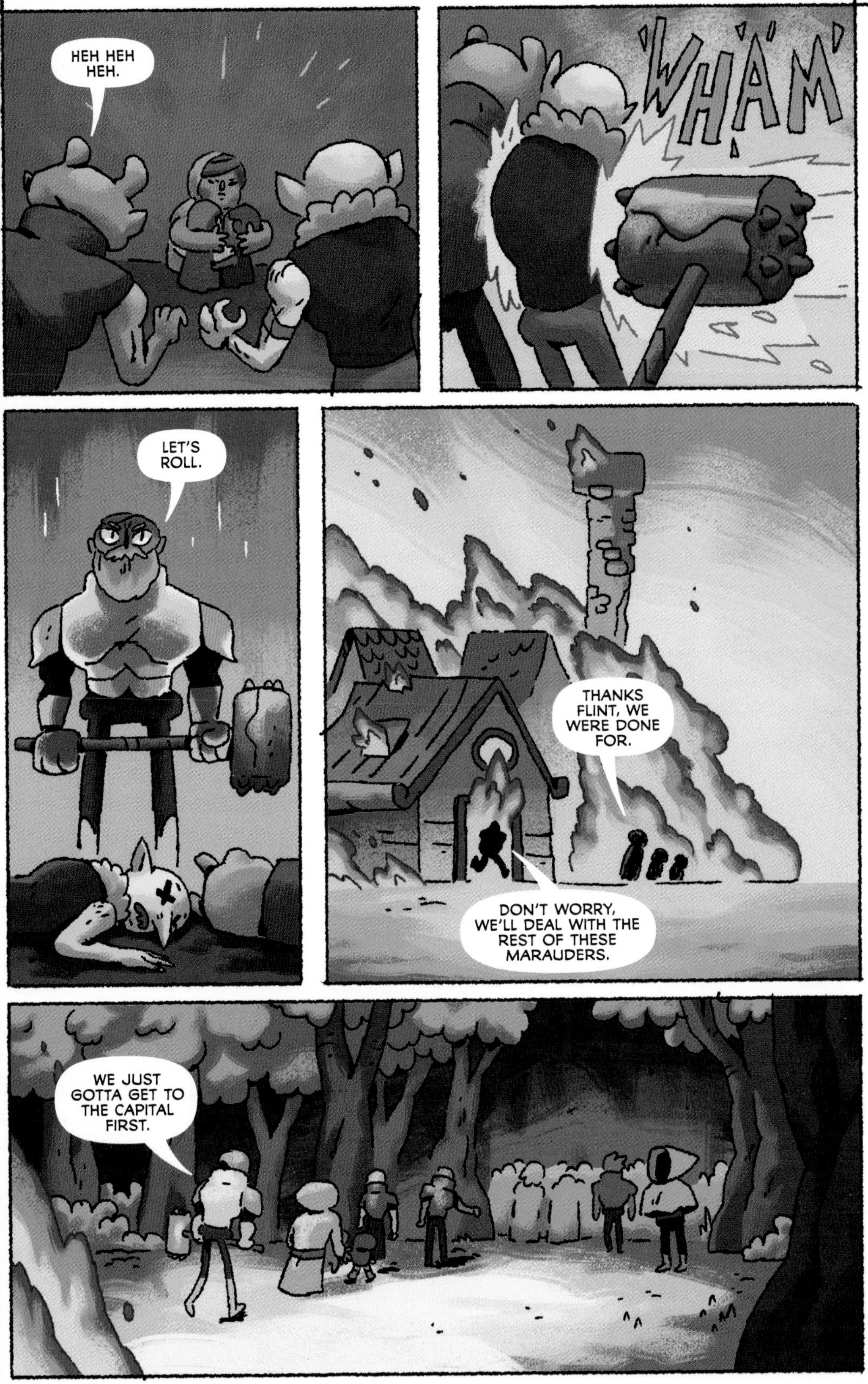
HEH HEH HEH.
WHAM
LET'S ROLL.
THANKS FLINT, WE WERE DONE FOR.
DON'T WORRY, WE'LL DEAL WITH THE REST OF THESE MARAUDERS.
WE JUST GOTTA GET TO THE CAPITAL FIRST.

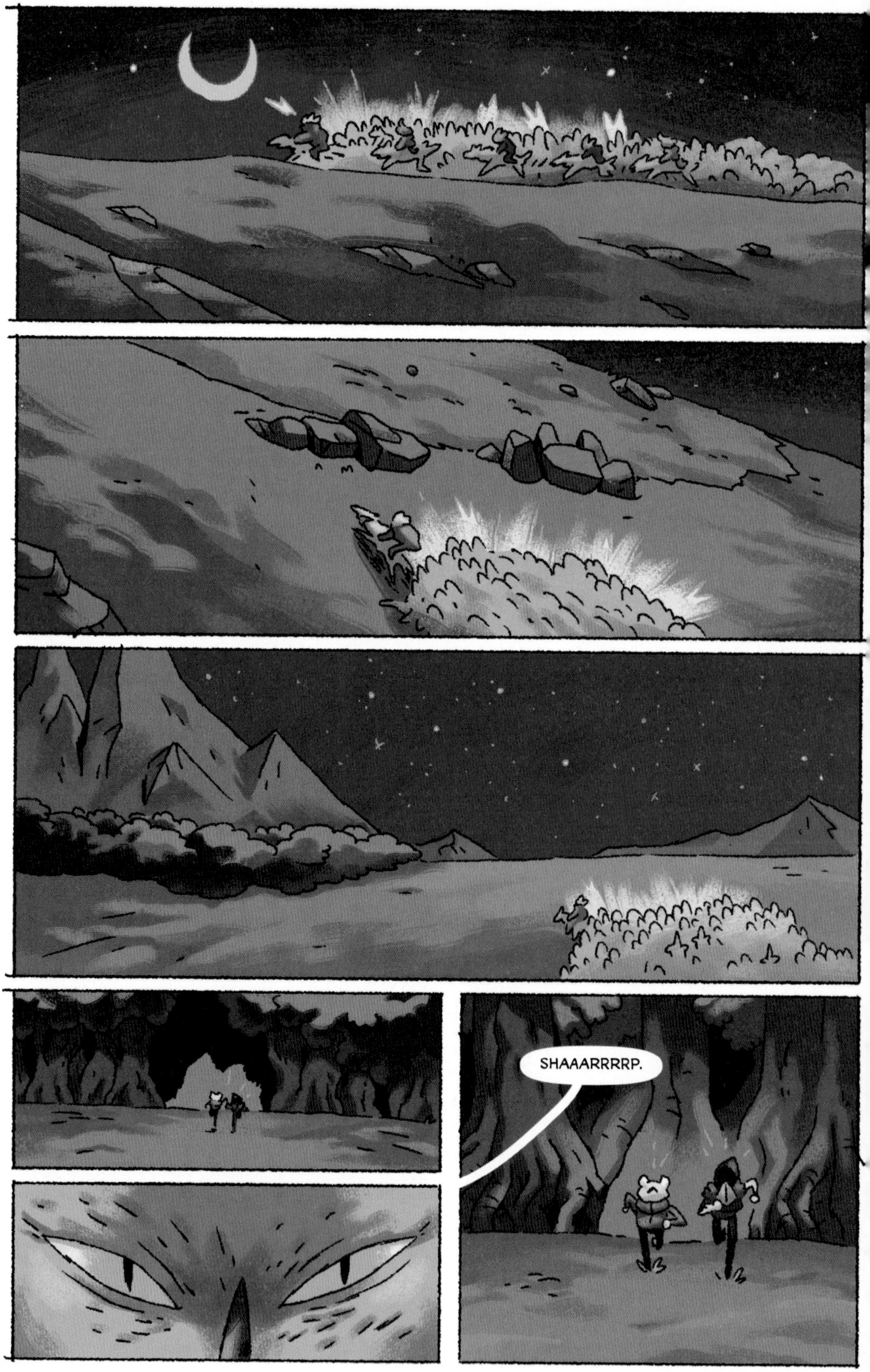
SHAAARRRRP.

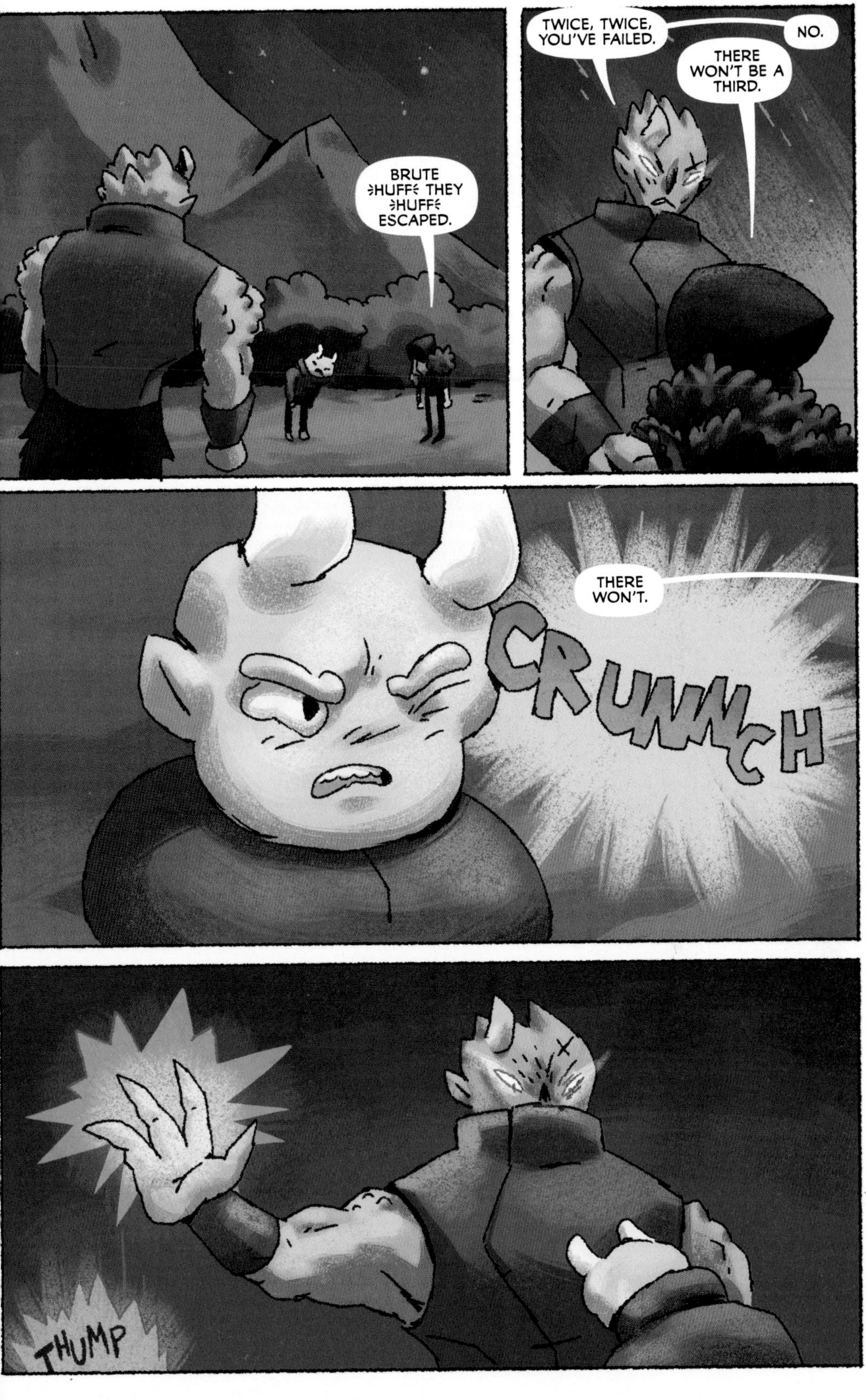
BRUTE
⋟HUFF⋞ THEY
⋟HUFF⋞
ESCAPED.
TWICE, TWICE, YOU'VE FAILED.
NO.
THERE WON'T BE A THIRD.
THERE WON'T.
CRUNNCH
THUMP

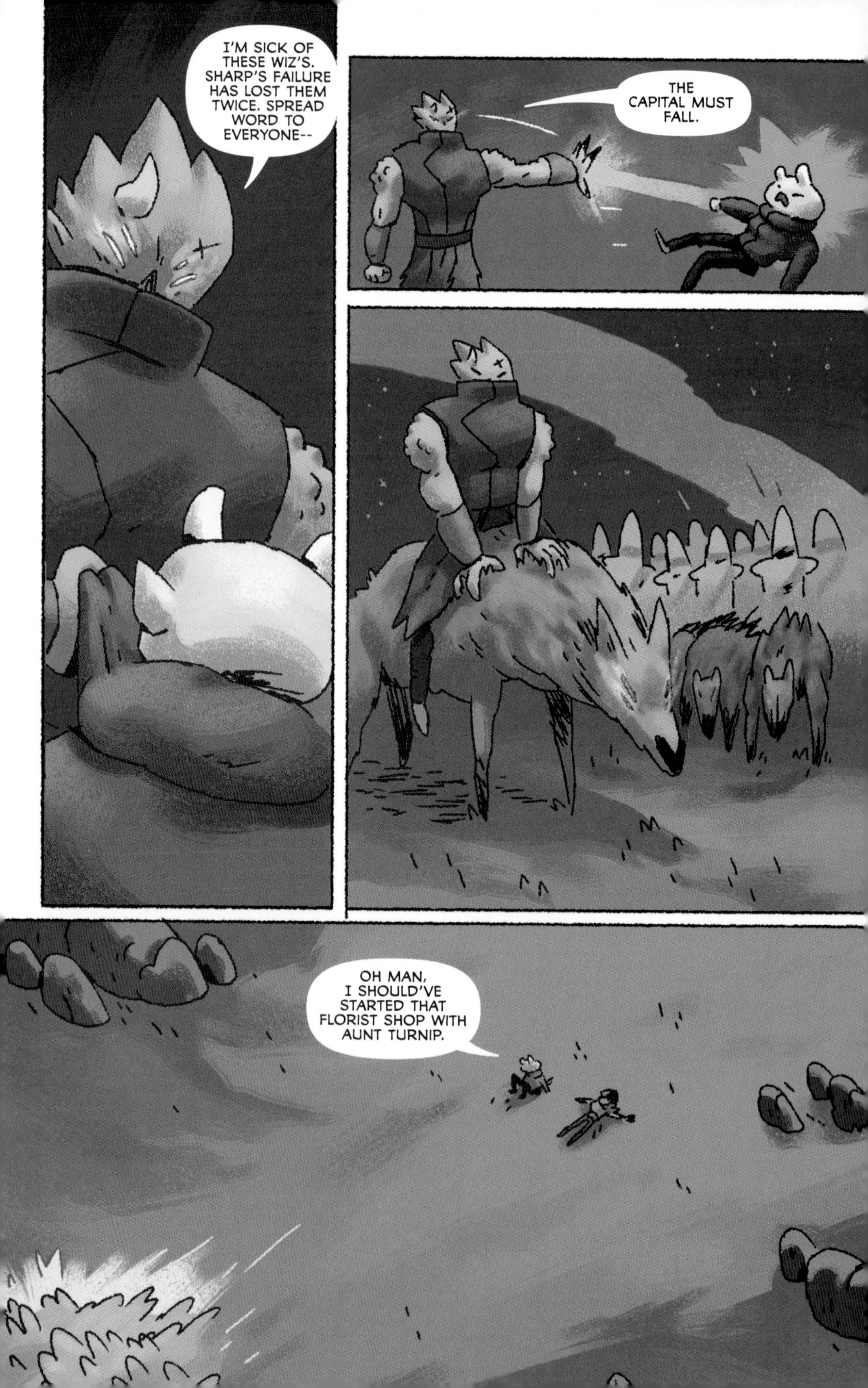
I'M SICK OF THESE WIZ'S. SHARP'S FAILURE HAS LOST THEM TWICE. SPREAD WORD TO EVERYONE--
THE CAPITAL MUST FALL.
OH MAN, I SHOULD'VE STARTED THAT FLORIST SHOP WITH AUNT TURNIP.

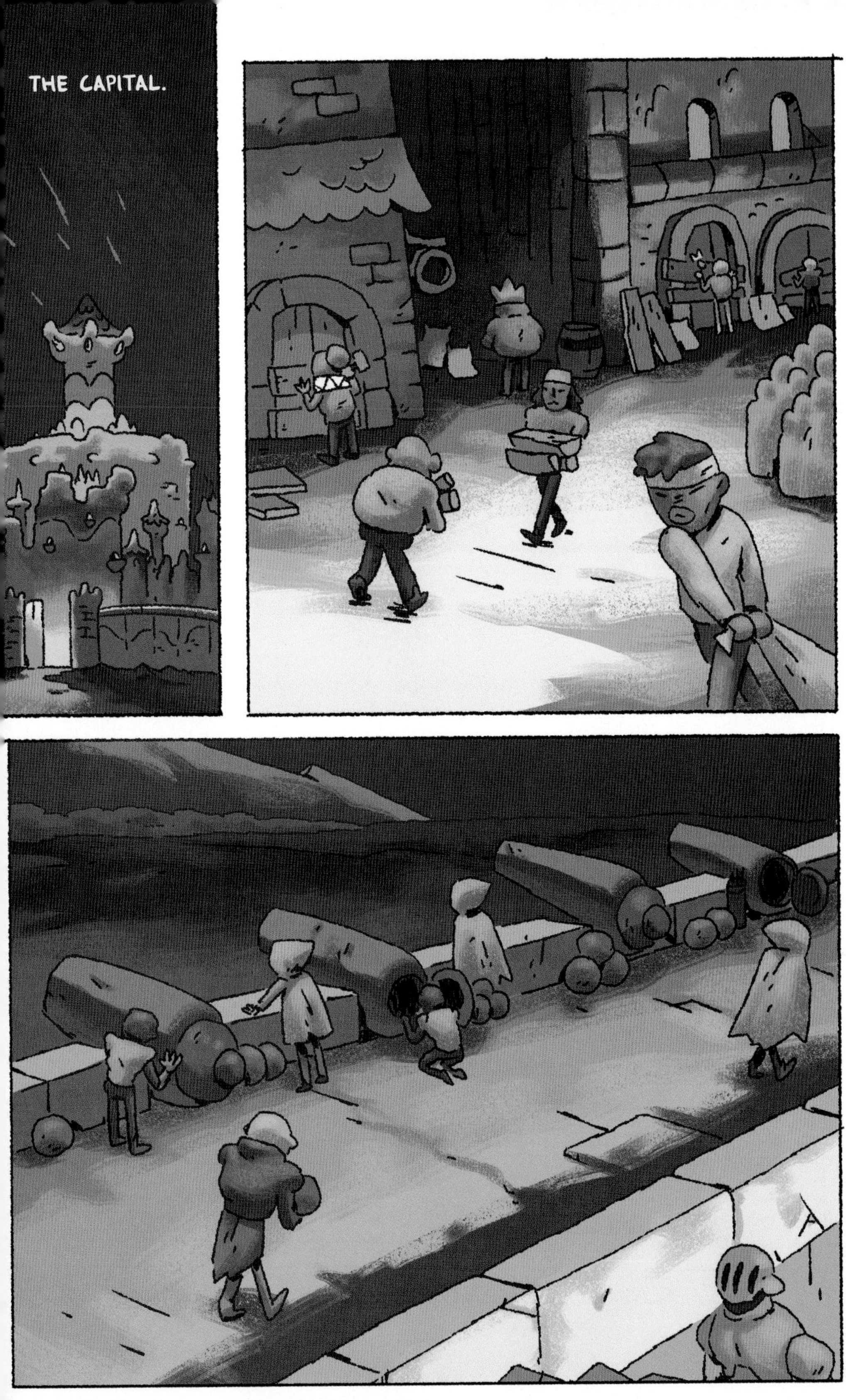
THE CAPITAL.

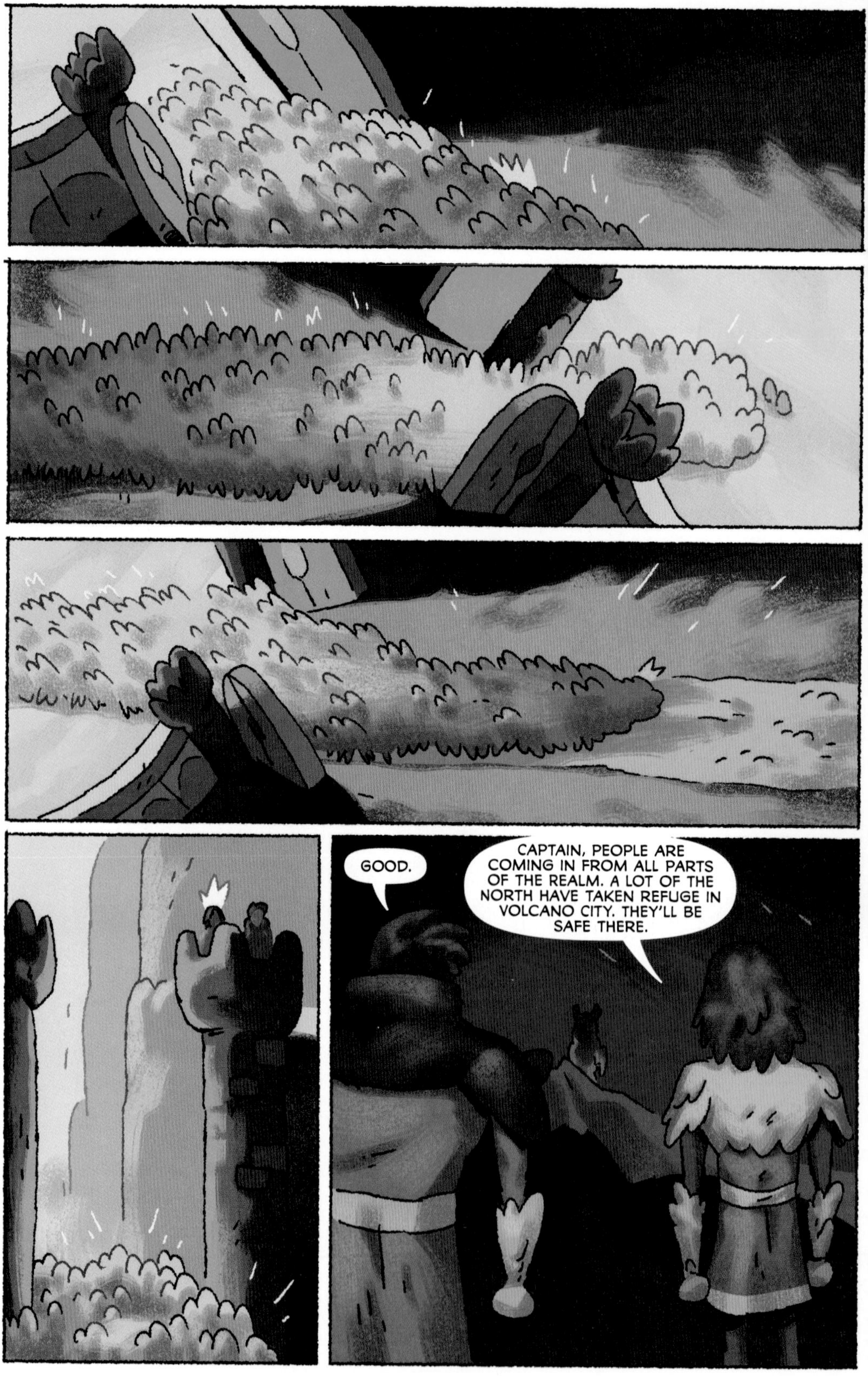
GOOD.
CAPTAIN, PEOPLE ARE COMING IN FROM ALL PARTS OF THE REALM. A LOT OF THE NORTH HAVE TAKEN REFUGE IN VOLCANO CITY. THEY'LL BE SAFE THERE.

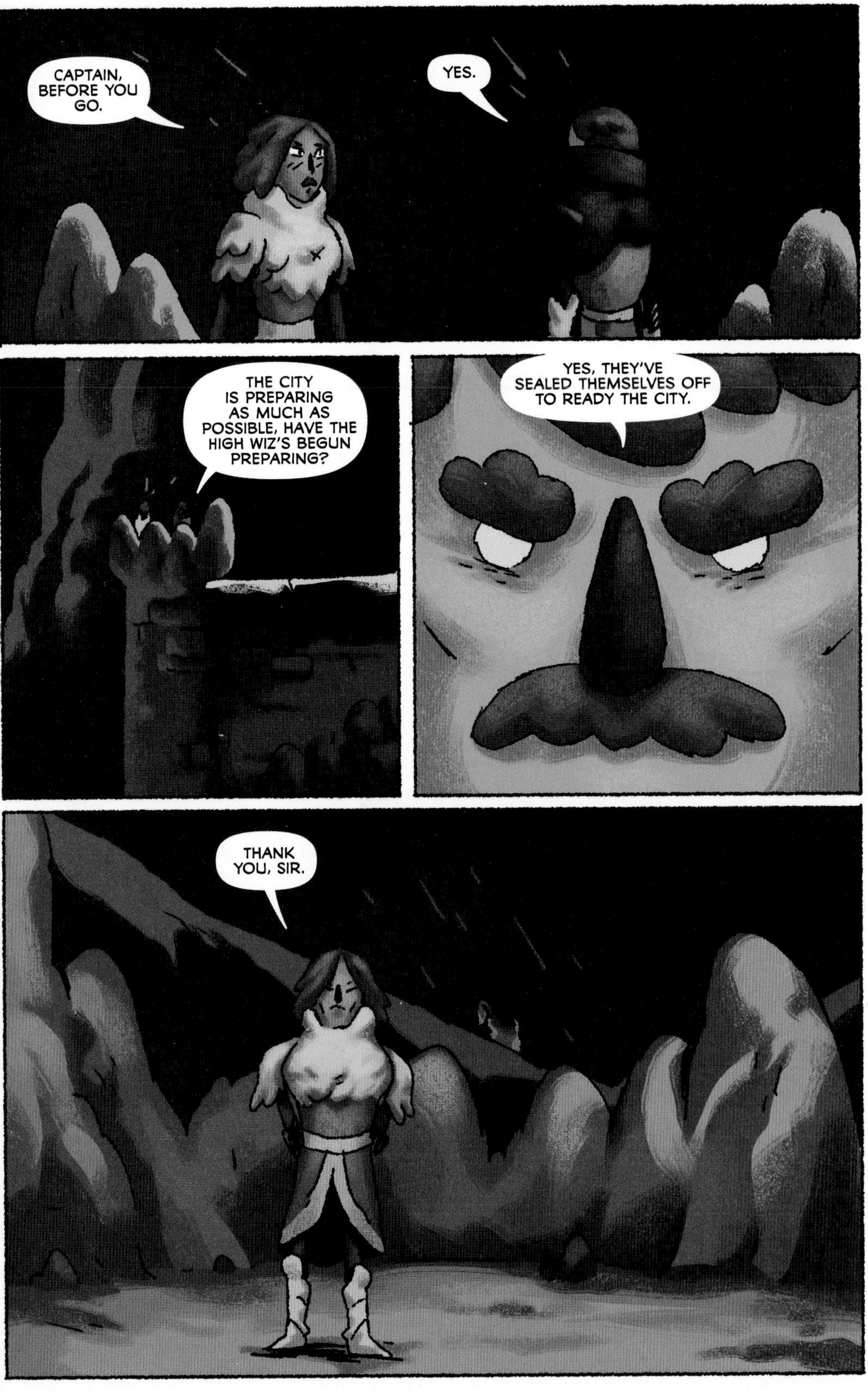
CAPTAIN, BEFORE YOU GO.
YES.
THE CITY IS PREPARING AS MUCH AS POSSIBLE, HAVE THE HIGH WIZ'S BEGUN PREPARING?
YES, THEY'VE SEALED THEMSELVES OFF TO READY THE CITY.
THANK YOU, SIR.

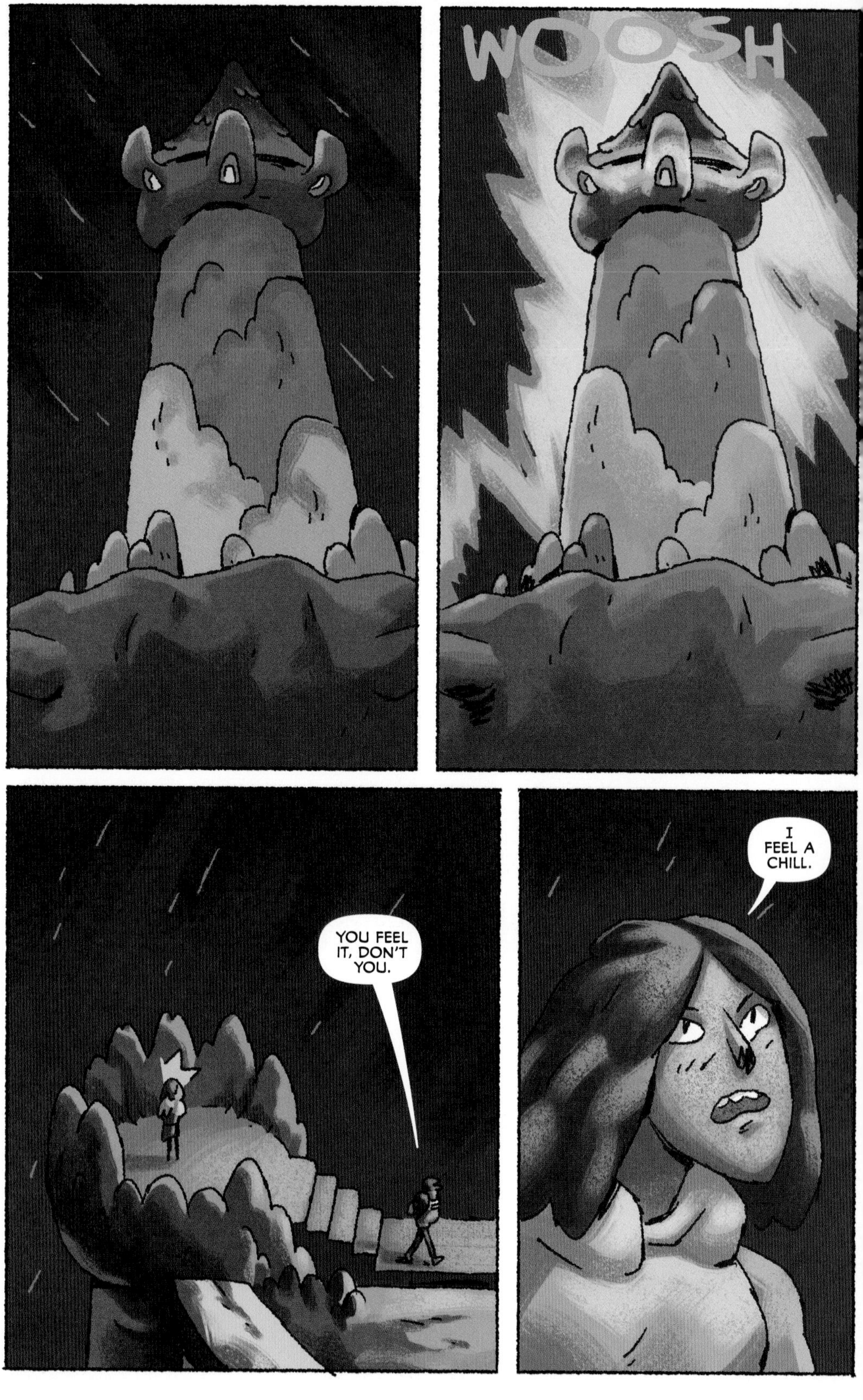
WOOSH
YOU FEEL IT, DON'T YOU.
I FEEL A CHILL.

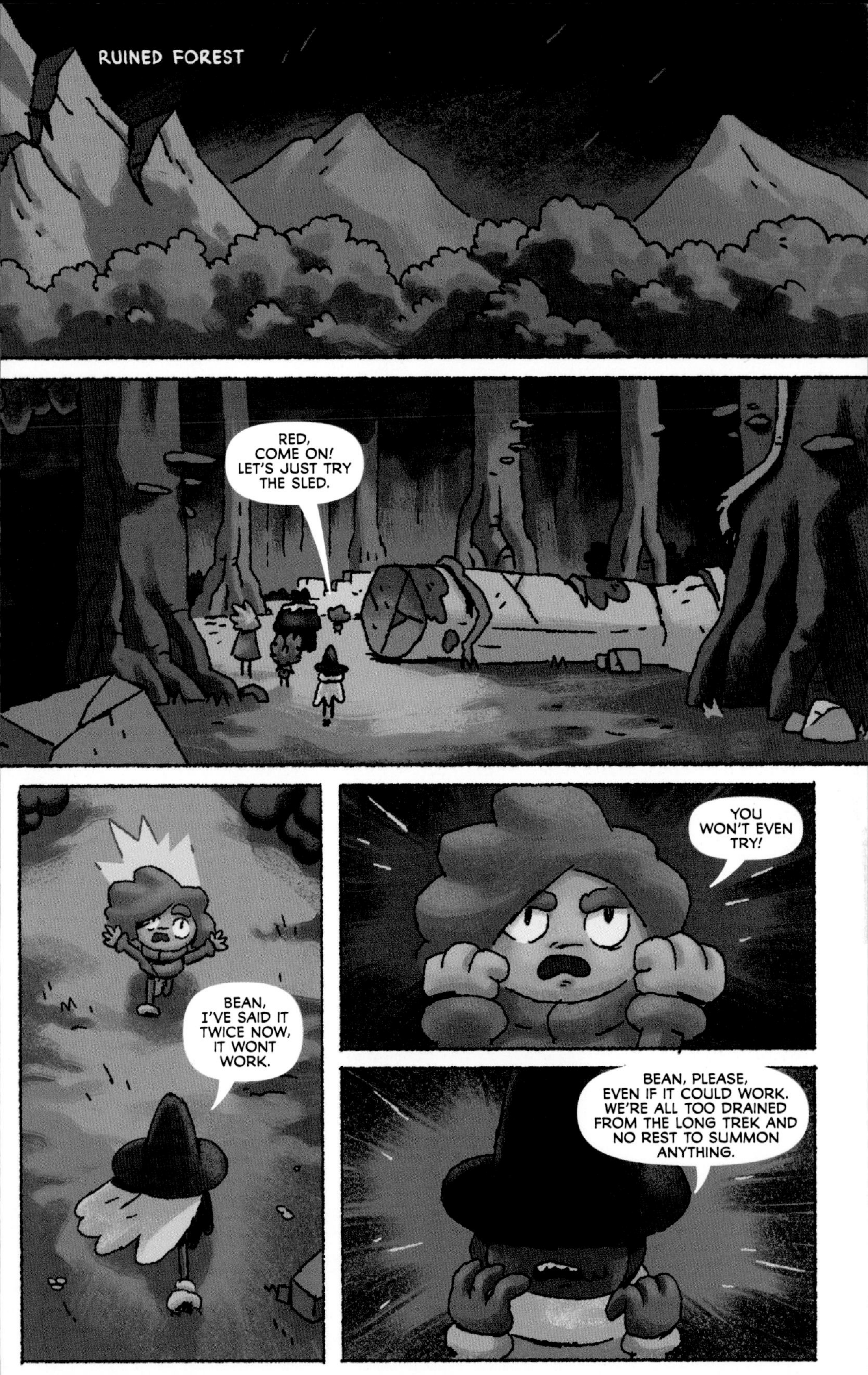
RUINED FOREST
RED, COME ON! LET'S JUST TRY THE SLED.
BEAN, I'VE SAID IT TWICE NOW, IT WONT WORK.
YOU WON'T EVEN TRY!
BEAN, PLEASE, EVEN IF IT COULD WORK. WE'RE ALL TOO DRAINED FROM THE LONG TREK AND NO REST TO SUMMON ANYTHING.

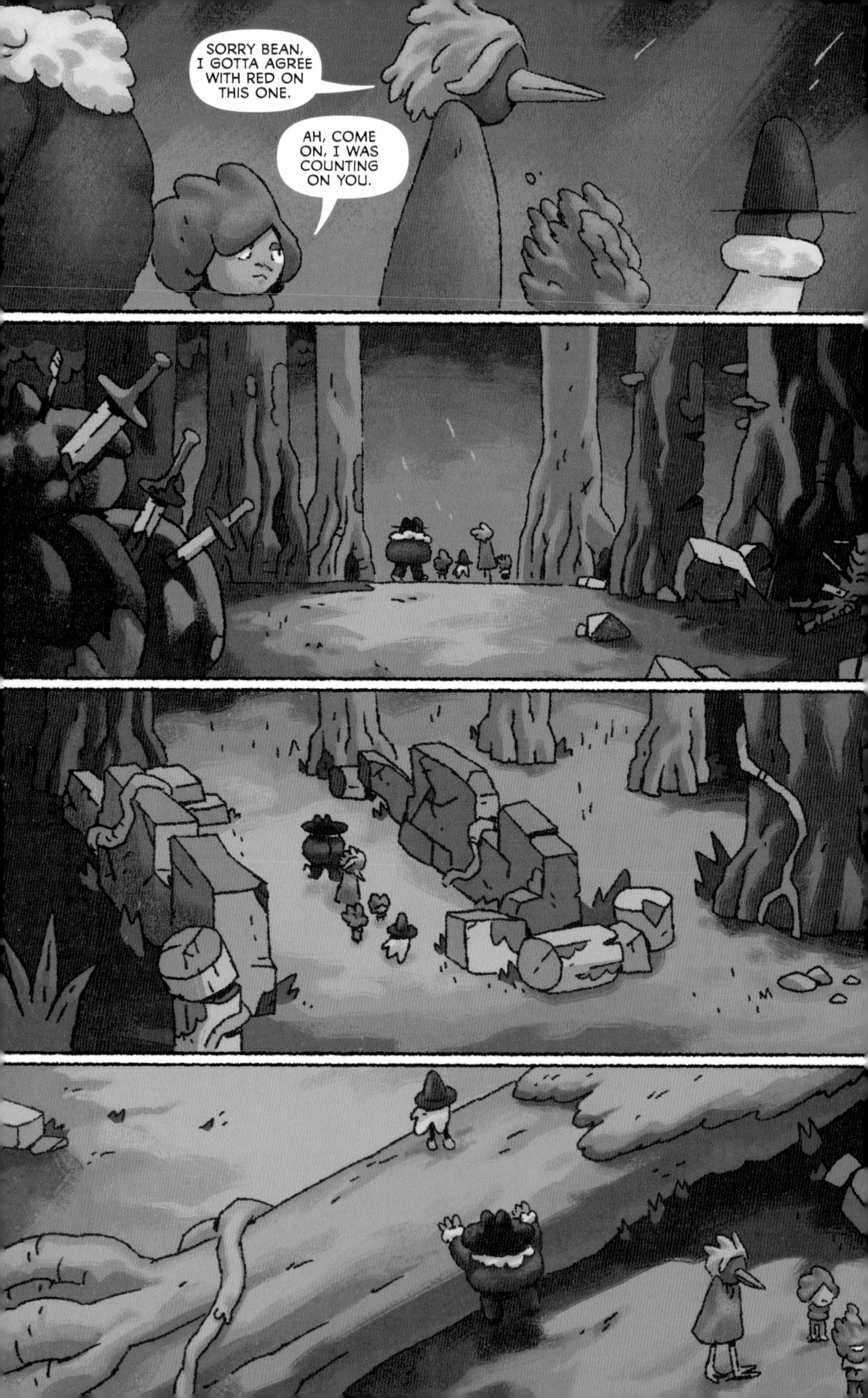
SORRY BEAN, I GOTTA AGREE WITH RED ON THIS ONE.
AH, COME ON, I WAS COUNTING ON YOU.

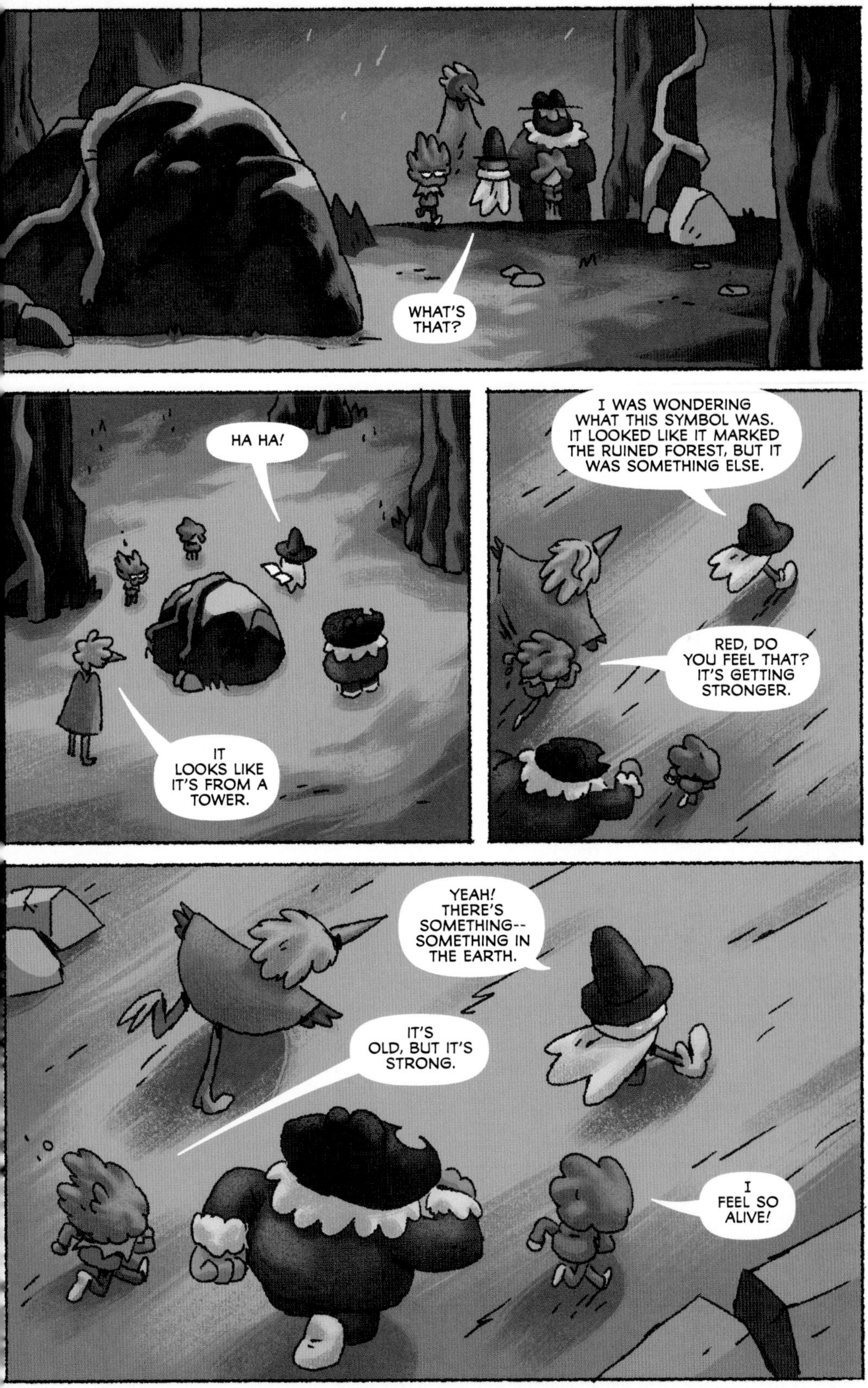
WHAT'S THAT?
HA HA!
IT LOOKS LIKE IT'S FROM A TOWER.
I WAS WONDERING WHAT THIS SYMBOL WAS. IT LOOKED LIKE IT MARKED THE RUINED FOREST, BUT IT WAS SOMETHING ELSE.
RED, DO YOU FEEL THAT? IT'S GETTING STRONGER.
YEAH! THERE'S SOMETHING-- SOMETHING IN THE EARTH.
IT'S OLD, BUT IT'S STRONG.
I FEEL SO ALIVE!

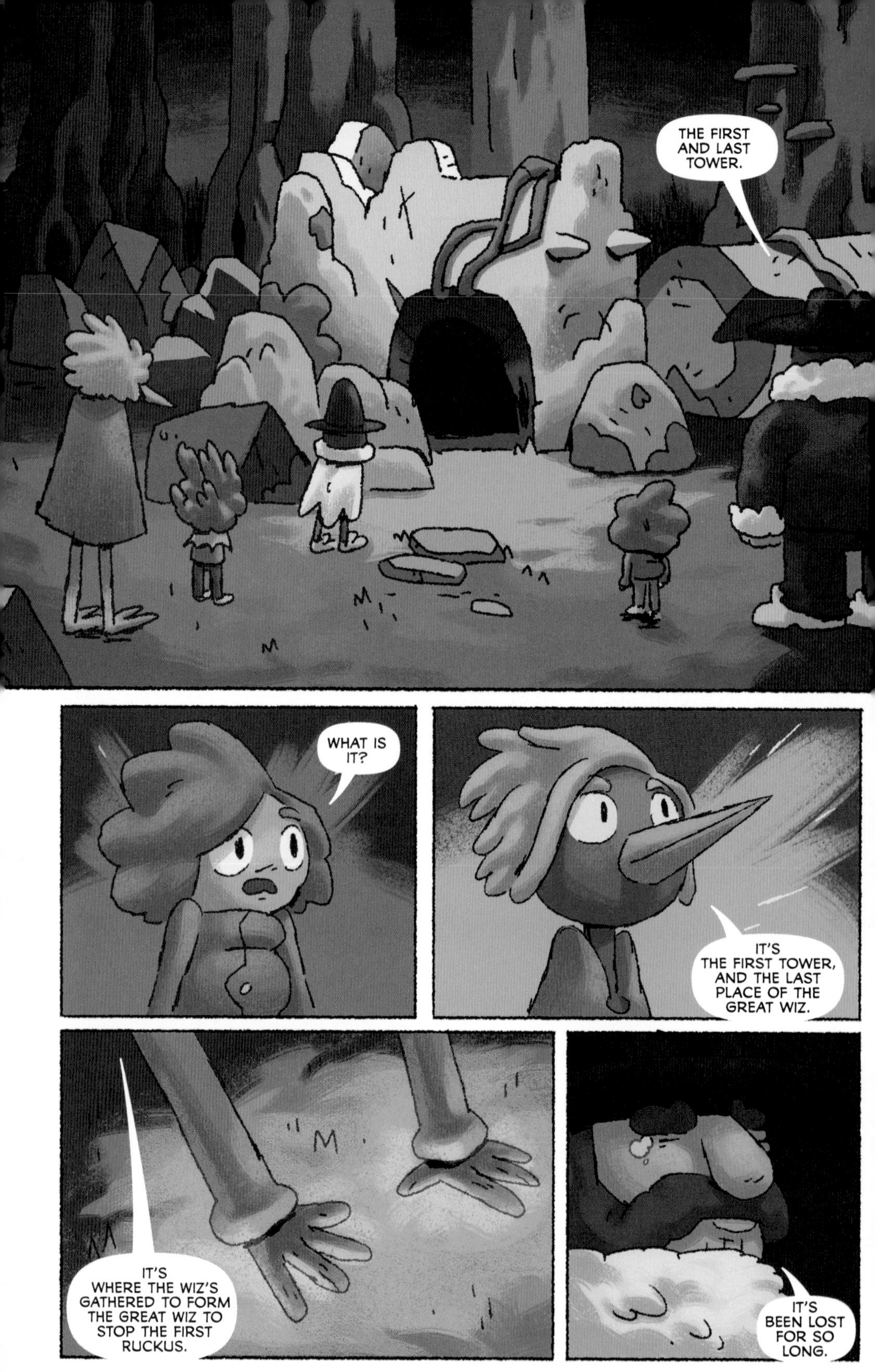
THE FIRST AND LAST TOWER.
WHAT IS IT?
IT'S THE FIRST TOWER, AND THE LAST PLACE OF THE GREAT WIZ.
IT'S WHERE THE WIZ'S GATHERED TO FORM THE GREAT WIZ TO STOP THE FIRST RUCKUS.
IT'S BEEN LOST FOR SO LONG.

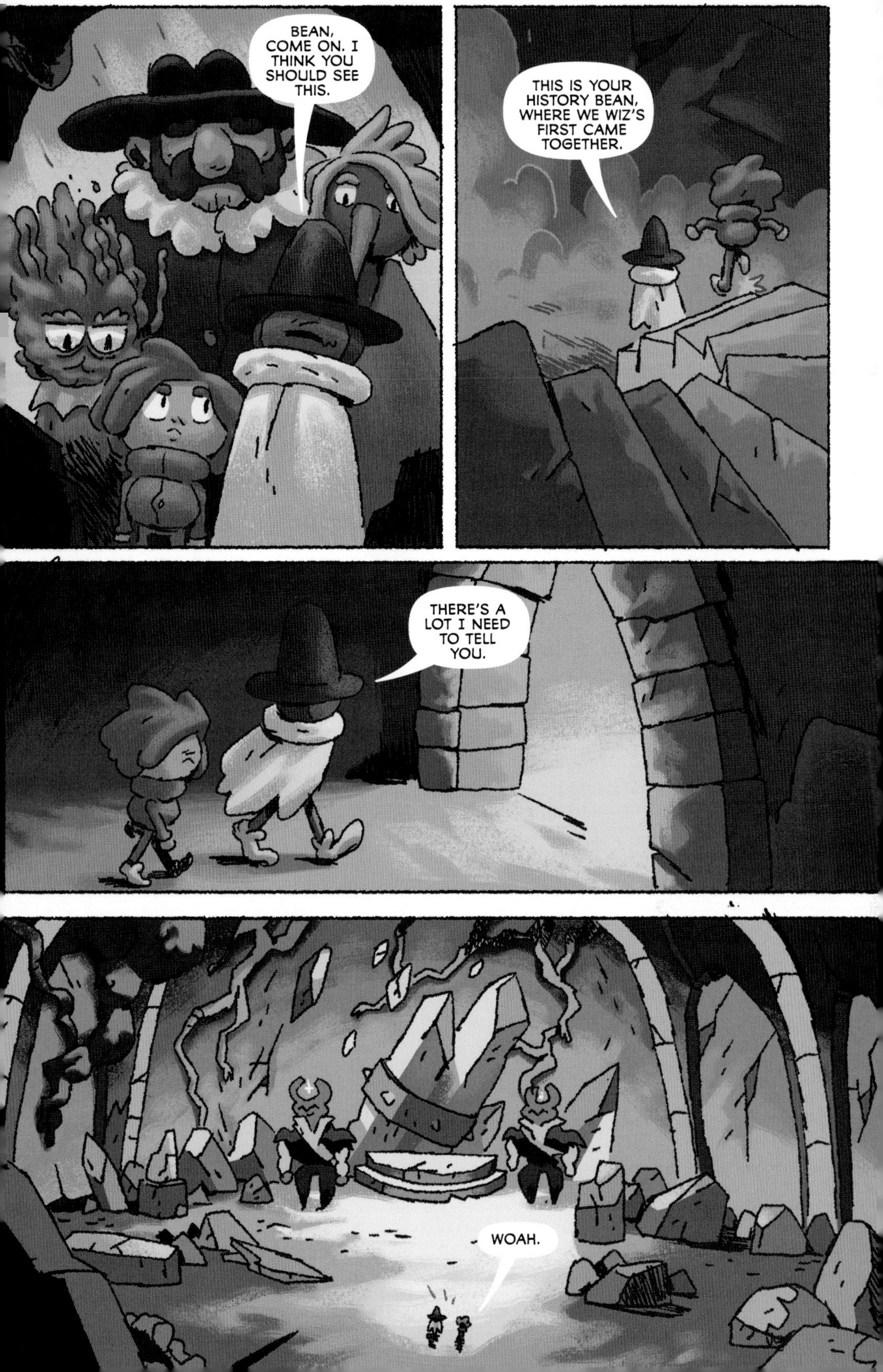
BEAN, COME ON. I THINK YOU SHOULD SEE THIS.
THIS IS YOUR HISTORY BEAN, WHERE WE WIZ'S FIRST CAME TOGETHER.
THERE'S A LOT I NEED TO TELL YOU.
WOAH.

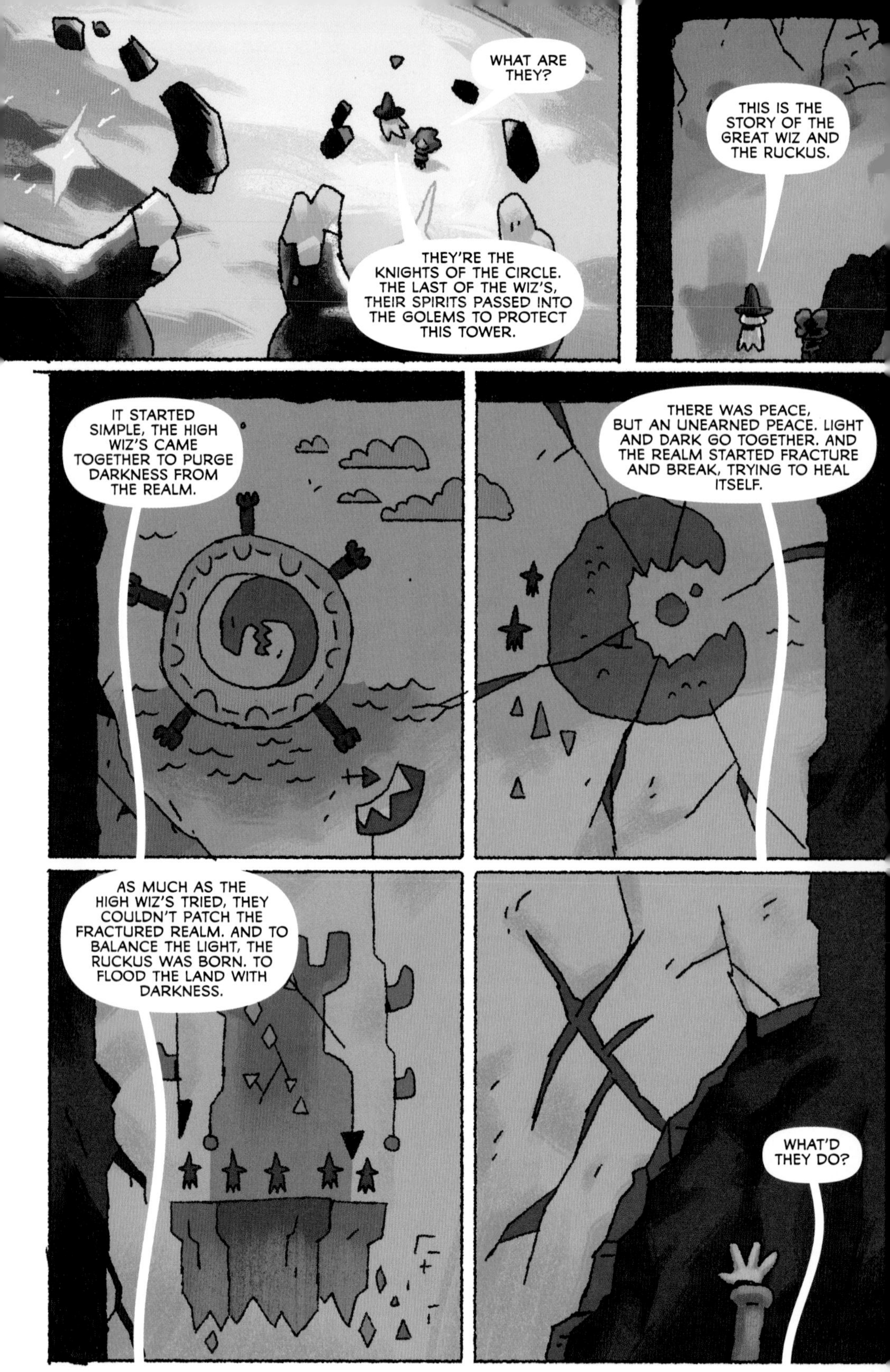
WHAT ARE THEY?
THEY'RE THE KNIGHTS OF THE CIRCLE. THE LAST OF THE WIZ'S, THEIR SPIRITS PASSED INTO THE GOLEMS TO PROTECT THIS TOWER.
THIS IS THE STORY OF THE GREAT WIZ AND THE RUCKUS.
IT STARTED SIMPLE, THE HIGH WIZ'S CAME TOGETHER TO PURGE DARKNESS FROM THE REALM.
THERE WAS PEACE, BUT AN UNEARNED PEACE. LIGHT AND DARK GO TOGETHER. AND THE REALM STARTED FRACTURE AND BREAK, TRYING TO HEAL ITSELF.
AS MUCH AS THE HIGH WIZ'S TRIED, THEY COULDN'T PATCH THE FRACTURED REALM. AND TO BALANCE THE LIGHT, THE RUCKUS WAS BORN. TO FLOOD THE LAND WITH DARKNESS.
WHAT'D THEY DO?

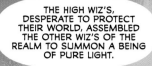

THE HIGH WIZ'S, DESPERATE TO PROTECT THEIR WORLD, ASSEMBLED THE OTHER WIZ'S OF THE REALM TO SUMMON A BEING OF PURE LIGHT.

THE WIZ'S WERE LOST IN THE SUMMON, BUT THE COST WAS WORTH THE WIN. THE GREAT WIZ WAS BORN AND DEFEATED THE RUCKUS.

AFTER THAT IT WAS AGREED THAT WIZ'S SHOULDN'T MEDDLE WITH THE NON-MAGICAL WORLD. BUT, INSTEAD, WOULD BE WATCHERS OF THE REALM, PROTECTING IT FROM UNNATURAL THINGS NOT MEANT FOR MERE MORTALS, LEAVING THE REALM VULNERABLE TO ITS OWN DEVICES.

LOST?

THESE TWO GUARDIANS HERE ARE THE LAST OF THAT TIME. OLD TIMER WAS WITH THEM THAT DAY OF THE SUMMON, THEY HAD HIM STAY BACK SO HE COULD PREPARE THE WORLD INCASE IT HAPPENED AGAIN. THESE TWO HERE, THEY SAVED US ALL THAT DAY.

WHAT DO YOU MEAN, LOST?

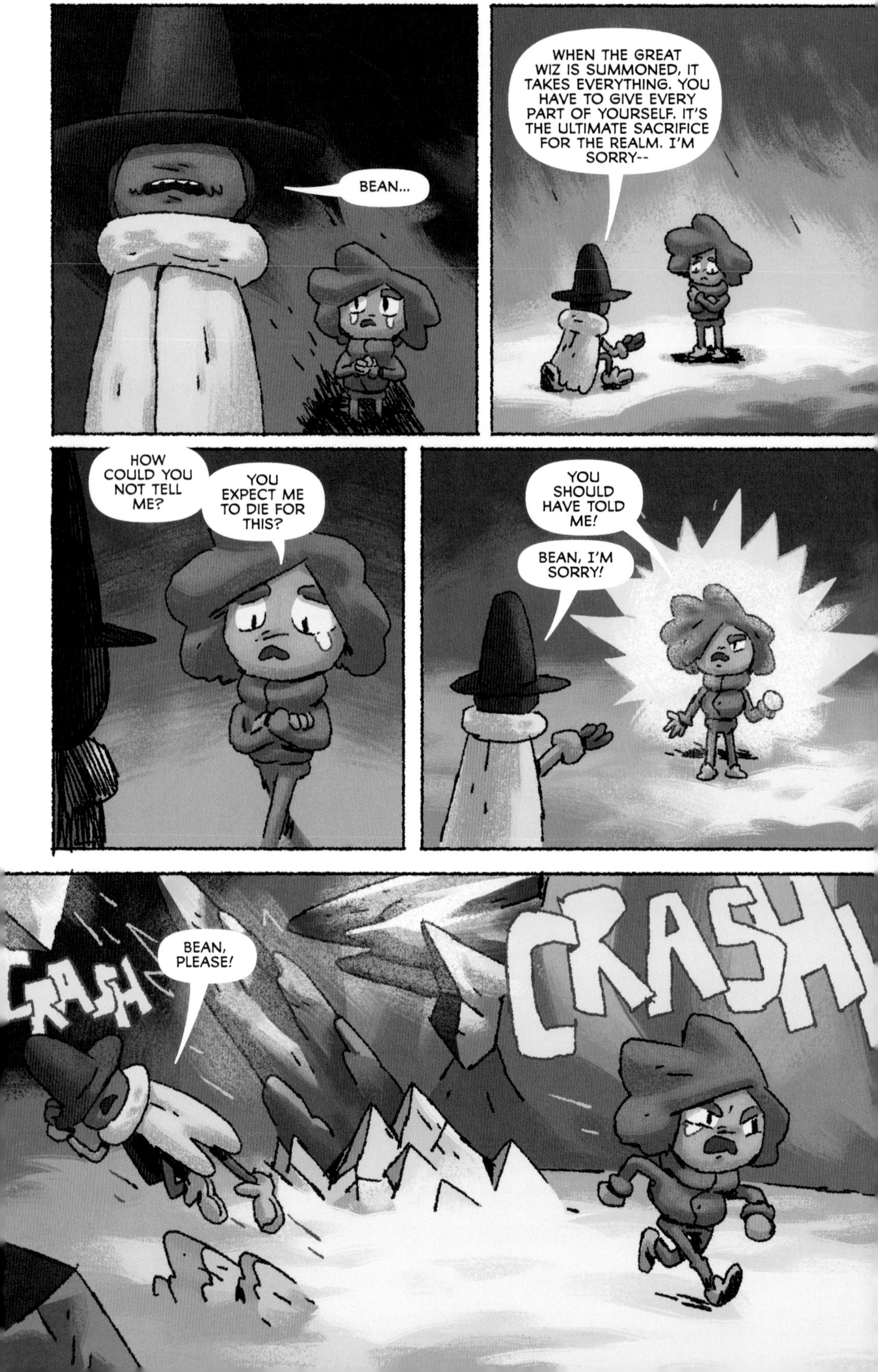
BEAN...
WHEN THE GREAT WIZ IS SUMMONED, IT TAKES EVERYTHING. YOU HAVE TO GIVE EVERY PART OF YOURSELF. IT'S THE ULTIMATE SACRIFICE FOR THE REALM. I'M SORRY--
HOW COULD YOU NOT TELL ME?
YOU EXPECT ME TO DIE FOR THIS?
YOU SHOULD HAVE TOLD ME!
BEAN, I'M SORRY!
CRASH
BEAN, PLEASE!
CRASH

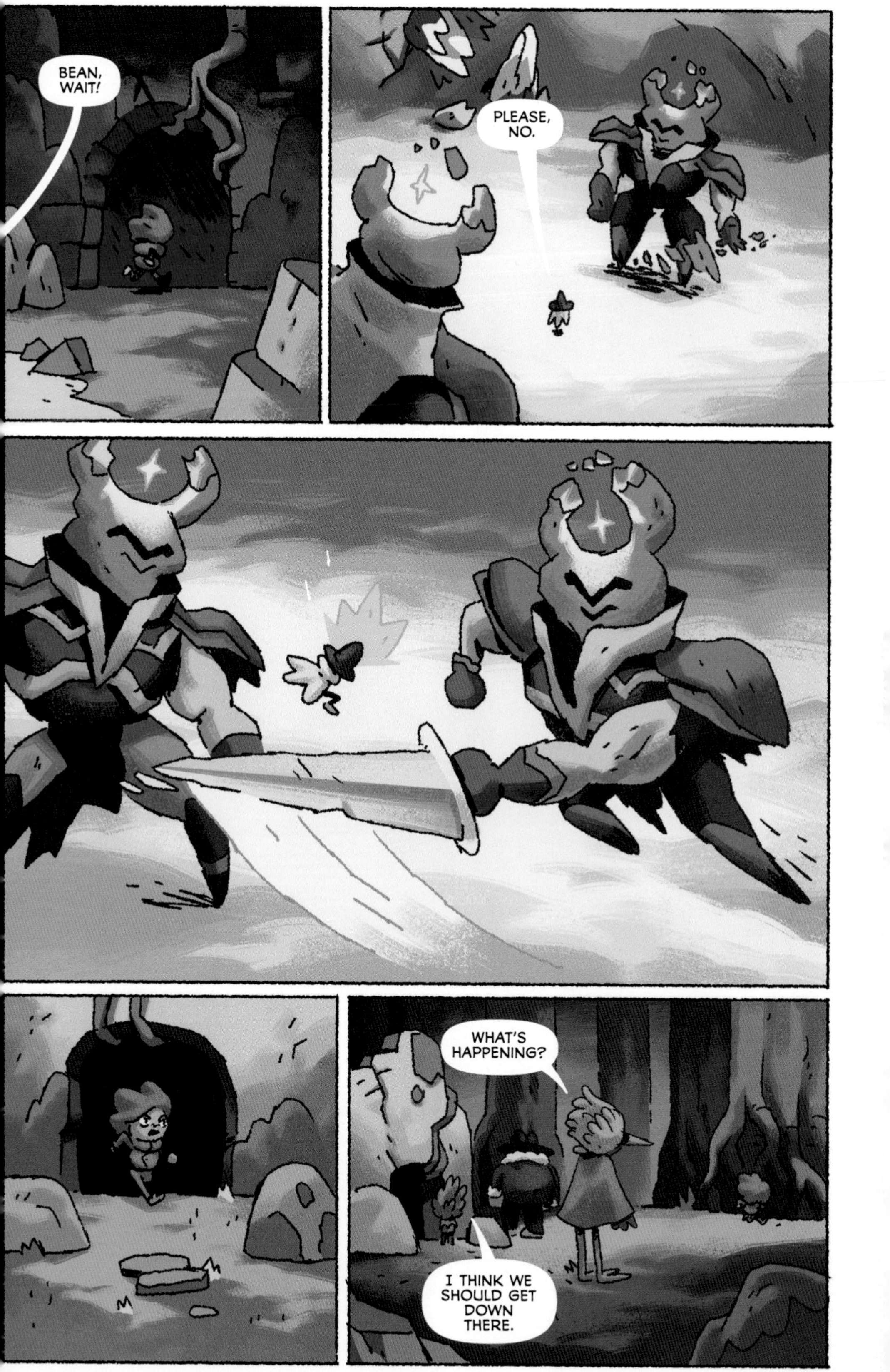
BEAN, WAIT!
PLEASE, NO.
WHAT'S HAPPENING?
I THINK WE SHOULD GET DOWN THERE.

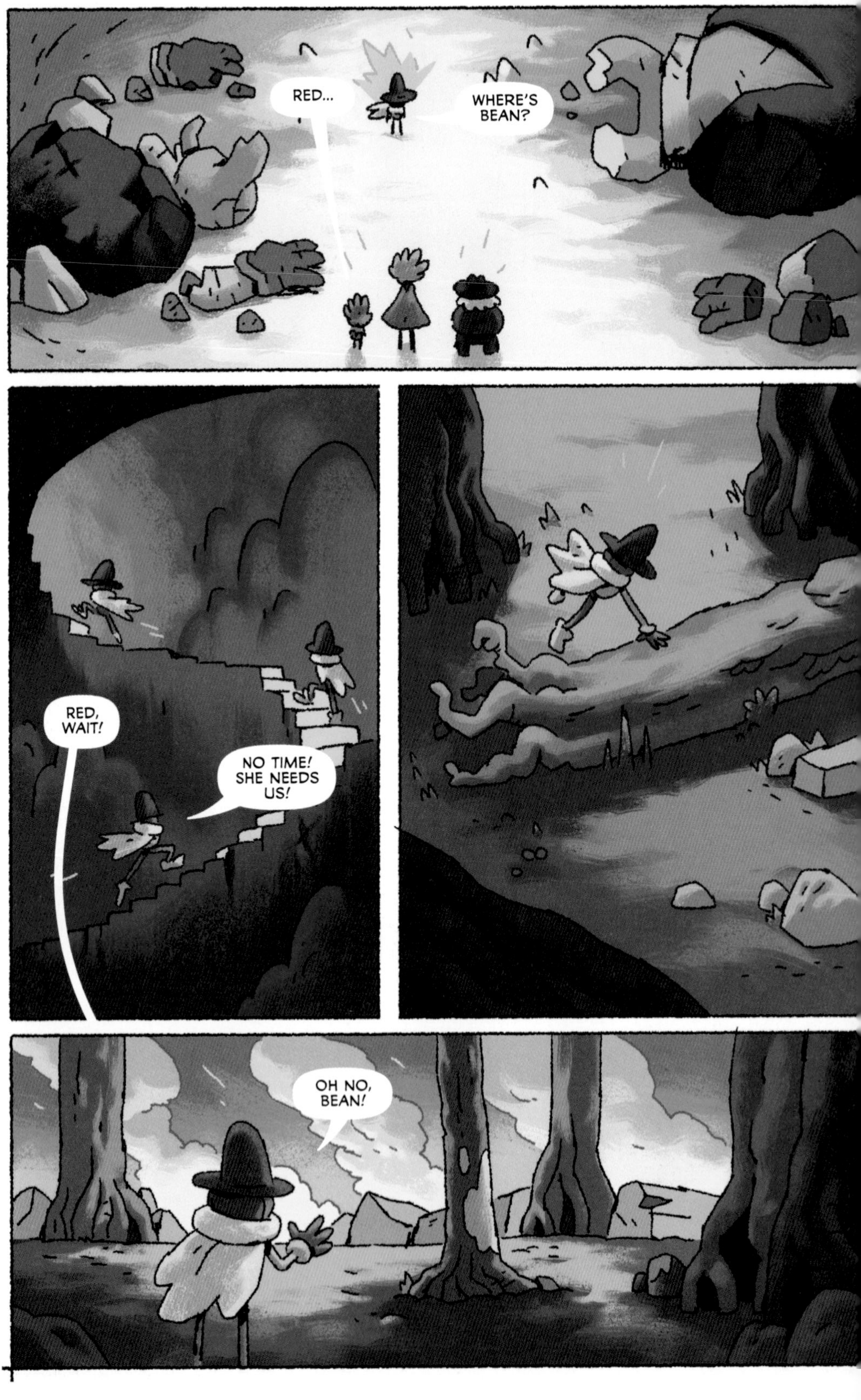
RED...
WHERE'S BEAN?
RED, WAIT!
NO TIME! SHE NEEDS US!
OH NO, BEAN!

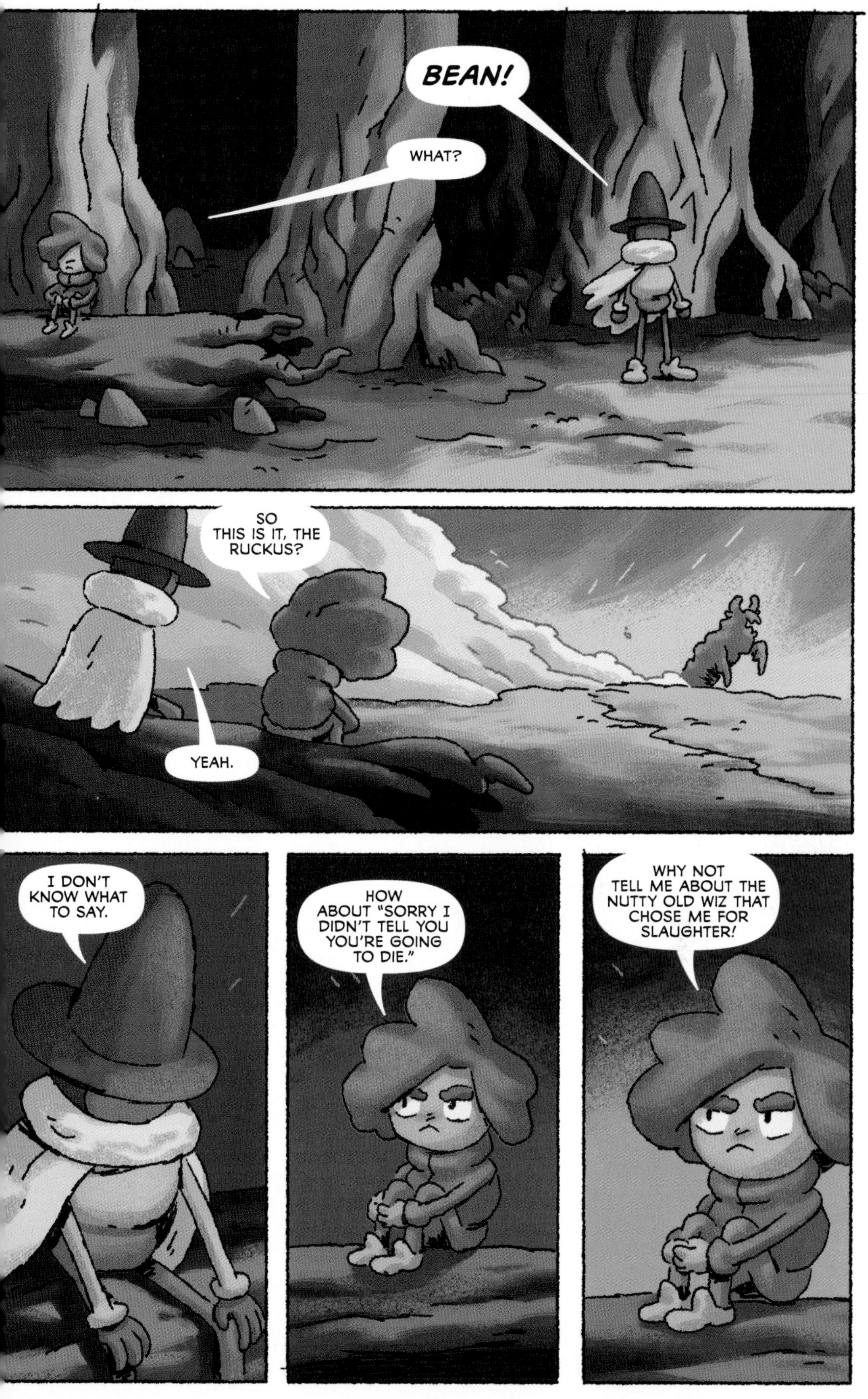
BEAN!
WHAT?
SO THIS IS IT, THE RUCKUS?
YEAH.
I DON'T KNOW WHAT TO SAY.
HOW ABOUT "SORRY I DIDN'T TELL YOU YOU'RE GOING TO DIE."
WHY NOT TELL ME ABOUT THE NUTTY OLD WIZ THAT CHOSE ME FOR SLAUGHTER!

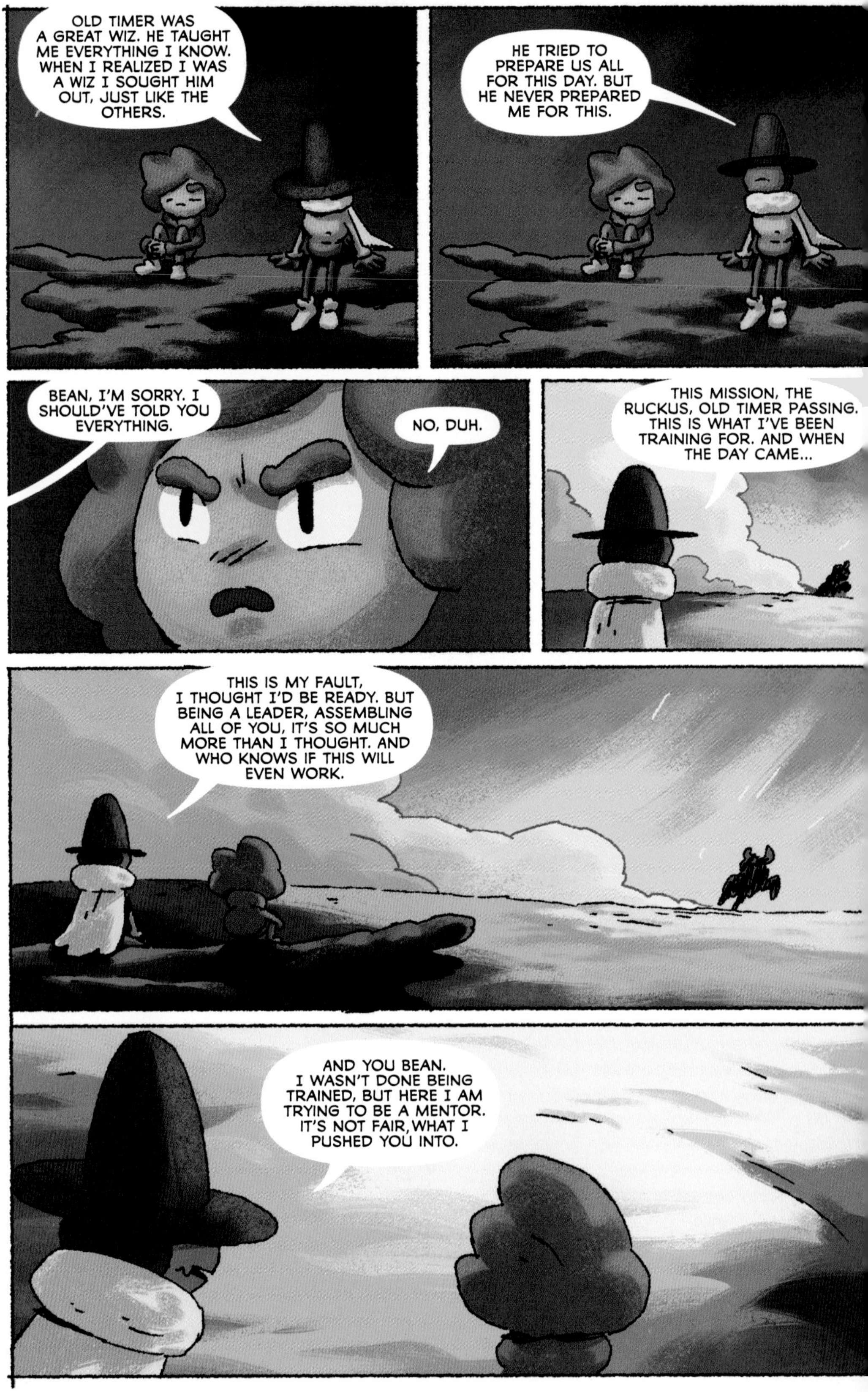
OLD TIMER WAS A GREAT WIZ. HE TAUGHT ME EVERYTHING I KNOW. WHEN I REALIZED I WAS A WIZ I SOUGHT HIM OUT, JUST LIKE THE OTHERS.
HE TRIED TO PREPARE US ALL FOR THIS DAY. BUT HE NEVER PREPARED ME FOR THIS.
BEAN, I'M SORRY. I SHOULD'VE TOLD YOU EVERYTHING.
NO, DUH.
THIS MISSION, THE RUCKUS, OLD TIMER PASSING. THIS IS WHAT I'VE BEEN TRAINING FOR. AND WHEN THE DAY CAME...
THIS IS MY FAULT, I THOUGHT I'D BE READY. BUT BEING A LEADER, ASSEMBLING ALL OF YOU, IT'S SO MUCH MORE THAN I THOUGHT. AND WHO KNOWS IF THIS WILL EVEN WORK.
AND YOU BEAN. I WASN'T DONE BEING TRAINED, BUT HERE I AM TRYING TO BE A MENTOR. IT'S NOT FAIR, WHAT I PUSHED YOU INTO.

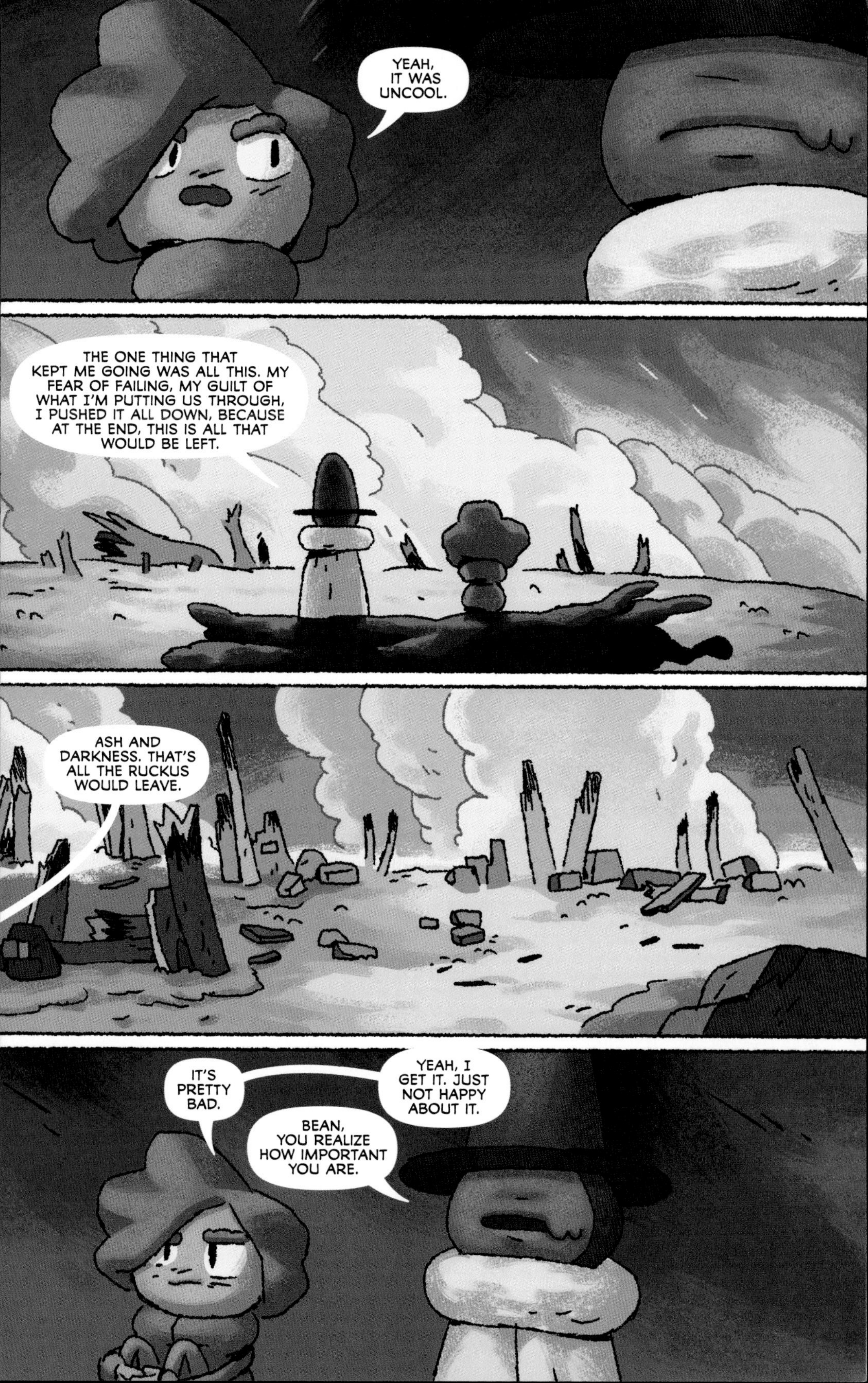
YEAH, IT WAS UNCOOL.
THE ONE THING THAT KEPT ME GOING WAS ALL THIS. MY FEAR OF FAILING, MY GUILT OF WHAT I'M PUTTING US THROUGH, I PUSHED IT ALL DOWN, BECAUSE AT THE END, THIS IS ALL THAT WOULD BE LEFT.
ASH AND DARKNESS. THAT'S ALL THE RUCKUS WOULD LEAVE.
IT'S PRETTY BAD.
YEAH, I GET IT. JUST NOT HAPPY ABOUT IT.
BEAN, YOU REALIZE HOW IMPORTANT YOU ARE.

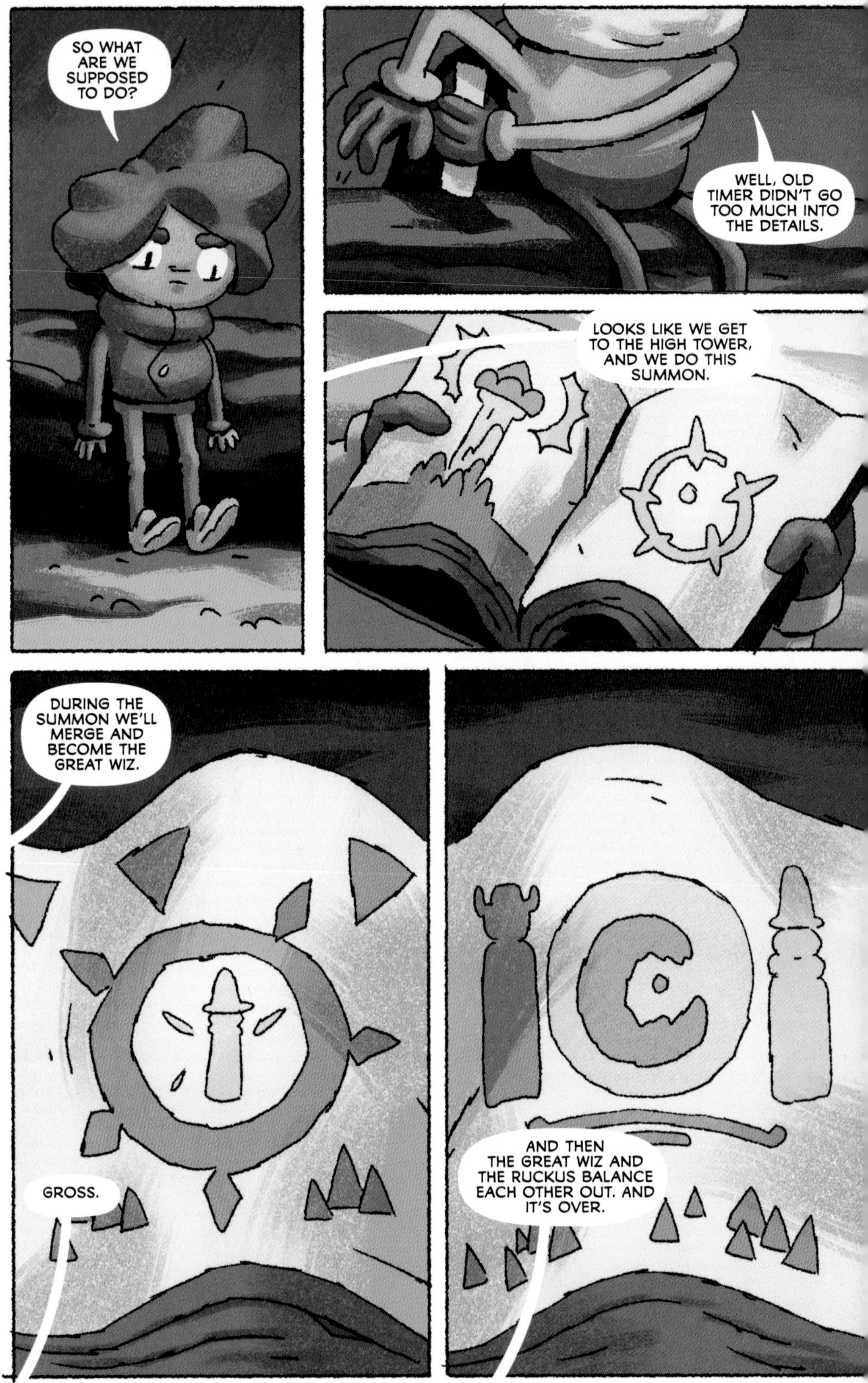
SO WHAT ARE WE SUPPOSED TO DO?
WELL, OLD TIMER DIDN'T GO TOO MUCH INTO THE DETAILS.
LOOKS LIKE WE GET TO THE HIGH TOWER, AND WE DO THIS SUMMON.
DURING THE SUMMON WE'LL MERGE AND BECOME THE GREAT WIZ.
GROSS.
AND THEN THE GREAT WIZ AND THE RUCKUS BALANCE EACH OTHER OUT. AND IT'S OVER.

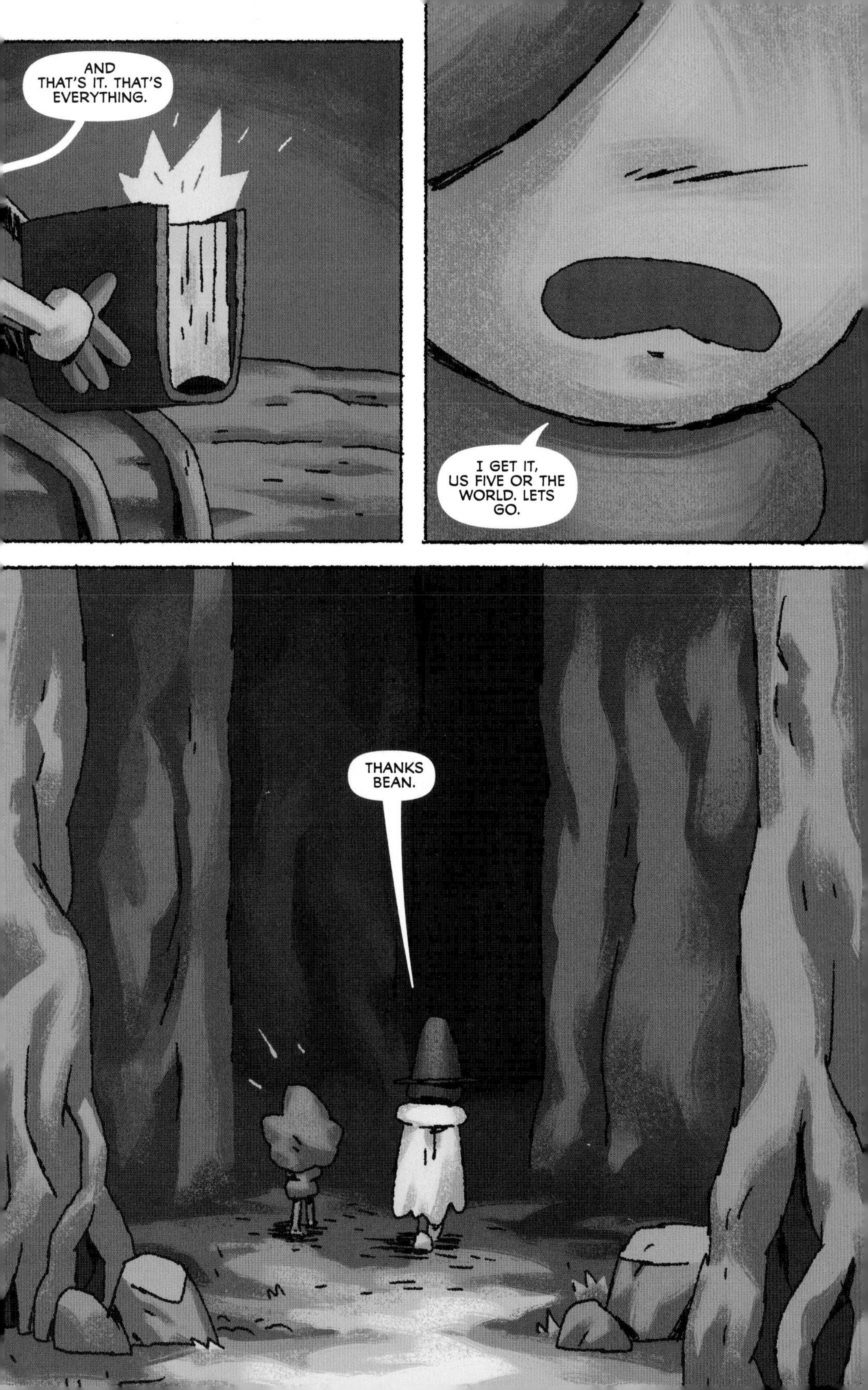
AND THAT'S IT. THAT'S EVERYTHING.
I GET IT, US FIVE OR THE WORLD. LETS GO.
THANKS BEAN.

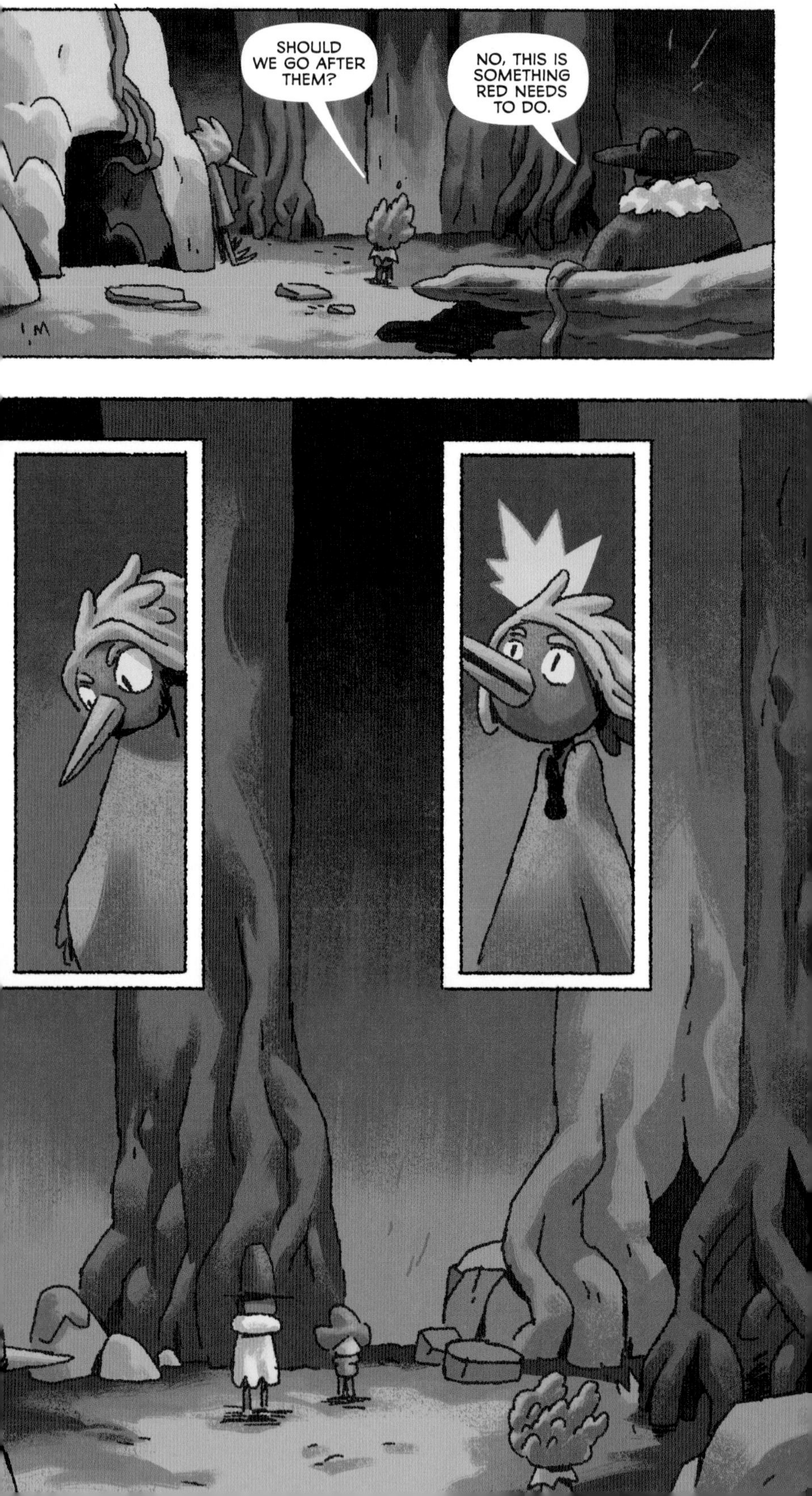
SHOULD WE GO AFTER THEM?
NO, THIS IS SOMETHING RED NEEDS TO DO.

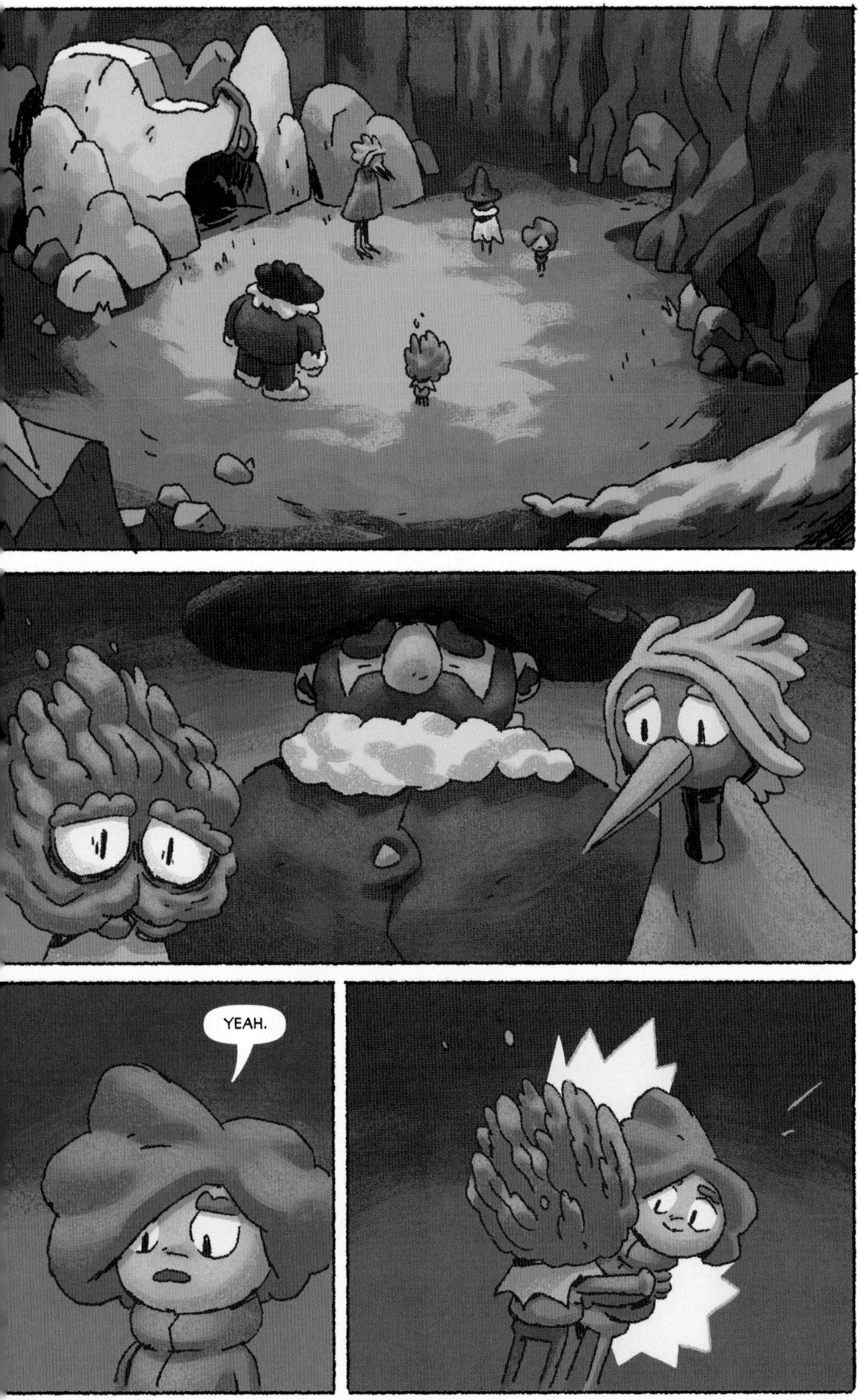
YEAH.

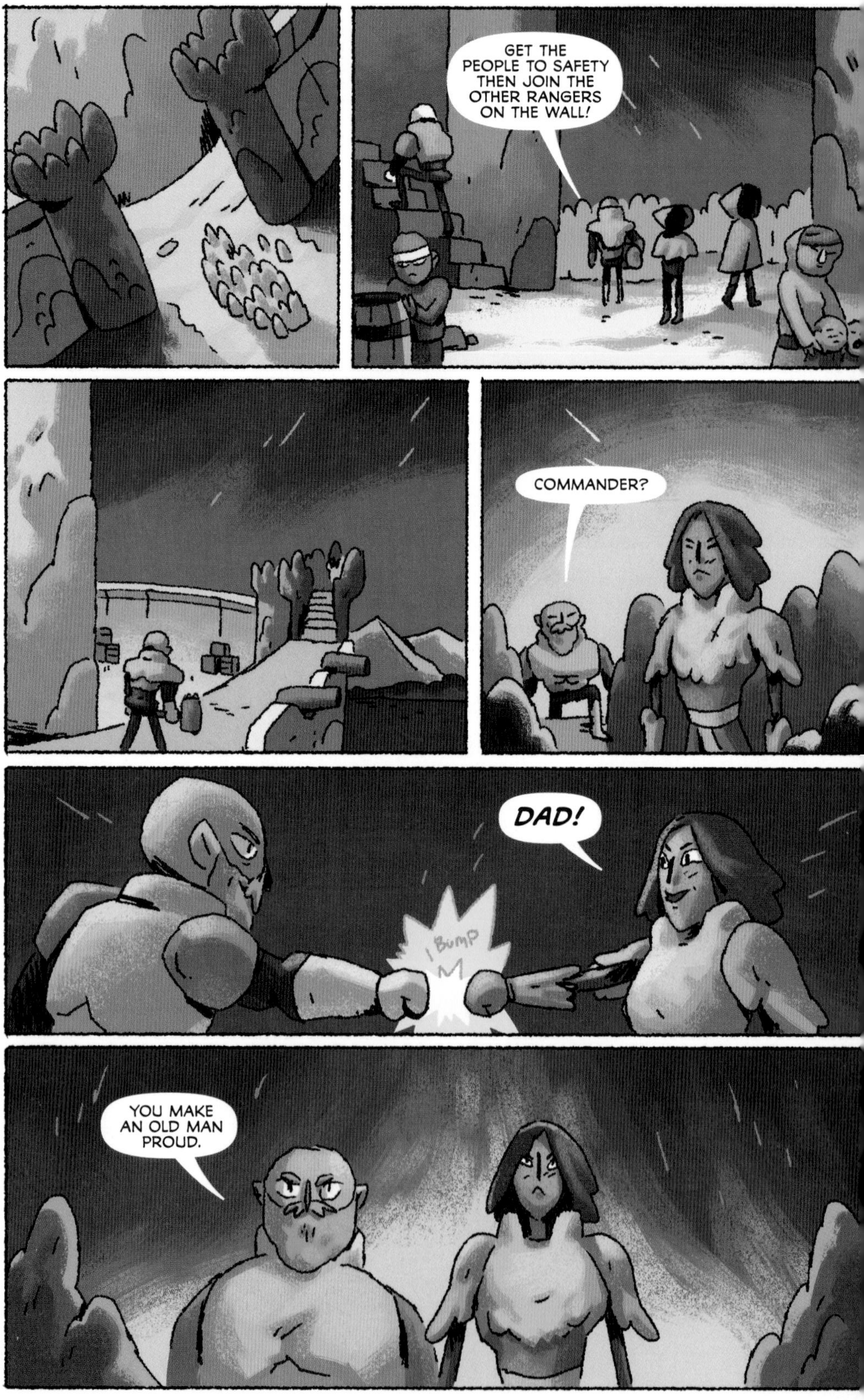
GET THE PEOPLE TO SAFETY THEN JOIN THE OTHER RANGERS ON THE WALL!
COMMANDER?
DAD!
BUMP
YOU MAKE AN OLD MAN PROUD.

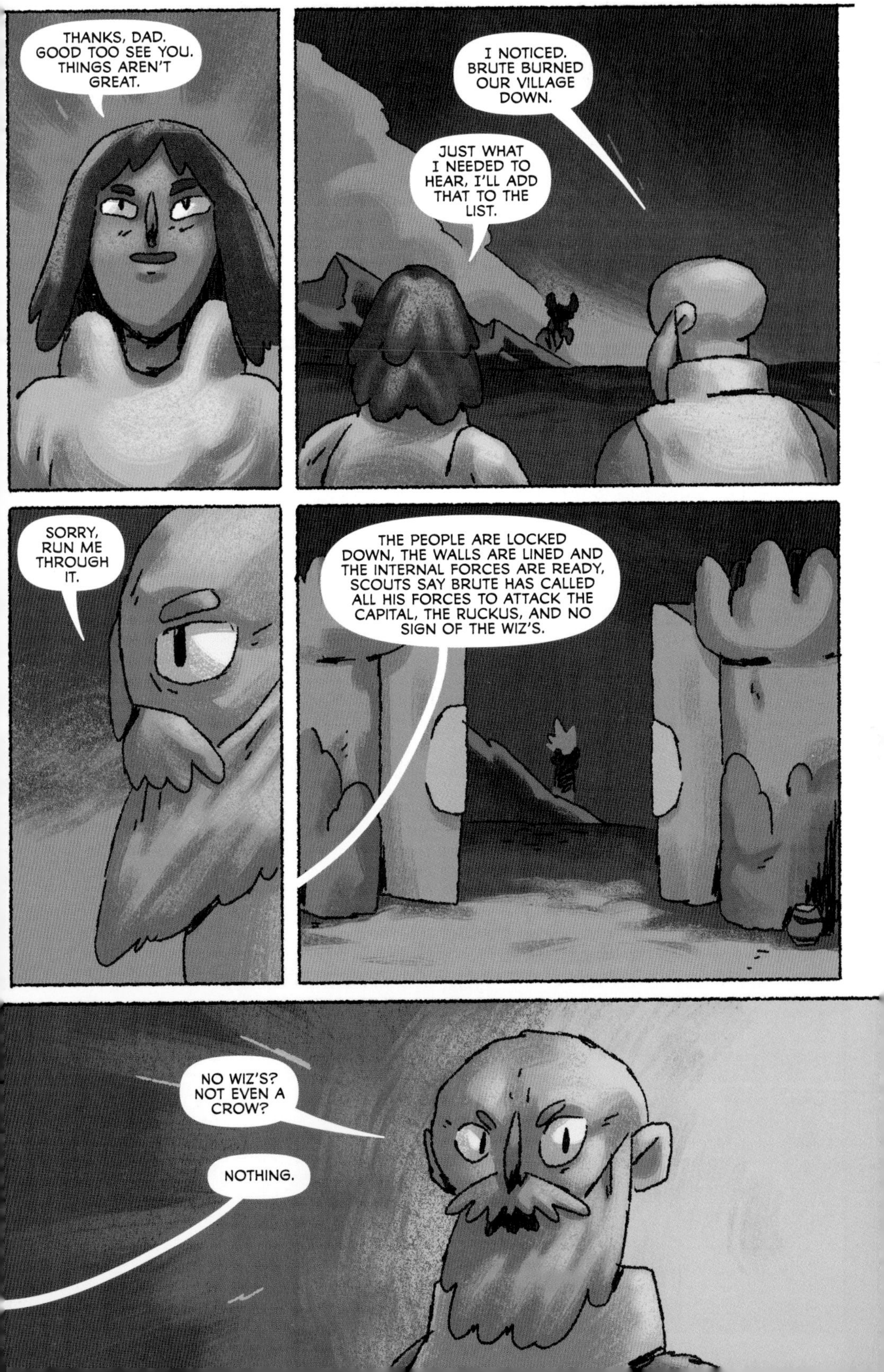
THANKS, DAD. GOOD TOO SEE YOU. THINGS AREN'T GREAT.
I NOTICED. BRUTE BURNED OUR VILLAGE DOWN.
JUST WHAT I NEEDED TO HEAR, I'LL ADD THAT TO THE LIST.
SORRY, RUN ME THROUGH IT.
THE PEOPLE ARE LOCKED DOWN, THE WALLS ARE LINED AND THE INTERNAL FORCES ARE READY, SCOUTS SAY BRUTE HAS CALLED ALL HIS FORCES TO ATTACK THE CAPITAL, THE RUCKUS, AND NO SIGN OF THE WIZ'S.
NO WIZ'S? NOT EVEN A CROW?
NOTHING.

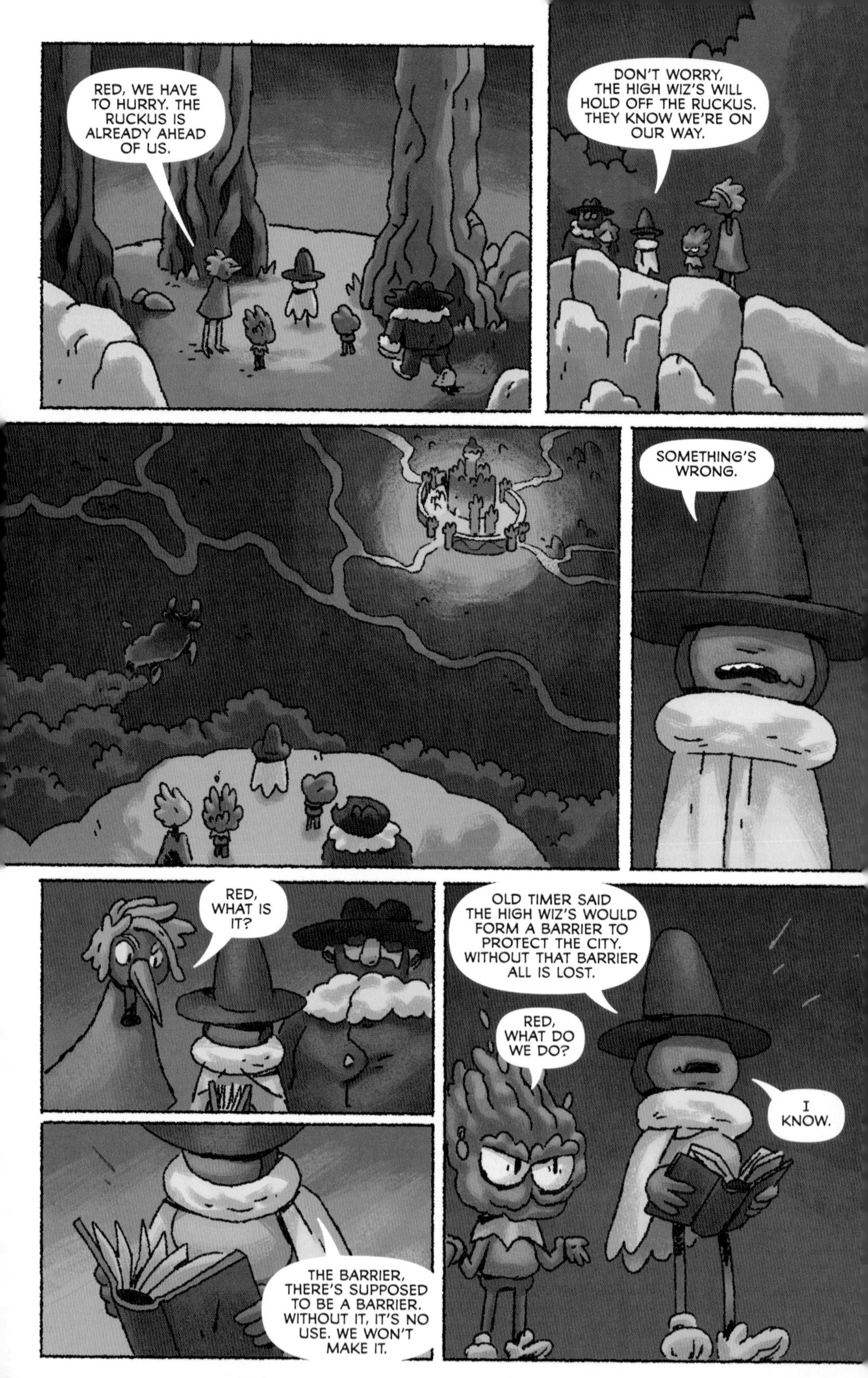
RED, WE HAVE TO HURRY. THE RUCKUS IS ALREADY AHEAD OF US.
DON'T WORRY, THE HIGH WIZ'S WILL HOLD OFF THE RUCKUS. THEY KNOW WE'RE ON OUR WAY.
SOMETHING'S WRONG.
RED, WHAT IS IT?
THE BARRIER, THERE'S SUPPOSED TO BE A BARRIER. WITHOUT IT, IT'S NO USE. WE WON'T MAKE IT.
OLD TIMER SAID THE HIGH WIZ'S WOULD FORM A BARRIER TO PROTECT THE CITY. WITHOUT THAT BARRIER ALL IS LOST.
RED, WHAT DO WE DO?
I KNOW.

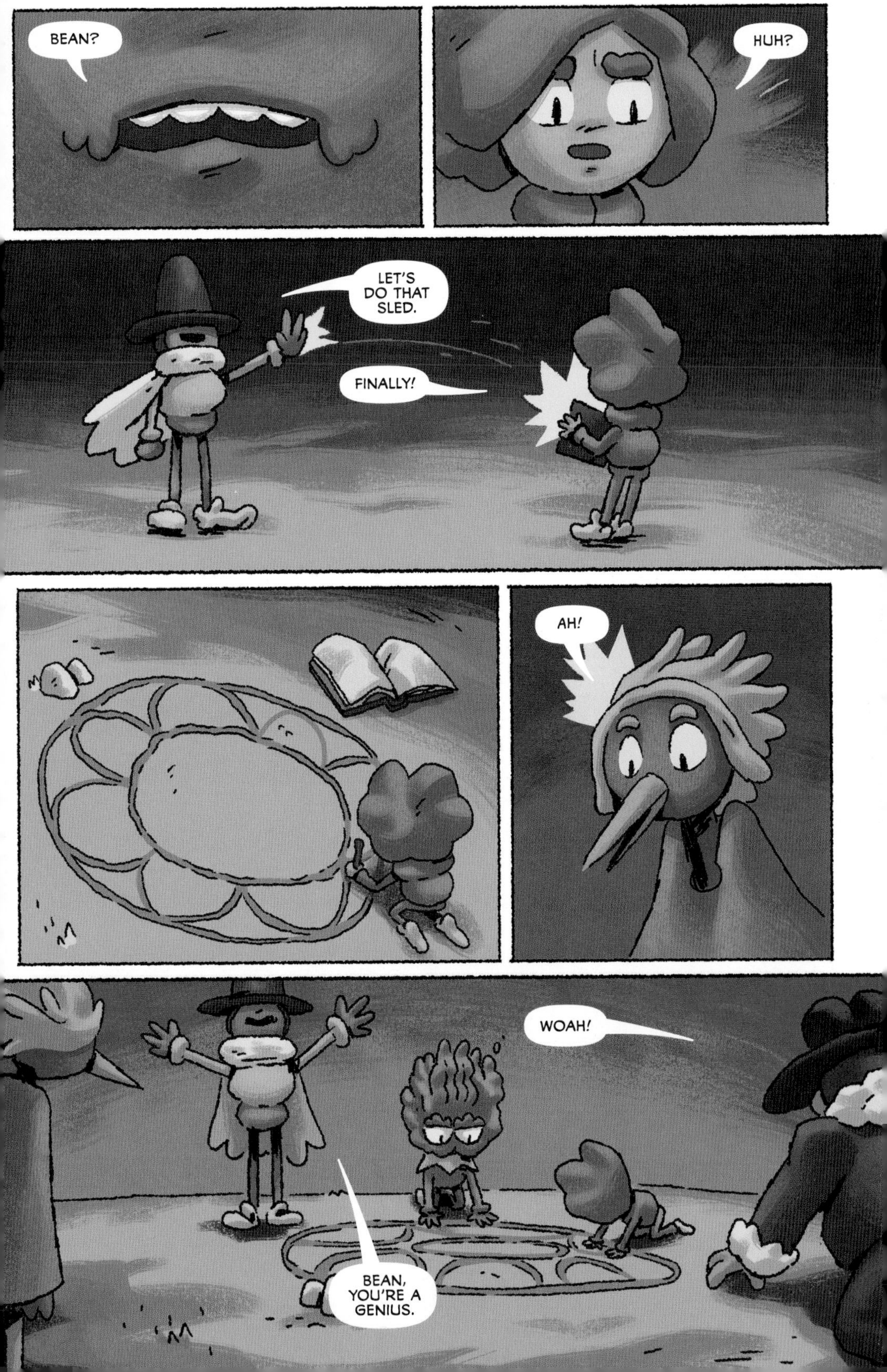
BEAN?
HUH?
LET'S DO THAT SLED.
FINALLY!
AH!
WOAH!
BEAN, YOU'RE A GENIUS.

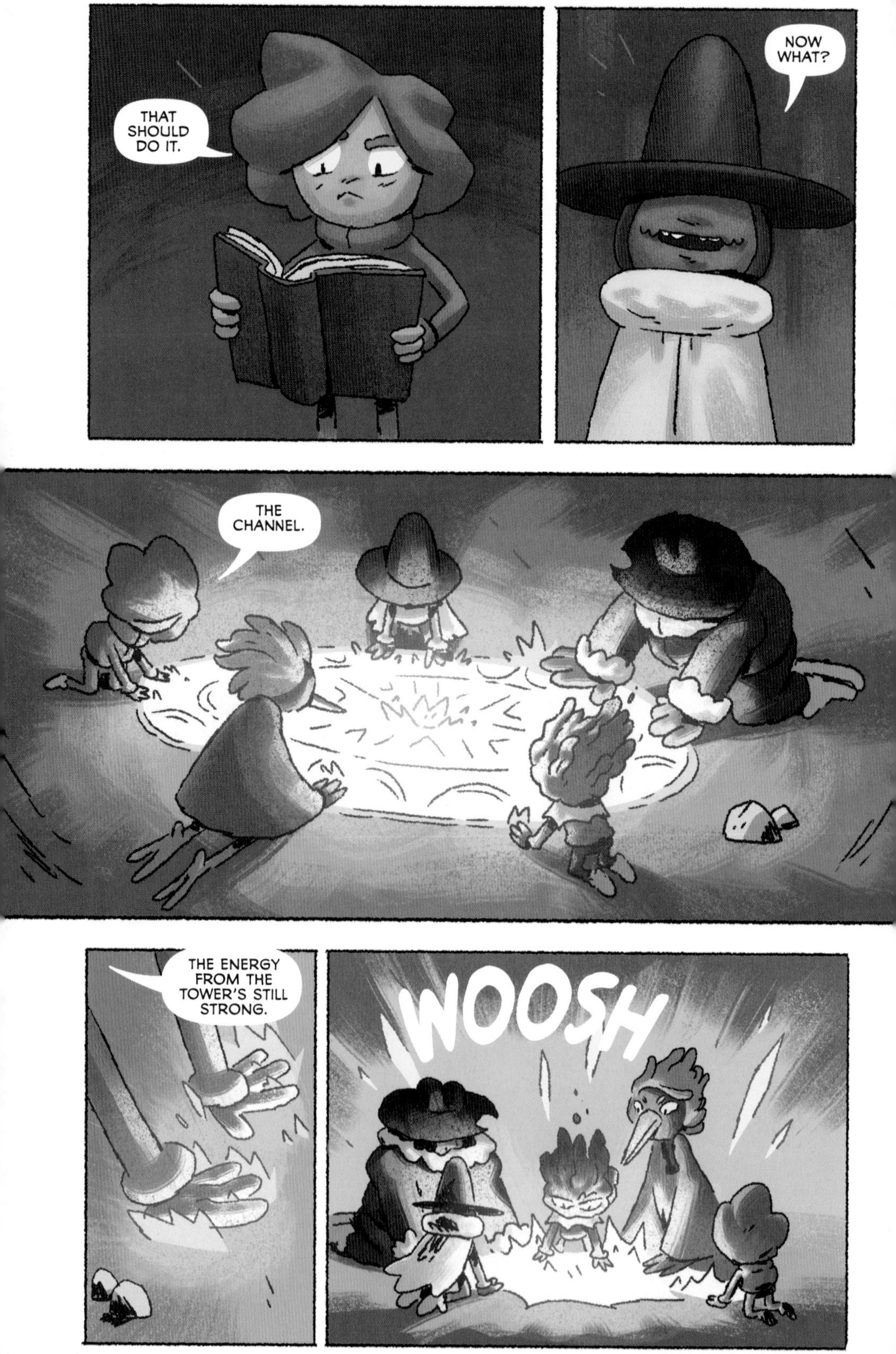
THAT SHOULD DO IT.
NOW WHAT?
THE CHANNEL.
THE ENERGY FROM THE TOWER'S STILL STRONG.
WOOSH

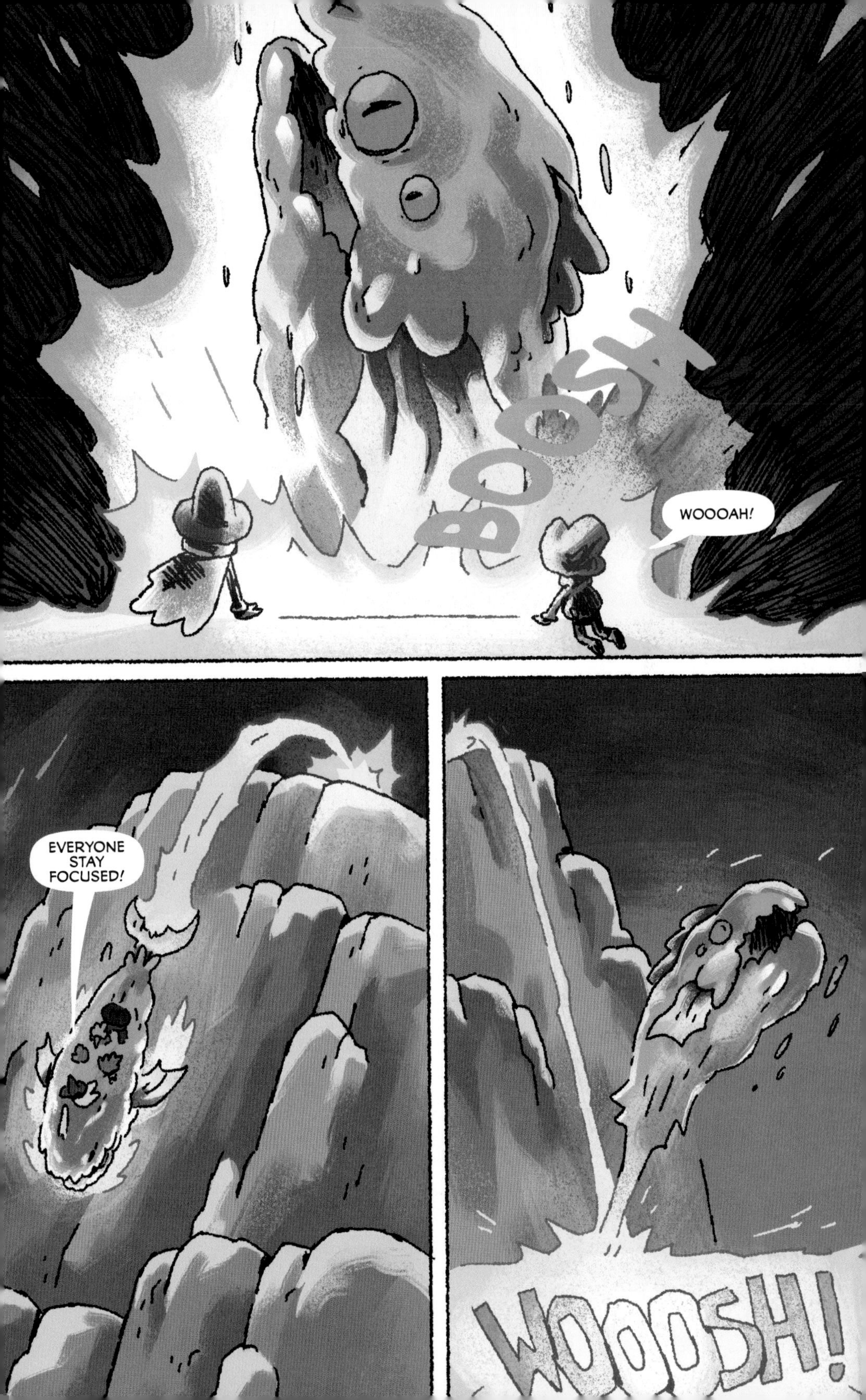
BOOSH
WOOOAH!
EVERYONE STAY FOCUSED!
WOOOSH!

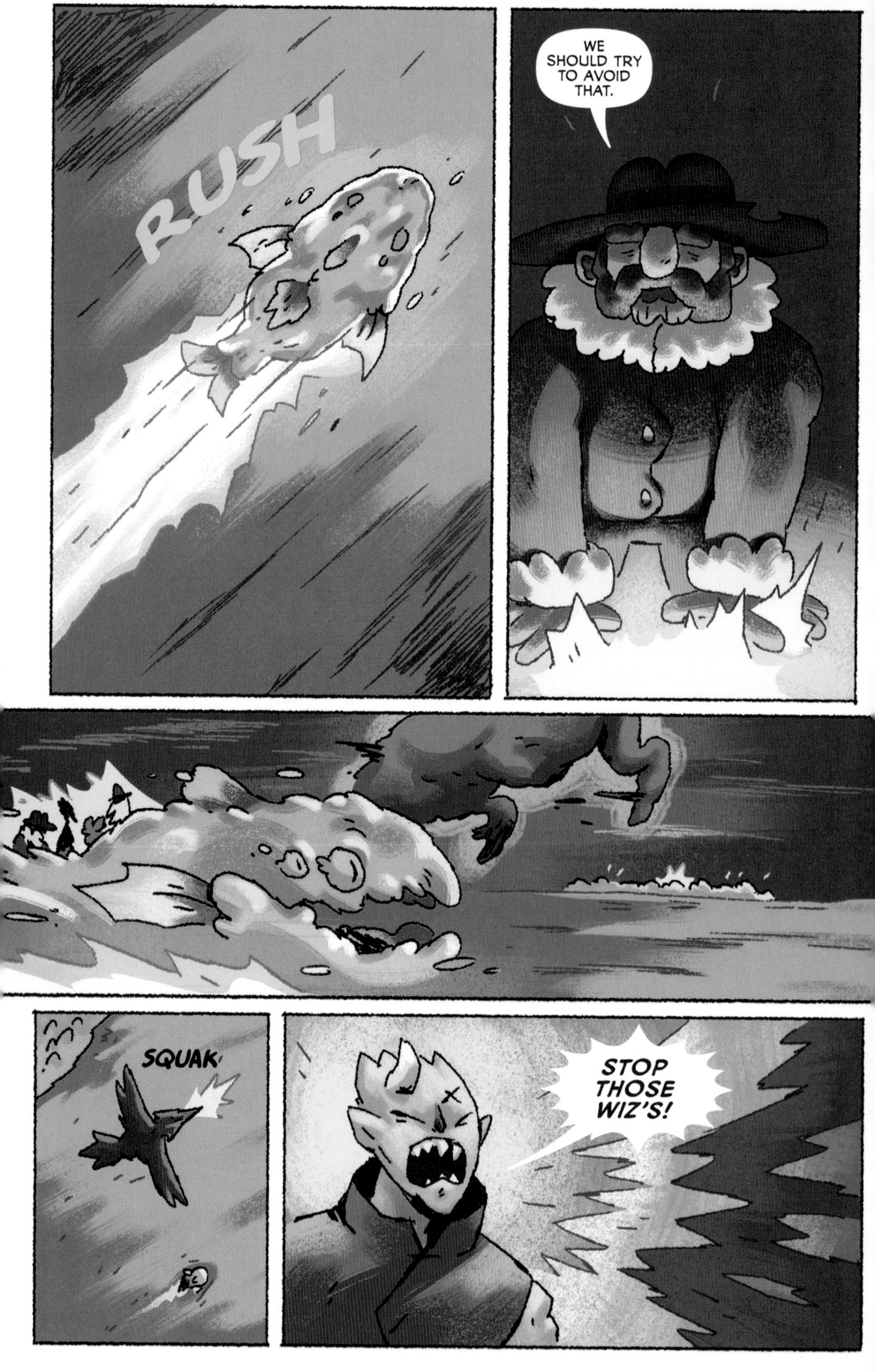
RUSH
WE SHOULD TRY TO AVOID THAT.
SQUAK
STOP THOSE WIZ'S!

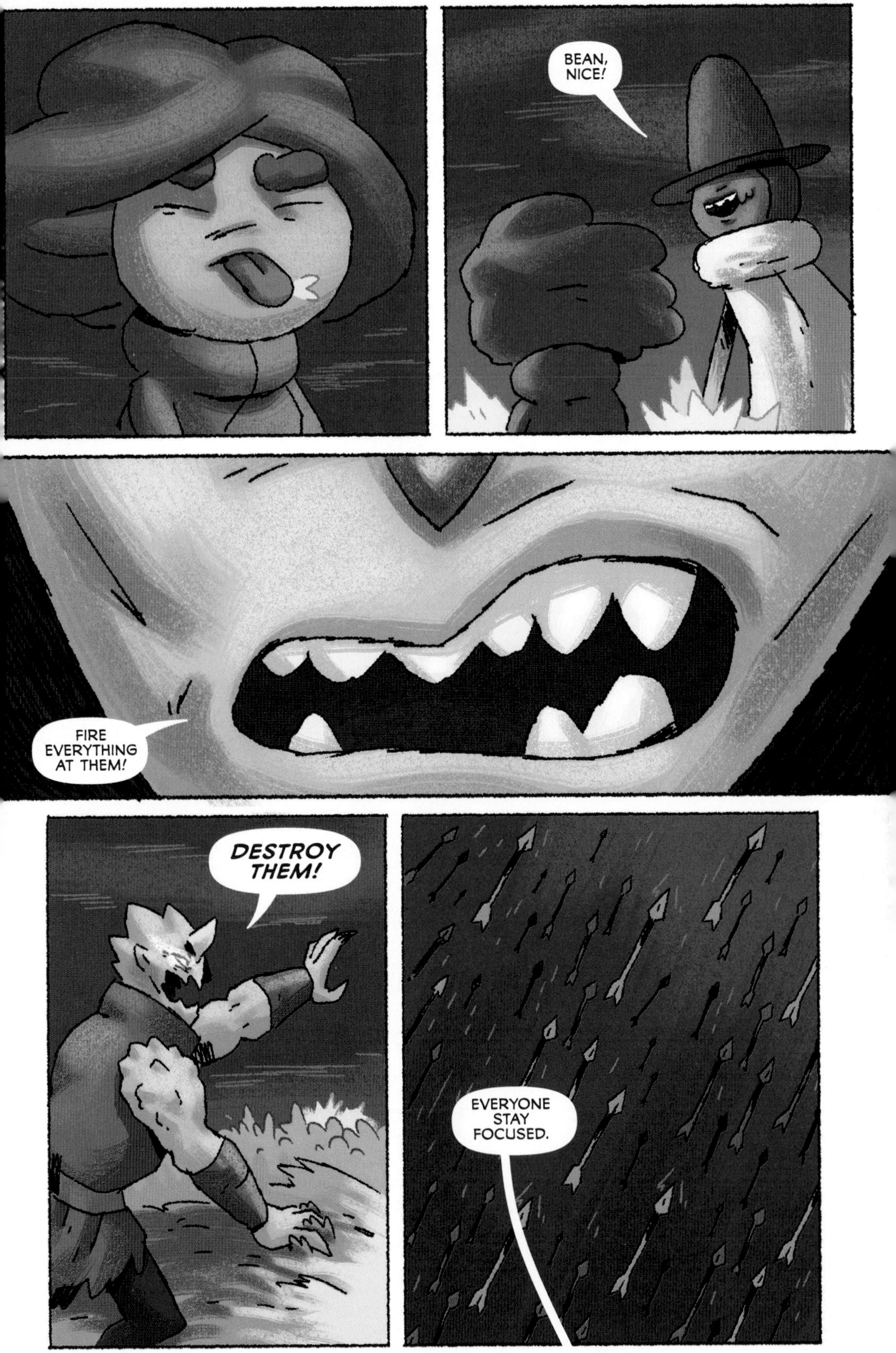
BEAN, NICE!
FIRE EVERYTHING AT THEM!
DESTROY THEM!
EVERYONE STAY FOCUSED.

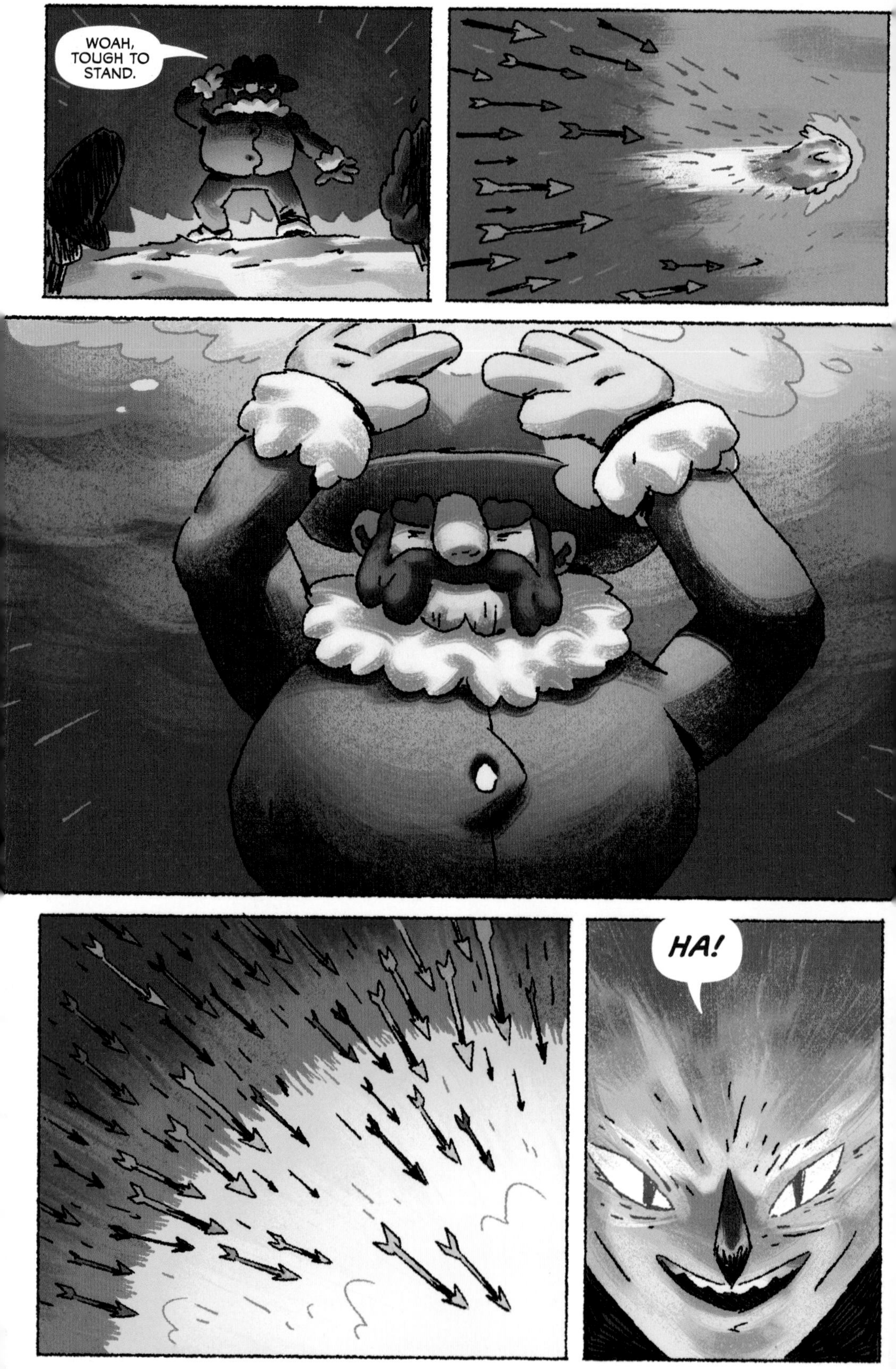
WOAH, TOUGH TO STAND.
HA!

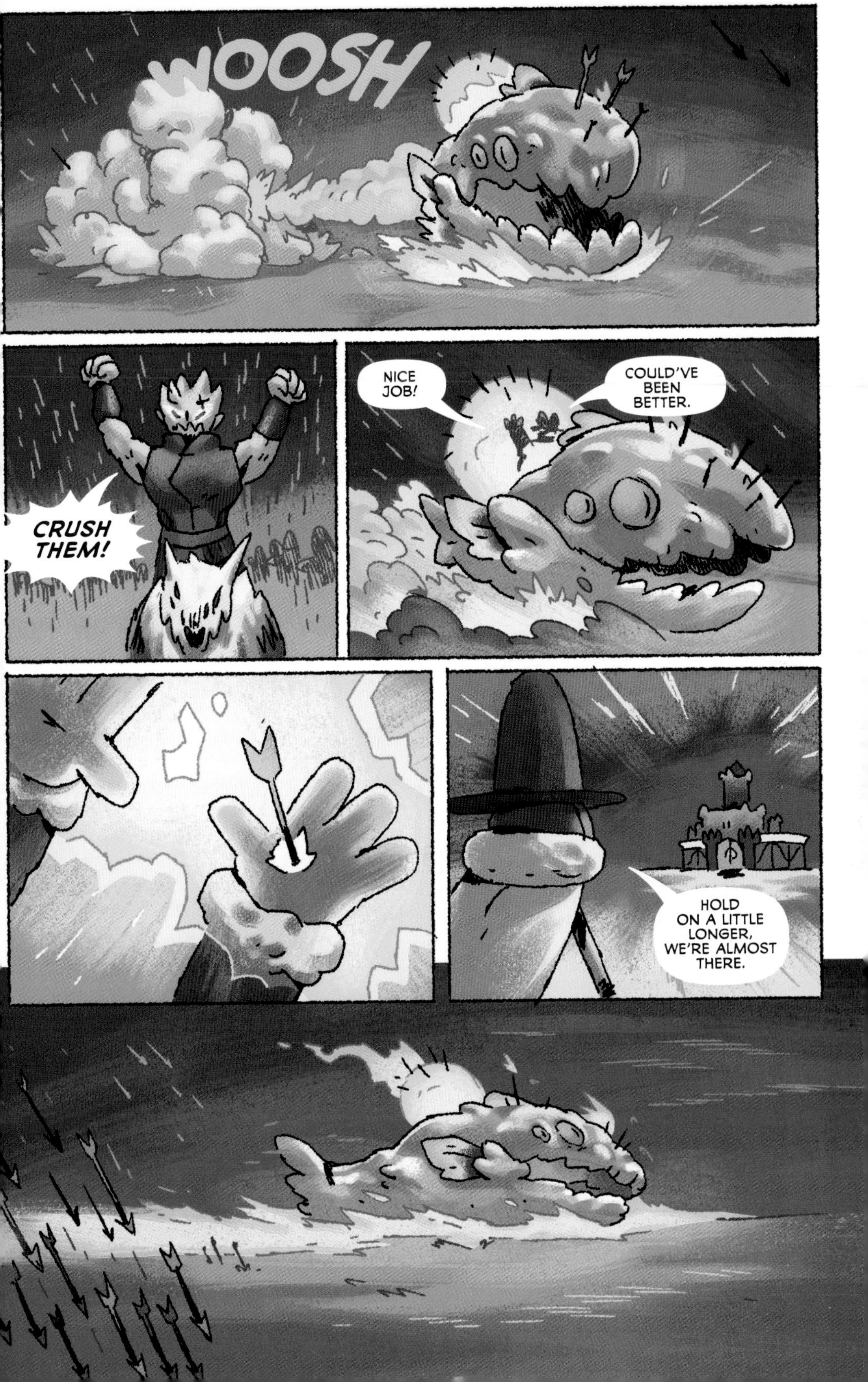
WOOSH
CRUSH THEM!
NICE JOB!
COULD'VE BEEN BETTER.
HOLD ON A LITTLE LONGER, WE'RE ALMOST THERE.

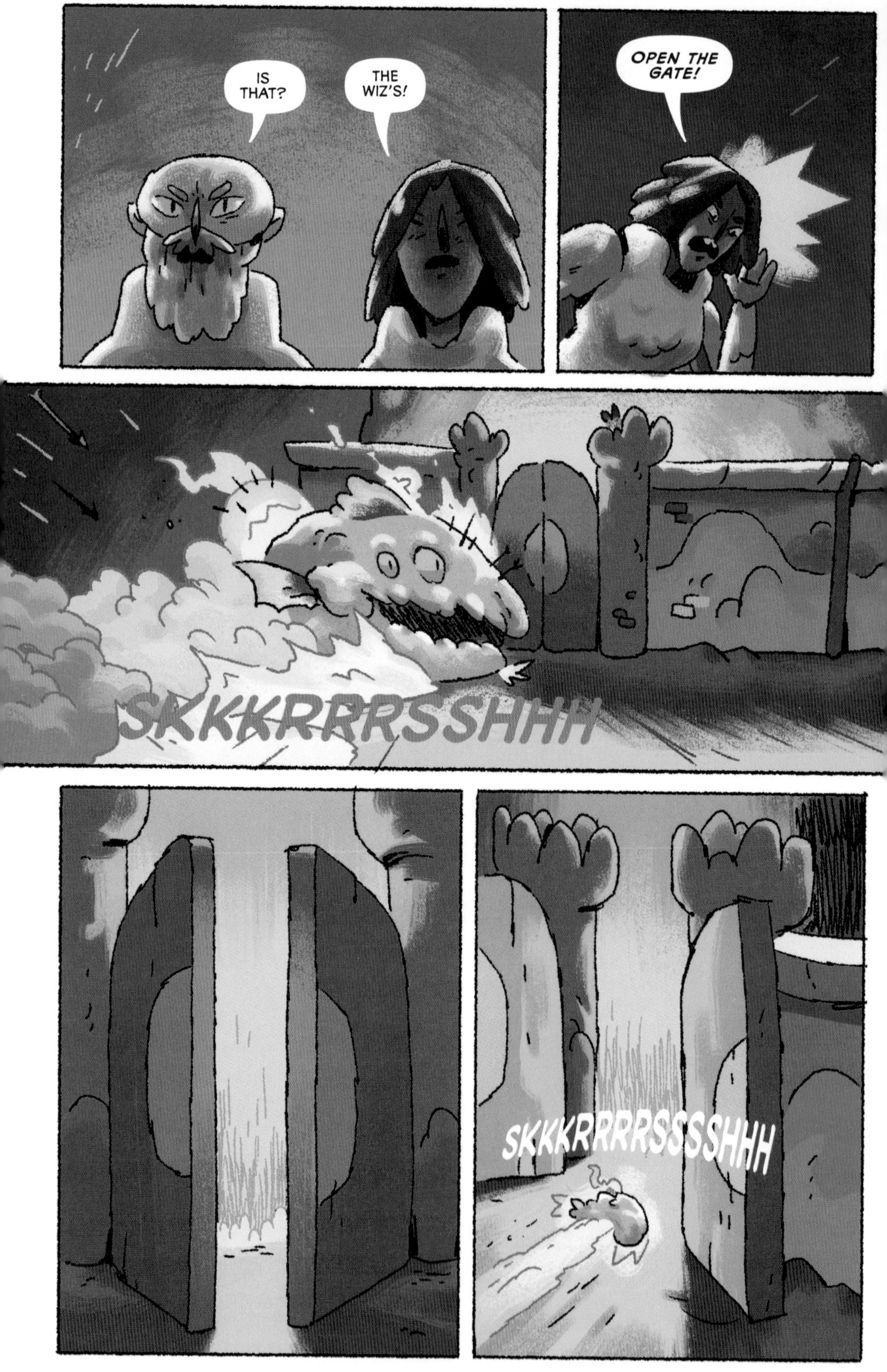
IS THAT?
THE WIZ'S!
OPEN THE GATE!
SKKKRRRRSSHHH
SKKKRRRRSSSSHHH

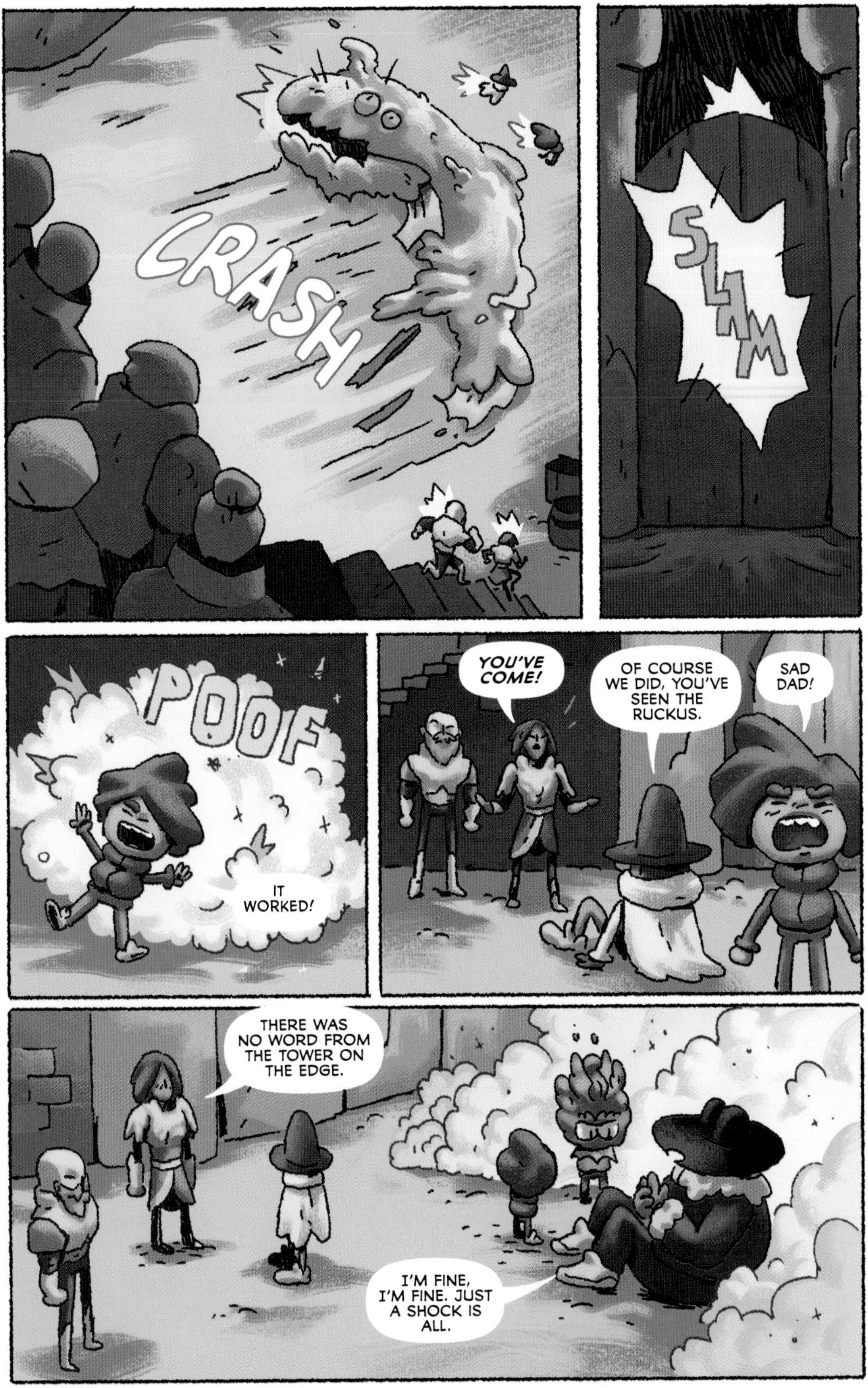
CRASH
SLAM
POOF
IT WORKED!
YOU'VE COME!
OF COURSE WE DID, YOU'VE SEEN THE RUCKUS.
SAD DAD!
THERE WAS NO WORD FROM THE TOWER ON THE EDGE.
I'M FINE, I'M FINE. JUST A SHOCK IS ALL.

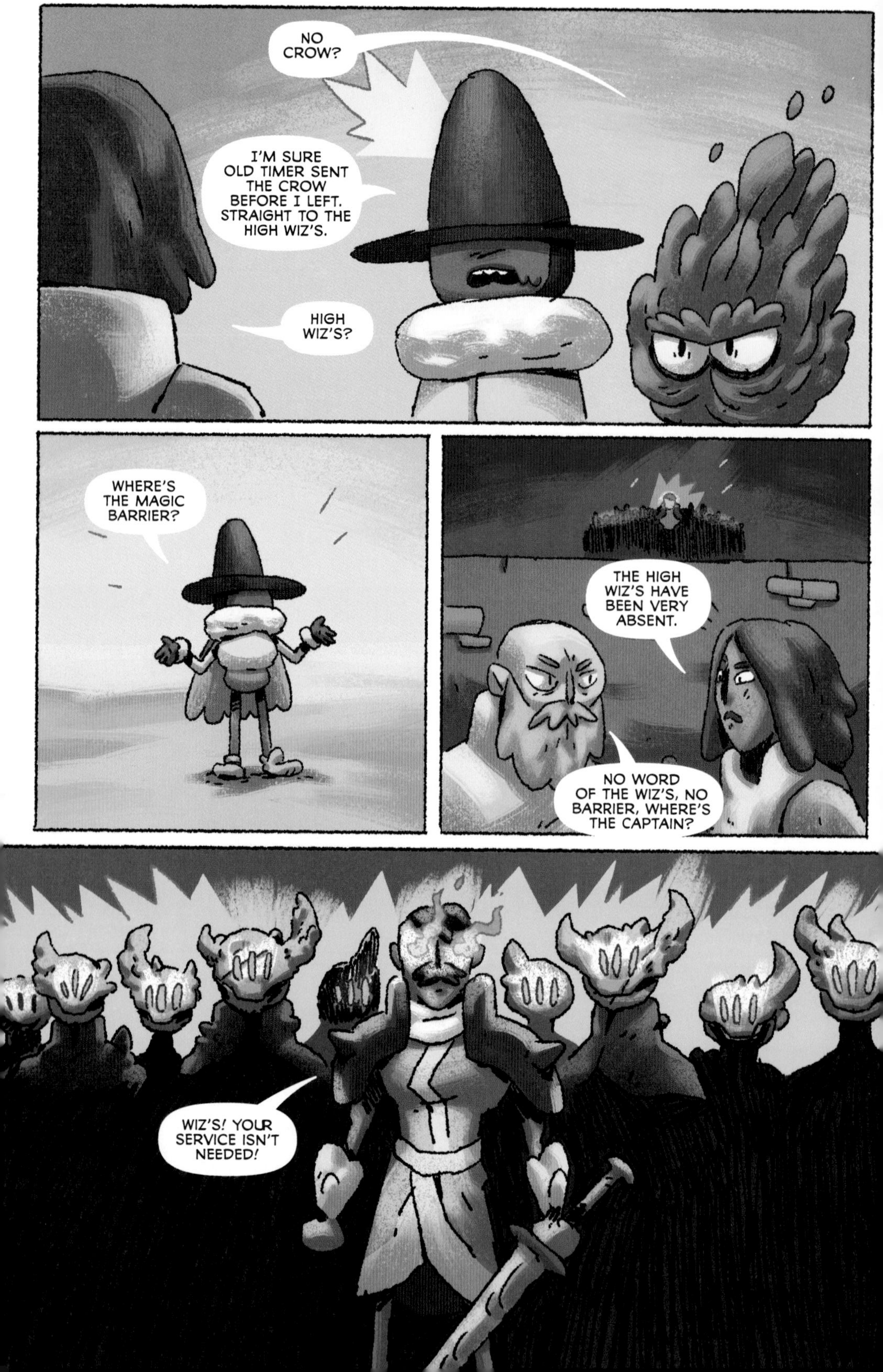
NO CROW?
I'M SURE OLD TIMER SENT THE CROW BEFORE I LEFT. STRAIGHT TO THE HIGH WIZ'S.
HIGH WIZ'S?
WHERE'S THE MAGIC BARRIER?
THE HIGH WIZ'S HAVE BEEN VERY ABSENT.
NO WORD OF THE WIZ'S, NO BARRIER, WHERE'S THE CAPTAIN?
WIZ'S! YOUR SERVICE ISN'T NEEDED!

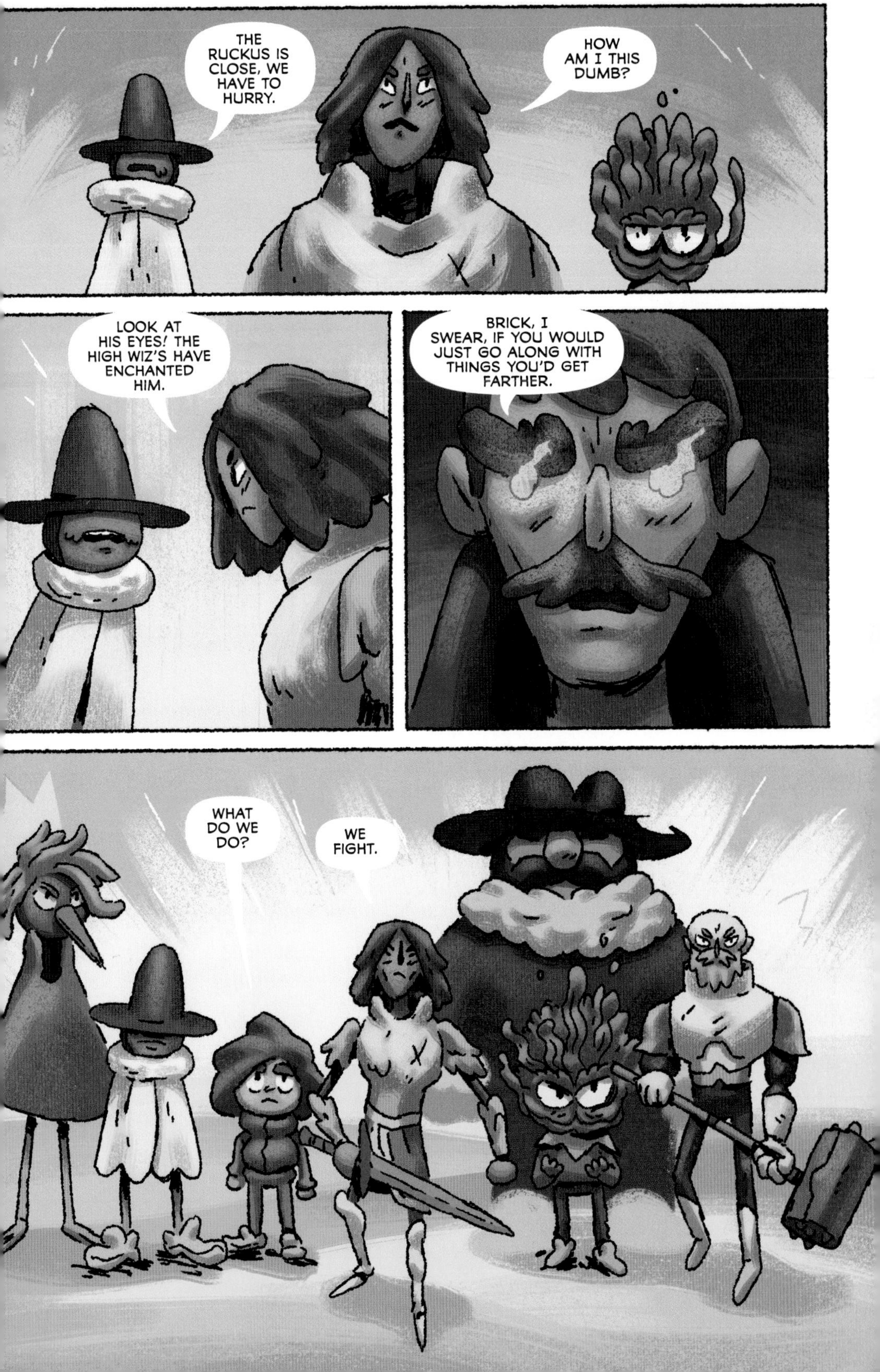
THE RUCKUS IS CLOSE, WE HAVE TO HURRY.
HOW AM I THIS DUMB?
LOOK AT HIS EYES! THE HIGH WIZ'S HAVE ENCHANTED HIM.
BRICK, I SWEAR, IF YOU WOULD JUST GO ALONG WITH THINGS YOU'D GET FARTHER.
WHAT DO WE DO?
WE FIGHT.

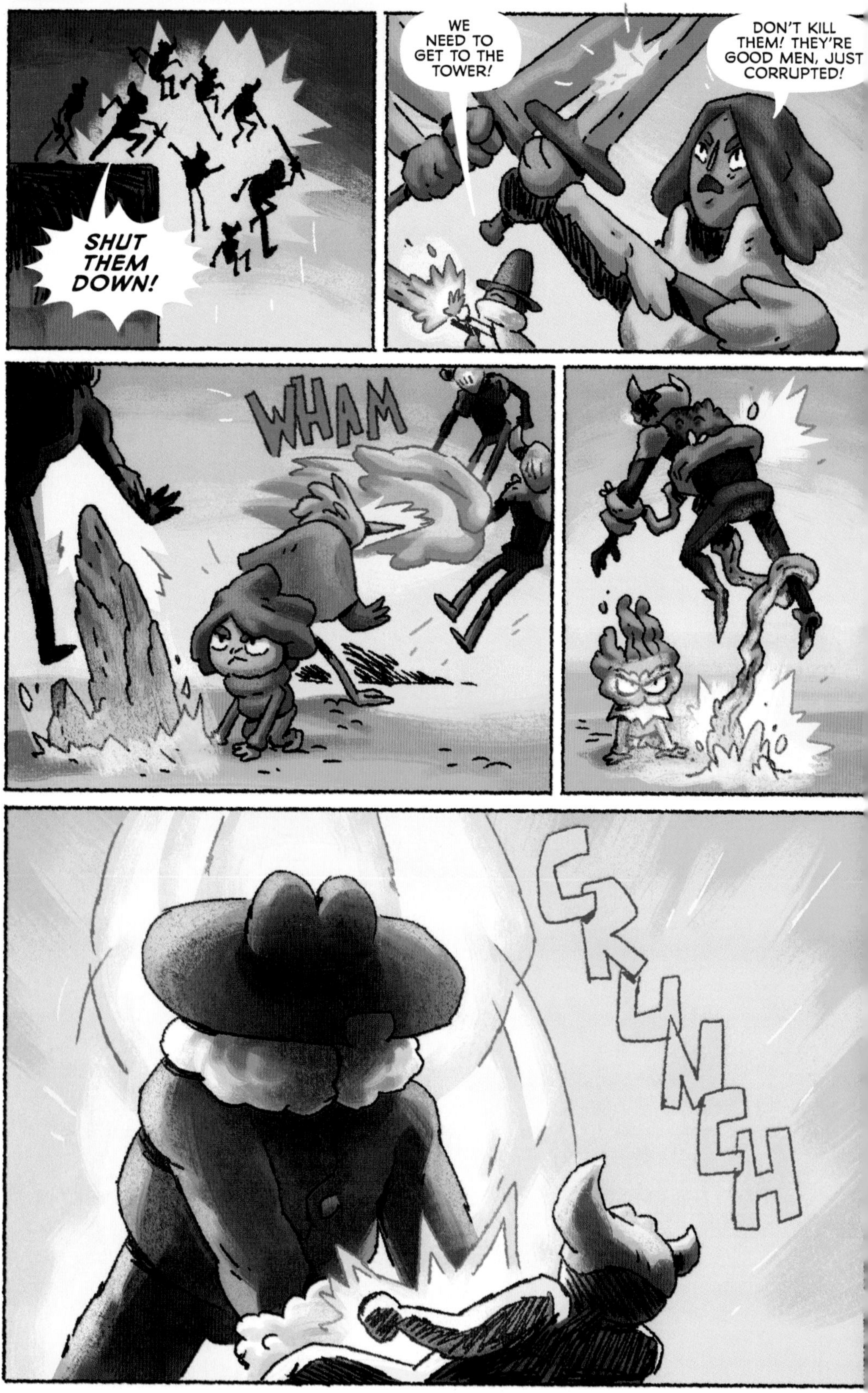
SHUT THEM DOWN!
WE NEED TO GET TO THE TOWER!
DON'T KILL THEM! THEY'RE GOOD MEN, JUST CORRUPTED!
WHAM
CRUNCH

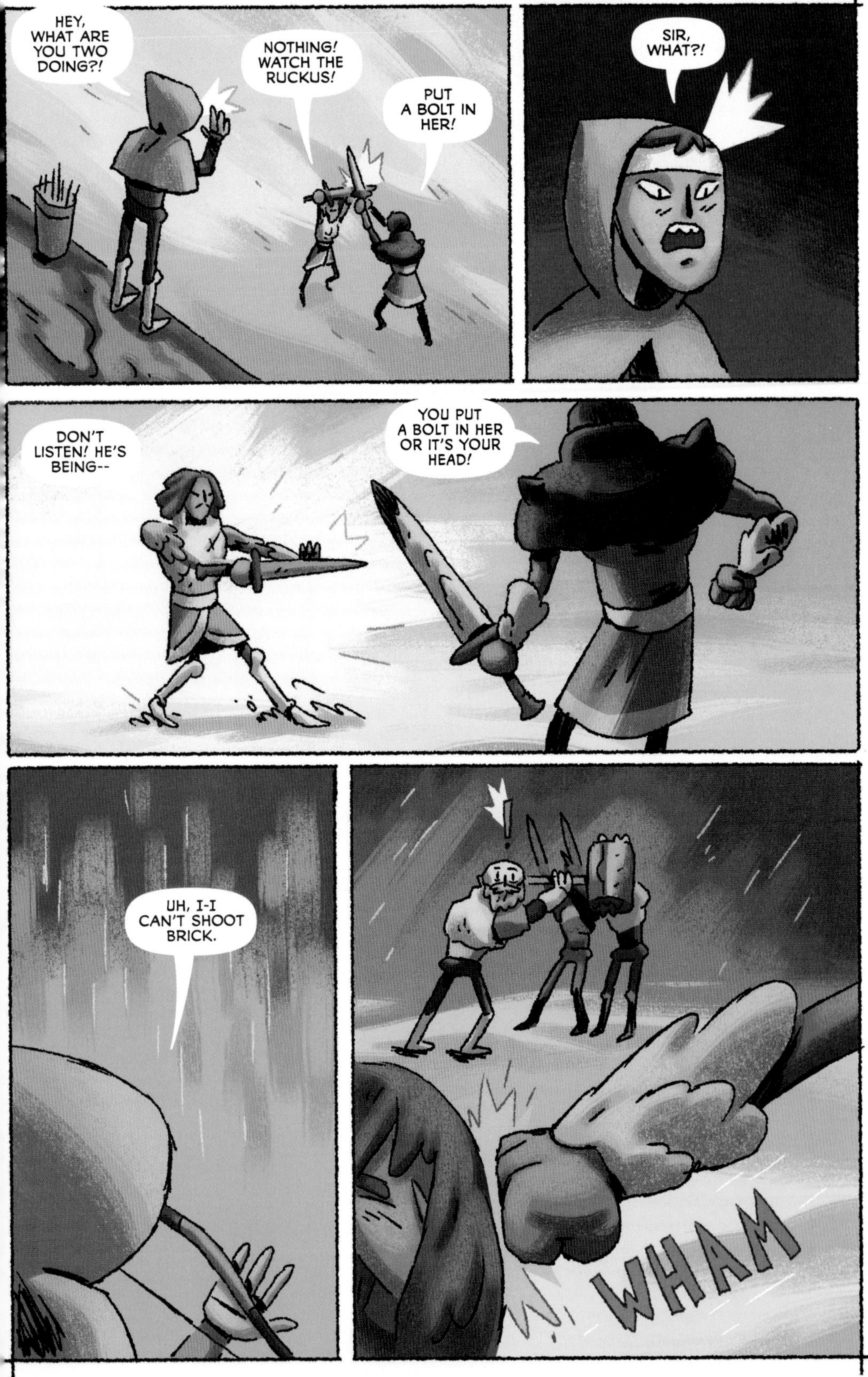
HEY, WHAT ARE YOU TWO DOING?!
NOTHING! WATCH THE RUCKUS!
PUT A BOLT IN HER!
SIR, WHAT?!
DON'T LISTEN! HE'S BEING--
YOU PUT A BOLT IN HER OR IT'S YOUR HEAD!
UH, I-I CAN'T SHOOT BRICK.
!
WHAM

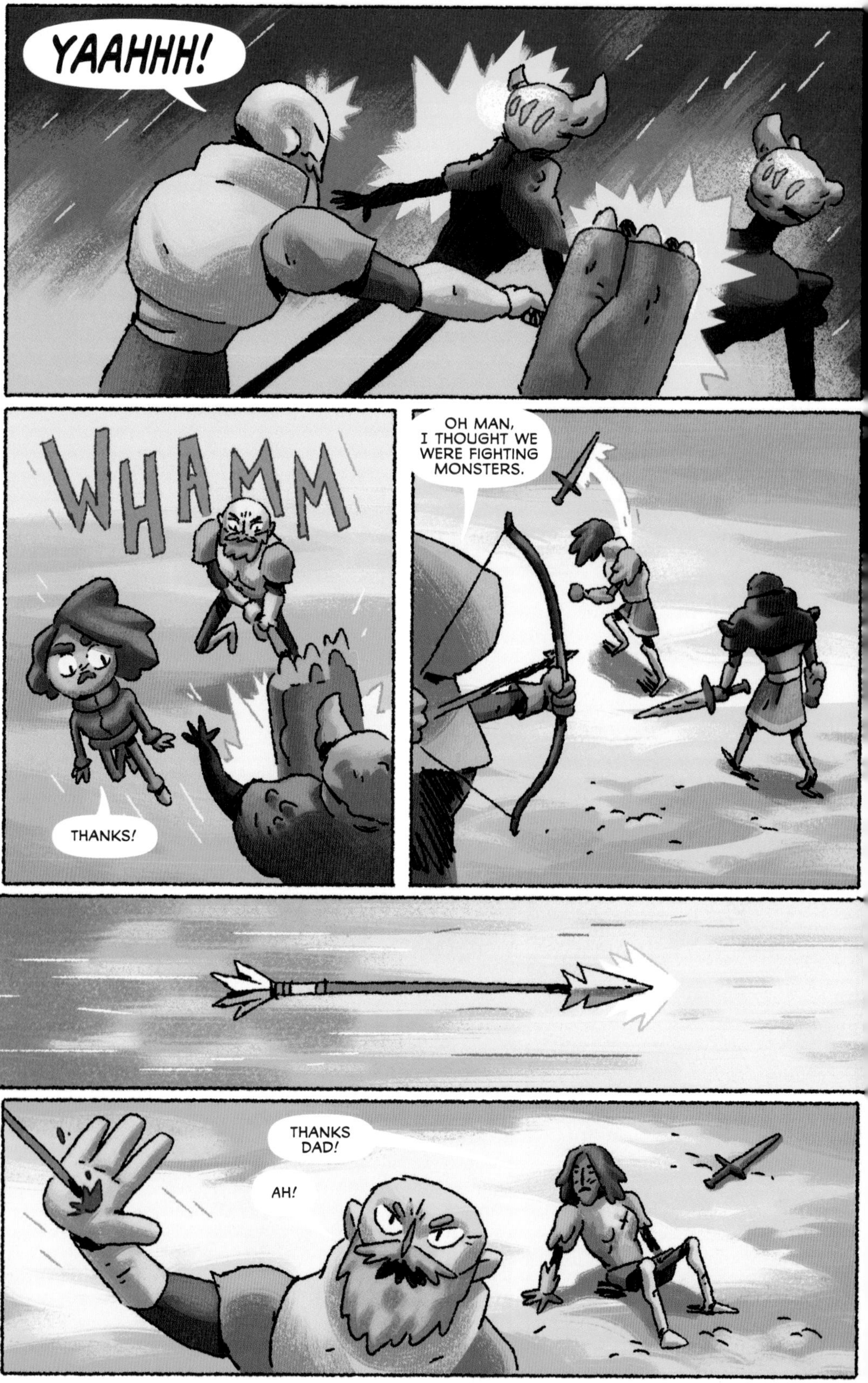
YAAHHH!
WHAMM
THANKS!
OH MAN, I THOUGHT WE WERE FIGHTING MONSTERS.
THANKS DAD!
AH!

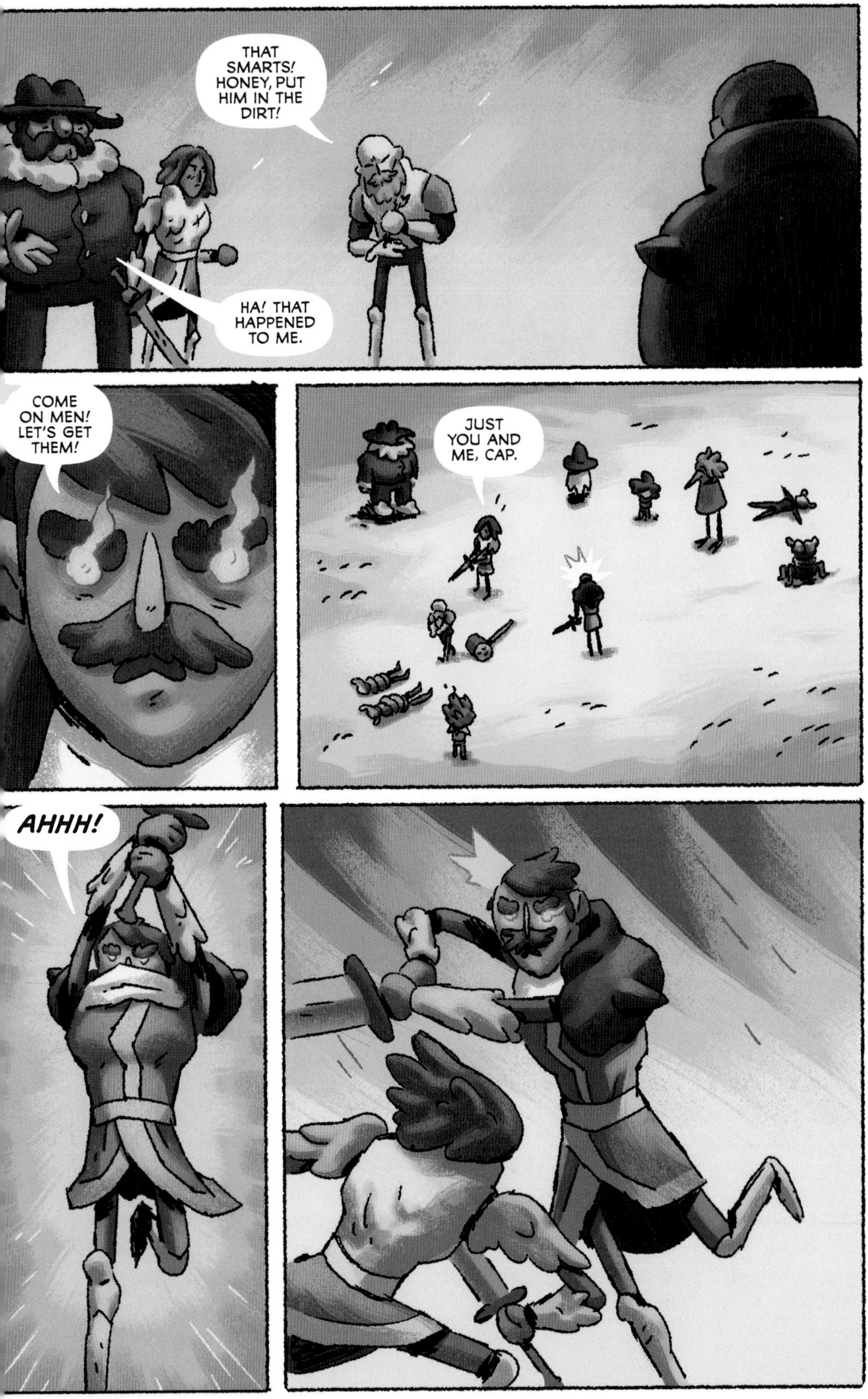
THAT SMARTS! HONEY, PUT HIM IN THE DIRT!
HA! THAT HAPPENED TO ME.
COME ON MEN! LET'S GET THEM!
JUST YOU AND ME, CAP.
AHHH!

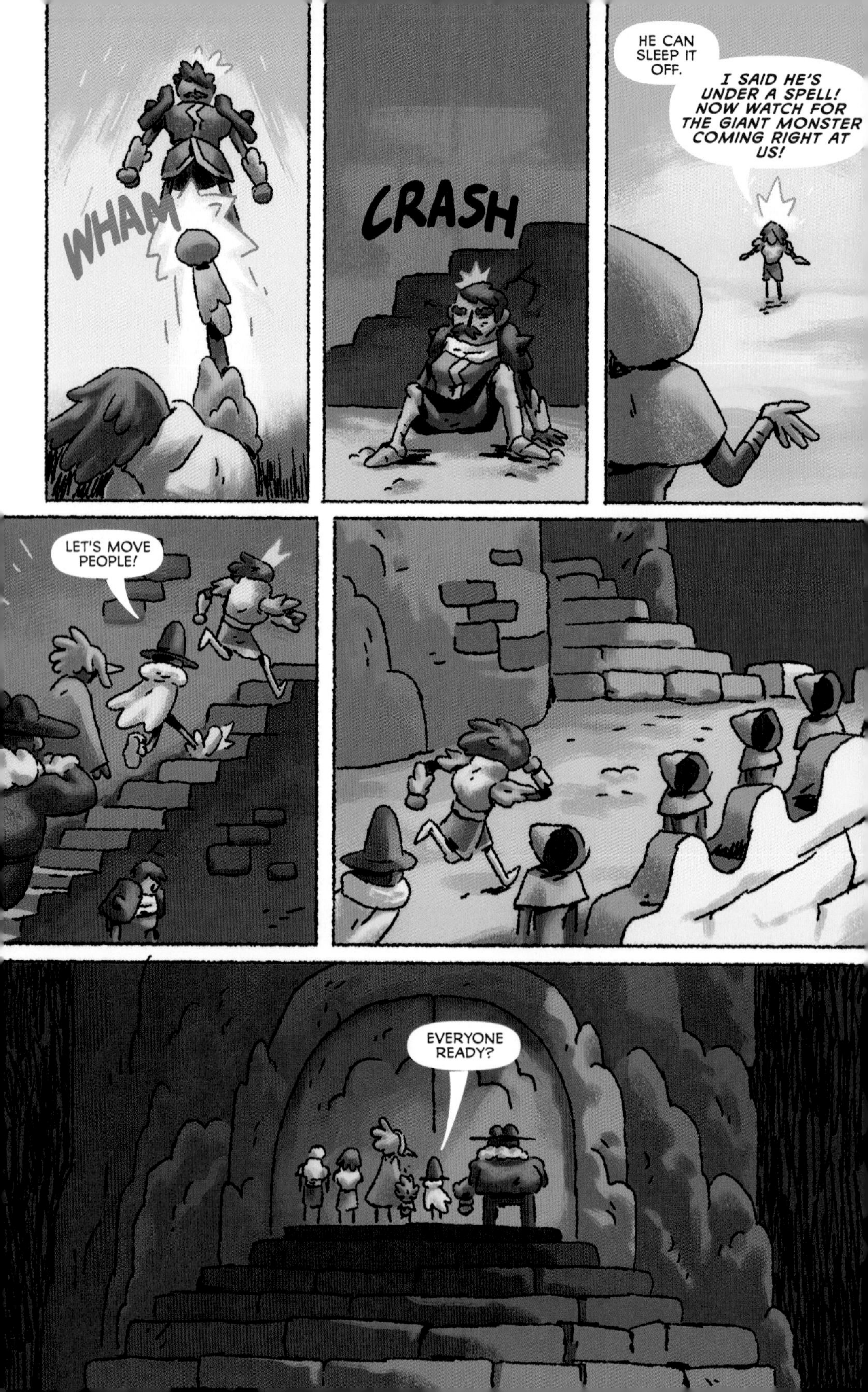
WHAM
CRASH
HE CAN SLEEP IT OFF.
I SAID HE'S UNDER A SPELL! NOW WATCH FOR THE GIANT MONSTER COMING RIGHT AT US!
LET'S MOVE PEOPLE!
EVERYONE READY?

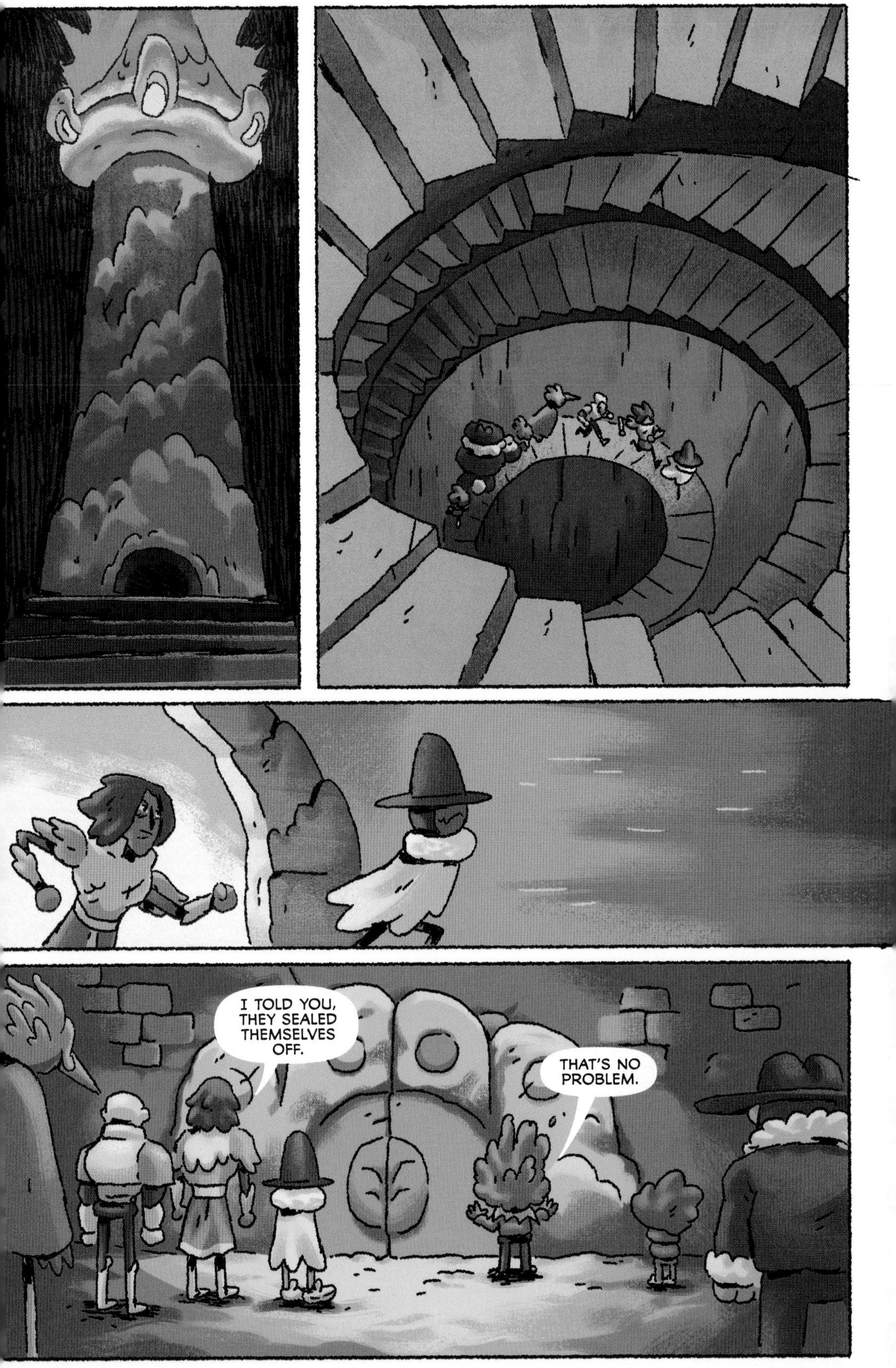
I TOLD YOU, THEY SEALED THEMSELVES OFF.
THAT'S NO PROBLEM.

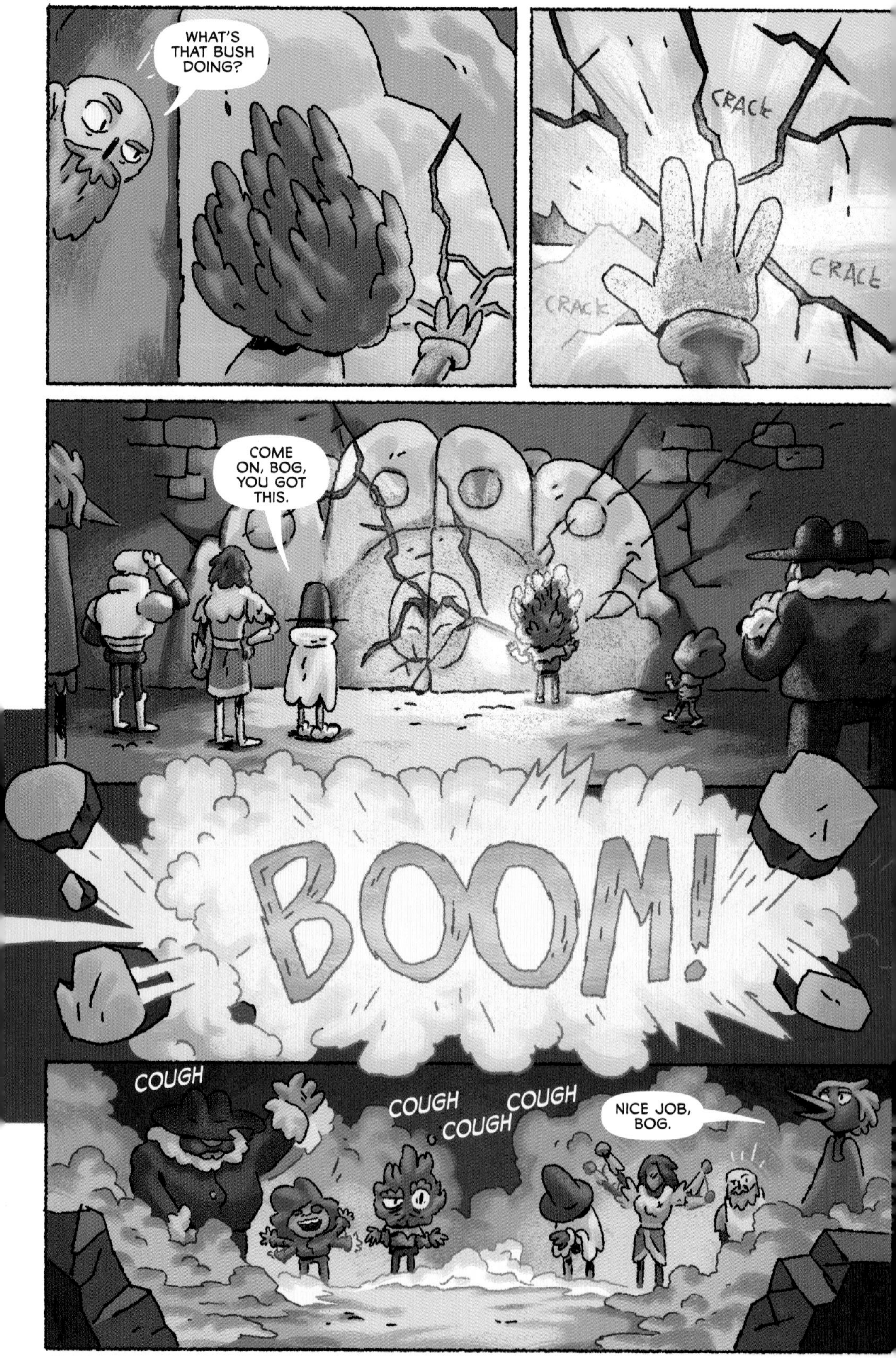
WHAT'S THAT BUSH DOING?
CRACK
CRACK
CRACK
COME ON, BOG, YOU GOT THIS.
BOOM!
COUGH
COUGH
COUGH
COUGH
NICE JOB, BOG.

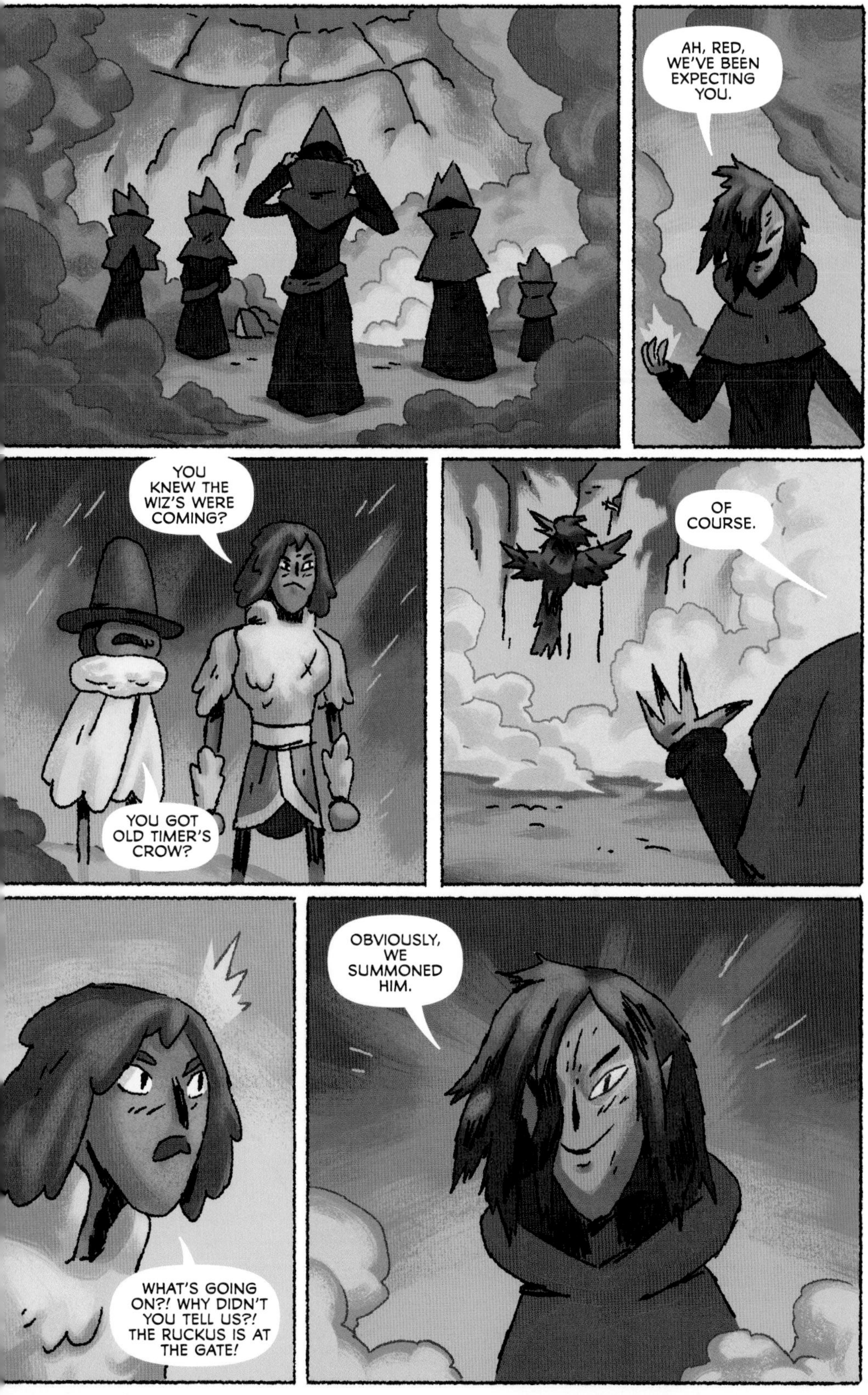
AH, RED, WE'VE BEEN EXPECTING YOU.
YOU KNEW THE WIZ'S WERE COMING?
YOU GOT OLD TIMER'S CROW?
OF COURSE.
WHAT'S GOING ON?! WHY DIDN'T YOU TELL US?! THE RUCKUS IS AT THE GATE!
OBVIOUSLY, WE SUMMONED HIM.

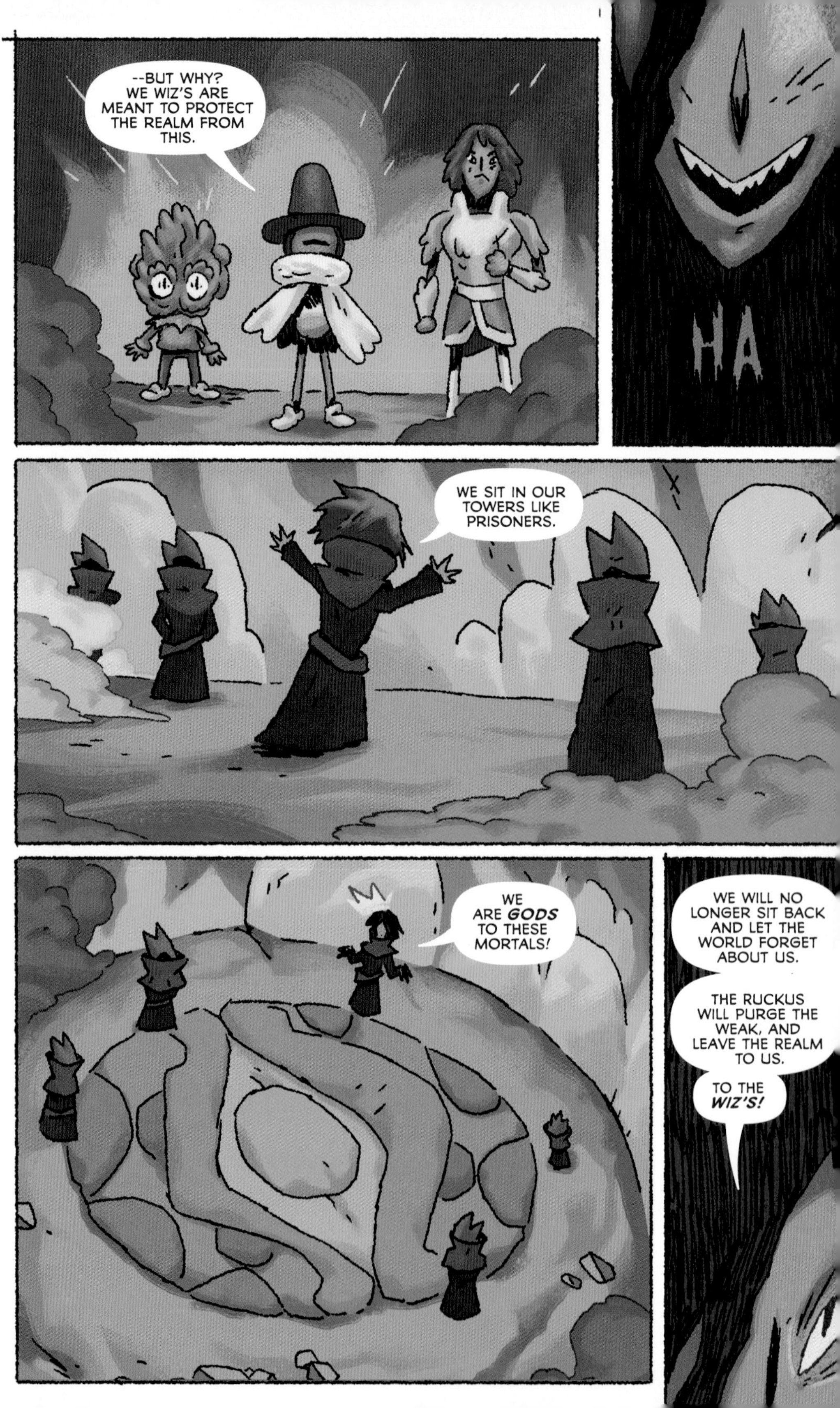
--BUT WHY? WE WIZ'S ARE MEANT TO PROTECT THE REALM FROM THIS.
HA
WE SIT IN OUR TOWERS LIKE PRISONERS.
WE ARE *GODS* TO THESE MORTALS!
WE WILL NO LONGER SIT BACK AND LET THE WORLD FORGET ABOUT US.
THE RUCKUS WILL PURGE THE WEAK, AND LEAVE THE REALM TO US.
TO THE *WIZ'S!*

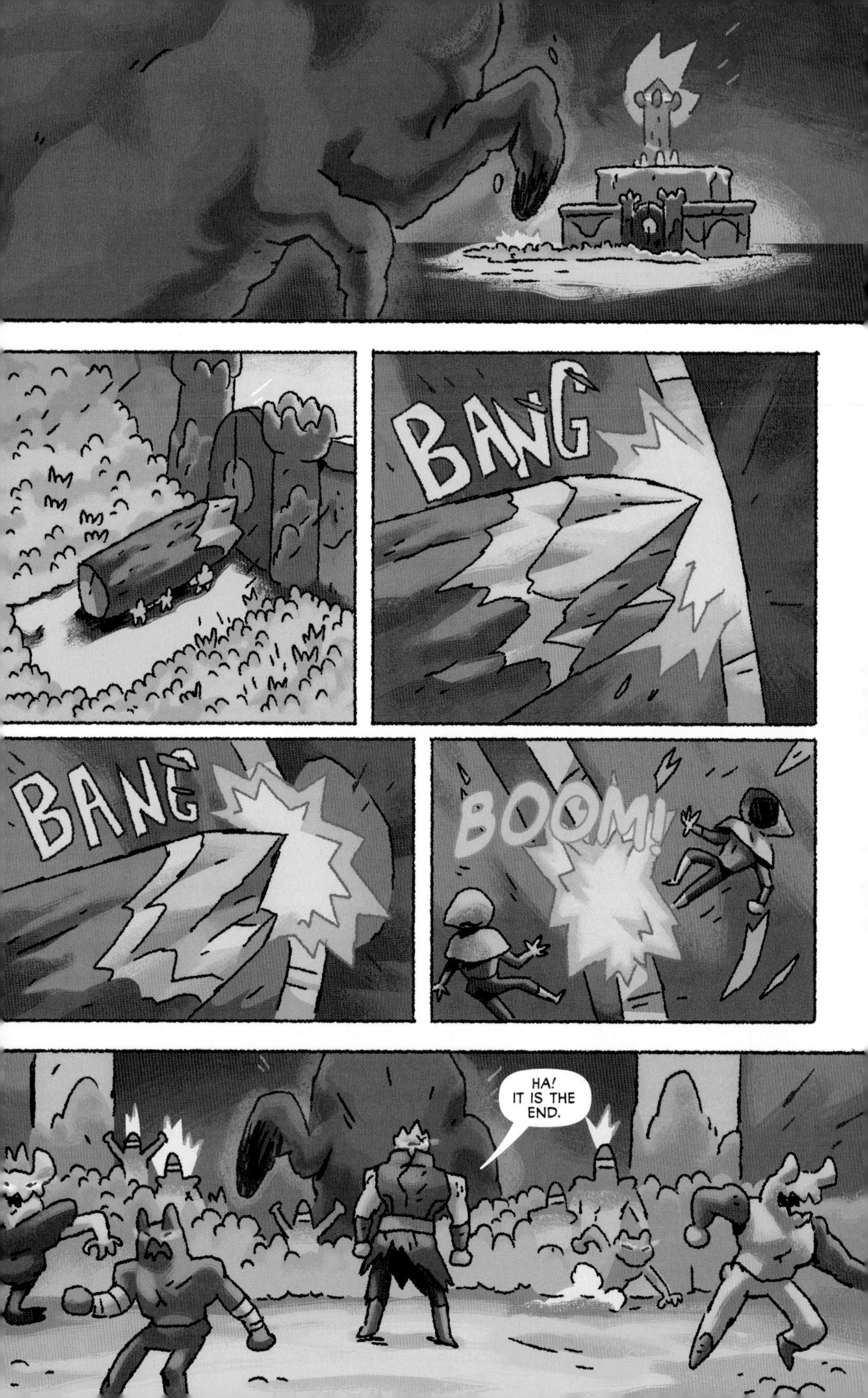
BANG
BANG
BOOM!
HA! IT IS THE END.

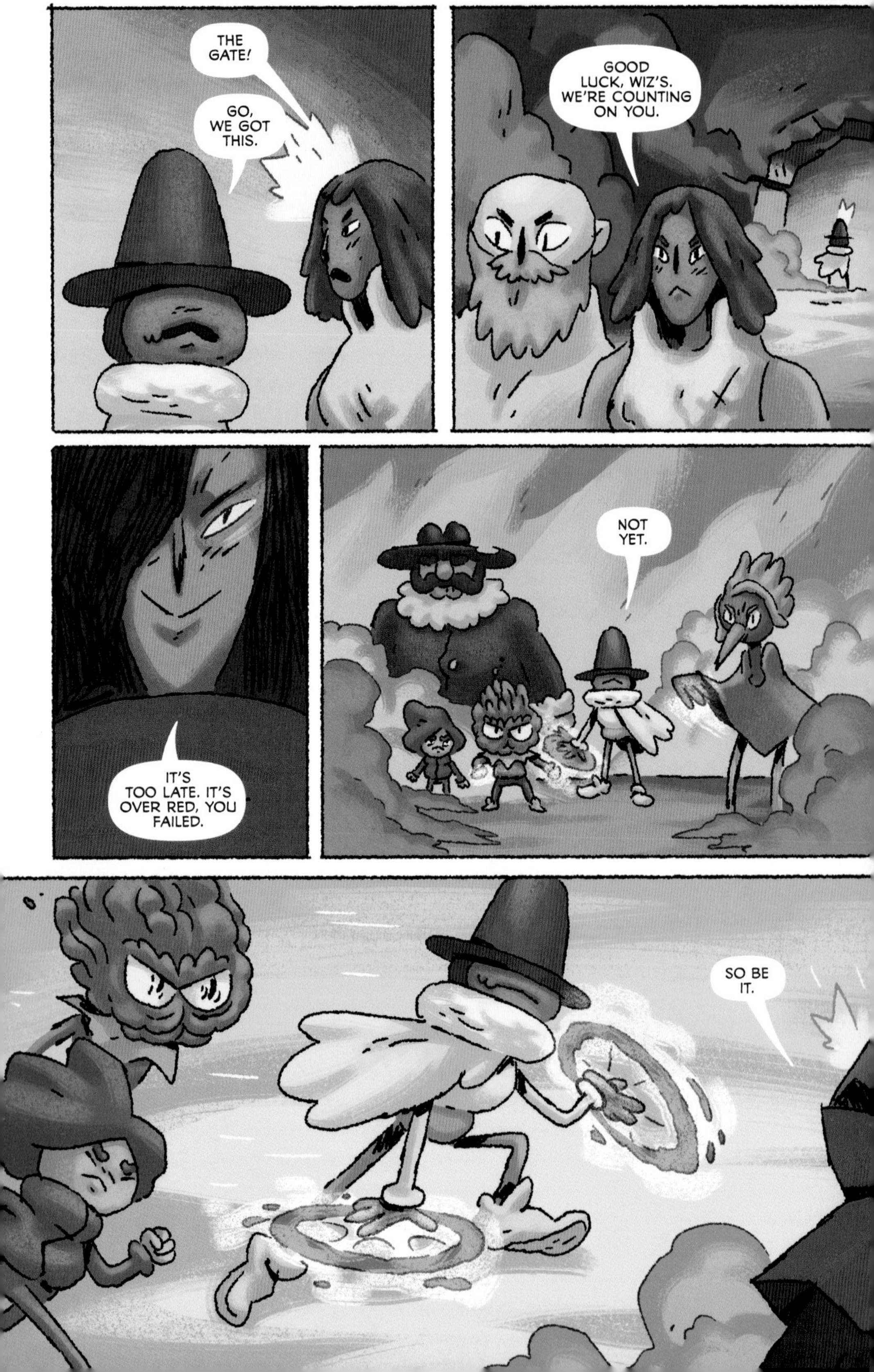
THE GATE!
GO, WE GOT THIS.
GOOD LUCK, WIZ'S. WE'RE COUNTING ON YOU.
IT'S TOO LATE. IT'S OVER RED, YOU FAILED.
NOT YET.
SO BE IT.

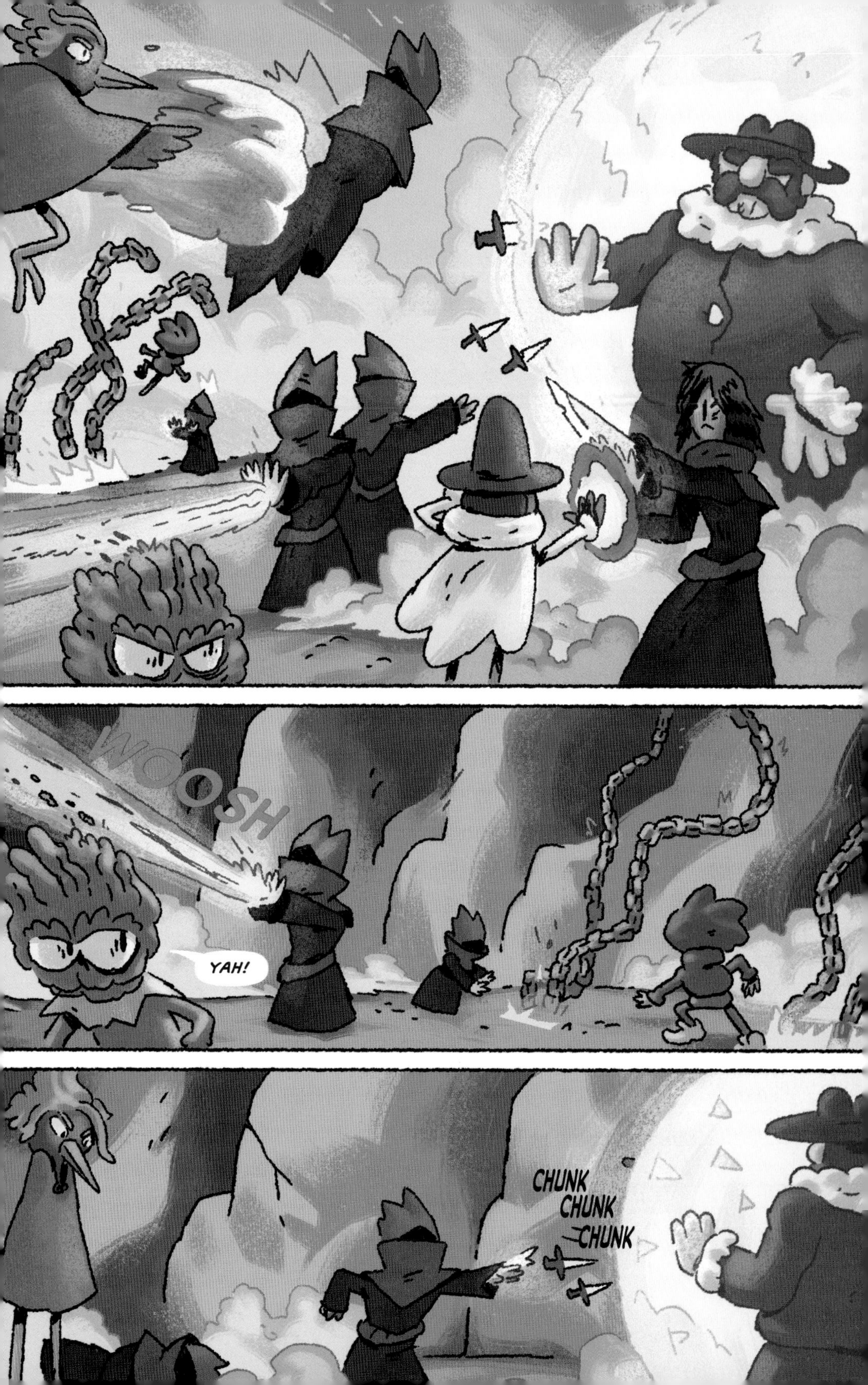
WOOSH
YAH!
CHUNK
CHUNK
CHUNK

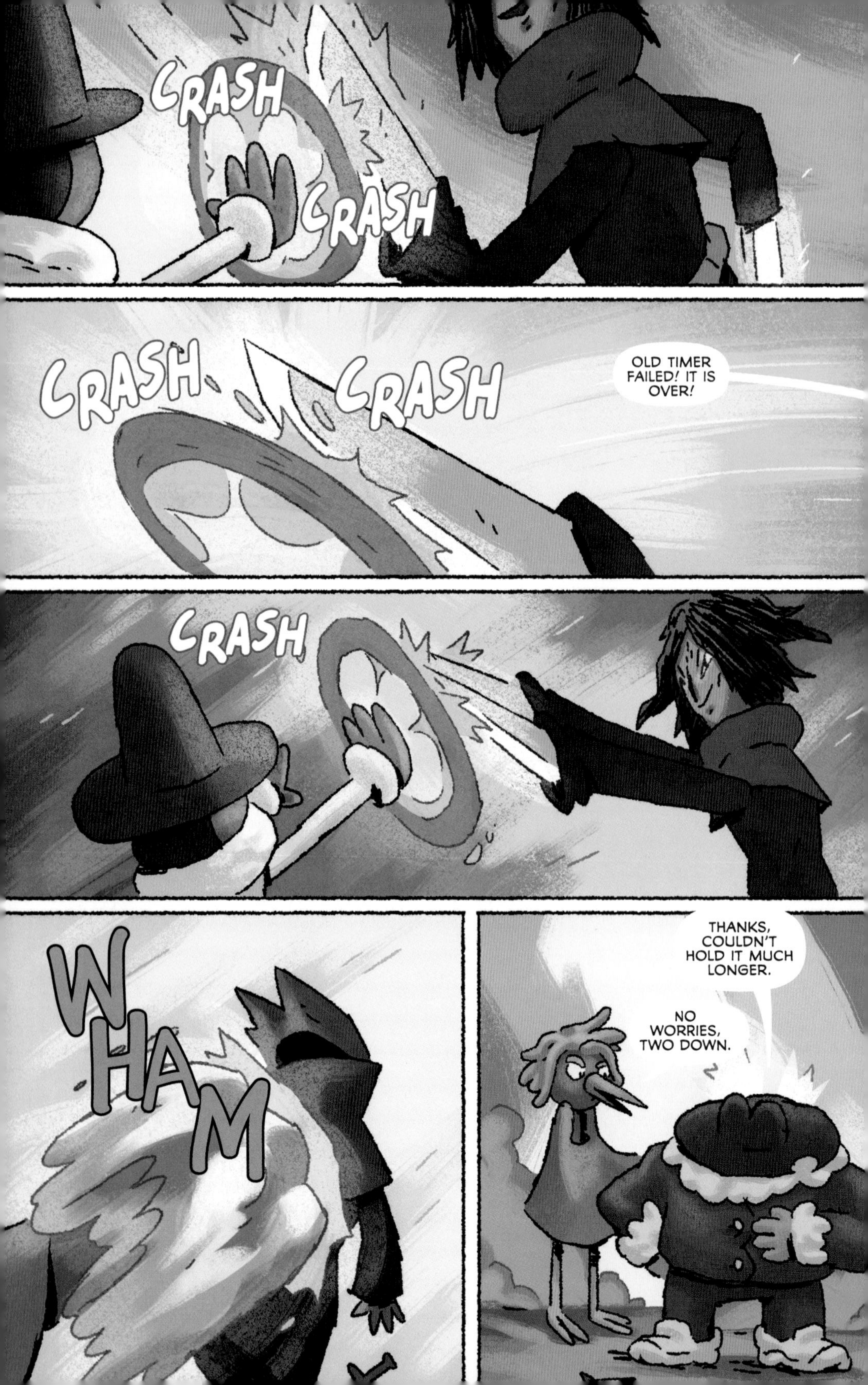
CRASH
CRASH
CRASH
CRASH
OLD TIMER FAILED! IT IS OVER!
CRASH
WHAM
THANKS, COULDN'T HOLD IT MUCH LONGER.
NO WORRIES, TWO DOWN.

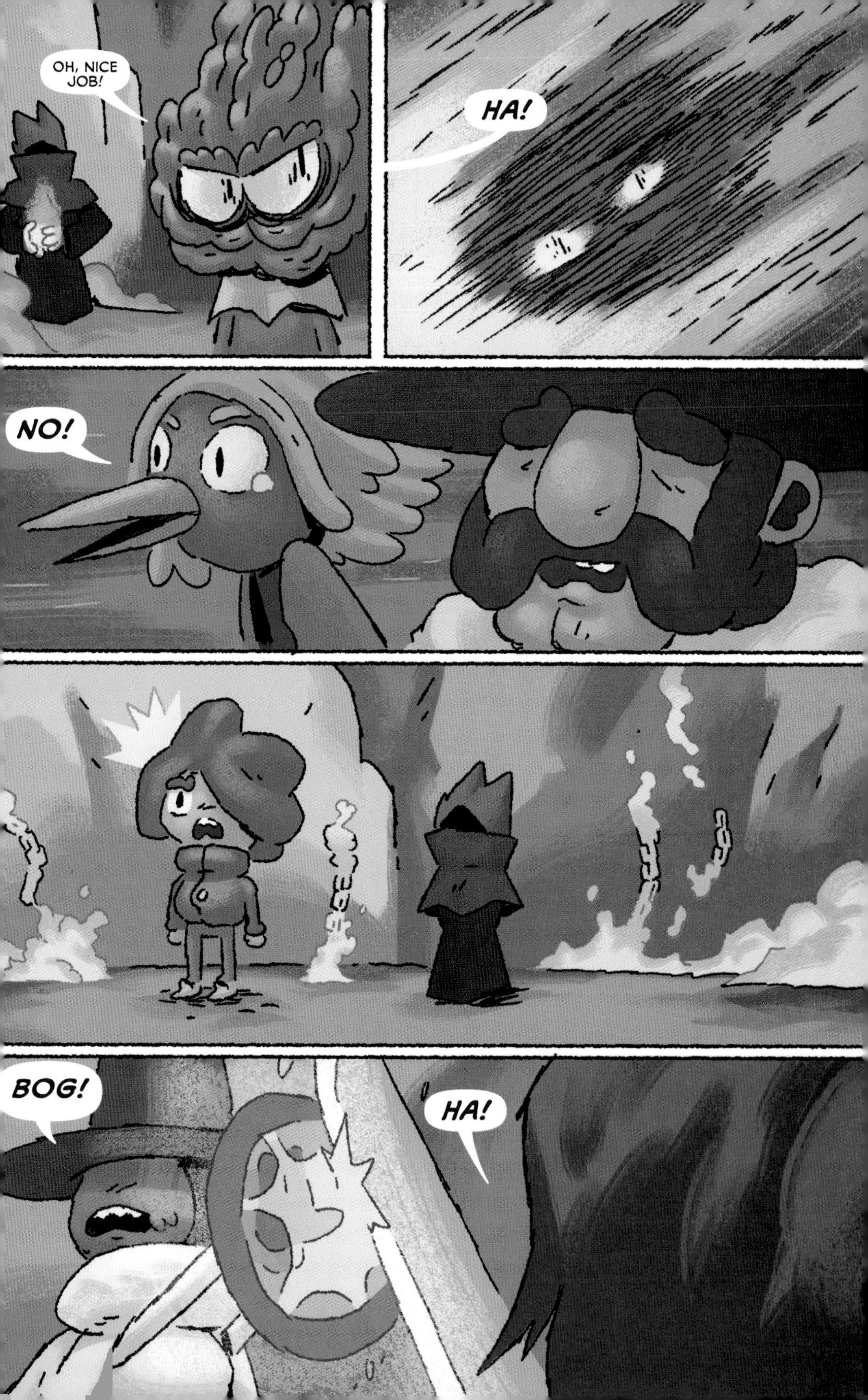
OH, NICE JOB!
HA!
NO!
BOG!
HA!

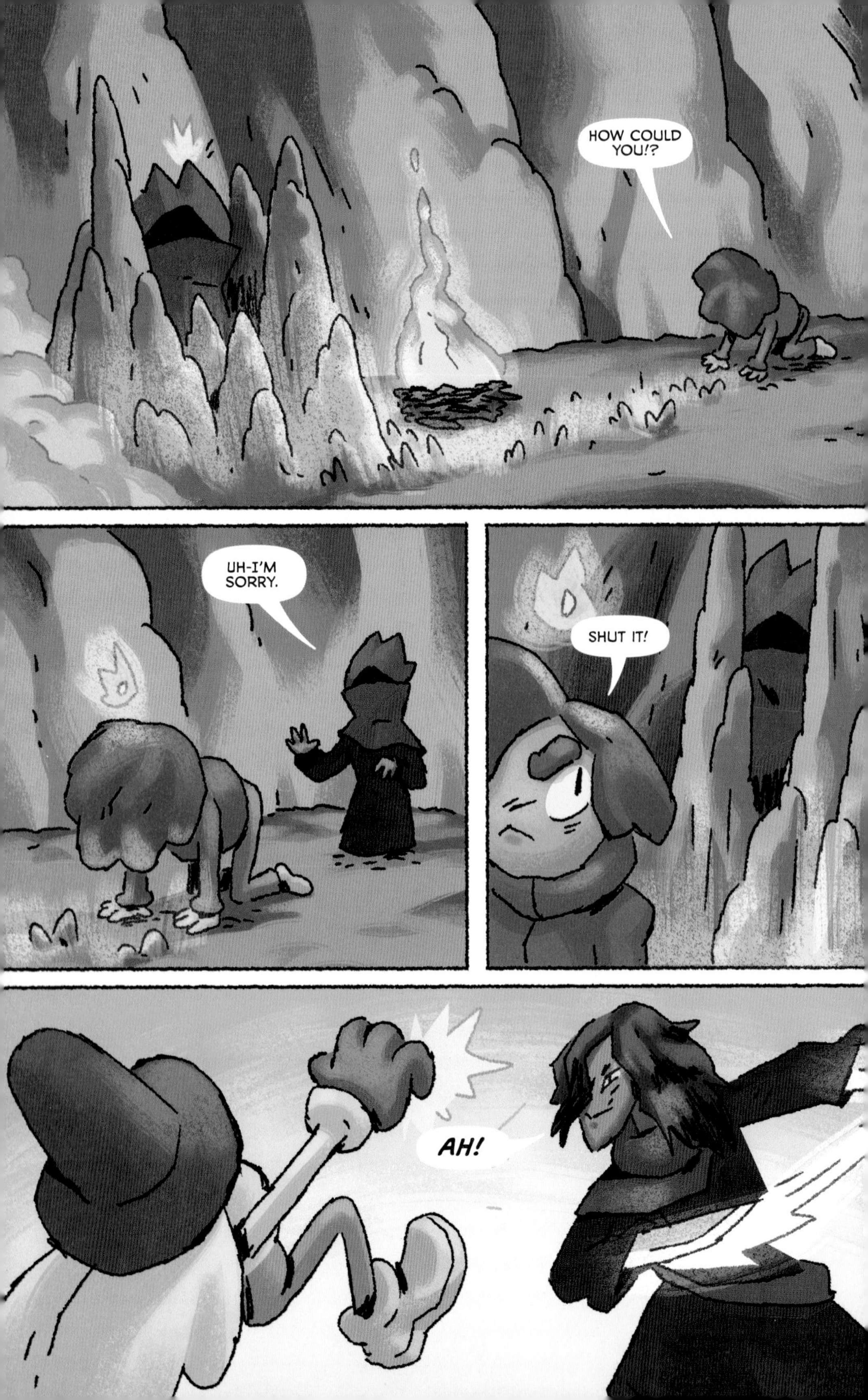
HOW COULD YOU!?
UH-I'M SORRY.
SHUT IT!
AH!

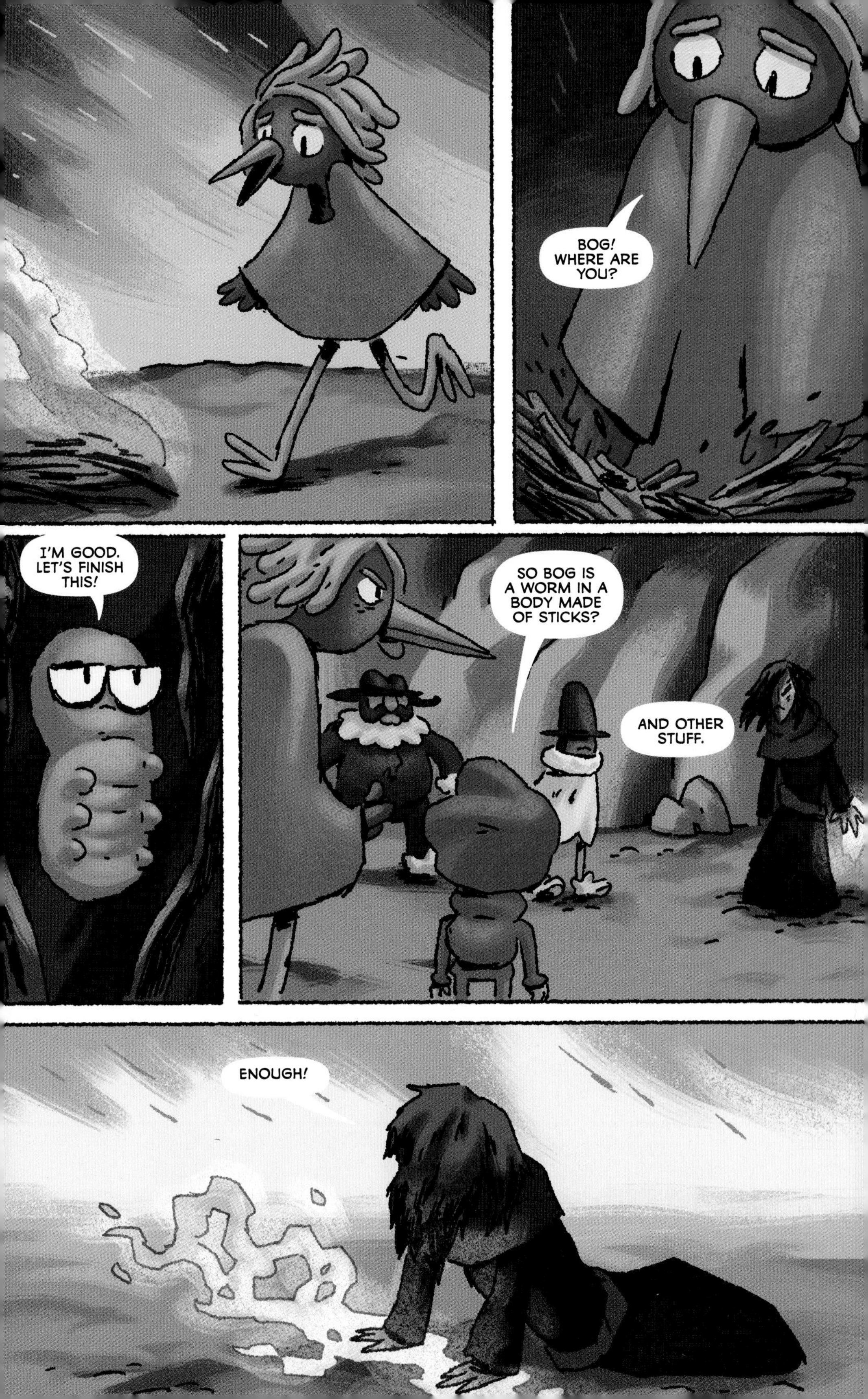
BOG! WHERE ARE YOU?
I'M GOOD. LET'S FINISH THIS!
SO BOG IS A WORM IN A BODY MADE OF STICKS?
AND OTHER STUFF.
ENOUGH!

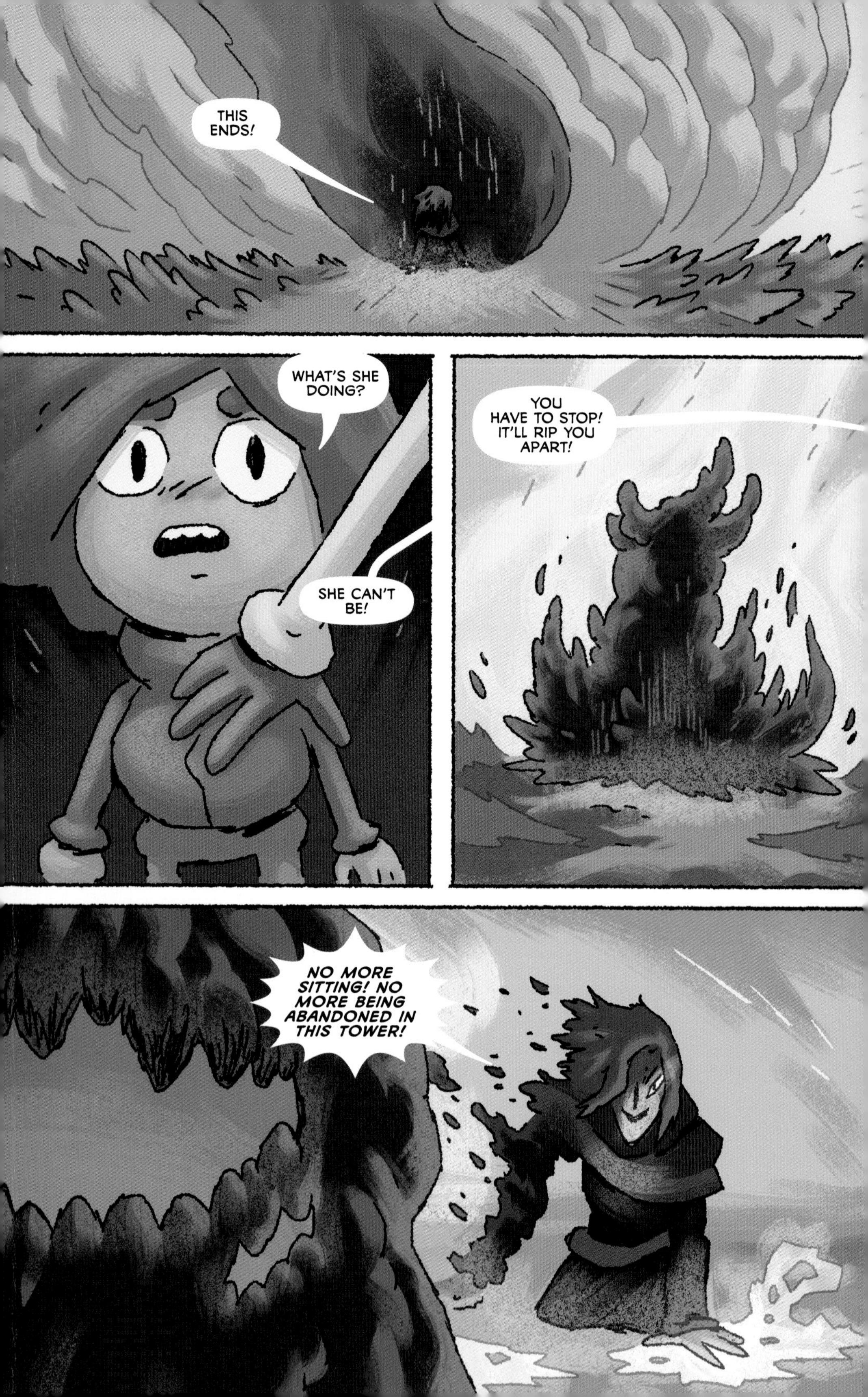
THIS ENDS!
WHAT'S SHE DOING?
SHE CAN'T BE!
YOU HAVE TO STOP! IT'LL RIP YOU APART!
NO MORE SITTING! NO MORE BEING ABANDONED IN THIS TOWER!

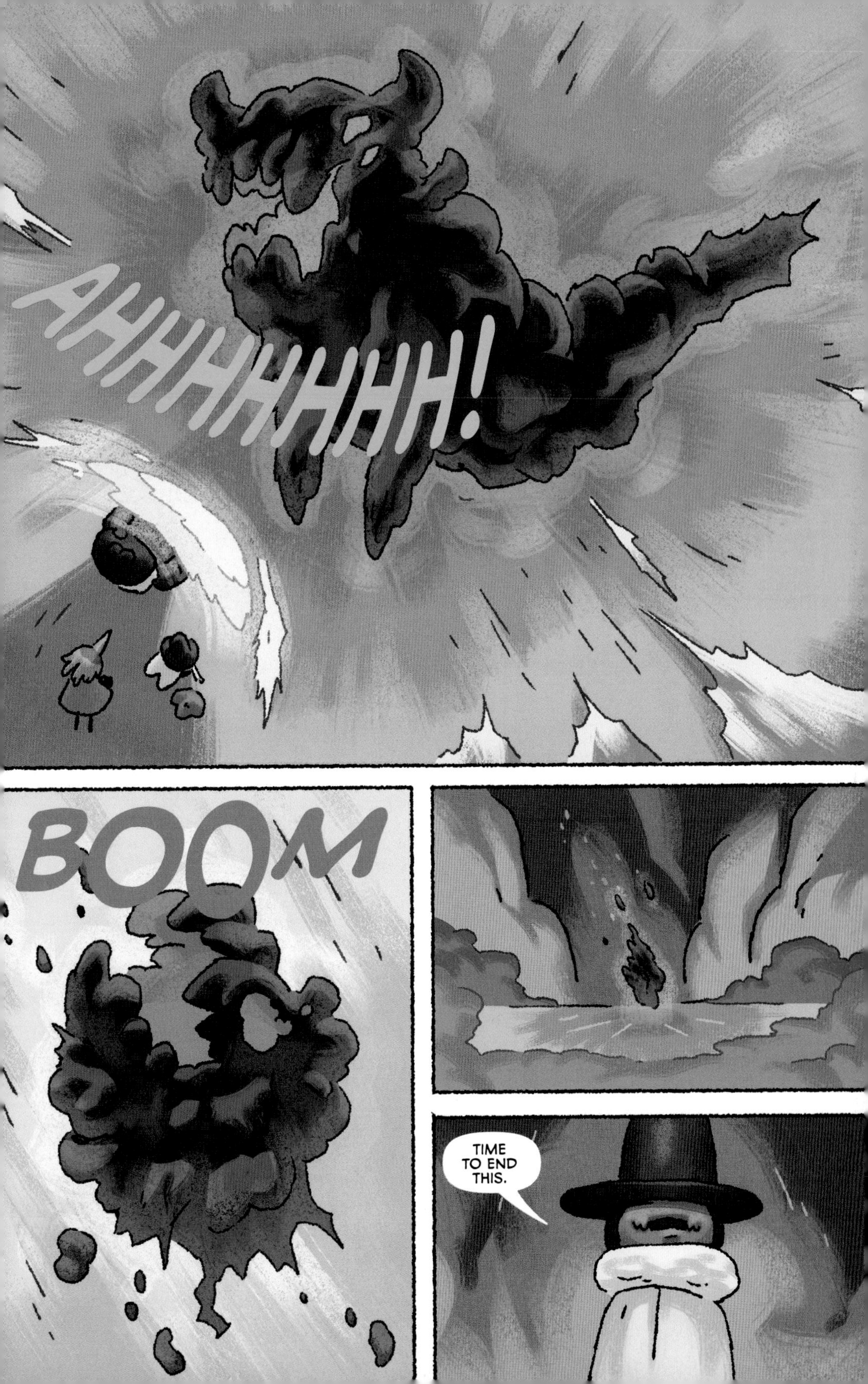
AHHHHHHHH!
BOOM
TIME TO END THIS.

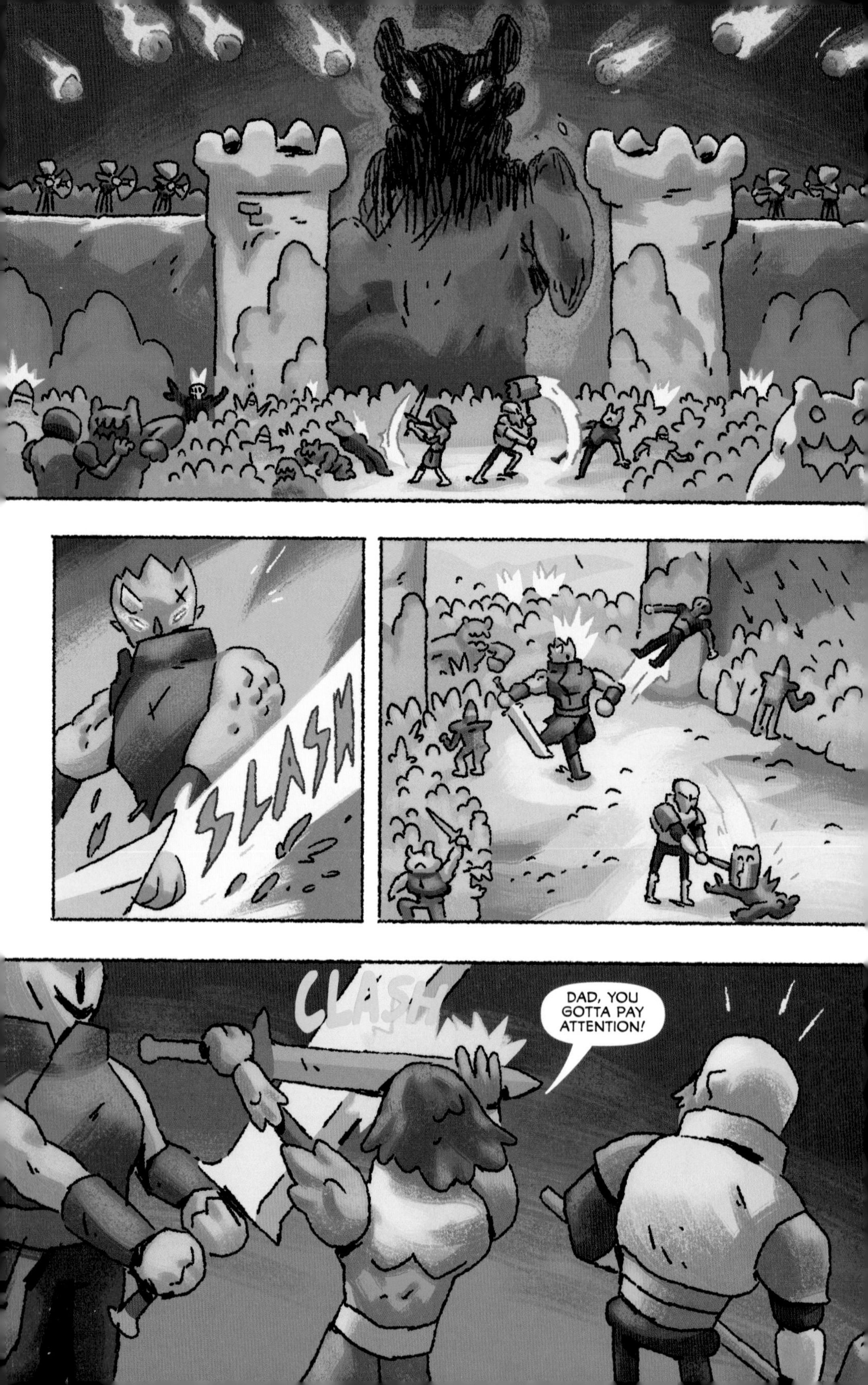
SLASH
CLASH
DAD, YOU GOTTA PAY ATTENTION!

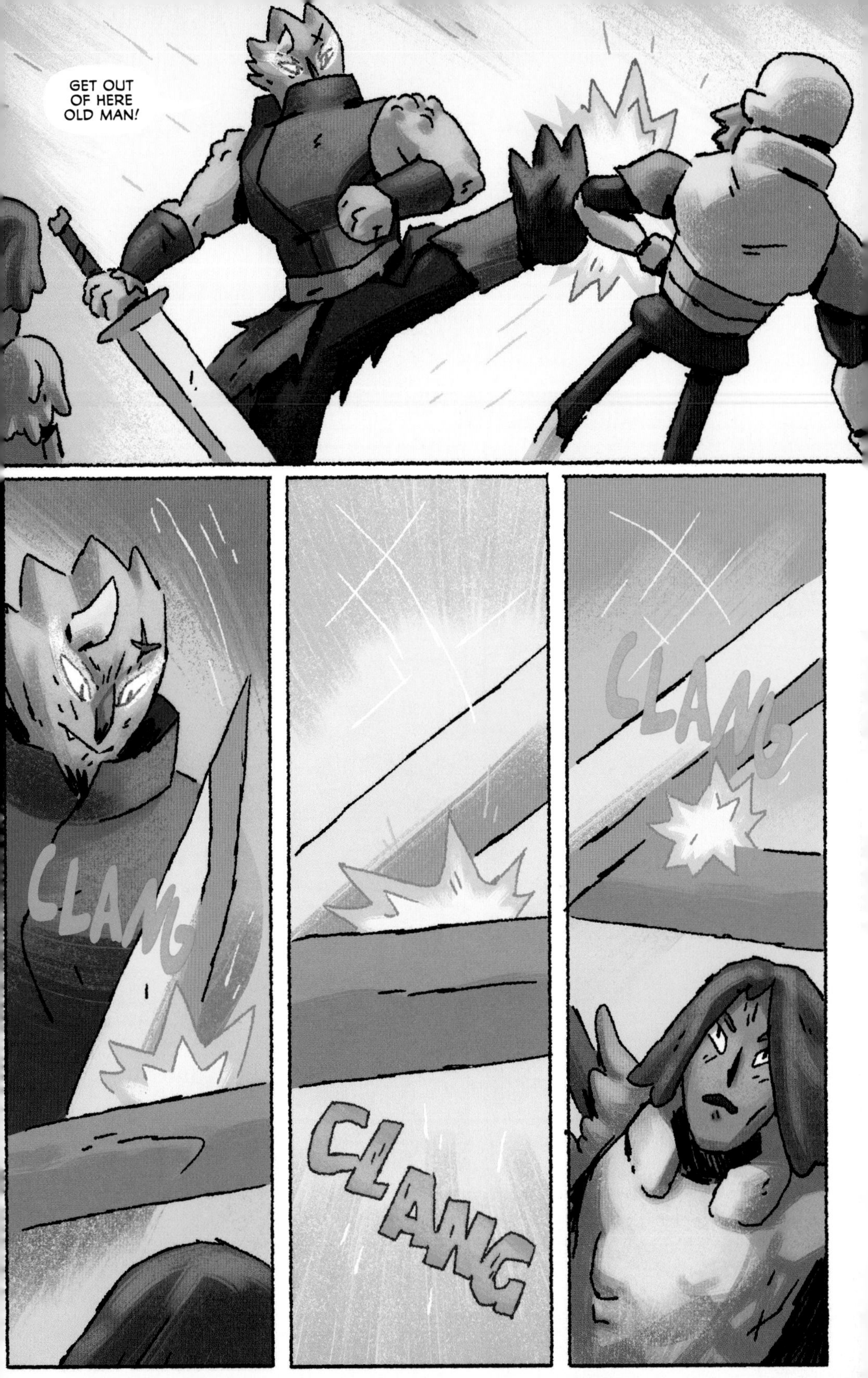
GET OUT OF HERE OLD MAN!
CLANG
CLANG
CLANG

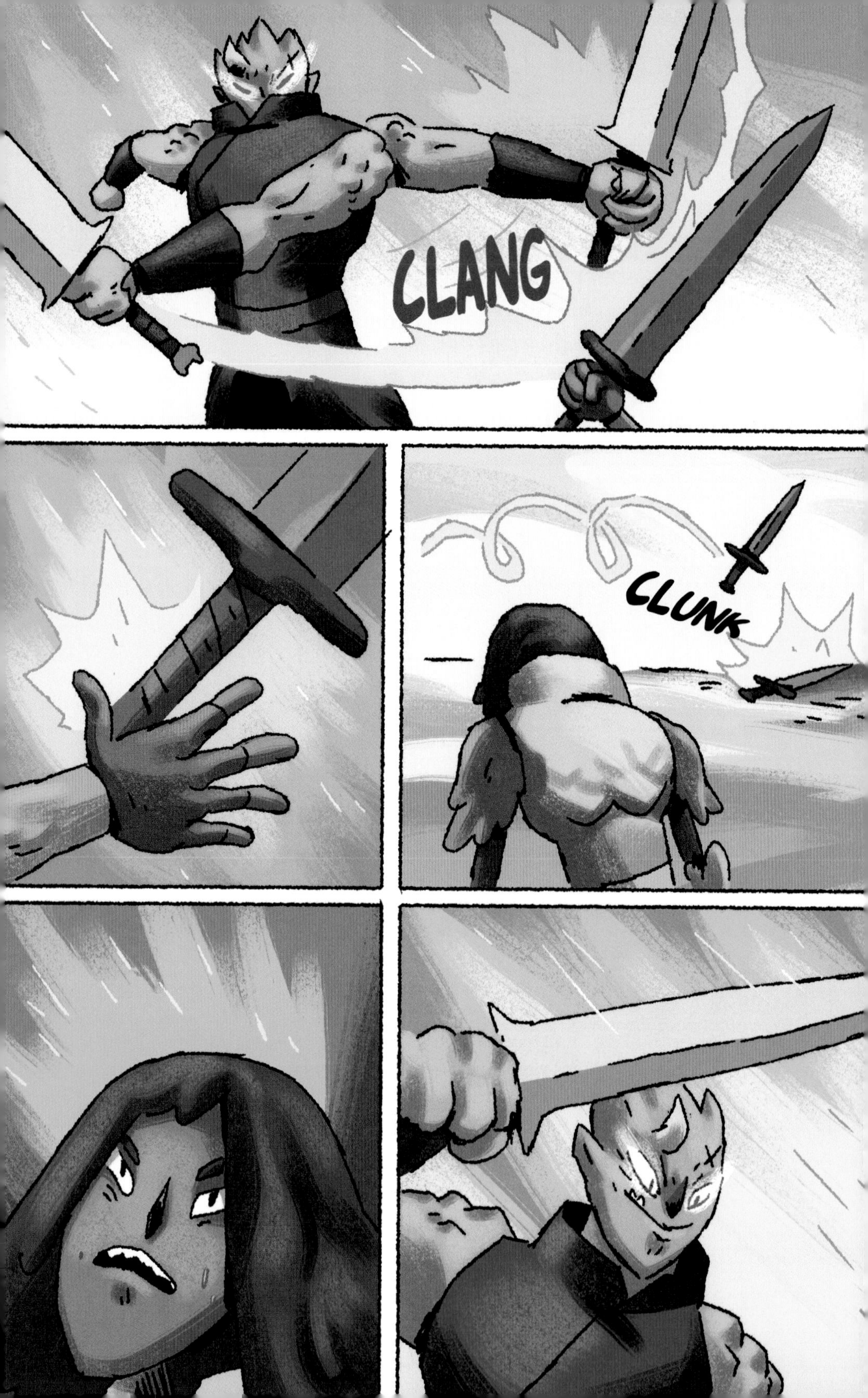
CLANG
CLUNK

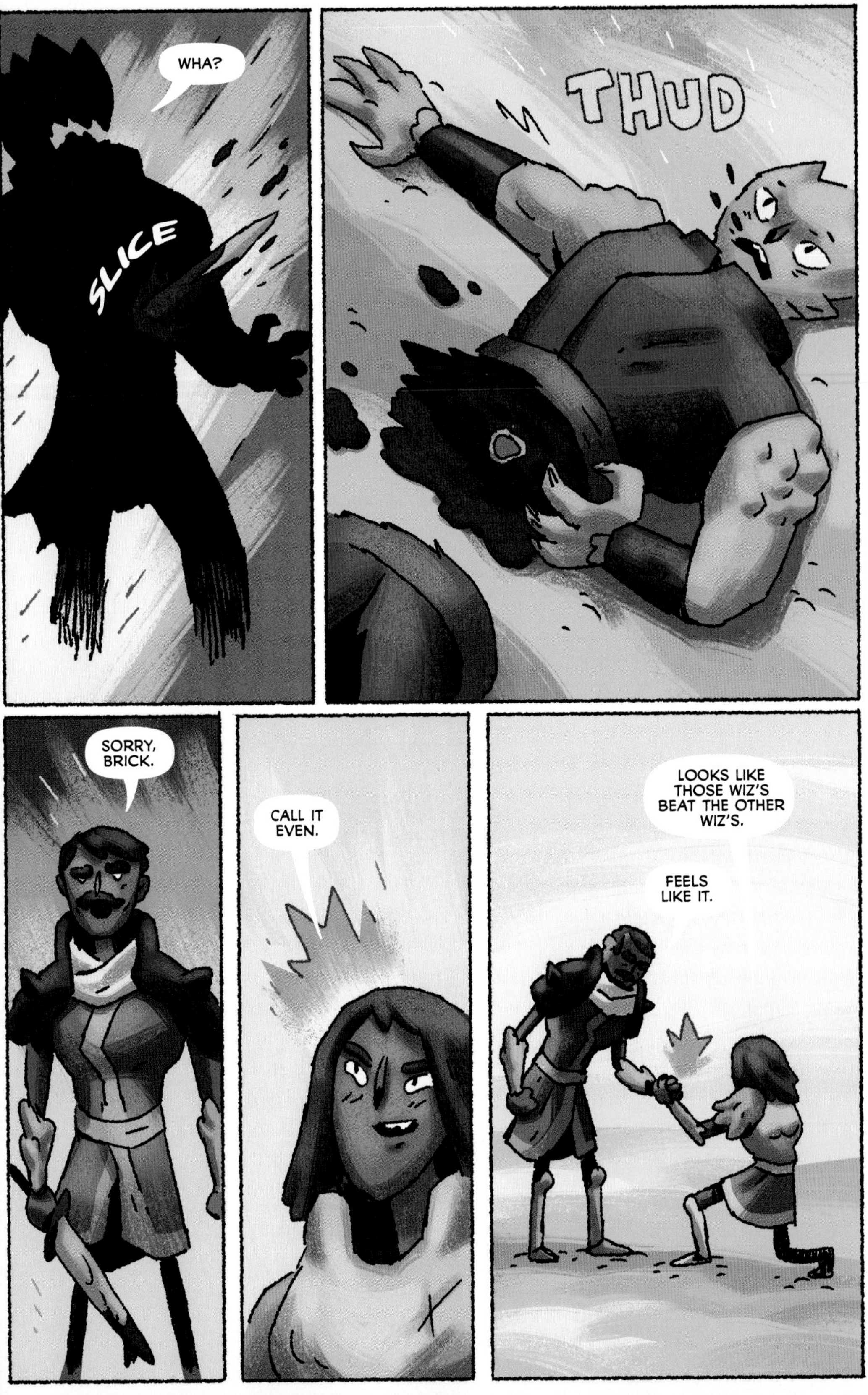
WHA?
SLICE
THUD
SORRY, BRICK.
CALL IT EVEN.
LOOKS LIKE THOSE WIZ'S BEAT THE OTHER WIZ'S.
FEELS LIKE IT.

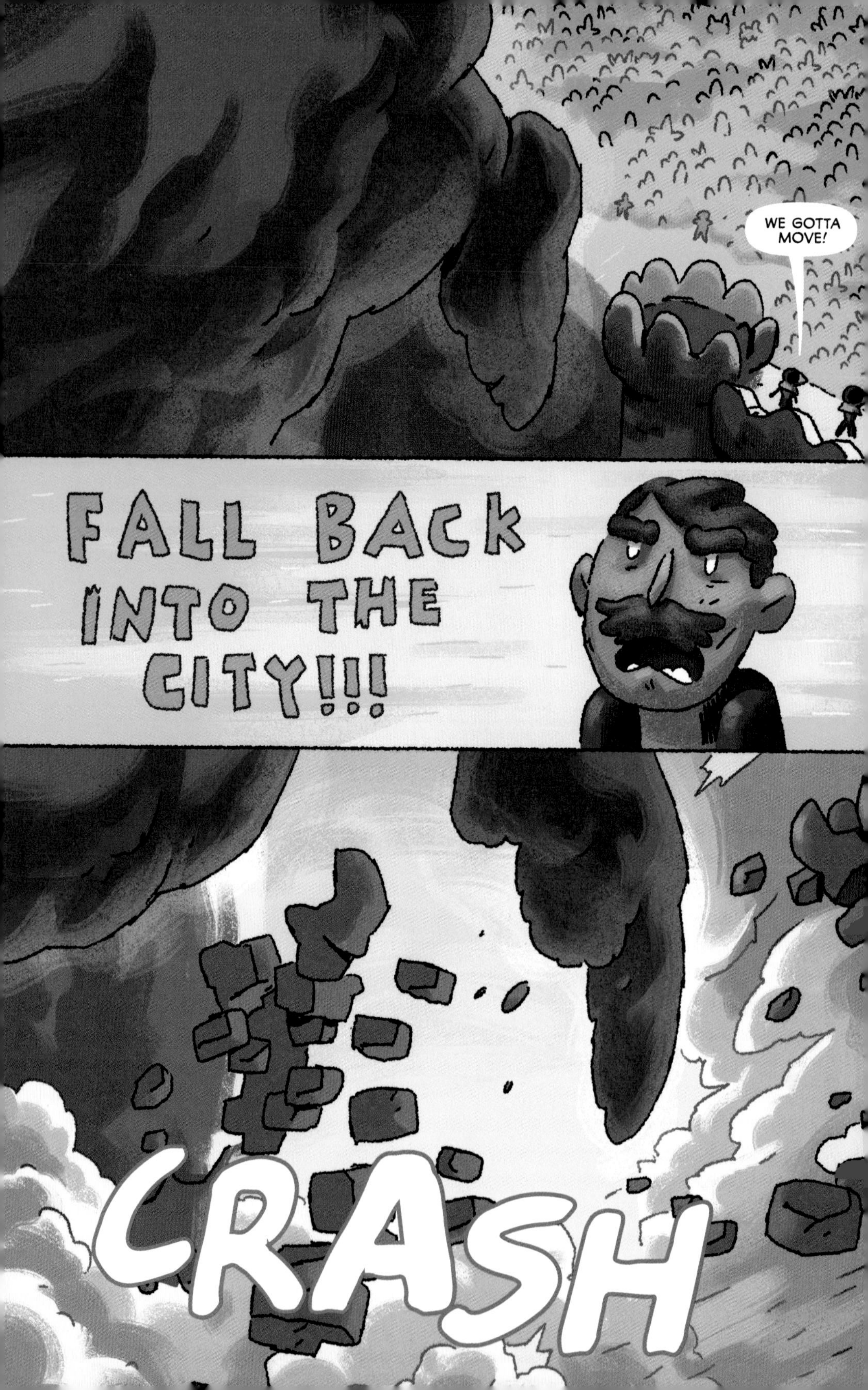
WE GOTTA MOVE!
FALL BACK INTO THE CITY!!!
CRASH

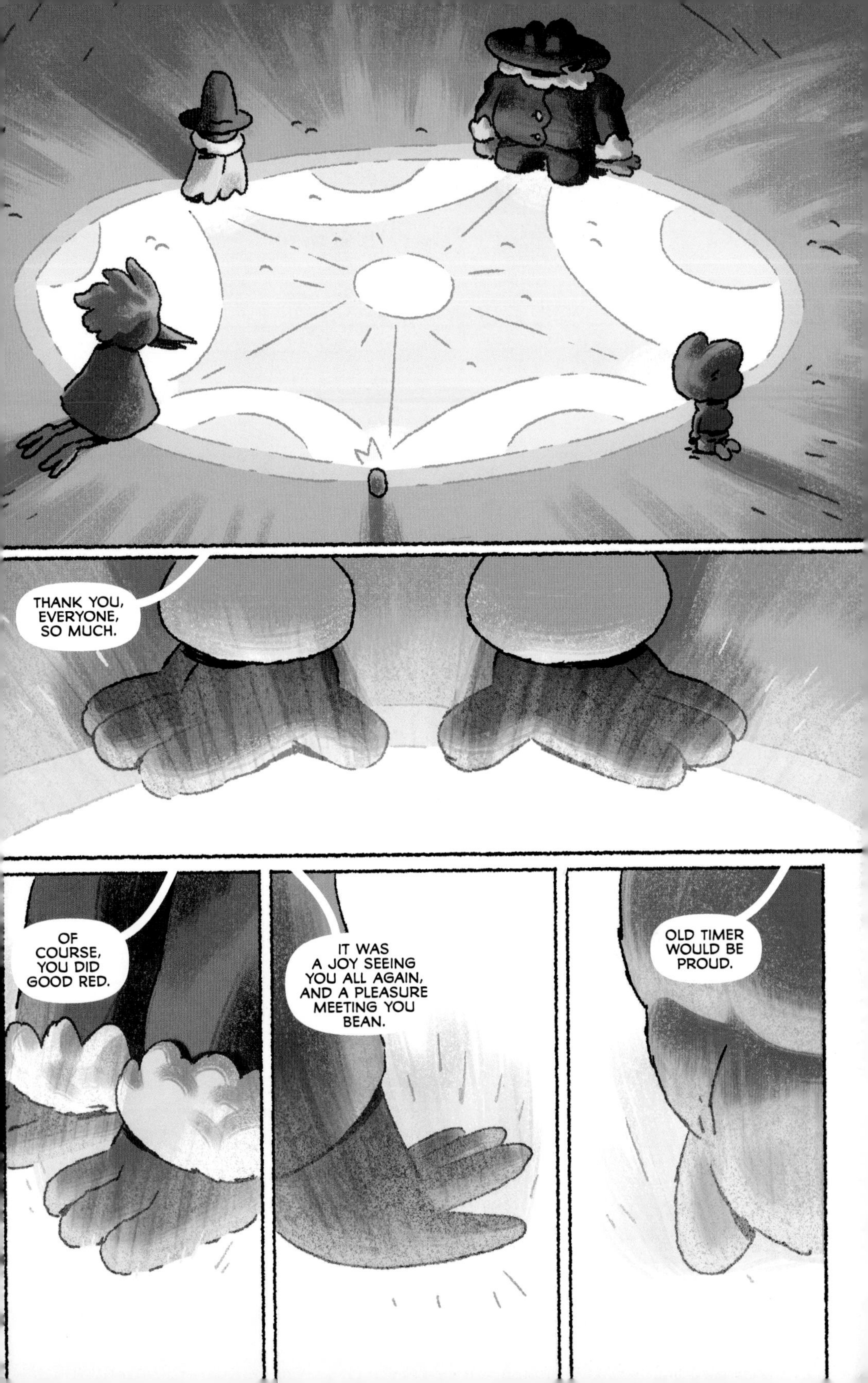
THANK YOU, EVERYONE, SO MUCH.
OF COURSE, YOU DID GOOD RED.
IT WAS A JOY SEEING YOU ALL AGAIN, AND A PLEASURE MEETING YOU BEAN.
OLD TIMER WOULD BE PROUD.

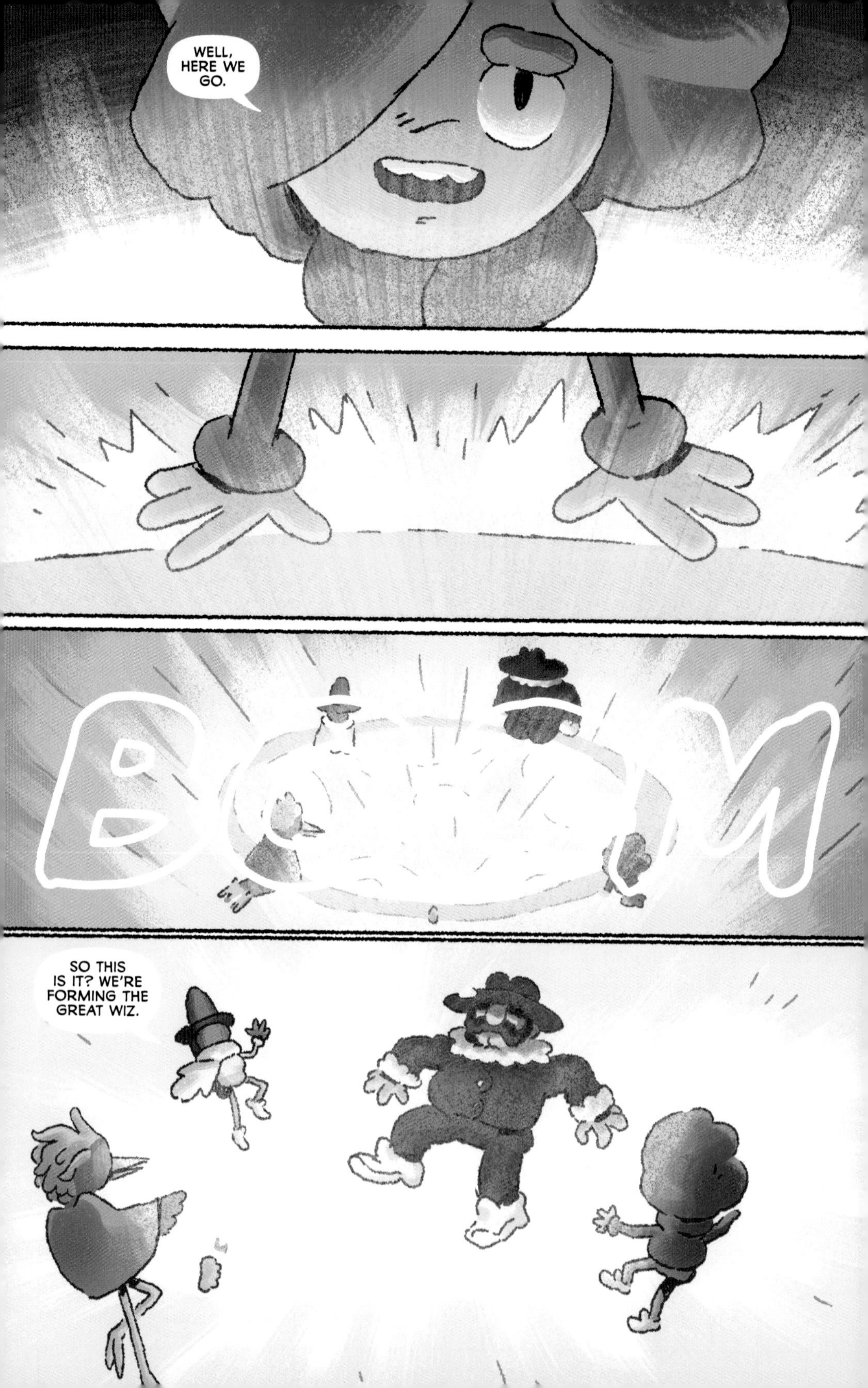
WELL, HERE WE GO.
BOOM
SO THIS IS IT? WE'RE FORMING THE GREAT WIZ.

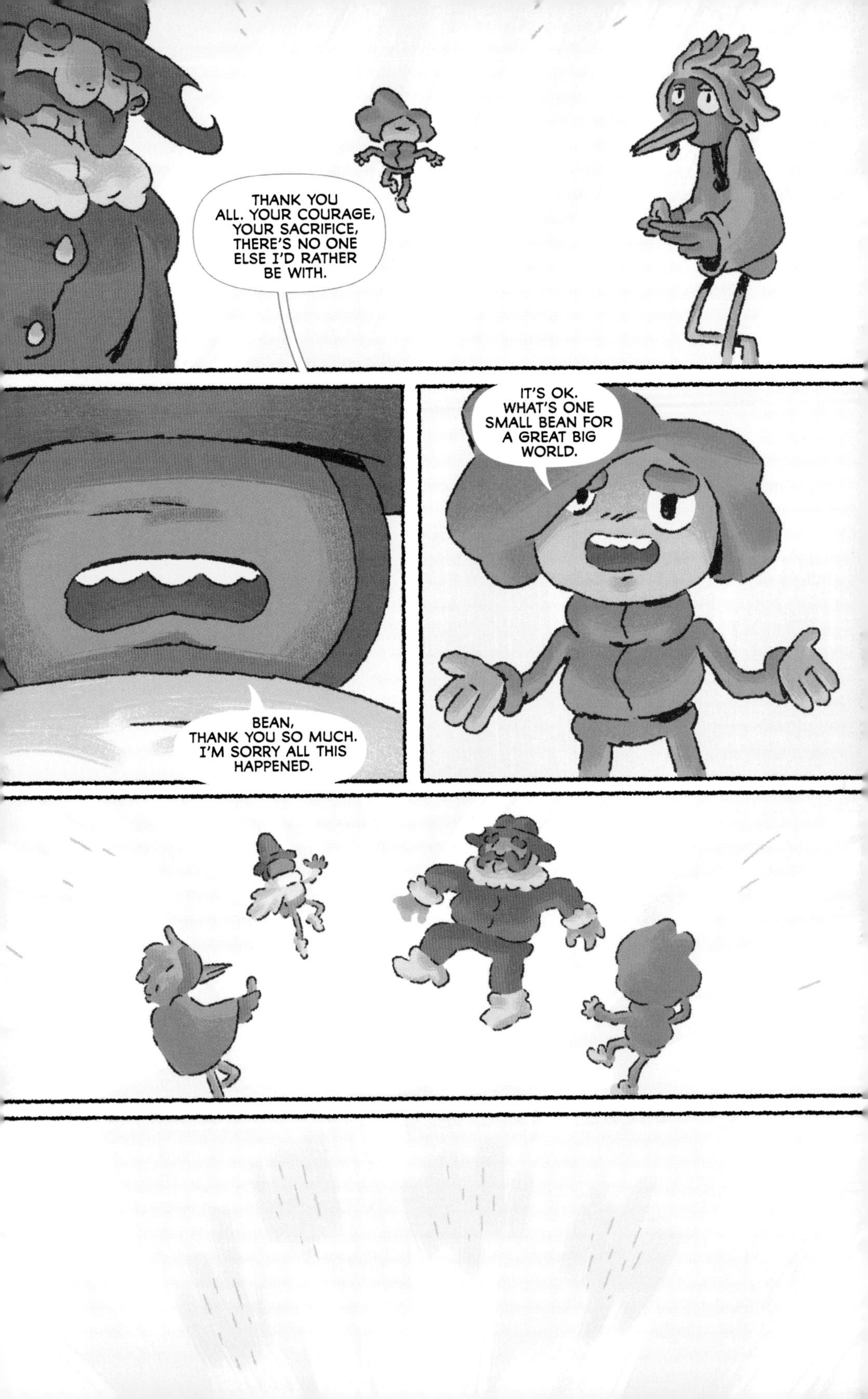
THANK YOU ALL. YOUR COURAGE, YOUR SACRIFICE, THERE'S NO ONE ELSE I'D RATHER BE WITH.
BEAN, THANK YOU SO MUCH. I'M SORRY ALL THIS HAPPENED.
IT'S OK. WHAT'S ONE SMALL BEAN FOR A GREAT BIG WORLD.

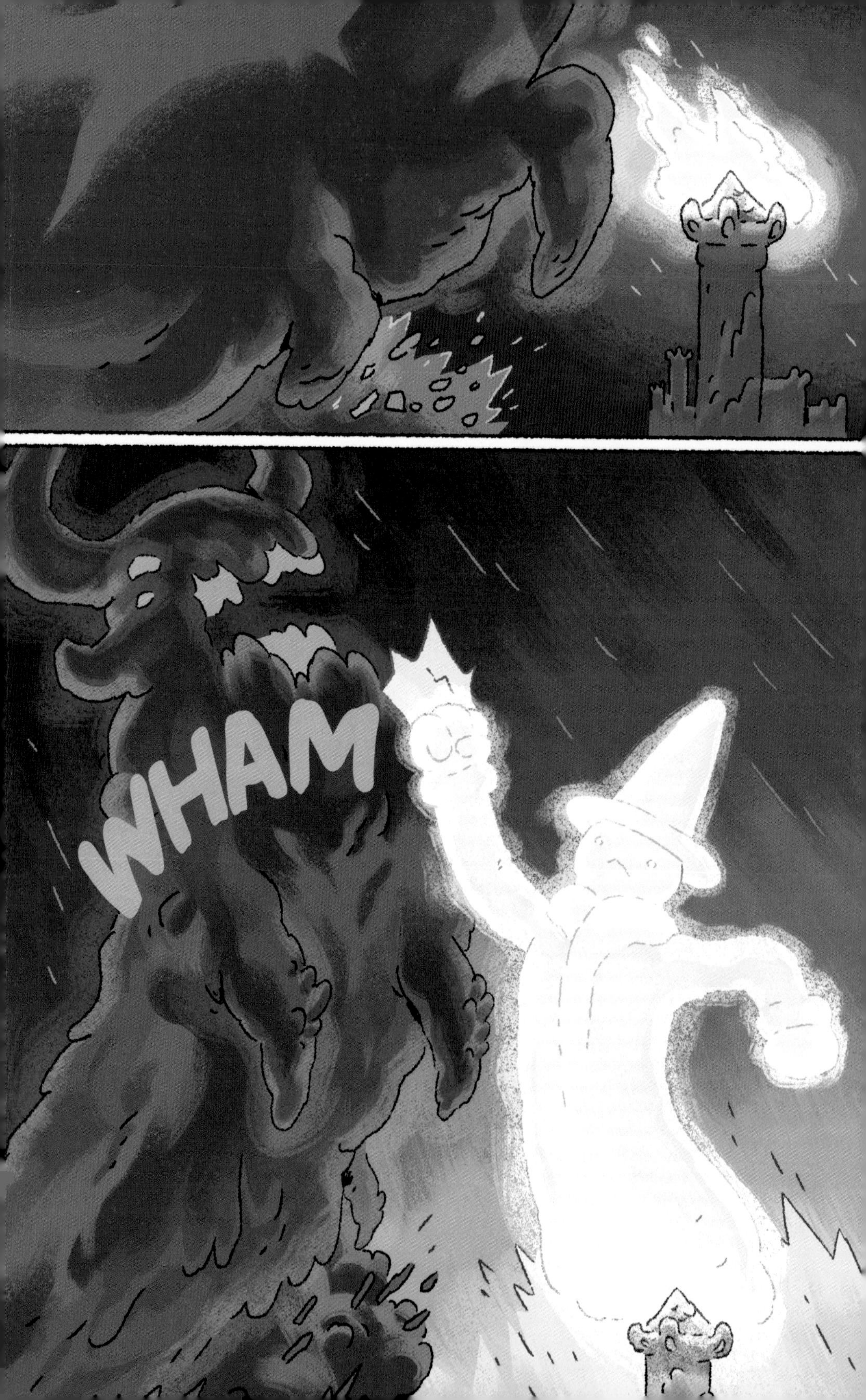
WHAM

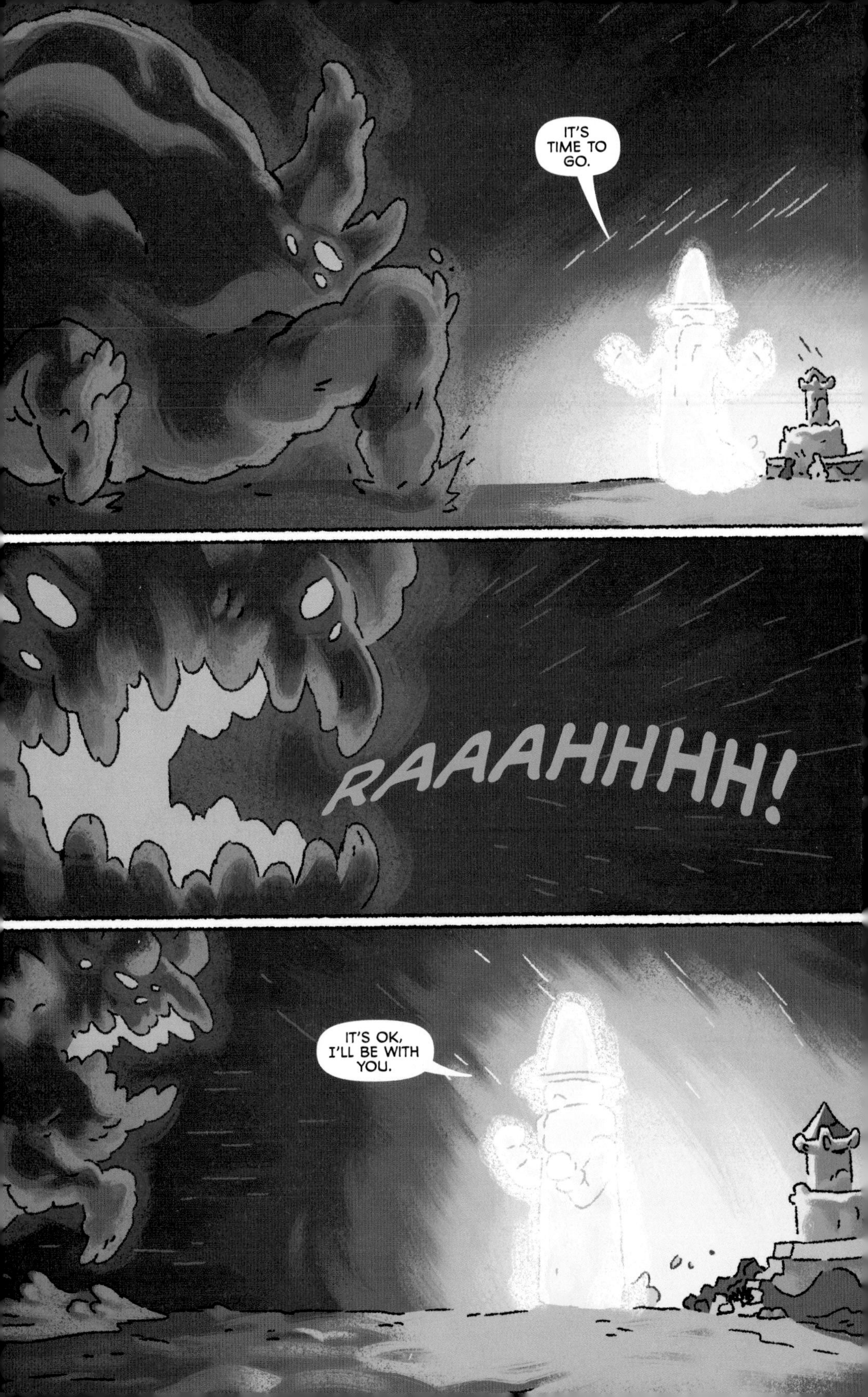
IT'S TIME TO GO.
RAAAHHHH!
IT'S OK, I'LL BE WITH YOU.

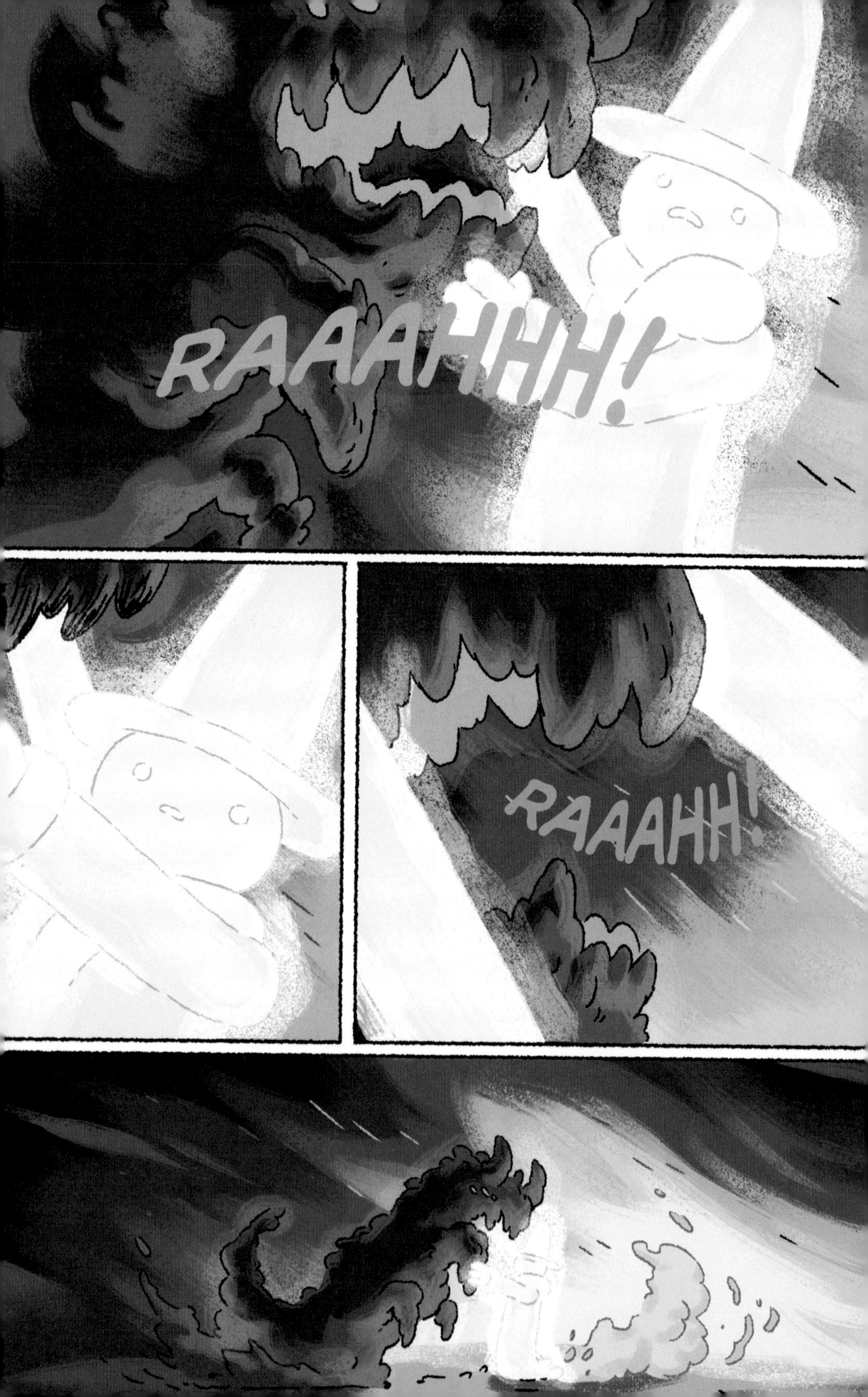
RAAAHHH!
RAAAHH!

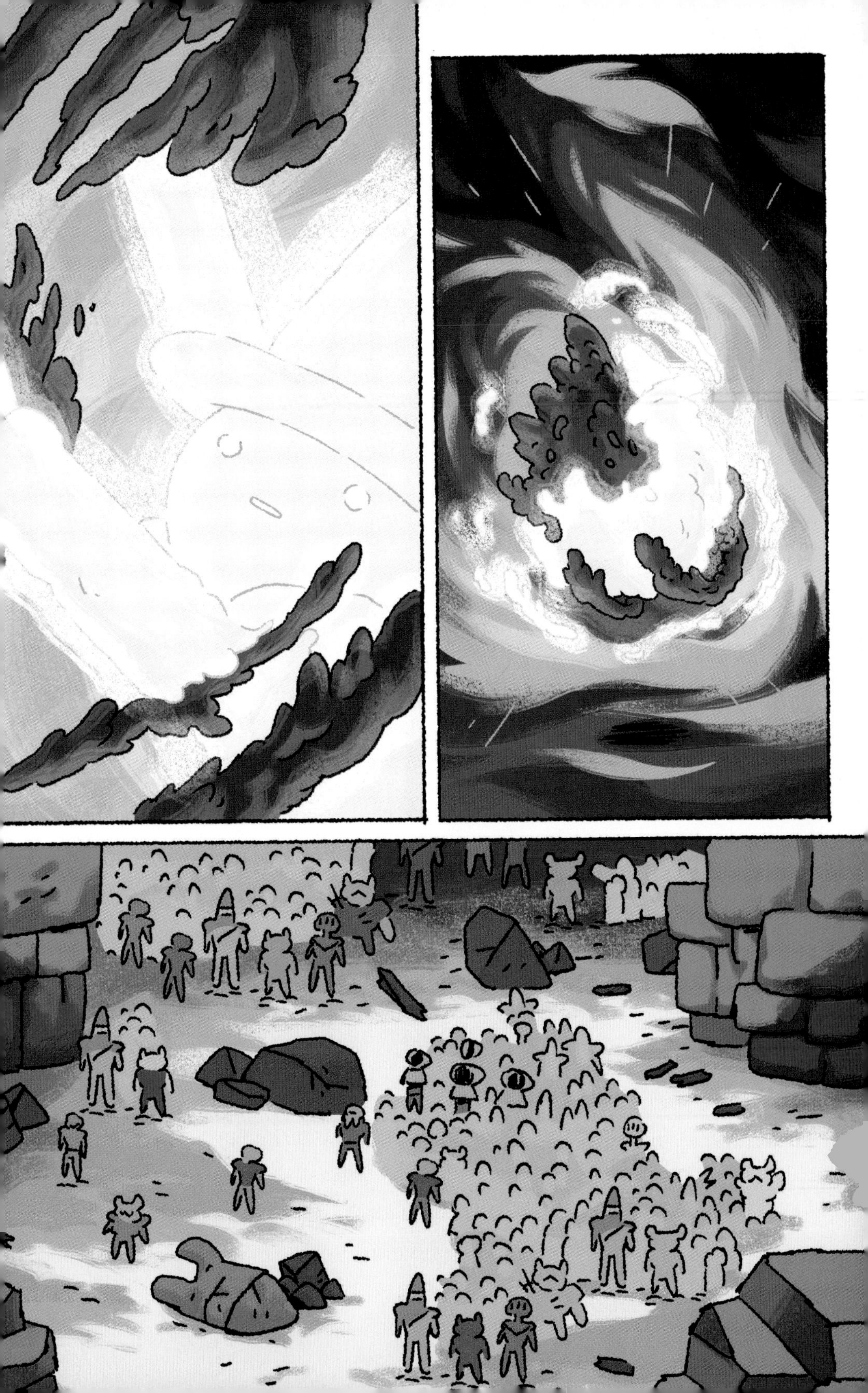

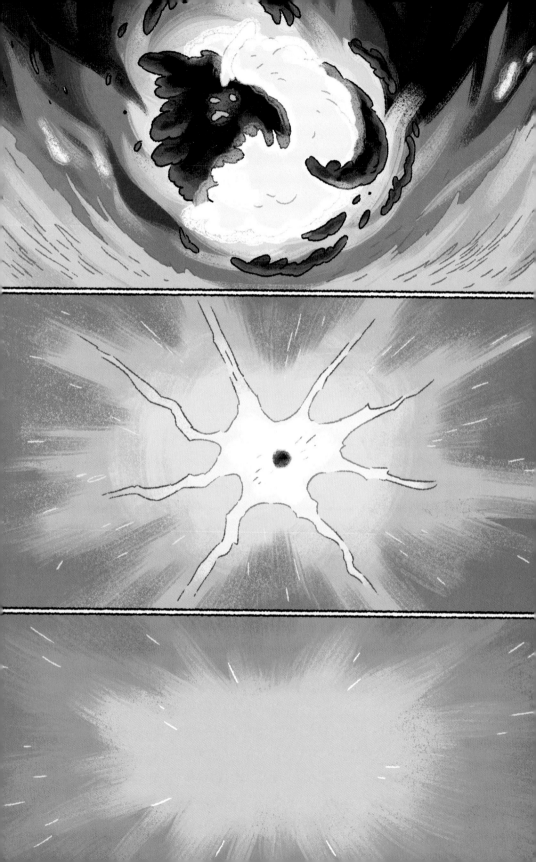

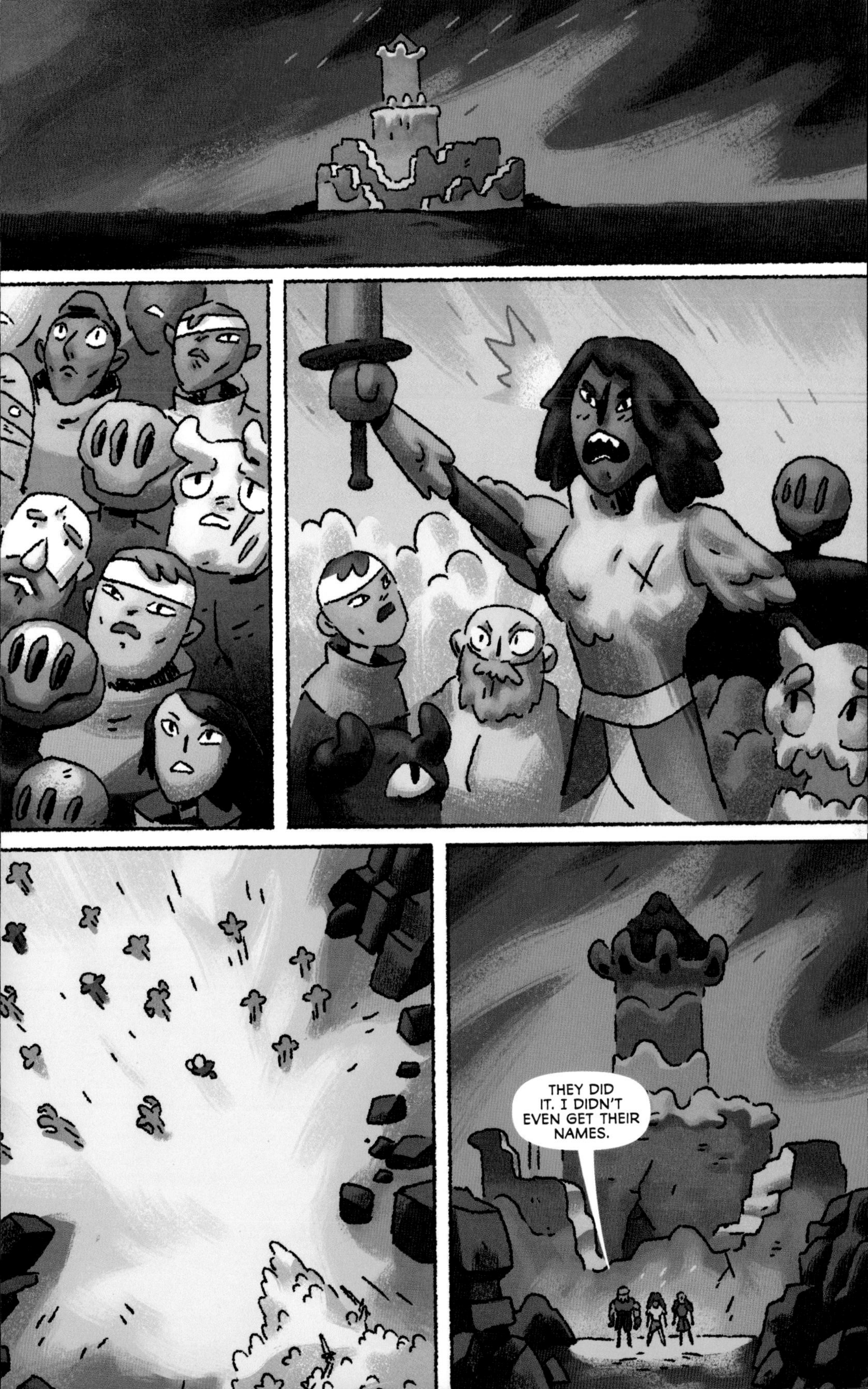
THEY DID IT. I DIDN'T EVEN GET THEIR NAMES.

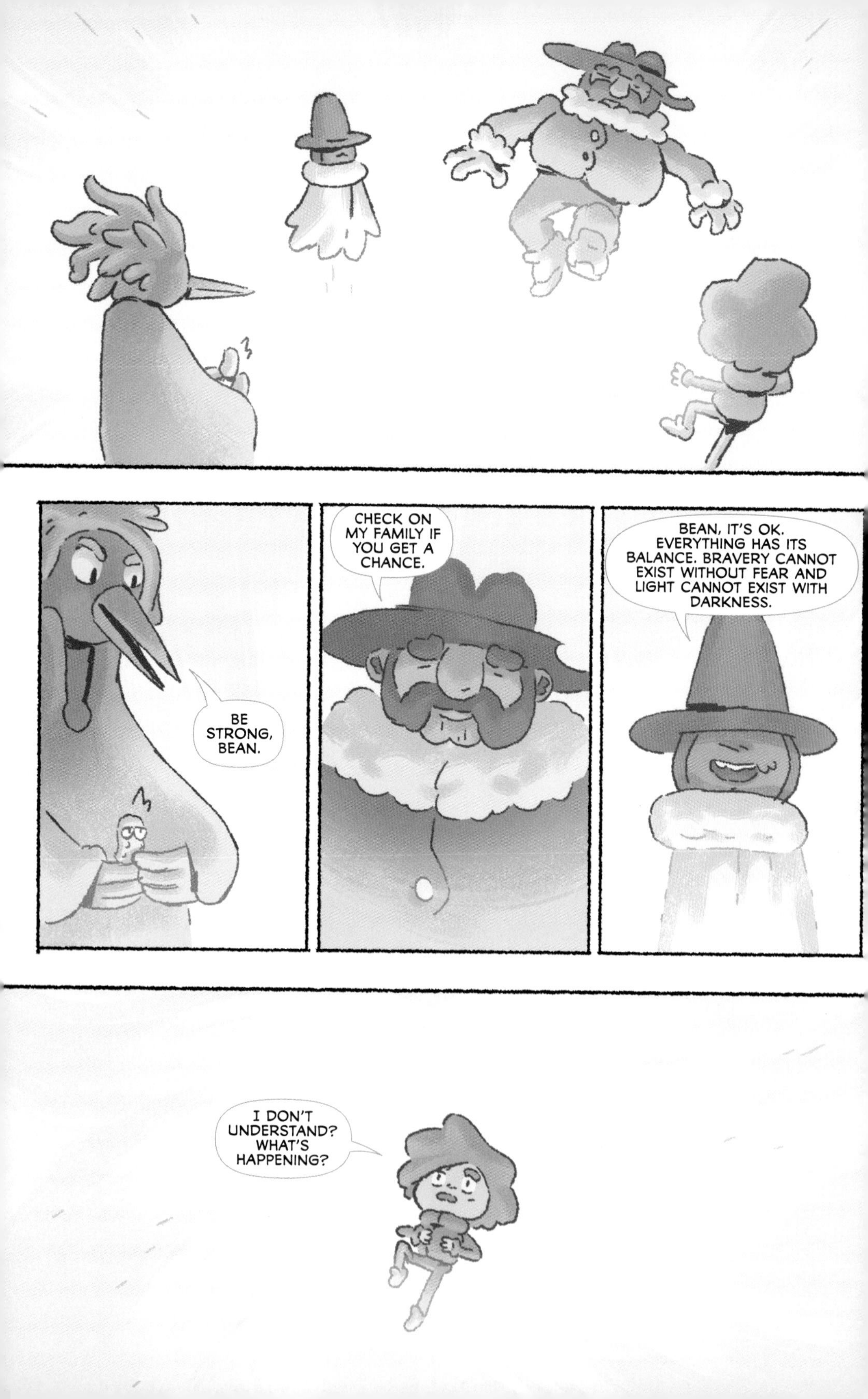
BE STRONG, BEAN.
CHECK ON MY FAMILY IF YOU GET A CHANCE.
BEAN, IT'S OK. EVERYTHING HAS ITS BALANCE. BRAVERY CANNOT EXIST WITHOUT FEAR AND LIGHT CANNOT EXIST WITH DARKNESS.
I DON'T UNDERSTAND? WHAT'S HAPPENING?

HEY.
AH!
IT'S OK, JUST WANTED TO CHAT.
UH...HI.
YOU'RE A PRETTY IMPRESSIVE KID. RED TOLD ME ALL ABOUT YAH.
WHAT'D HE SAY?
JUST LOTS OF GOOD STUFF, SAVED THE DAY A COUPLE TIMES, GOOD AT MAGIC. JUST A GENERAL GOOD PERSON.

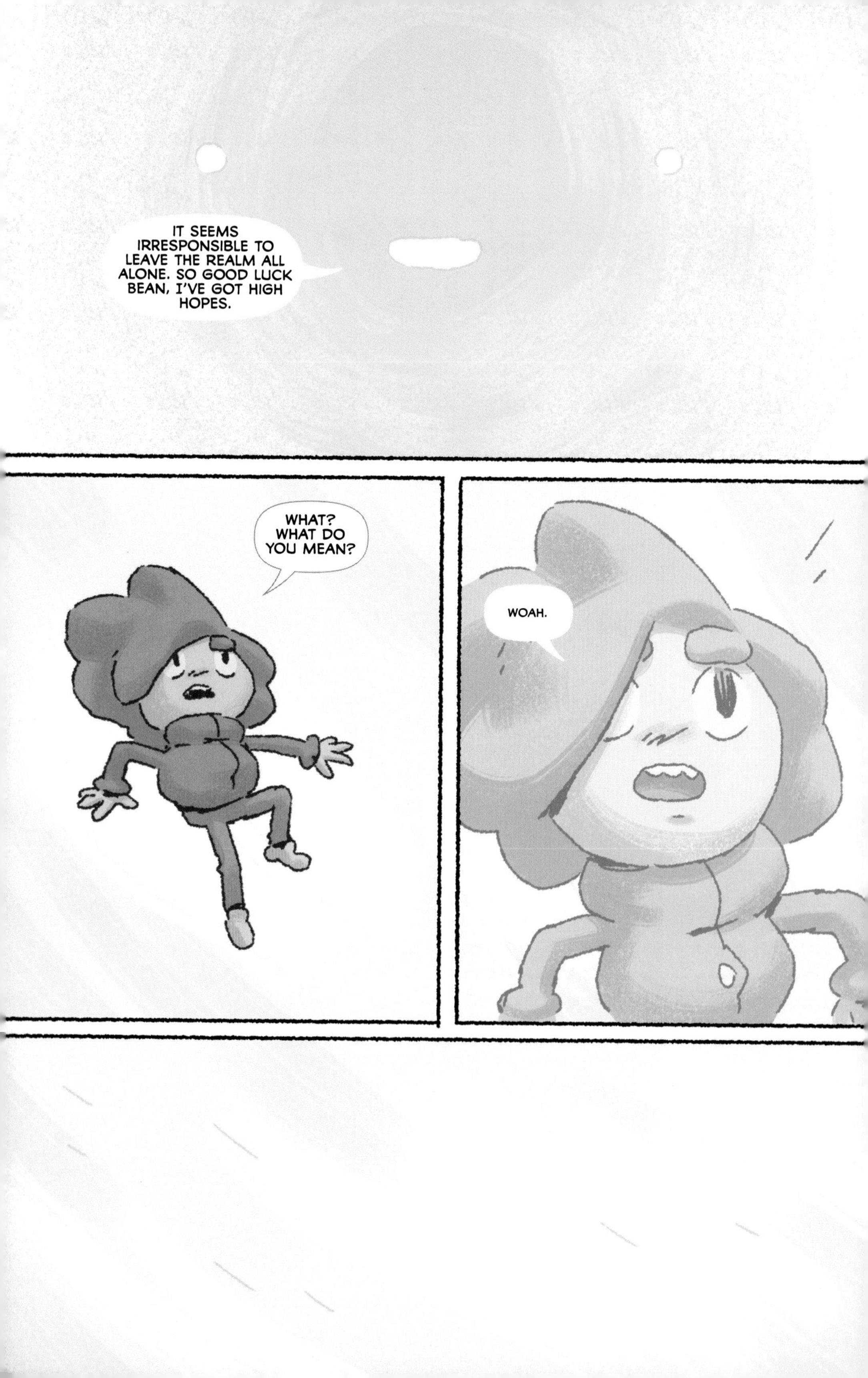
IT SEEMS IRRESPONSIBLE TO LEAVE THE REALM ALL ALONE. SO GOOD LUCK BEAN, I'VE GOT HIGH HOPES.
WHAT? WHAT DO YOU MEAN?
WOAH.

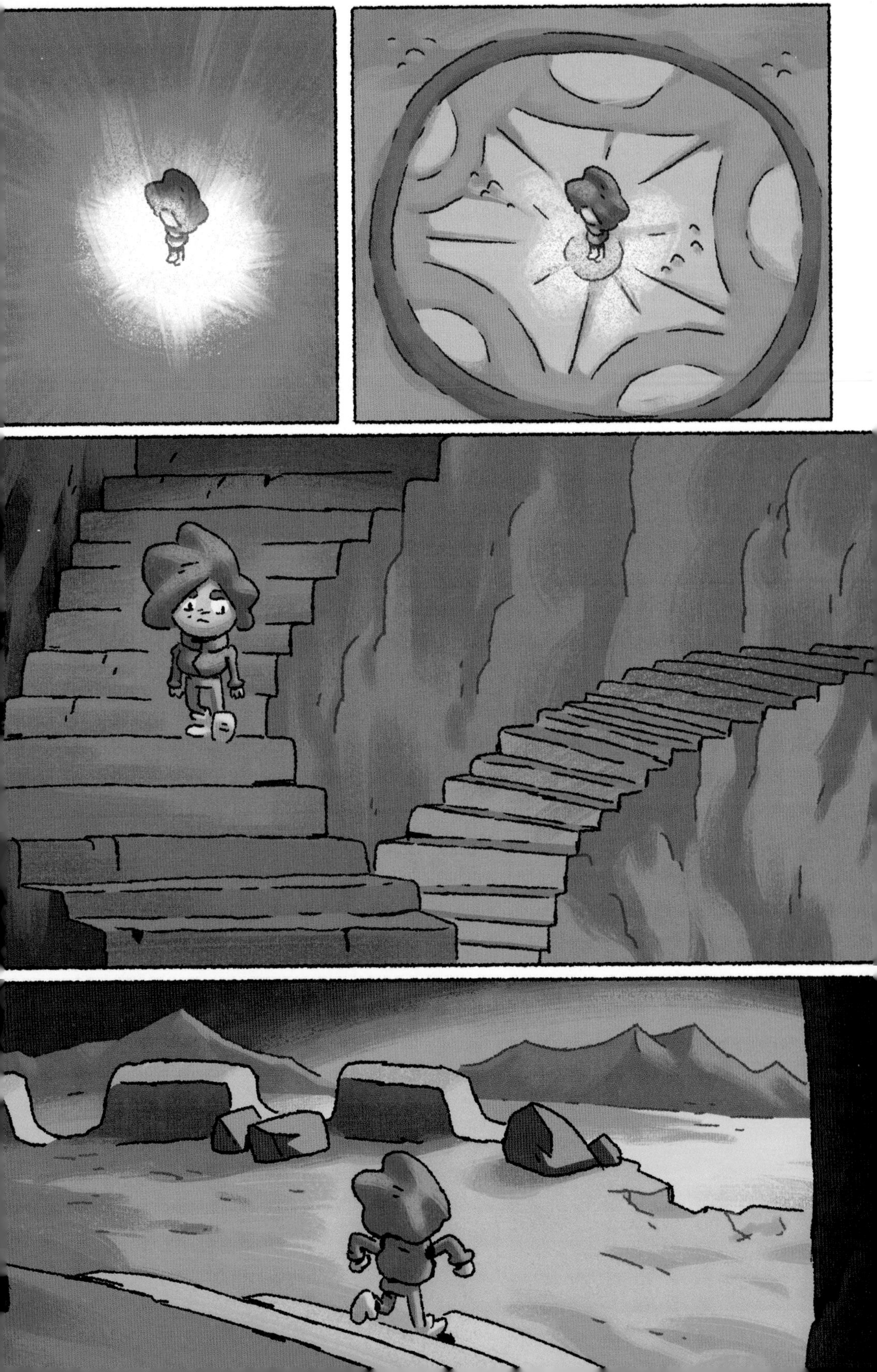

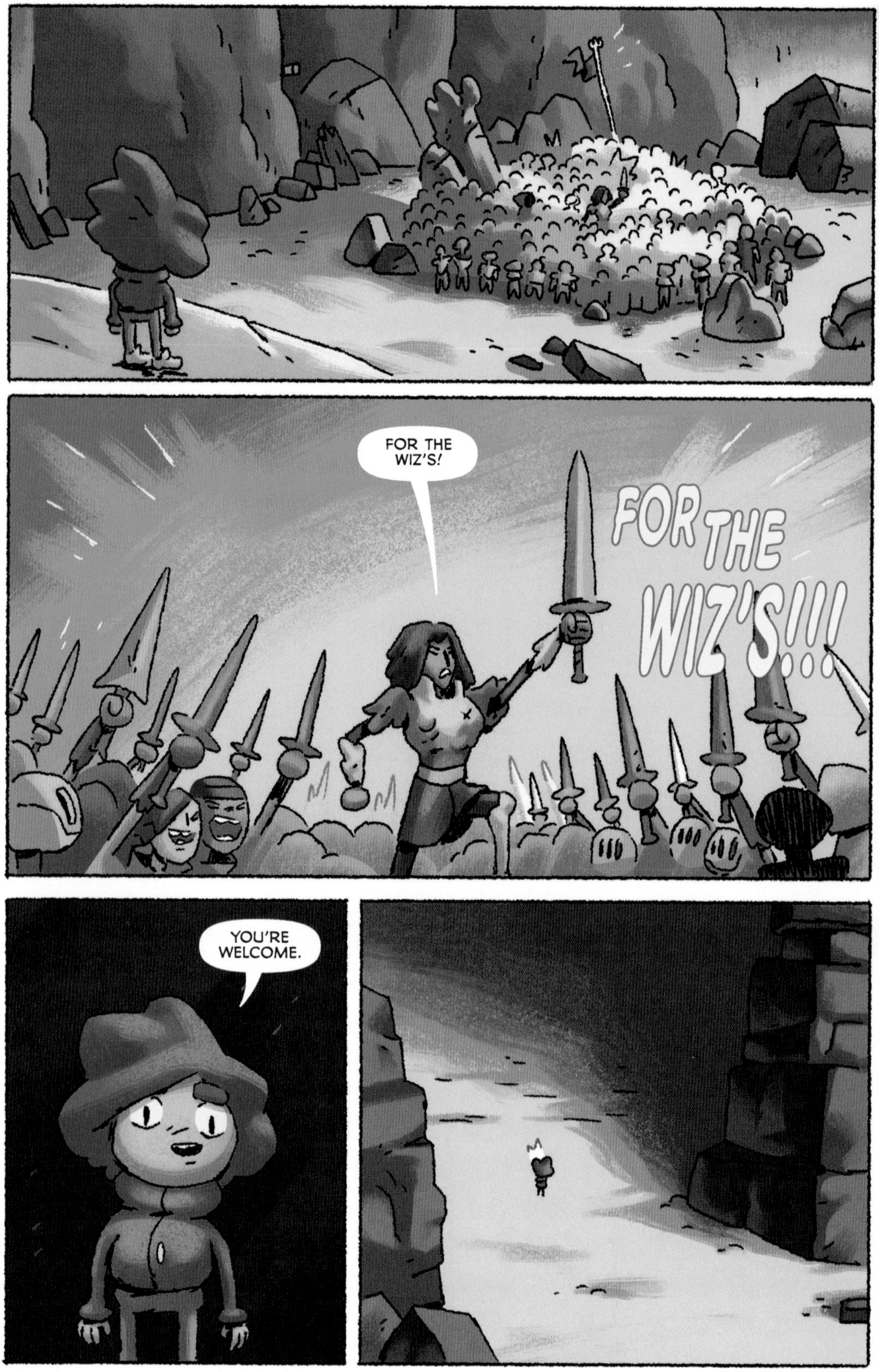
FOR THE WIZ'S!
FOR THE WIZ'S!!!
YOU'RE WELCOME.

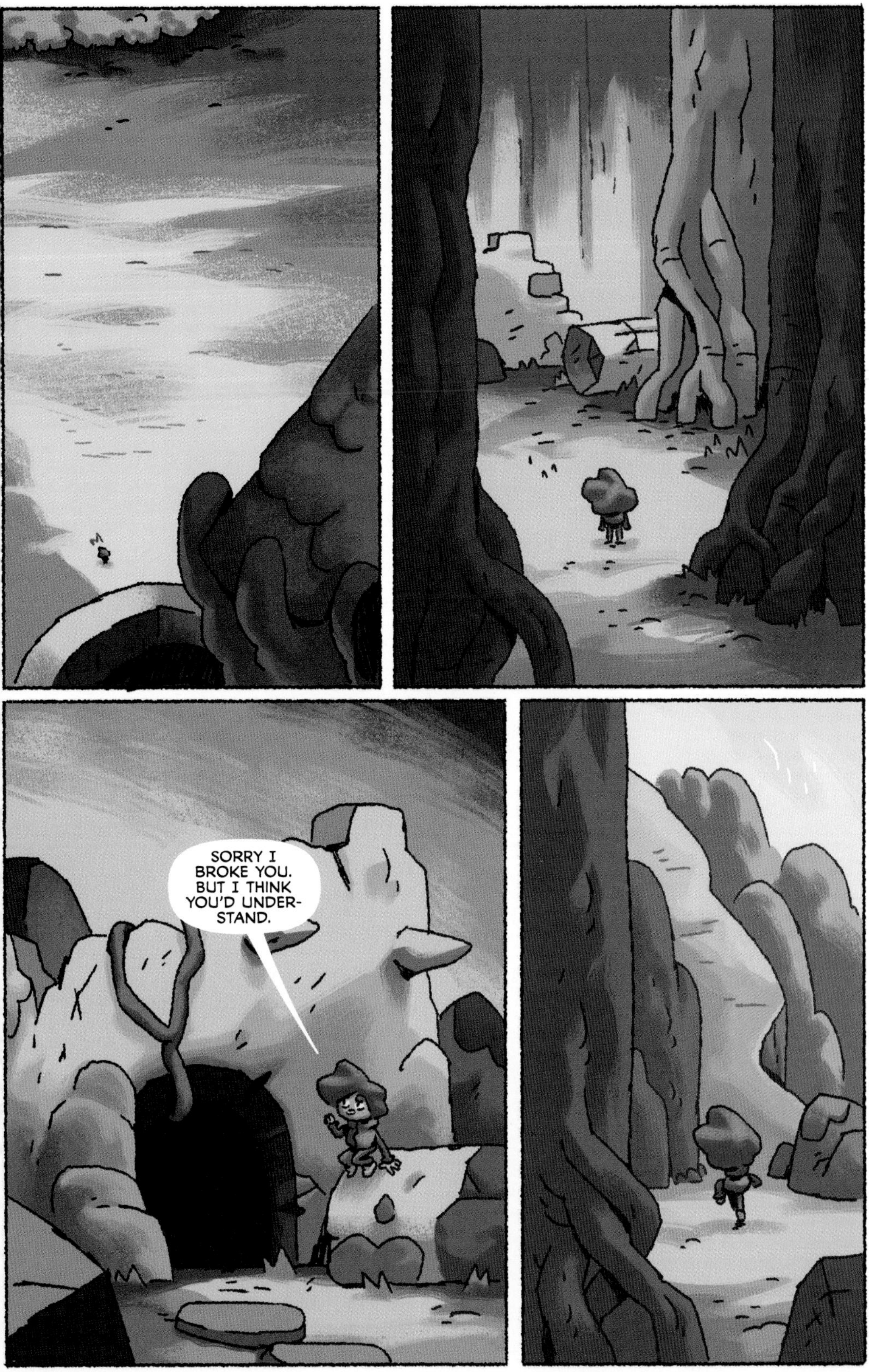
SORRY I BROKE YOU. BUT I THINK YOU'D UNDER-STAND.

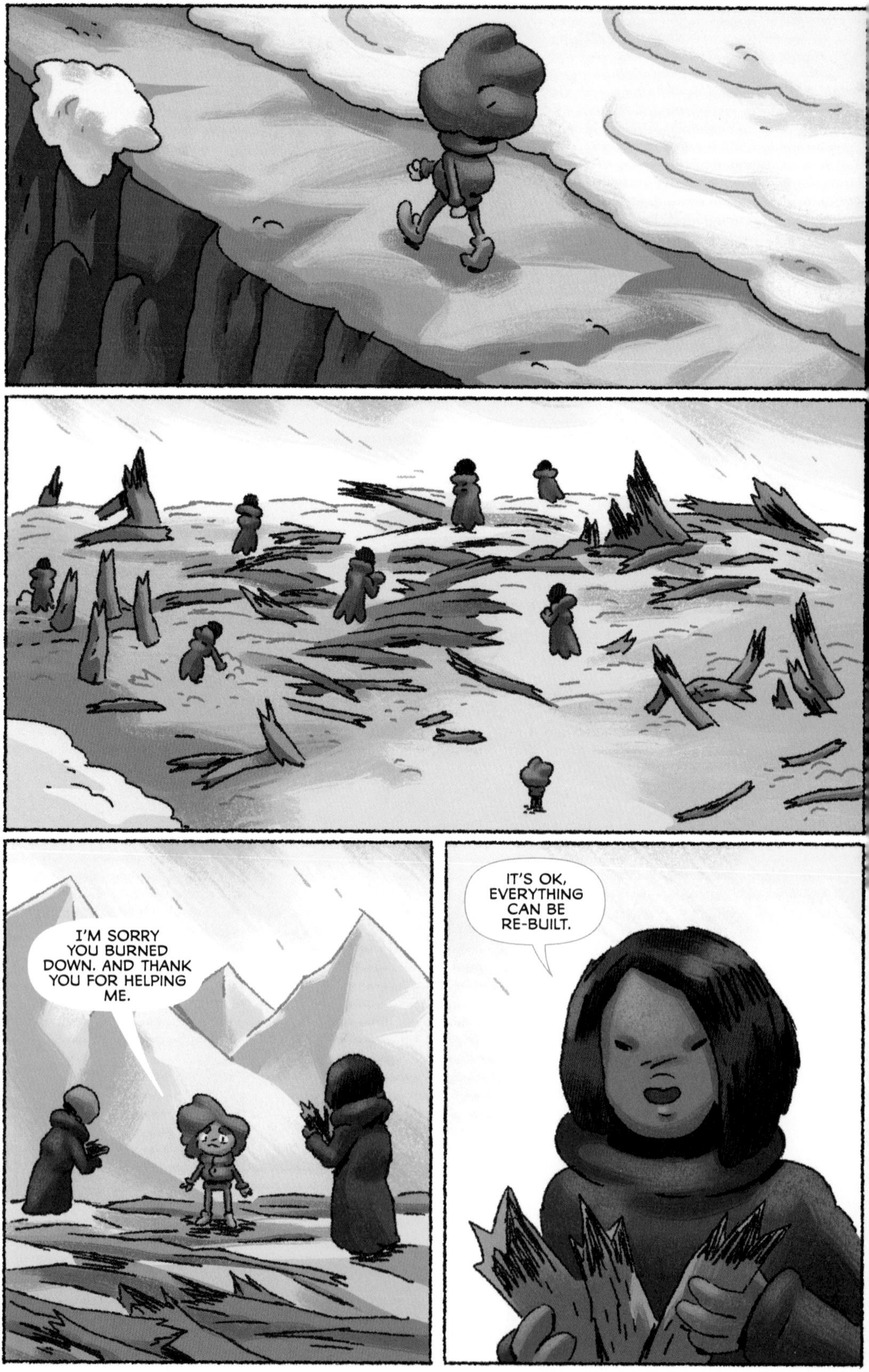
I'M SORRY YOU BURNED DOWN. AND THANK YOU FOR HELPING ME.
IT'S OK, EVERYTHING CAN BE RE-BUILT.

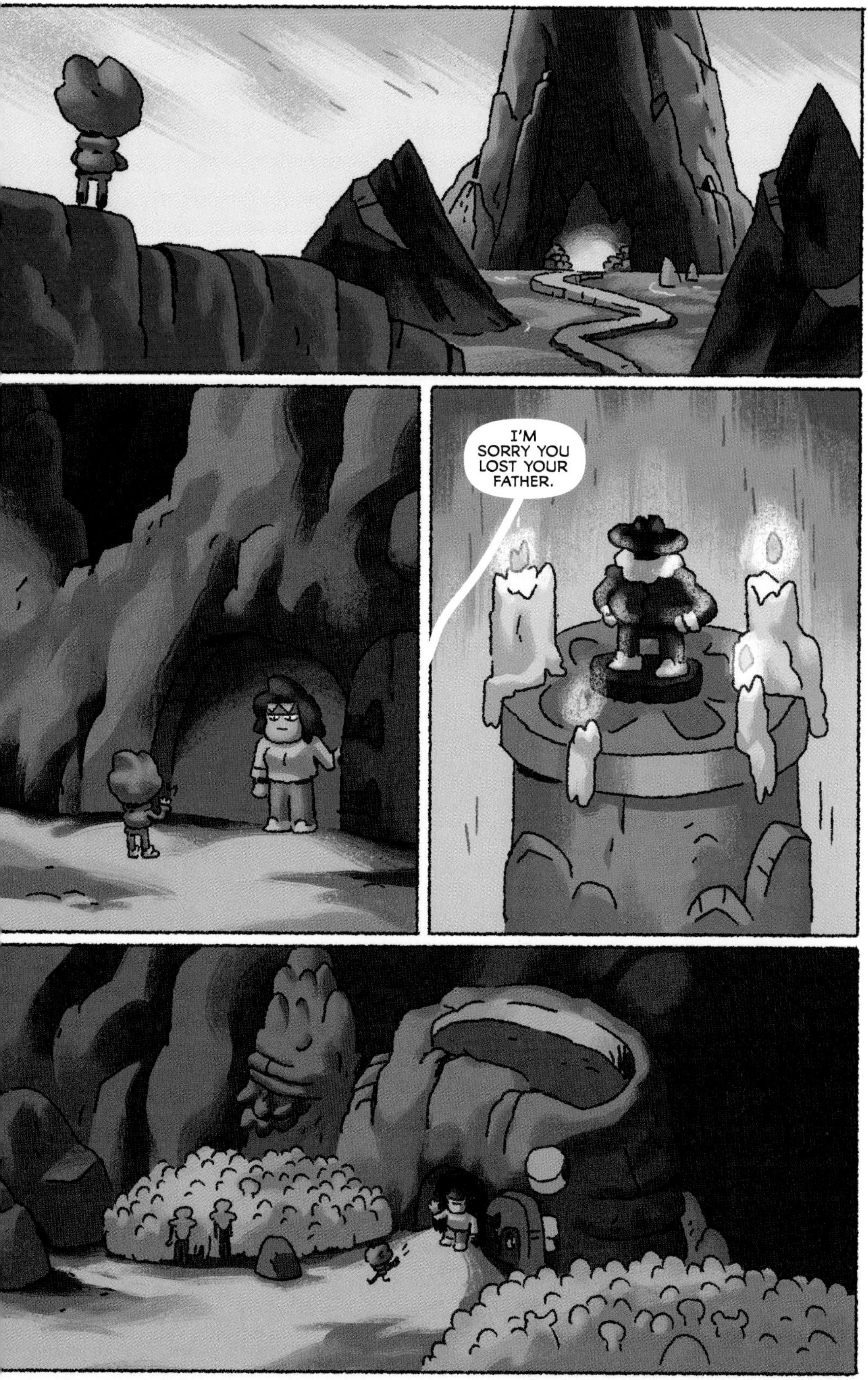
I'M SORRY YOU LOST YOUR FATHER.

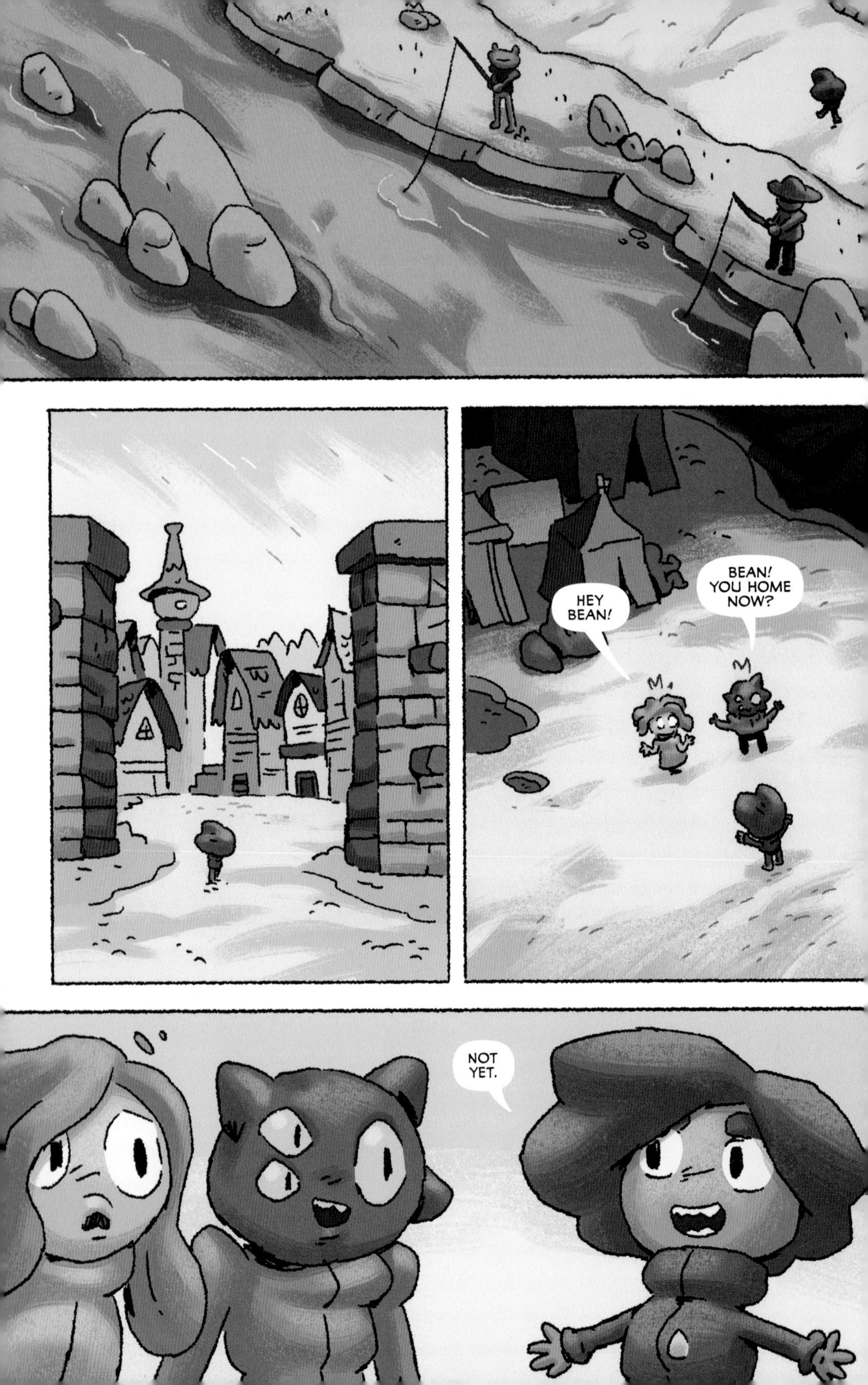
HEY BEAN!
BEAN! YOU HOME NOW?
NOT YET.

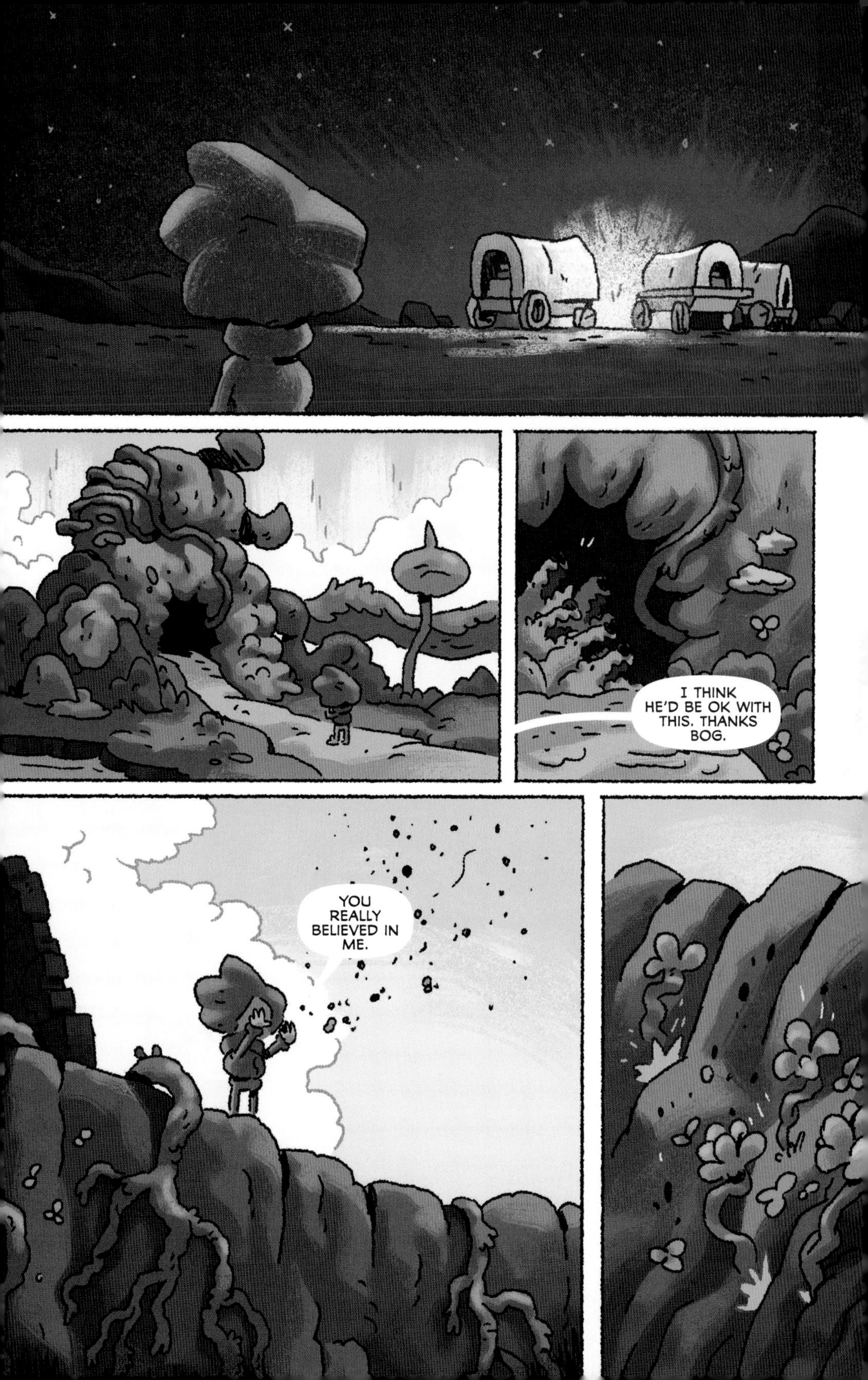
I THINK HE'D BE OK WITH THIS. THANKS BOG.
YOU REALLY BELIEVED IN ME.

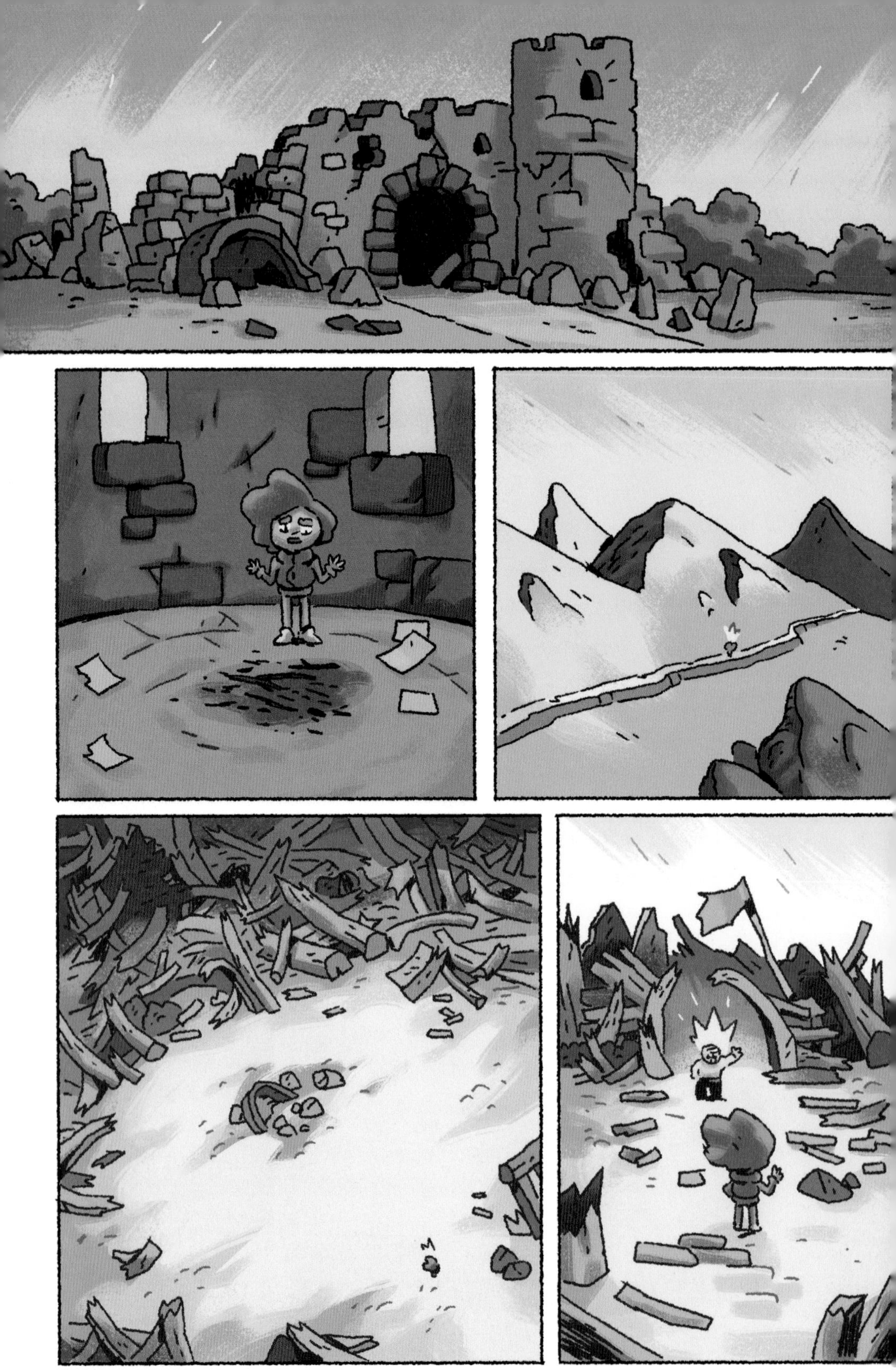

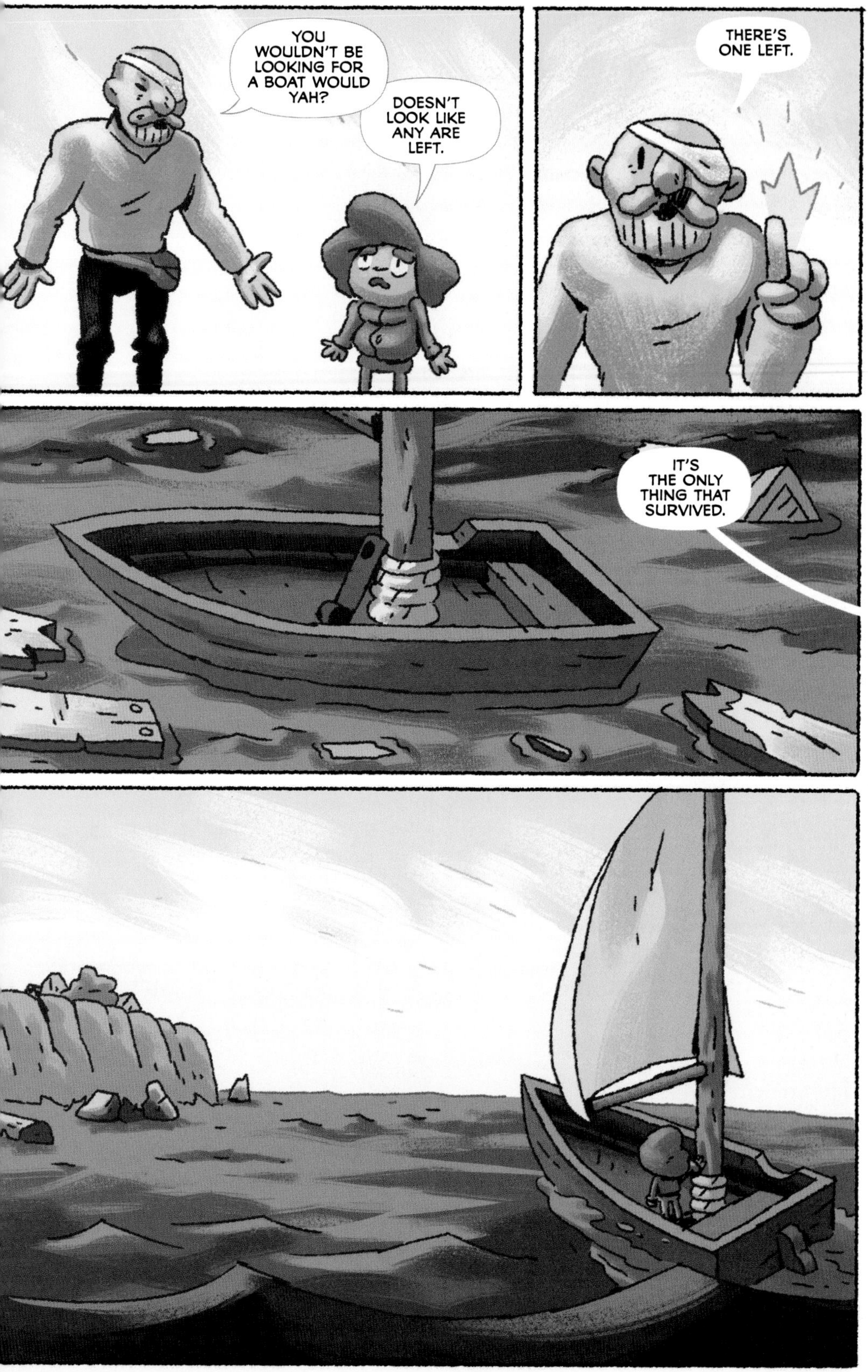
YOU WOULDN'T BE LOOKING FOR A BOAT WOULD YAH?
DOESN'T LOOK LIKE ANY ARE LEFT.
THERE'S ONE LEFT.
IT'S THE ONLY THING THAT SURVIVED.

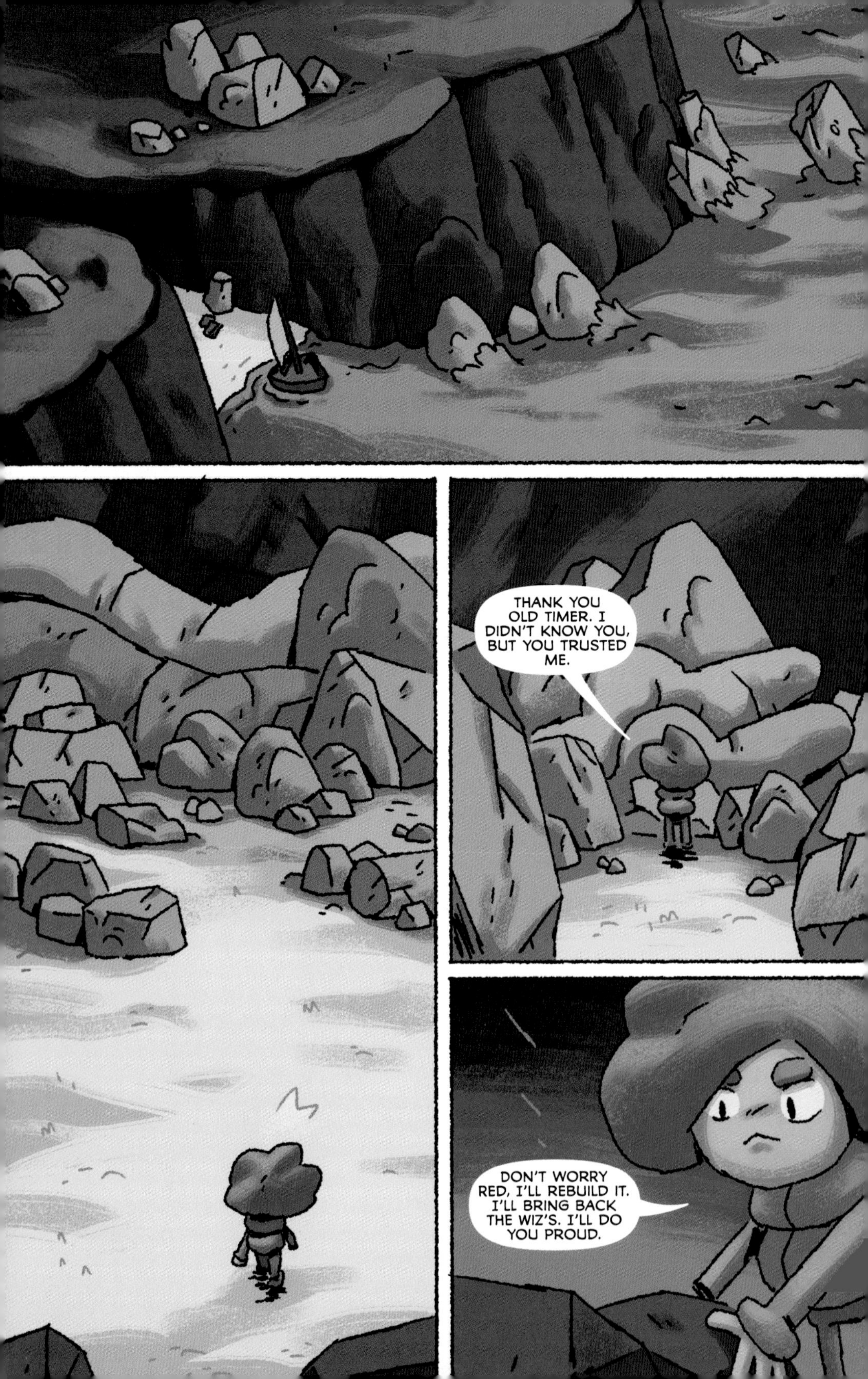
THANK YOU OLD TIMER. I DIDN'T KNOW YOU, BUT YOU TRUSTED ME.
DON'T WORRY RED, I'LL REBUILD IT. I'LL BRING BACK THE WIZ'S. I'LL DO YOU PROUD.

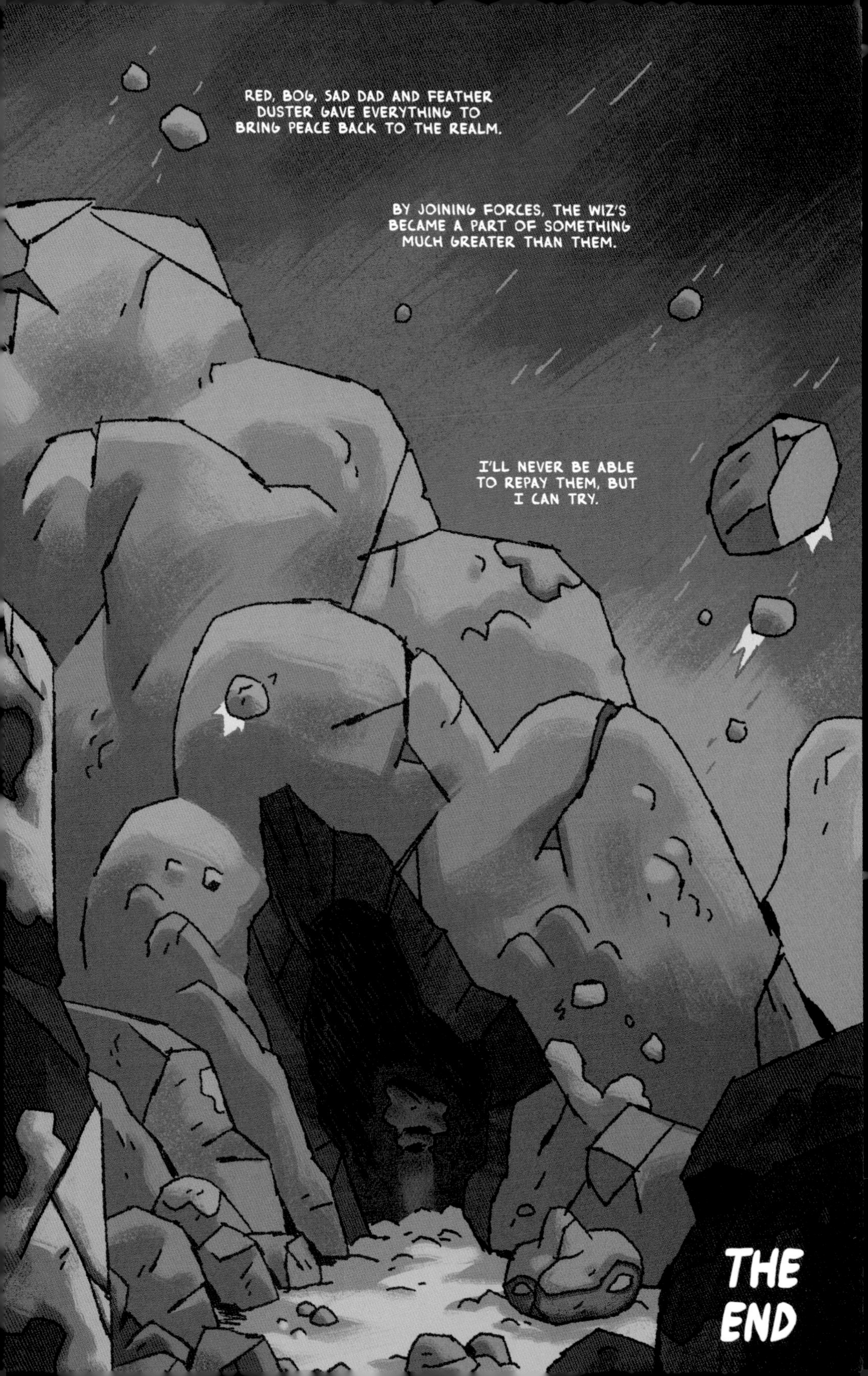
RED, BOG, SAD DAD AND FEATHER DUSTER GAVE EVERYTHING TO BRING PEACE BACK TO THE REALM.
BY JOINING FORCES, THE WIZ'S BECAME A PART OF SOMETHING MUCH GREATER THAN THEM.
I'LL NEVER BE ABLE TO REPAY THEM, BUT I CAN TRY.
THE END

DISCOVER
EXPLOSIVE NEW WORLDS

Adventure Time
Pendleton Ward and Others
Volume 1
ISBN: 978-1-60886-280-1 | $14.99 US
Volume 2
ISBN: 978-1-60886-323-5 | $14.99 US
Adventure Time: Islands
ISBN: 978-1-60886-972-5 | $9.99 US

The Amazing World of Gumball
Ben Bocquelet and Others
Volume 1
ISBN: 978-1-60886-488-1 | $14.99 US
Volume 2
ISBN: 978-1-60886-793-6 | $14.99 US

Brave Chef Brianna
Sam Sykes, Selina Espiritu
ISBN: 978-1-68415-050-2 | $14.99 US

Mega Princess
Kelly Thompson, Brianne Drouhard
ISBN: 978-1-68415-007-6 | $14.99 US

The Not-So Secret Society
Matthew Daley, Arlene Daley,
Wook Jin Clark
ISBN: 978-1-60886-997-8 | $9.99 US

Over the Garden Wall
Patrick McHale, Jim Campbell
and Others
Volume 1
ISBN: 978-1-60886-940-4 | $14.99 US
Volume 2
ISBN: 978-1-68415-006-9 | $14.99 US

Steven Universe
Rebecca Sugar and Others
Volume 1
ISBN: 978-1-60886-706-6 | $14.99 US
Volume 2
ISBN: 978-1-60886-796-7 | $14.99 US

Steven Universe & The Crystal Gems
ISBN: 978-1-60886-921-3 | $14.99 US

Steven Universe: Too Cool for School
ISBN: 978-1-60886-771-4 | $14.99 US

**AVAILABLE AT YOUR LOCAL
COMICS SHOP AND BOOKSTORE**
To find a comics shop in your area, visit www.comicshoplocator.com
WWW.BOOM-STUDIOS.COM